AMBITION TO SAVOR

A Lone Thorn Novel

B.B.E. Gwyn

Book Cover Design by Getfast

Book Cover Illustration by B.B.E. Gwyn

Map Design by Shepengul

Chapter Art and Scene Break Illustrations by B.B.E. Gwyn

First edition 2024

To those who love bringing characters to life in tabletop roleplaying games and collaborative storytelling.

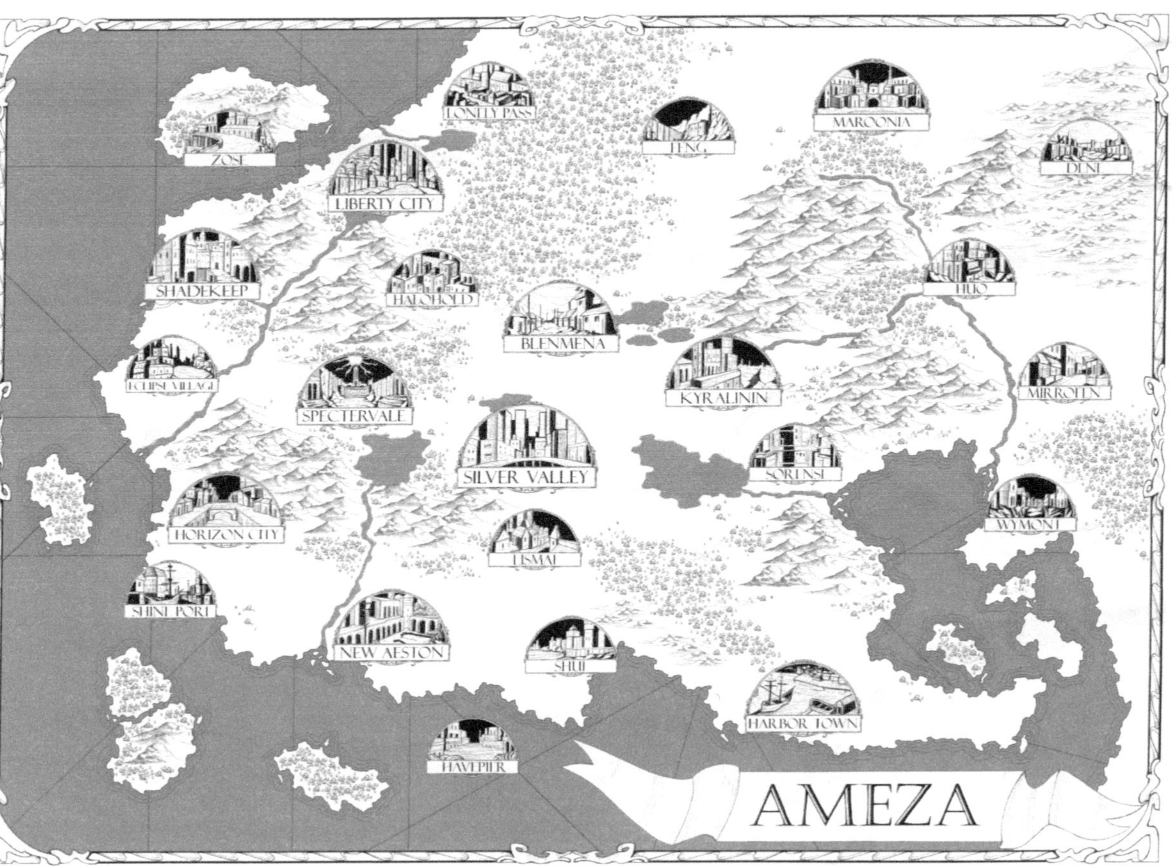

ZOSE
LONELY PASS
TENG
MAROONIA
DUNE
LIBERTY CITY
SHADEKEEP
HALOHOLD
BLENMENA
HUO
ECLIPSE VILLAGE
SPECTERVALE
KYRALININ
MIRROLEN
SILVER VALLEY
SORENSE
HORIZON CITY
WYMONT
LISMAI
SHINE PORT
NEW AESTON
SHUI
HARBOR TOWN
HAVEPIER
AMEZA

CHAPTER 1

Corruption. Mutiny. Absolute villainy was occurring within the walls of his beloved establishment.

Jonathan Tessier had little reason to complain of late. Profit margins were rising, his customer base was expanding, and the recent annual health inspection had wrapped up swimmingly with no findings. After years of fatiguing work and plowing through stress, things were supposed to be looking up for his pride and joy, the Taverne Tessier.

However, walking down the street on this early autumn morning, he was feeling neither proud nor joyous. He could see his restaurant across from him as he stood waiting at the intersection, its pristine exterior of royal blue and beige surrounded by trees of warm hues. When he first renovated the place, he had aimed for a clean and regal appearance inside and out, so even if he could not boast of its size, the feeling of elegance, class, and beauty would still be conveyed.

And now it was filthy. Metaphorically speaking, of course.

The walk signal lit up, and Jonathan looked both ways to ensure the road would be safe for his passage. Did he spend an excessive portion of his allotted walking time turning his head and eyeing the stationary cars around him before crossing? Yes, but he could hardly be blamed. If everyone adhered to the laws as they were supposed to, people like him would not have to squander away energy for the most mundane of activities.

He reached the other sidewalk and turned right to approach the entrance of the restaurant. Its name flashed brilliantly in gold lettering, bringing him a fleeting moment of comfort.

Tension rapidly returned to his muscles, and his jaw and shoulders tightened painfully as he walked inside and shrugged off his thick coat. He looked around at the soft, pastel blue walls, the slate gray floorboards, and the furniture in various shades of rich brown and pale yellow. His waiters busied themselves with preparing the dining room and the outdoor seating area for the upcoming lunch rush, so he only offered them a brief greeting before his gaze panned over to the host station.

"You have finally returned, Elenora," he said to the woman there as she clocked in. Her mere presence helped to ease his persistent sense of dread, though not completely. "How was your vacation?"

Elenora Kerras was a middle-aged woman, short in stature, and she had a cheerful presence in stark contrast to his own. She had been the head chef at Taverne Tessier almost since its grand opening. Given how reliable she was, Jonathan had no idea what he would have done without her. She had brought decades of experience with her, and Jonathan was quietly convinced this had kept his business afloat during those grueling early days. Her chef's uniform fit her stout body well, and a few grays gracefully adorned her dark violet hair. She looked up and grinned widely at her boss, waving jovially as he stepped closer.

"I really needed the break, but I'm so ready to get back into it. You missed me, didn't you, Mr. Tessier?" Elenora reached out a hand in a silent offer to take his coat. "And you're here a little earlier than usual. I sure hope things haven't completely fallen apart while I was gone."

Jonathan shook his head, declining her gesture. "Things certainly could be better, but I am relieved to have you back. I have something I need to discuss with you," he said to her before he nodded once and turned briskly to head upstairs. "If you find a moment, please come to my office." He groaned as he went, eliciting a surprised noise from her.

He wanted to sigh as he entered his office and draped his things over the top of his chair. The room was small, but organized with filing cabinets behind his desk, a drawer unit to the side with a file rack and a printer placed on top, and a couple of plush armchairs for employees he needed to chat with. Sliding into his desk chair and booting up his computer, Jonathan thought only of the menu he would have to manage for the following week. He had already been forced to hurriedly draft one up two days ago to address a midweek emergency in which he discovered there was an alarming discrepancy in the restaurant's inventory. Many ingredients of the highest quality and with the biggest price tags, including premium truffles and caviar, had all disappeared soon after he had acquired them without ever making their way into the dishes served to valued customers.

Naturally, the first thing Jonathan did was check the security camera footage in the hopes it would be easy to catch the culprit on video. Instead, he was left confused. He could not pinpoint where the opportunity to steal ingredients would have arisen; the storage room could only be accessed during operational hours and was locked at any other time, eliminating the possibility that a patron or some other external party could have done the dirty deed.

He remembered the onslaught of headaches he felt when he realized he had no choice but to conclude the thief was one of his own staff. Surely he did not escape being bossed around as a simple line chef and working with awfully insipid menus a little over five years ago just to wind up facing blatant insubordination now. The team he had so meticulously interviewed contained a lawless individual who had slipped through the cracks of his otherwise impeccable scrutiny. One member had dared to win over his confidence just to steal from right under his nose—

A knock against the pane of his glass office door interrupted his brewing irritation as he typed away at next week's menu. It must have been at least the tenth time in just the last two days that he could feel his blood boiling purely at the thought of this betrayal.

Elenora opened the door, peeking her head in before she fully stepped inside and walked over to the armchair across the desk from Jonathan.

"You always look so serious, but today is something else," she remarked with an amused grin as she sat down and got comfortable. "Oh, how I missed you and the Taverne. What did you want to talk to me about?"

His one solace was that he could trust Elenora, even if she had not been away on vacation during the time of the thefts.

Jonathan gave her a wry smile. "You recall how we wanted to introduce more gourmet dishes into our menus?"

She nodded. "Can't hurt business to cater to wealthy customers," she said agreeably, then immediately appeared concerned. "Oh, no. Don't tell me. Did it not go down well with the rich folk?"

"We never even had the chance to find out," he told her grimly. "The expensive ingredients were stolen shortly after I had obtained them." He quickly filled her in on the progress of his investigation and the obvious conclusion he had reached.

Elenora let out a sigh and shook her head. "You really think one of our own did this?"

"I hate to say it, but I cannot imagine how anyone else could have. Only employees can access the storage room freely without drawing suspicion."

"That's disappointing."

He felt the head chef's pain, and he watched her forehead crease as her face fell. She treated the team as a beloved family and carried a motherly disposition toward them. She made a habit of inviting them out on day trips of shopping or mini-golfing or bar hopping, all to spoil them, while he considered his competitive compensation package to be enough of a favor. Aside from

Elenora, they were all just hirelings to him, so he found it easier to be angry instead.

"Do you have any suspicions about who it could be?" he asked.

"Goodness, no. I can't even imagine." She paused, then lowered her voice. "What are you going to do?"

"I do not yet know," he said. "But we especially cannot afford to order any more truffle varieties until this is resolved."

"Should we ask everyone if they know anything?"

Jonathan shook his head. "I wanted to keep my investigation a secret, and I hardly think it is a good idea to expose it now. It might cause the thief to lie low for a while, only to strike again when the moment is right."

"Well, then, what are you thinking of doing?"

"Perhaps we could trap them. . . bait them out?" He pushed his chair back, getting up to pace around the narrow room with his hands clasped behind his back. "But our budget has no room for anything other than our current week's menu."

Elenora's gaze followed him as she tapped a finger to her chin, thinking deeply. "I wonder if you could pretend something is expensive. When it really isn't?"

Jonathan creased his brow at this suggestion. His employees were all knowledgeable in the culinary space. He would not hire for anything less. As he mulled this over, his eyes glanced up at the clock on the wall.

"It will have to be a plan we expand on later. We should get ready to open for lunch."

She nodded in agreement, joining him in standing up. "It feels like we're starting a bit of an undercover operation," she said, her tone of voice far too excited for what Jonathan considered a weighty matter.

They headed back downstairs to help prepare the dining areas and the kitchen, and when it was an hour before noon, they were ready to open their doors to customers.

The emergency menu Jonathan prepared offered a variety of salads, soups, and stews; main lunch entrées; and desserts. He aimed for his restaurant to always feature high-quality ingredients popular throughout the nation of Ameza, and to utilize them in fusion recipes that pulled inspiration from many of the world's best culinary cultures. On top of delectable recipes, excellent customer service and a luxurious atmosphere were priorities Jonathan made certain his staff knew to uphold. Today's ingredients were of rather common rarity due to the thefts, but his skillful kitchen team seemed to be handling things well, and customers were satisfied nevertheless.

For most of this lunch shift, Jonathan remained at the station to handle host duties, occasionally heading into the kitchen to lend his aid whenever the chefs were feeling overwhelmed. At one point while he was there, one of the waiters, Ransley, snuck in a moment between taking orders and delivering food to request his attention.

"I might be wrong," Ransley said, sounding a little panicked, "but I think we just had a critic come in."

Jonathan frowned. "Is that so? Who?" he asked.

"I think he's the one that's called Labey."

It took a moment for him to register, but the restaurant

owner clicked his tongue disapprovingly at the mention of this name. It was dreadful timing that a critic should visit and add to his already heightened levels of anxiety. While he would always value the opinions of top gourmet chefs as superior, there were only a handful of food critics whose reviews he could respect. Trevor Labey's were not among them. The articles he published online tended to be far too dramatic and exaggerated to warrant being taken seriously, but they had somehow become very popular with the general public, regrettably so.

He had to decide swiftly between giving Trevor Labey extra attention, risking criticism over special treatment of a critic, or continuing with normal restaurant operations as if he were a regular customer.

Not one to be fond of pretenses, Jonathan promptly exited the kitchen to find this guest. Another waiter was currently noting Labey's order: crunchy quinoa salad, potato leek soup, a stir-fry rice bowl for his main entrée, and tropical fruit salad for dessert. He stood by until the waiter finished and marched past him to entrust the order to the kitchen.

"Good afternoon, sir," Jonathan greeted as he approached Labey's table.

The man looked up and studied him in silence for a moment before he nodded. "Afternoon. And you are?"

"My name is Jonathan Tessier. I am the humble owner of this restaurant and honored to be serving you today." He dipped his head in a polite bow. "I must be upfront, as your distinguished reputation precedes you, Mr. Labey. We are infinitely grateful that you decided to pay our restaurant a visit, but I must inform you that we will be aware of who you are as we work to provide you with the best possible experience."

He endured another quiet pause before the critic nodded once more. "Very well. Thank you for your honesty. I hope to enjoy my meal."

Though the response seemed favorable, Jonathan hesitated to feel any relief as he returned the nod and retreated into the kitchen's tense atmosphere. Ransley had warned the rest of the staff, and the team was now on high alert while preparing Labey's food. Jonathan weaved his way through chefs shuffling back and forth between stations and stoves to rigorously examine the dishes and give his final approval before they could be presented to the table. His taste tests concluded that the crunchy quinoa salad and potato leek soup were up to par, and the stir-fry bowl and fruit salad were excellent even by his strict standards.

A few of the waiters took turns bringing these approved dishes to the critic, and Jonathan eventually slinked out of the kitchen, not wandering too far from it but enough for a vantage point from which to spot any of Labey's reactions toward his lunch.

Jonathan frequently thought customers tended to linger a bit too long when having a meal at his restaurant, limiting the establishment's already modest capacity from serving more guests. Hosting a critic seemed to magnify this sentiment. He knew he was spending far too much time sneaking glances at Labey during his meal and carefully observing him for any signs of either approbation or disdain.

And yet he felt he learned nothing from keeping such a watchful eye. The critic offered no clues in his expressions while he ate, and a stifling mood loomed over the staff as they continued to look after the other customers in the dining room. The tension persisted after the man finished eating, paid with a respectable tip, and departed, even up until the end of the lunch shift.

"I certainly did not think we would be on the radar of famous critics to begin earning visits from them," Jonathan said dryly when he had settled back in his office with Elenora. The team was downstairs cleaning up before they would enjoy a break for two to three hours. Most of them would be back on the clock for dinnertime.

"No?" Elenora tilted her head. "Doesn't this fit right in with your picture of success?"

He frowned. "Big names like his typically want to be patrons of even bigger names."

"Imagine that, your little Taverne is already making it big. Who would have guessed?" The head chef let out a laugh, only for it to be followed by a heavy sigh. "I can't say I had a good time, though. I can't remember ever feeling this stressed. The pressure was just so suffocating."

He nodded in agreement as he picked up a silver spoon and used it to stir the tea he had prepared to calm his nerves. "Unfortunately, there will be no relaxation for us until Labey's review becomes public, and perhaps not even then. We have enough to deal with as it is."

"Right, the stolen ingredients," she said, eyeing his cup. "Thank goodness they didn't dare take away your weird weed tea."

"You wound me, Elenora. Milkweed tea being unpalatable to you ordinary folk does not diminish my taste for it. Our attention should be on the culprit, the one who has conducted a truly distasteful act."

She snorted. "I still don't think asking everyone some questions about it is the worst idea. Maybe someone saw something. Besides, you already stopped buying those expensive ingredients. What if the thief caught on and is so on guard that we can't even bait them anyway?"

Jonathan furrowed his brows. "Then should I not have put a pause on our supply?"

"Not that hindsight will help you, but it was a pretty strong reaction, and dare I say it, maybe a bit hasty. I'm no thief, but I could imagine thinking you might be on to me."

He appreciated her honesty, but her word choice sat poorly with him. It painted his course of action as potentially misguided, mistaken even, and he would not be eager to admit such a fact. Instead of addressing this directly, he decided to entertain her preferred method of solving this issue.

"And you believe you can accurately read every one of our staff? How would you discern for sure who is lying?" he asked. "You know I regard your leadership highly, but even then, I doubt that mere intuition is sufficient. I would rather catch them red-handed with irrefutable evidence."

The woman sighed, leaning back in her armchair and lifting her hands to rest behind her head. "This is tough. I'm just afraid that we'll run ourselves dizzy trying to catch this thief and waste so much time and money that it gives you even more grief," she said, her expression softening with genuine concern. "I would hate for this to eat away at us from the inside."

"We still should wait," he insisted. "Once we start to execute your plan, there is no taking it back. I think I should look into rare ingredients that might be so tempting that the thief throws out all inhibitions and goes for the bait. If that fails, then we can begin your interrogations."

Elenora frowned slightly as she thought this over, eventually letting out a breathy chuckle. "You're so careful for your age," she remarked. "But you do have a point. Mind-melding with our staff can only go so far." She nodded. "Let's try it, then."

He refrained from mentioning that he was less than fifteen years younger than she was, or that age had nothing to do with how scrupulous someone should be. After agreeing that she should maintain her usual duties so as not to rouse suspicion, Elenora departed from the office to enjoy what was left of her break.

When dinner came around, it was a shift of a more typical nature, and while busy, thankfully uneventful compared to lunch. Jonathan took every opportunity in between rushes to check online for Labey's post about the Taverne, but he found no results.

The review came in the next morning. The moment Jonathan walked in the door, signaling his usual late-morning arrival, Elenora scurried over to him with her phone in hand, the food journal that Labey wrote pulled up on the screen. He did not spare a moment to take off his coat as he read the post right away, the two of them slowly inching upstairs together toward his office while he did.

Labey called the Taverne's food "uninspired, basic, and a disappointment in the culinary world due to its unremarkable presentation and lack of creativity." The critic claimed that his experience was no different from any average restaurant, and it had no chance of standing out with such plain ingredients.

Any positive words Labey might have used in his essay slipped into Jonathan's periphery to be forgotten. Though he was not surprised by the critic's excessively harsh rhetoric, Jonathan's indignation burned over this unwelcome review being the first one of its kind he had ever received.

"Read the comments," Elenora said when he was about to hand her phone back to her. "Under the post."

He would have rather that there were no comments at all, but Labey's virality always drew in heightened engagement from his followers at a minimum of dozens of comments. The consensus from the feedback at the end of the web page was that Labey visiting a boring restaurant was not unexpected and that they were thankful they would not have to waste the time to visit.

"If it were not for the thief, we could have had a menu that actually impressed him," he said, nearly seething.

Elenora could do nothing to hold back her uneasy laughter as she took back her phone, her eyebrows lifting with worried sympathy. "I'm so sorry. This is becoming such a string of bad luck," she said, patting his arm. "I'm sure it'll get better. At least he didn't say our food was disgusting."

He wondered if that might have been less painful, as mediocrity was perhaps the worst quality to have for sensationalism. As bizarre as people were, some might have been interested in sampling restaurants with extremely bad reputations.

When the rest of the team clocked in, the pair went back downstairs so Jonathan could gather them all into the kitchen for a brief meeting. After he relayed the contents of the critic's review, he attempted to reassure everyone that they would overcome this setback.

A chef called Orla spoke up. "What if this really hurts business? Won't our jobs be in trouble?" The other chefs—Danna, Henry, Rhea, and Marshall—also appeared concerned that this could put them out of work.

"Let's not be so negative, everyone," Elenora said. "We can still count on our good location and the fact that most people won't even see Labey's review."

"I don't know about that," Ransley said. "Online reviews have more impact these days. Otherwise, I might not have recognized Mr. Labey."

"I feel like it wasn't that long ago when critics actually tried to disguise themselves," Elenora remarked. She earned a few blank looks from her younger colleagues.

"Really?" Ransley asked. "They couldn't have been completely anonymous. Wouldn't smaller, local restaurants be unfairly caught off guard? Having easy access to the most popular critics' identities rewards everyone who takes the time to keep up with the industry."

"You knew, but we still got a negative review, Ransley," Orla reminded him.

The group of nine, including the other waiters—Finley, Natalie, and Yevina—began chatting among themselves, raising concerns about the menu and how it would be unfair for them to lose their jobs over it. The incoherent commotion escalated to the point that Elenora and Jonathan had difficulty regaining their attention.

"Quiet!"

With a frustrated clearing of his throat, Jonathan waited as his staff settled down into a stunned silence.

"I understand your worry," he said. "As the owner, of course I share in that. But it would benefit us very little to allow this to discourage us. I will be doubling my efforts to introduce better ingredients and ensure this never happens again. As a matter of fact, there are some ingredients I could acquire that not many people have heard of, and some can even be sold for their weight in gold. I will work on marketing and our public image. We will recover from this review and take it one step at a time, starting with today."

The doubt lingered in most of their expressions, but the team soon reluctantly acknowledged his speech and dispersed throughout the restaurant to begin getting ready for another lunch shift. Jonathan passed by Elenora for one last short exchange of words.

"I will be upstairs if you need me," he told her, apologetic that he would have to leave her in charge of preparations. "I have a few important calls I must make."

CHAPTER 2

JONATHAN'S SPEECH HAD BEEN about catching any misplaced curiosity that he might be bringing in even more ingredients of golden value, rather than about comforting his employees.

Despite being opposed to Elenora's idea to read minds, he could not resist trying it once. If the lure he threw out had earned him better insight into who his thief could be, he probably would not be outside the city right now trudging through fields of dry and unkempt grass. To his dismay, nearly everyone had engaged in behaviors that his eager scrutiny deemed suspicious. One individual did not look as disappointed about the review as the others did, another pondered aloud about the specific prices of the ingredients Jonathan alluded to, someone else glanced awkwardly around the kitchen during the racket. Nothing of what he noticed helped him. It was inconceivable that all his staff should be guilty of this heinous crime together.

After informing Elenora he needed to step away, he had gone back to his office to get in touch with some old associates. A life raised in nobility was but a remnant of his childhood, one he willingly left behind a long time ago when he realized how wealth without struggle afforded people time to buy misery with cash. Even so, there were some things he never lost, like the etiquette ingrained in his mannerisms.

Jonathan flipped through an old contact book, one of the very few things he took from among his father's possessions while he rejected the rest. The list had been largely trimmed to leave only individuals he could foresee being useful, a move made out of practicality over sentimentalism. He picked up the phone, dialing every number that caught his eye until someone picked up.

"Using your name to demand a favor? You're just like your father," the gruff voice on the other end grumbled.

Jonathan grimaced, but quickly reminded himself to treat the associate like they were something more than a scrawled name, an artifact of an old business partnership.

"I would not ask if I did not absolutely need your assistance," he said.

"You said you wanted help boosting your restaurant's reputation?"

"Yes. Anything in the way of improving public image, if you could. Or connecting me with other reputable critics."

"Well, it's going to cost you, you know."

"What do you want in return?"

"A favor for a favor," the associate said. "Even if you're not your dad, having a Tessier in my debt is pretty enticing."

"What kind of favor?" Jonathan asked.

"I don't know yet. I'm sure it'll be something simple. Whenever I feel like calling it."

"I want it clearly outlined in writing."

He hoped the next person who answered his call would leave a less bitter taste in his mouth.

"You need my help, dear? So out of the blue?"

"I apologize for bothering you," he said. "I need some information about any valuable ingredients that are both accessible and in demand."

"Can't we have a nice conversation and catch up first? I was so fond of Lady Tessier. She threw the best parties and treated me well. To think her little boy's all grown up and doing business of his own."

Jonathan gritted his teeth, apathetic and impatient.

"Perhaps another time? As you know, running a business is multiple full-time jobs."

Pleasant laughter sounded through the phone. "Very well. I may know merchants who offer such ingredients, but they're expensive. Considering they're so difficult to obtain."

"That is fine."

"I can find more options for you, if you'd give me some time."

"Of course. Anything helps."

He managed to secure a few more calls, all marginally helpful to his goal. At the end of his efforts, he decided trying to order new ingredients would not be easy on the budget. There had been, however, an economical alternative suggested to him.

He could acquire the supply with his own two hands.

What began as leaving his head chef in charge for a few minutes extended to imploring her to handle the entire lunch shift. Elenora had been hesitant to shoulder such responsibility, but one look at his eyes seemed to convince her that the matter on his mind held great importance. He rushed out the door to prepare for the journey, fetching a few of his dustier belongings along the way, and took a cab past Silver Valley's city borders. The driver took him as far as they could until the roads became unmanageable.

Jonathan then walked through the fields toward a lake a few miles north of the capital. The grass stood up to his thighs, and bits of the blades snagged the fibers of his trousers to give the dark material a chaotic pattern of yellow speckles.

He had heard long before there was an abundance of lotuses that grew in and around this lake, but he had just been enlightened that an exceptional variety could be hidden within the other plants. He never had a reason before to come all the way out here to verify any of this, and he could only hope it would not be an utter waste of his time when he already loathed being away from his busy restaurant. As he came closer, he could see how the flowers generously decorated the lake, from its shores to all across its water's tranquil deep blue surface.

Once he reached the lake, he began by walking along its edge, carefully studying the lush plants that grew around its verdant banks. He poked at a few of the lotus flowers of beautiful pinkish hues with the tip of the silver rapier he had brought along with him, wanting to see if the provocation would allow him to detect any abnormalities in the blossoms.

He covered the full circumference of the lake within half an hour, unable to find anything out of the ordinary after staring so critically at hundreds, maybe even thousands, of flowers. It made him a little nauseous, and he quickly arrived at the dreadful conclusion that he might have to rent a boat to travel farther in.

There was a small boat rental shop nearby, its dull exterior of metal and wood exposed behind peeling white paint showing evidence of being worn out by the weather. He briefly wondered if it earned enough business to stay up for much longer, considering the stillness of the lake. It was without a doubt a beautiful sight, but too far from any city to make the trip here a reasonable one. Boats of maybe two or three distinct types were stationed around a ragged dock in front of the shop. As Jonathan approached, he could see a faded wooden sign designating this facility as the Purity Lake Boat Rental.

He walked inside and asked the shopkeeper if he could rent out a smaller boat fit to sail toward the center of the lake. Though the keeper appeared to be of a grumpier disposition and was not keen to help in the slightest, he eventually guided Jonathan to choose a deck boat but offered shallow instructions on how to operate it.

As soon as he started the boat, Jonathan had trouble steering it as it jerked erratically. To add to his frustration, the shopkeeper had come outside in his idleness to observe him and began yelling at him from the shore.

"What're you doing, you dunce?" the shopkeeper shouted gruffly. "Why're you taking out a boat if you can't even sail it?"

"There is a first time for everything," Jonathan called back, his tone of voice laden with annoyance. "Or should I simply give up and ask for a refund?"

"You ain't getting a refund over my dead body!"

Ignoring the keeper's crude language, Jonathan focused his attention on getting the vehicle under control, and though it was graceless, he managed to handle it smoothly enough to glide slowly across the water. The flowers that floated on its surface bobbed away to make room for the boat to travel through.

Each minute of practice that he endured had him getting better accustomed to navigating the boat, and when he reached the central area of the lake, he felt confident he could resume his search. The shopkeeper was still watching him from land, but Jonathan was determined to not glance in his direction, so the next time he happened to face the shop, he saw the man had finally gone.

He picked a random spot to stop the boat and continued to prod at the nearby blossoms with his sword. When he received no reaction from the buds, he drove to another spot in the water and attempted it again. Nothing.

When he moved toward a third spot, beginning to trace a triangular path in the middle of the lake, a glistening spark of unusually bright light broke up the monotony of his vision. Narrowing his eyes, he sailed toward the source, realizing that one flower among the bunch stood out from the rest. Instead of pale pink gradients, this flower had a metallic sheen across its petals that bounced the light of the afternoon sun toward him, and as he navigated closer, the colors of the blossom danced between vibrant hues of purples, blues, yellows, and reds.

Without thinking, Jonathan used his rapier to prick at it a couple of times, until the petals suddenly closed around the tip of the weapon with the ferocity of a vise grip. He managed to pull his sword free before letting out a panicked yelp when the boat started moving without his input. His hand darted to the side of the watercraft to grasp it tightly as it was being pushed away with the ripples, and he realized that not only had the strange flower risen up high above him in a matter of seconds, it was in fact only the pistil of a much larger lotus flower, this one with a corolla of brilliant white and measuring a span of approximately thirty feet between the points of opposite petals.

His attention was not kept on this new flower for long. A seedpod broke through the surface of the lake as an extension of this flower, sharing very few characteristics with a typical lotus receptacle. This pod featured a gaping mouth of sharp fangs, reminiscent of carnivorous plants, but really only those that belonged in nightmares. The water dripping from its wide orifice looked like the drool of a famished animal, and the holes that would normally house the seeds could be mistaken for dozens of jet-black eyes.

It lunged at him with frightening speed and succeeded in closing its jaws around his left arm. The fabric of his thick coat hindered the plant-beast's attack, though its longer and sharper fangs drew blood underneath his clothes. The blooming sting of pain snapped him out of his state of shock as he jerked violently away. The seedpod pulled itself in and appeared to be winding up for another ruthless attack.

Jonathan held his rapier steady in front of himself, drawing on energy from within his hand to focus on the thin blade. What began as tendrils of muted blue aura that floated around his grip and wrapped around the rapier abruptly shifted into silvery metal, condensing to transform the skinny sword into a giant vegetable knife.

Taking hold of the helm once more, Jonathan had the boat dash back toward the plant, barely dodging out of the direct path of the seedpod's second vicious lunge. As he sailed toward its stem, he resolutely held out his weapon, its shape transformed to better deal with this type of creature. The blade sliced cleanly through its thick stem as he whizzed past, and the truncated seedpod fell limp, plunging from its tall height into the water.

Just out of reach of the resulting splash and rippling waves, Jonathan cautiously circled the base of the plant and waited. Everything became calm.

Once he brought the boat to a full stop, he let out a groan as he released his hold on the helm and clumsily fell to his knees. Even with a warning to how dangerous encountering a chomping lotus could be, nothing could prepare his nerves for charging directly at it. It had been years since he last got up to silly antics like this that put him in the way of danger, and he could not decide if the thrill was worth it.

He stood and sailed closer to the now motionless plant. As soon as he figured it was within reach, he went to the edge of the boat and grabbed the intact stem of the flower, trying to pull at it and promptly realizing that it was firmly rooted to the bottom of the lake. He exerted more strength to yank it out, but being an individual of unimpressive brawn, he instead slipped on the wet surface of the boat and fell completely and unceremoniously into the water.

What a tiresome inconvenience. This struggle had best be worth paying for a new coat, at a minimum. He did not need to come up for oxygen, so he swam deeper toward the root of the lotus and used his weapon to loosen the dirt around it. It required significant effort, and he felt the soreness beginning to form within his arm muscles, but the rhizomes came loose where he could easily pull them up from the soil. The dark water heavily obscured his sight, but even through the murk, he could see how beautifully opalescent the rhizomes' skins appeared from the tiny amount of light they could catch.

With a total of four roots tucked in various coat pockets, Jonathan swam up to the boat, tossing over what he could to lighten his weight as he clambered back on board. He sat with a tired slouch on the side of the boat, lifting his hand to brush back his hair, the water having made it stringy, flat, and a little bit darker than his usual icy blue.

Being soaked was quite the nuisance for him and his tailored outfit, but turning to see how magnificently the irides-cent colors of the precious lotus stems sparkled under the afternoon sunlight reminded Jonathan of the reward that would await him. His rapier had returned to normal when the technique he used to transform it faded away, so he used a regular kitchen knife to chop the rhizomes in half, a better size to store them away in his bag. He decided he should take apart the giant white flower too. He could probably craft something exquisite from it.

Now that he had learned how to handle one of these beasts, he reasoned he should try his luck at locating another chomping lotus. He had already submerged himself under the water once, so what was one more time?

The second round went smoothly by comparison. Jonathan knew what kind of blossom to search for, how to prepare for when the beast would aggressively emerge from the lake's surface, how to decapitate the seedpod with satisfying efficiency after reforming the wider blade over his sword, and how to enter the water gracefully since it proved useless to try dislodging the plant's roots all the way up from the boat.

After the excitement of his hunt died down, he soon felt the weight of his physical and magical exertion. He was completely drained, but he had a total of eight lotus roots and two flowers to show for it. Once he finished sectioning off all the parts of these quirky plants into more compact pieces and storing them away, he lay down on his back across the open area of the boat deck and closed his eyes.

The sun was still fairly high in the sky, and Jonathan hoped the warmth of the sunlight would dry his clothes as he rested.

Jonathan was rusty; he was unsure he missed this kind of life. He had not done anything close to this since opening his restaurant. He had put away his rapier, fully dedicating his blades to chopping and dicing ingredients, rather than the slicing required for fights. Those first few years were the most precarious, and when despair would have been the prize that awaited him if his dreams had fallen apart—if he had failed—he became a workaholic.

But he was still a Mercenary. He had gotten his License over a decade ago, back when he was in his early twenties, thinking the coveted profession would be his best bet in securing a lavish amount of funds in a short amount of time for his true passion. And it worked. It helped him avoid debts and lease a desirable location that had been the perfect jumpstart to drawing in hungry customers.

Now that his restaurant was enjoying some stability in patronage, provided Labey had not managed to inflict too much of a dent in its reputation, Jonathan's thoughts wandered to whether or not he could go back to Mercenary work. It would no doubt still be for the sake of his restaurant rather than to run errands for the wealthy, where pursuing unusual beasts for revolutionary ingredients and exploring dangerous sites to discover exotic recipes would replace playing host and helping to wait tables.

"Well," he muttered to himself, "it is hardly a decision worth making now." There was still too much to attend to at the Taverne for him to make an abrupt occupational transition.

He lifted his arm to check his wristwatch for the time. Its quality craftsmanship had survived the water immersion he carelessly subjected it to. The lunch shift must have just finished by now, and it would soon be getting close to dinner. More than three hours had passed since he left the Taverne. His skin was beginning to prickle through his layer of sunscreen protection. He should head back.

Driving the boat toward the dock outside the rental shop, Jonathan found a place to park it before he moved the sheath of his sword behind his hip. He did not want to offer more reasons to be yelled at. The bag with his valuable cargo that he heaved onto his shoulder helped to further obscure it from view.

The shopkeeper studied him with clear disdain when he entered the shop to return the boat keys, his hair and clothes still damp.

"Are you some type of lunatic?" the keeper asked him, the scratchiness in his voice growing proportionately with his increasing volume. "I do not approve of you swimming in the lake! You stupid city folk, thinking you can do whatever you want."

Jonathan did not think his own pride was worth the energy to argue with this man. "It was an accident," he said wearily. "You saw how I lacked skill in driving the boat in the first place. I sincerely apologize." He held out the keys.

Jonathan felt a slight sting along his fingers as the man snatched them out of his hand with no delicacy at all.

"Get out of here," the keeper snarled. "Why can't I have normal customers for once?" He continued to grumble incoherent complaints under his breath about his urban-dwelling clientele.

With a shrug, Jonathan left the shop and called for an intercity cab to meet him back where he was dropped off. By the time he plodded through the fields to reach the dirt roads again, the vehicle was there waiting to bring him into the capital. Luckily for him, the driver did not seem to mind that he was not as dry as the grass around them.

Once they were back in Silver Valley, he instructed the driver to take him to his apartment complex. Before returning to his restaurant, he desperately wanted to shower and change his clothes. There were few things worse to him than appearing downright unpresentable.

When he removed his coat and shirt, he finally laid eyes on the bite marks left behind on the skin of his forearm and the trails of dried blood where it had dripped around the wounds. They were not as severe as the pain led him to believe at the time, but certainly not pretty to look at. He quickly cleaned the mess and bandaged his injuries, which of course became a tad cumbersome to keep out of the water of an otherwise warm and rejuvenating shower.

The tears left behind in the fabrics of his shirt and coat by the chomping lotus's fangs rendered them unsuitable for him to ever wear again, but he figured he should rid them of the blood that had soaked into them and donate them so someone else could make sure they did not go to waste. He was about to get ready to soak his clothes in cold water to wash out the stains when his cell phone rang. Frowning as he decided whether or not to take the call, he begrudgingly tossed the clothes into the sink as he went to look at his phone.

Elenora.

"Hello?" he answered. "Is something the matter?"

"Mr. Tessier." Her gentle voice came through with a negligible static effect. "Do you plan on returning to the restaurant soon? We, um. Someone... who seems super important just called and said she would be coming in. Didn't leave a name, though."

"Coming in now? In between shifts?"

"Yeah. She said we won't want to miss this opportunity."

His brow knitted in confusion, but he could detect a similar uncertainty within her voice too. "Very well. I was going to come in anyway; I will simply hurry back," he said. His sullied clothes would have to wait their turn to be saved.

CHAPTER 3

"OH, GOOD, YOU'RE HERE," Elenora said with a huge sigh of relief when Jonathan stepped inside the restaurant at around half past four in the late afternoon. She spoke hurriedly and with a fluctuating timbre, as if she had not yet recovered from a frenzy. "Having to deal with anything outside the safety of my little kitchen makes me so nervous, you have no idea. I was terrified I was going to screw something up!"

He gave her a repentant smile. There was no doubt in his mind that she handled things splendidly while he was gone. She merely lacked the confidence she most definitely deserved to have. "Even if you did, I think I would be able to forgive you."

"Then I'll forgive you for abandoning me," she said with a mock pout, at which he chuckled lightly.

A clean dress shirt and coat concealed his bandaged wounds, and the bag containing the spoils of his lotus battle hung from his shoulder.

"When did the person who called say they were going to arrive?" he asked.

"In about ten minutes. The conversation is a blur to me, but I remember her asking if we'd be able to help with a special order."

As a small business, he would consider himself and his team quite flexible, even if the timing came about rather inconveniently. There were really no hard rules for what customers could try asking of them, the restaurant technically being closed notwithstanding. It was only a matter of how far he would have to go to ensure their satisfaction.

"Did everyone else already leave for break?"

Elenora nodded.

"Alright, then I will be back in a moment. I want to leave this up in my office," he said, gesturing to his shoulder bag.

When he returned, their guest had been let inside by Elenora and was sitting at one of the tables, waiting for him. The head chef stood awkwardly at an arm's length in a timid silence with her hands passively clasped in front of her.

He could guess why. The woman who had come to visit them wore a custom black dress of fancy materials adorned with ribbons and mesh that contoured her elegant form better than anything he had seen even his own mother wearing. She was an older lady, with white streaks in her short black hair, sunken cheeks, and a sharp gaze that caused him to start when she looked up at him. It was clear she held high status.

"Hello," he began, voice raspy before he cleared his throat. "Hello, ma'am," he tried again, accented with a respectful bow of his head. "What brings you to our humble restaurant?"

The smile she gave in response caused him to shiver, but he did not think she looked unkind. It was more of a dull sorrow that he saw in her piercing hazel eyes.

"I wanted to come here because we have found ourselves in quite a bit of a bind," she answered. "I am Lucille Askew, sister of the recently departed Clifton Askew."

Jonathan recognized the second name as one belonging to the national treasurer who served here in Silver Valley. He did not keep up with politics closely enough to have been aware of the man's passing.

He directed his gaze to the floor. "My condolences, Lady Askew."

"Thank you," she said. He attempted to gauge her voice for a standout emotion, but he could only read indifference from it. "The caterer we booked for his memorial service decided to pull out rather last minute, much to our further dismay. So, I have come to you with an urgent request, if that is within your capacity."

Catering was a service so few asked of the Taverne that he barely remembered they offered it. If he recalled correctly, he had not updated the catering menu in several months.

"How urgent?"

"By tomorrow morning. I am willing to pay any expedited fee."

When he looked up and glanced at Elenora, she had her eyebrows raised with interest. Before either of them could answer, Lucille spoke up again.

"I actually came across Trevor Labey's review of your restaurant, which is how I found you."

For a few seconds, he could do nothing but stare blankly at her. "You. . . you saw the review and chose to come here all the same?"

Her chuckle was soothing and pleasant. "Indeed. We do not have many options with the availability we need, and your lovely chef here told me over the phone that you might be able to help me." The glance she gave Elenora forced the latter to avert her gaze from what seemed to be inadvertent intimidation. This reaction did not seem to bother Lucille, though. "Besides, having this emergency on our hands means I do not seek to take any risks. An 'uninspired' restaurant is a more reassuring option than one that does too much."

Jonathan frowned at her answer and suppressed a grimace. "We never wanted to be described in that manner," he admitted. "It was awful timing. We often aim to experiment with flavors that may not be for everyone. In fact, we just obtained a supply of a new ingredient I would love to incorporate, if you would be willing to entertain it, ma'am." He thought this might be the perfect opportunity to truly impress someone belonging to the elite and squash the allegations that his restaurant was boring.

"What is this ingredient?"

The way she studied him through this exchange was nothing short of intense, and it was all he could do not to rudely look away. It was in those moments she gazed so directly at him that he understood why Elenora displayed such a shy demeanor. "A rare variant of the lotus root. You can sample the dish we use it in, and if it is not to your liking, then we will not include it." His bluff relied on the testimonies of those associates, and he hoped to not regret trying to impress her.

She said nothing for a few moments, appearing to consider his proposal. Eventually, she dipped her head in a gesture of acceptance. "Very well. That sounds reasonable to me."

Jonathan went to fetch paper and a pen from the host station so he could write out some fresh options for Lucille to choose from. He listed various finger sandwiches, salads, a few types of meat and cooked vegetable platters, and a couple of appetizer selections.

While she mulled over her choices, he used the phone next to the cash register to call in his staff. Because he needed everyone to come in earlier than the usual dinner start time to handle this order on top of their upcoming rush, he offered generous overtime rates that would undoubtedly be covered by the lavish Askew budget, which succeeded in pulling the entirety of his team back to the restaurant within half an hour. What a relief his staff was so easy to motivate. Even the wait team could lend a hand with tasks around the busy kitchen, especially in packing up the food and preparing it for delivery.

He then sat with Lucille to answer any of her questions and discuss the finer details of her preferences. Prices, quantities, and recipe adjustments to take allergies into consideration. She seemed satisfied with his suggestion to use the rare lotus roots in a cooked vegetable platter as well as a salad, both of which she would taste before giving her final approval. As he went to retrieve his bag and bring it to the storage room, he calculated that the recipes he had in mind would require using around half of the eight rhizomes he had just acquired.

When their doors opened for dinnertime, Jonathan and Elenora shifted from working on the catering to handling orders from their other customers, while the rest of the team continued on. He reasoned that his chefs had already gained a type of rhythm in their work, and it would be best not to disturb them from it. After about an hour, the waiters also began transitioning to helping with their regular guests, and the kitchen became divided in responsibilities. Lucille was invited to wait in the employee break area upstairs so she would not be bothered by their bustling dining room.

In between bringing out dishes to their patrons, Jonathan started noticing strange movements from one of his chefs. Rhea was hovering around the kitchen garbage can for much too long to simply be throwing scraps away, and her gaze was so focused on something inside the bin that she did not catch him looking in her direction. He split his concentration between chopping vegetables and glancing up every so often to observe her behavior.

Finley came into the kitchen to pick up orders, but Rhea pulled him aside and whispered something Jonathan was too far away to hear. The waiter then walked over to tie up the garbage bag and take it outside to the alley where they kept their dumpsters, even though it was alarmingly clear to Jonathan that the bag had not been filled enough to require disposal.

Cautious instinct had him flagging Elenora over, though he hesitated when he saw that Rhea now had her focus directed at him. She even dared to move closer under the pretense of resuming work so she would be within earshot. He could not yet tell Elenora what he saw.

"Would you mind taking over for me here when you have the

chance?" he asked her instead. "I want to check on the progress of our catering." The head chef readily agreed, and they proceeded as normal, though the knowledge of Rhea's and Finley's suspicious activities mentally gnawed away at him. He could only hope his acting was convincing enough for Rhea not to realize that he had been alerted to her conduct.

Finley walked back inside and moved with purpose toward his rightful place in the dining room. Rhea carried on with her cooking with no further signs of irregularity. Jonathan found no opening to talk with Elenora and could not do much more than keep all his staff busy and distracted to ensure they would not move out of line for the rest of the shift.

A few minutes before the restaurant would close for the night, Lucille reappeared downstairs and called for Jonathan's attention. Somewhere in the typical chaos of their labor, the chefs managed to set aside small portions of the lotus salad and vegetable platter that Jonathan tasted and approved for a waiter to bring up to her. Handling the evening's split duties meant he had no time to be present when she tried these experimental dishes, so she must have come here now to share her feedback.

He went to meet her right outside of the kitchen with a tense expression that refused to leave his face, even when she told him he could relax.

"I also ordered a couple of other items from your menu. I had gotten a bit peckish," she said with some amusement in her tone. He had not expected her to be so lighthearted about her ordeal.

"I hope everything met your expectations." No sooner had he finished his sentence than he wished to amend his words. Her expectations must have already been set low thanks to the critic's review.

"Truth be told, I do not believe your restaurant to be as mediocre as Labey wrote it off to be. It may not hold the same prestige as my regular picks, but it does have potential."

He was too afraid to rejoice, in case he might have heard her incorrectly. "Really?"

"Yes. I think your Taverne is a promising newcomer to the culinary scene. That man craves attention and is shortsighted in his reviews, but he knows nothing about your future." She made a point to glance around. "This place is rough and unrefined, and perhaps might benefit from a space less cramped, but with some proper investment, I can envision you doing very well."

If gasping did not require a heavy intake of air, he would have done so in response to her favorable appraisal. Her esteemed social status made these half compliments something he yearned to hear. "Thank you for your kind words, ma'am."

"Should Clifton's memorial service be a success as far as the catering is concerned, I will see what I can do to assist you with your reputation and investment. Though I cannot promise it will be easy, as it may require you to earn more favor with my family and social circle," she said, a sly smile resting on her lips. "Our Askew name tends to be misleading, but you can trust us to deal straight with you. Clifton did not serve so many years without having earned genuine approval from the public."

Jonathan knew better than to ever put blind confidence in someone with great wealth, though any benefit he could squeeze out of the rich would be difficult for him to refuse.

He expressed his sincere gratitude again, and the lady left before they locked the doors and began their cleanup routine. Extra tasks were given to Rhea and Finley, plus a couple of the other staff to hide his attempt to keep his suspects occupied and inside the walls of the restaurant for as long as he could. A few complaints were tossed his way, but everyone complied before he had the chance to lose his temper.

This gave him the chance to pull Elenora aside to the storage room under the guise of taking inventory. With the door closed, he shuffled through items on the racks while she checked the refrigerator.

"I saw Rhea talking discreetly with Finley," he told her in a hushed voice. "Then Finley took a half-empty trash bag outside, probably with a lotus root inside it."

She wordlessly gave him a look that prompted him to continue.

"Once everyone begins to go home, if you see either of them—" He stopped himself. This entire time, he had anticipated a single culprit. With an alliance between a chef and a waiter, his suspicions were being proven otherwise, and for the worse. "Actually, if you see anyone go out through the kitchen's back door instead of our main entrance, I want you to call the police while I stall."

"Whoa, hold on. What do you mean by 'stall'?" Elenora asked. "I don't like the sound of that. Seems a little dangerous, Mr. Tessier."

He hummed, moving over to the box where he had placed the lotuses when he brought them back downstairs. There were only three roots inside.

"Maybe," he said. "Then you should also guard access to our knives, just in case."

Her face scrunched up with disbelief. He could see that she wanted to ask if he was crazy, but she said nothing.

"Of course, if it gets dangerous, your priority should be getting yourself to a safe place."

"Absolutely not," she said in the familiar incensed lilt she usually only used when a customer had been unfair to someone on their team. "If they try anything to hurt you, I'll be ready to knock them out myself."

Jonathan recognized her protective mother-bear spirit, but he was surprised to have that vigor dedicated to him even at the expense of their own coworkers. As the owner and an individual who would not tolerate any nonsense, he never had an issue dealing with unreasonable patrons, so he did not think he would see a time when Elenora would fight for his honor. He appreciated it deeply.

His usually stern composure softened. "This is a really terrible idea," he said sheepishly. "I would not forgive myself if you got hurt. But I need to be sure."

She cracked a smile and nodded once. "At least you're aware. There's nothing I hope more than we're wrong about Rhea and Finley. But if they are stealing from us, then I have no problem putting them in their place."

Having confirmed through the remaining quantity of rhizomes that someone had taken advantage of the evening's mayhem to act again, Jonathan left the storage room first and went to sit at one of the tables, where he would be perfectly positioned to watch the front door while he reviewed the day's profits.

If it had not been for the catering order, they would have performed noticeably worse than yesterday. Disappointing, but much too soon to attribute it to Labey's review. It could go either way. Maybe it was a singular bad day, or maybe until he was able to counteract the critic's influence, he could only rely on regular customers who with their previous positive dining experiences at the Taverne would not be driven away by one online post.

Yevina and Natalie were the first to leave together, engrossed in cheery conversation as they waved goodbye to their boss and exited through the front doors. How blissfully ignorant they were of the dirty scoundrels in their midst. Both had been waitresses at the Taverne for about three or four years, making them a part of the roster that had stayed for more than one anniversary.

The average tenure of any restaurant employee was not more than a few months, so his establishment enjoyed a fairly impressive retention rate. Hiring new staff to replace those who left or were fired after just a year was still far from a pleasant experience for him. Between getting to know new people and the logistical hassle of having to change the team every now and then, he never concerned himself with developing anything beyond a professional relationship with his staff. But he valued employees like those two, who stuck around long enough for him to say he could trust them.

He thought about Rhea Obie, a chef that he hired about eleven months ago. She was a woman of similar age to his, in her thirties, who had a proper decade of experience when she interviewed with him. Her long dark brown hair was neatly tied up whenever she was in the kitchen, and her doe-like green eyes matched her quieter disposition. She did not take to the humor or ebullience the rest of the team relished in, and he had thought that meant she was a serious artisan, one dedicated to the craft, with a comparable attitude to his.

Finley Ebrar was a younger employee, in his mid-twenties, but had been at the Taverne for almost two years. He had been a seasonal worker turned semipermanent when he showed consistent performance and a desire for more hours. Despite his stockier build, he was able to move with impressive speed and grace between tightly spaced tables. Jonathan did wish that Finley shaved his dark stubble more often, but he had thought the waiter's dedication had more than made up for a less ideal grooming routine, so he never commented on it.

To think he had so innocently construed these characteristics of theirs as propitious rather than as masks to hide their traitorous intentions. They were only biding their time under facades of devotion for an opportunity to blindside the person who provided them employment.

Jonathan had to remind himself it was too early to draw conclusions based on his frustrations. Granted, the thieves were defiling his ambitions to be a revolutionary culinary force whose claim to fame would be his creation of legendary new recipes. Given how hard it had been for him to get a decent night's sleep ever since the thefts began, it was not easy to wave away these negative thoughts that were beginning to form about Rhea and Finley before their collective guilt was confirmed.

Henry was the next to leave, then Danna, and soon Ransley and Marshall. Within an hour after closing, Orla became the last to head home, aside from his pair of suspects.

When he saw Finley pass by him next, Jonathan had to conceal any hint of surprise that might have flickered across his face. The waiter did as the others and bid farewell as he also walked out through the main entrance. It was now quite dark this late into the night, but Jonathan watched carefully through the front windows of the restaurant as Finley strolled down the street, illuminated only by streetlamps until he was out of sight.

It was in observing Finley's relaxed state that Jonathan noticed a shadowy individual he did not recognize standing on the sidewalk across the street. The figure was hunched over and facing the restaurant head-on.

At this hour, there were often very few people still wandering these particular streets in favor of ones with bars and resorts. Those who happened to be around walked with clear destinations in mind and did not linger nor take more than a fleeting interest in a closed restaurant. Jonathan stepped closer to the windows to get a better view, though he realized too late that his curiosity might have been detected by the stranger when they began tilting their head forward like they were trying to peer inside.

He moved over to the tables away from the front of the restaurant and began straightening them. Not that he needed to, since the flower vases and tablecloths were already oriented with excellent precision. He only wanted to appear busy and keep his hands occupied until he meandered his way to the kitchen.

With a firm grip on a knife-sharpening rod, Elenora hurried to speak. "Rhea just went out through the back door when she thought I wasn't looking," she said. "I don't think she knows that I saw her leave."

Something was definitely going down. They needed to act fast.

"Call the police now," Jonathan instructed her. "And I will leave it to you whether you want to interfere. But please, do not do so until you hear me knock three times on this door."

He then unhooked one of the hanging cast-iron skillets and took it with him as he hurried back to the dining room.

CHAPTER 4

THE SHADOWY FIGURE WAS no longer where Jonathan first saw them when he went to check the front windows again.

They had stalked over to the nearby crosswalk and were currently waiting for the chance to move to this side of the street. Standing at a distance from the windows where the illumination from outside would not catch him, Jonathan tried to peer out and follow the stranger's path from a rather disadvantageous angle.

As he expected, they turned right and began walking toward the Taverne. Jonathan stepped back farther to ensure he would not be easily seen. He lost sight of the suspicious individual in the process, but he anticipated he would witness them walk by the building anyway in just a few seconds.

Much to his chagrin, they did no such thing.

Jonathan all but pressed himself against the glass to scan the outside. He stared at the street in disbelief, which was now completely empty. The lurker had vanished.

Surely they had no reason to turn around and go an entirely different direction. Or worse yet, if they were somehow involved with whatever was going on with Rhea, that could mean they dared to sneak behind the restaurant instead, like a dirty, scurrying little rat.

Before he rushed to go outside, Jonathan retrieved his phone using his unoccupied hand and had it start recording audio as a precaution. He then left the restaurant still holding the cast-iron pan near his chest, keeping close to the wall as he skulked quietly through the alley between buildings.

He stopped short when he reached the corner, hearing a familiar voice in the process of confirming his speculations.

"Finley and I managed to snatch up a rare lotus root," Rhea said. "When I first saw it, all I could think of was how beautiful it was, and I knew it would fetch a pretty price."

The voice that responded was scratchy and harsh, so he could not imagine it belonging to anyone other than that shady figure. "Is that so?"

"You better not try to cheat me out of a good price, Wisp," Rhea said. "I know this one should be worth a lot."

"We'll see. Where is it?"

"Finley should be here soon to help me get it out of the trash."

So, the waiter left through the front door only to deceive. A shame Finley had the guile to spend on deeds like this. Jonathan did not have to wait long, and as he moved the skillet so it was mostly hidden behind his back, he slipped his phone into a coat pocket and rounded the corner soon after he heard the waiter joining his conspirators.

"Oh? What is this?" Jonathan said to draw their attention. "Rhea? Finley? What is going on here?" He did not enjoy having to feign ignorance, but these crooks had taken him for a fool and forced him to play along. After this was all done with, and hopefully that would be very soon, he would not have to engage in their wicked game anymore.

The chef and waiter gave him that helpless-deer-in-head-lights look before they scrambled for excuses as to why they would be loitering behind the restaurant instead of already headed home.

"Mr. Tessier! W-we just wanted to. . ." Rhea began, glancing between the two people accompanying her in her apparent crimes. Thanks to the light from a small lamp over the restaurant's back door, Jonathan could see now that the lurker who went by Wisp was another man. He was hunched over and presumably of older age, as evidenced by the salt-and-pepper beard exposed under a hood that hid the majority of his face. "An item of mine went missing, so we were just looking around for it. We didn't want to bother you after such a busy day," Rhea managed to utter.

Jonathan raised a brow at this blatant lie. He knew he needed to keep his voice calm, but it was agonizing to suppress his anger. In her deceit, she had somehow spun this situation around to paint herself as the one who lost something. How dare she. He was the one who was made to suffer from their thoughtless actions.

"Is that so?" he asked. "Unfortunately, I seem to have also misplaced something of mine. You see, it is quite valuable, and I worry that it was disposed of in the rush."

The three of them visibly stiffened, but he would not let them off the hook so easily.

"Well, tell me what it is you have lost, and maybe we can help each other."

Rhea spoke first, as she had no other choice. "A—A bracelet. . ." Even she did not seem convinced of her own tale, stuttering and fidgeting where she stood. No proper chef would be wearing jewelry around their hands while handling food. Had she truly lost it, it would not be out here, so far from her belongings.

Jonathan lowered his head in disappointment, choosing not to honor her with a response. Instead, his eyes moved between her and Finley as he watched the latter's expression of guilt increase with each passing second.

"Do I not pay you both well?" he asked them. "And with tips, your paychecks are that much more robust. You threw the lotus rhizome out on purpose, and I assume you were also the ones who stole the expensive ingredients from before. Do you mean to tell me that your greed led you to think this behavior is acceptable?"

"What are you going to do?" Finley finally spoke up, his voice shaking. "If you're going to fire us anyway, then no harm done, right? Your restaurant does not have enough prestige to be selling that kind of cuisine anyway."

"Yeah." Rhea joined in, bolstered by her cohort's daring words. "What an awful waste. Is this how you're spending money you could've given to us as bonuses?"

Jonathan narrowed his eyes. He had not expected such disrespectful aggression from his now former staff members. He could not have known that they held these grievances against him when they had been pretending to be satisfied with their employment.

"Leave everything alone, do not touch anything," he told them. "That goes for your friend there too. We will wait here for the police, so if you resist, I will not hesitate to use force."

All three of them stared at him incredulously.

"You?" Rhea said. "In a three against one? You're a fool and delusional."

Finley crossed his arms over his chest and stood tall in what Jonathan assumed was supposed to be an intimidating stance. "You should be careful with your words. I don't want to hurt you, but you know you wouldn't stand a chance against me. We'll be taking our loot and leaving."

It was not a debate that he was of average height and not nearly as muscular as Finley, but Jonathan knew they were still only ordinary people. He frowned when the ex-waiter began ambling over to the dumpster but said nothing as he eased himself toward the door and knocked on it thrice.

Elenora emerged behind him with her knife-sharpening rod at the ready, glancing around wildly to assess the situation. Jonathan raised his hand to brace himself against the door she almost smacked him with.

"Rhea! Finley!" she called out. "How could you do this against your own restaurant? And who is this guy? Nobody go anywhere, the police are on their way!"

Rhea groaned, clearly annoyed that someone else had come to interrupt their heist. "Well, we're obviously not going to be working here anymore. You know what?" she said, addressing

Finley and the shady merchant instead. "Let's just take care of them both and get out of here already."

There were times when a person might do something unexpected, but not entirely surprising. In all his caution, Jonathan had imagined that they would fight back if he were to catch them in the act but deemed it an unlikely possibility. When Rhea and Finley each pulled out their pocketknives and wielded them with the intent to harm, he understood that he had to make them wish they had run instead.

They charged at him first, but their amateur maneuvers were a cinch to dodge and block with his cast-iron pan. A sudden attack from Wisp, who had manifested a sharp-edged switchblade outside of Jonathan's peripheral vision, was the only one that found purchase, slicing a shallow but long cut across the back of his hand and drawing blood.

Jonathan winced and pulled away from them, though the wound was minor and he reacted quickly. His other hand became cloaked in his muted blue aura and he ran his fingers across the gash. The energy was hot against his skin as it cauterized the wound and stopped the bleeding in an instant.

In the next swift movement, he held out the pan, and tendrils of whitish smoke wafted from its cooking surface. The overwhelming aroma of fermented herring traveled through the cold night air, aimed at the three perpetrators who were in the process of charging him again.

Disoriented by the delicacy's awful stench, Rhea screamed as she recoiled and Wisp doubled over with a gaunt hand clasped around his nose. Though his face crumpled up from the smell and he stopped short in his run, a steadfast Finley seemed to be more resilient against Jonathan's olfactory assault.

"How dare you attack your own boss after stealing from him!" Elenora shouted furiously. She had been momentarily stunned from their audacious instigation of violence, but hastily snapped out of it as she ran toward Wisp, the one she likely had the least misgivings about fighting back.

When speaking of times someone was able to do something both unexpected and surprising, Elenora rapidly claimed that position as she lunged toward the hooded man. Jonathan wanted to stop her from jumping in where she could be severely hurt because he knew she was also not like him, but when she expertly swung her sharpening rod directly into Wisp's temple before he could recover from the stench, she did so with sufficient force to render him unconscious. Jonathan felt his worry dissipate in that instant. The strange man was devious enough to land a sneak attack, but he was not hardy enough to withstand the fury of a strong thwack upside the head. He collapsed into a heap and his knife clattered from his grip onto the dark asphalt.

Fueled by a level of rage Jonathan had never seen her possess, Elenora wasted no time in facing a distracted Rhea. He thought she would experience some remorse in so brutally knocking a man out cold, but she showed him that he should begin forming some new opinions regarding his dear head chef.

"How selfish do you have to be to hurt someone over some lousy vegetables?" she screamed as she swung the rod at Rhea. Elenora did not manage a clean hit this time, but as Rhea tried to block the blow, she was further shaken when the metal made contact with her forearm with painful speed, the sharp sound of the whack leaving those still conscious wondering if a bone had been broken.

Rhea yelled out in pain, hurling a fiery glare in Elenora's direction. "Will you shut up about it already?" Jonathan did not know she was capable of mustering such a snarl from what had once been a serene voice.

Undeterred, Elenora ruthlessly swung again, but Rhea had the sense to dodge and counter with her own attempt to shank her senior chef. With a fluid movement, Elenora brought the rod around to divert the course of Rhea's knife before it could stab her.

Jonathan felt torn on whether he should keep watching the women as they engaged in combat with each other or rush over to help. Finley was still standing, but his concern for Elenora's safety had left him wrought with an intense fear that they might end the night with a devastating tragedy. He could have sworn he saw an image of that knife plunging deep into Elenora's body flash through his mind despite the reality.

Spinning the handle of the pan in his hand, he dismissed the crippling fishy aromas and aimed an invigorating scent of peppermint at Elenora instead. It was one of her favorites.

He was not ignorant of the fact that the power he chose to train when he first began honing his aura and the abilities that came with it would raise eyebrows. Most of his peers desired explosive skills or tricks that resembled wizard magic of fantastical lore. When he designed one of his powers to conjure aromas from his aura that either boosted his allies' energy and concentration or debilitated his foes, he wanted to make the point to any naysayers that the sense of smell was not to be underestimated, either in culinary environments or the heat of battle.

As he surrounded Elenora in a scent he knew she passionately adored, he watched her inhale deeply with a fleeting look of surprise in one moment and pounce forward with focus in the next, where she found an opening to tackle Rhea onto the ground with careful precision and restrain her arms behind her back. Elenora snatched the pocketknife out of Rhea's hand and removed her own apron, using its strings to securely tie the struggling chef's wrists together.

Jonathan turned his gaze toward the lone Finley, whose eyes darted between his fallen partners and his former employer, not knowing whether to fight or flee. The prize of the valuable lotus root must have held a tempting grip on him that he chose the former. He rushed toward Jonathan and swung twice, striking at empty air both times as Jonathan weaved nimbly out of the way.

Before he even had the chance to retaliate, Elenora appeared, having snuck up behind Finley to swing her blunt weapon at him. Though the man displayed shock at her sudden arrival, instinct allowed him to block her strike in time. The moment Finley changed his focus, Jonathan struck him with the pan, aiming for a specific spot on his neck to dampen his strength and leave Finley dazed and wobbly rather than fully unconscious.

Elenora got to work as soon as Finley fell over, binding his arms behind his back using his own belt. She panted heavily throughout her task as the heightened levels of adrenaline that had rushed through her body during their scuffle were catching up to her now that it was over.

Jonathan walked to Rhea, and he found her squirming in an attempt to get back on her feet. He grabbed behind the collar of her chef's uniform and dragged her toward the wall, pulling her into a sitting position against it.

"You are staying right here until the police arrive," he said to her with a scowl. She looked like she wanted to say something biting in response, but since none of her mocking words from before had done her any service, she seemed to think better of it as she let her chin drop.

The cops finally arrived a few minutes later. Elenora handled most of the explanation regarding what had happened. Jonathan contributed simply to say that he could provide them with an audio recording, one that would prove not only the thefts, but that he and Elenora acted in self-defense.

He was vigilant with his word choice, making sure nothing he said could be deemed a lie. Elenora had no hesitations dressing up the story she gave to the police, so that they would think Jonathan had accidentally stumbled across the crime no sooner than minutes before the officers arrived, and that she only became involved when she heard commotion outside the kitchen door.

The police surveyed the scene for relevant clues and told them the situation was straightforward, but they still recommended at least one of them accompany the officers to the station for a full report. Elenora volunteered, so Jonathan attached the recording via text and sent it to her. He told the officers he was exhausted, and since he gave his evidence to Elenora, she should be more than capable of providing an adequate statement.

Once the three culprits, two thieves and a black-market salesman, were taken away and the cops departed with Elenora, Jonathan delicately rummaged in the half-empty trash bag to retrieve the stolen lotus rhizome. His face pulled into a grimace as he labored through the task.

He went into the kitchen with the lotus and used one of the sinks to wash it thoroughly. The breathtaking prismatic luster began to restore itself as the filth was rinsed away under the running water.

After he dried the root with paper towels and returned it to the box with the others, Jonathan checked the time. The altercation had only lasted a couple of minutes, if even that, having occurred with such fleeting intensity. The interaction with the police had taken half an hour at most. It was not even midnight yet.

If he had sustained more injuries than the one across the back of his hand, he might have considered simply heading home to rest. But he was fine, and his conscience beckoned him to wrap things up here in Elenora's place when she was working hard elsewhere for his sake. He was still basking in the substantial feeling of gratitude that she had emerged from the skirmish with not one scratch on her body, and he was beyond impressed with the way she had handled herself.

He made a mental note to ask her later where she learned to fight like that.

With the kitchen and dining areas tidied up, Jonathan went up to his office to deal with any administrative duties he could fit in before he needed to retire for the night. As he waited for his computer to wake up from standby mode, he reclined fully into his chair so the back of his head draped over the headrest and his chin pointed toward the ceiling.

Things were going to change around here. The constant agitation he felt during the last several days would be assuaged now that the perpetrators had been discovered and arrested, but that was hardly the end of the matter. He lost a reliable waiter and a capable chef, which would certainly alter the team dynamics and oblige him to begin searching for replacements.

He did not care much for how the other chefs and waiters might receive the news that they lost Rhea and Finley. They could adjust and move forward with very few issues. That was the nature of the hospitality industry. It was Elenora he most wanted to check in with later. The fierce look she had in her eyes when she fought was an image he could still clearly see in his mind.

With Wisp, her lack of hesitation was hardly something to be questioned. The man was an unfamiliar intruder and the only one with enough cunning to have actually hurt her boss. That her ferocity did not die down when she faced her own juniors was what stood out to Jonathan. Rhea might have been their newest employee, but her time at the Taverne had been plenty, and Elenora tended to bond fast with her coworkers.

There was also everything he imagined he would need to explain to Elenora, whose questioning looks he did not miss amid the action. The aromas that apparated from nowhere, the instant cauterization of his wound, maybe even where in such a short amount of time he had gotten the ingredient they used as bait. An ingredient so beautiful to behold he had not needed to announce its value for Rhea and Finley to fall into his trap.

Jonathan fixed his posture with a soft groan and checked his email inbox. One message timestamped as sent earlier in the evening was from his mother's doting friend. It contained a more thorough list of premium ingredients trending among foodies. He sorted through the list, eliminating those said to be located too far across the nation to obtain or those that did not particularly inspire him, and scrawled out ideas for each of the surviving contenders for possible menu items.

The other emails were mundane, except for one. His father's old associate claimed they had already arranged for a few other critics to pay the Taverne a visit in a week. The critics would be upfront about having been explicitly invited, and might not entirely undo the damage, but their ability to spotlight the restaurant to their audiences would be invaluable. Impressing them would dull the sting of Labey's negative feedback.

Jonathan did not recognize the names belonging to two out of the three critics, and he would not discredit their credentials for it, but he gawked at the third.

Lala Sweet. *The* Lala Sweet. Impossible.

The bottom right drawer of his desk contained a trove of newspaper clippings, printouts of online articles, and mementos of great accomplishments by esteemed culinarians. Little reminders of what he himself wanted to achieve. The top celebrity gourmet chef in Ameza with the endearing name provided more contributions to his collection than anyone else.

His veritable admiration for her far exceeded how ridiculous he normally would have thought her name to be. Praise for her restaurants and the unique taste of her cuisine had only escalated the past couple years, and that put her further out of his reach.

There was absolutely no way she would make the time to visit such a tiny, insignificant restaurant as his. Not a chance.

But what if this was the reality where it could happen? Perhaps there was that slim possibility he had underestimated the capabilities of the associate who cared to relay this information to him, as he had been inclined to do with most of these people. If the contents of this email turned out to indeed be reliable, Jonathan would just as vehemently refuse to forgive himself for letting this golden opportunity slip through his fingers as he would despise feeling a fool for being so gullible.

A glowing review from the one and only Lala Sweet would propel him into the renown he had been hungry for his entire career.

Such a grand reward was worth the minuscule risk. He replied with a declaration of his gratitude, a promise to connect the associate with his fellow Mercenaries, and an affirmation that he would be ready in time for their visit.

Maybe things, one by one, the mystery of the thefts and his restaurant's reputation, were beginning to sort themselves out in his favor.

CHAPTER 5

Elenora gaped, dumbfounded.

"Wait, hold on just a minute, Mr. Tessier," she said, waving a hand in front of her face as if the gesture could ward off her confusion. "Explain that to me one more time. Slower, please."

The two kicked off an earlier morning in his office, each of them settled in their usual spots. The staff members scheduled to work today were downstairs ensuring a safe delivery of the memorial service catering. They needed to get everything to the venue by nine.

"What I am getting at is that beyond the safety we enjoy in our metal cities, there are realms teeming with the kinds of mythical creatures and otherworldly herbs you only read about in children's books or fantasy novels," Jonathan said. "Many more that the average mind could not imagine."

The head chef frowned. Jonathan took it as an invitation to continue.

"Do you already know about those of us who can develop special abilities like the ones you saw me using last night? The healing of my wound, the aromas of food." He paused and she shook her head. "Different people choose different powers that align with their own talents and personalities, of course. The possibilities are immensely vast, but we call these 'magical' skills Avidea. They serve as the main grant that helps us access those wondrous realms."

"A grant?" she echoed. "I didn't know grants were magic. I only heard of them as being extreme physical techniques, for elite soldiers and law enforcement. I thought they weren't very safe?"

"Archaic grants were indeed extremely risky to their wielders. Avidea was developed to be a safer one that anyone can learn to use, although it is a much slower natural process that involves rigorous training."

"I see," she said. She exhaled deeply, briefly closed her eyes, and nodded when she reopened them. "Okay, let's say I agree this is all true. Mythical creatures and magic users are real. Why are you telling me?"

"I thought after what happened yesterday, it is time I be upfront with you," he said. "As someone I genuinely trust. For instance, I did not buy those lotus rhizomes from some merchant. To save money and time, I had to harvest them myself from a giant carnivorous plant found only in the lake miles outside the city."

Elenora furrowed her brow, saying, "What fairy tale are you going on about? So, you're saying you just found one of these giant plants. Just, out there. Was it dangerous?"

"It was. At first, I was unprepared. I had to fight it—"

"Fight it? Really?"

"Yes," Jonathan said. "It was manageable. But now I have a list of other rare ingredients that might be even more elusive. Can you picture it, Elenora? This could be the gourmet menu I have wanted for so long. And just in time for the critics' visit." He leaned forward over the desk in his enthusiasm. "With such a tight schedule, I wanted to know if you would be interested in joining me in my search. Even without Avidea, you handle yourself incredibly well in a fight."

"I just took some basic self-defense classes," she muttered in response to his praise. "But this... this feels like it's totally beyond me. Why can't we stick to the stuff we already know? Caviar? Bird's nests? A sprinkle of saffron or gold? Wouldn't that be good enough?"

And so, with urgency, Jonathan took Elenora down to the kitchen. He retrieved one of the lotus roots from storage, chopped a few thin slices from half of it, and sautéed those in olive oil. Even while they were cooking, the iridescent coloration across each slice was mesmerizing. He soon plated and served them to Elenora as they were. No additional dressings, no sauces, no seasonings.

The head chef had not vocalized a single comment throughout this process and continued on in that manner as she used chopsticks to pick up one of the slices and bring it to her mouth.

Jonathan observed her intently while she chewed. Her eyes quickly widened more and more with each passing second until she was done, her jaw left hanging open.

Neither of them said anything for a full minute. Her eyes seemed to water. He waited for her to articulate her reaction, but she had been stunned motionless.

The silence was finally broken by the loud clash caused when she slammed the chopsticks onto the counter.

"This is what we've been missing?"

He grinned widely.

"How is it so savory and complex, all on its own?" she asked, picking up her chopsticks again to help herself to another slice. "Hmm, it has all the essences of cream and curry. But you didn't add a single thing to it!"

"Not to mention the potential health benefits. Improved heart health and blood circulation," he added proudly, repeating what his mother's friend had claimed. A bit of online research found a handful of studies that confirmed the assertions.

After she had fully cleaned the plate, she confessed to him that she understood. She wanted to see for herself where food like that came from. Since an effort like this was unfamiliar territory for her, Jonathan suggested they search for the first ingredient on his list as a trial run, and determine at the end if she found it worthwhile to keep accompanying him.

In either case, he had only a week, and there was one more matter he had to address to allow him to concentrate wholly on that list.

"As you might be aware, Rhea Obie and Finley Ebrar are no longer on the team," Jonathan later told his staff after the catering delivery had been finalized. "They were caught stealing from the restaurant and have been arrested by the police. The investigation is ongoing."

He waited a few moments as they failed to resist murmuring among themselves. Elenora was the only one who had little reaction, having told him earlier that she was fine, and the police questioning had been the most boring part of last night.

"To recover from this as well as from the critic's review, Elenora and I will be handling some restructuring and other work behind the scenes. I have decided to close the restaurant for the next five or six days, but you will all receive your regular wages for this duration."

The more uninhibited employees dared to cheer at this news, but Jonathan disregarded it. He warned them to be prepared to execute a top-notch performance when they came back.

"Elenora, come with me to my cousin's tailor shop," he said once everyone else departed to enjoy their unforeseen paid leave. "I cannot in good conscience have anything like last night happen again with you so atrociously equipped."

Like him, Victoria Tessier had also left the wealth of their name behind. She spent considerable time in the wilderness playing nomad, but she often came back to the city to fulfill certain responsibilities. Her shop was a five-minute drive away by city cab. Jonathan and Elenora arrived there to find that today was one of their luckier days when the tailor welcomed them.

Victoria was often mistaken as Jonathan's younger sister, sharing his foxlike features and teal eyes that were characteristic of the noble family. She preferred to dye her pale hair a vivid hot pink instead, and wore bohemian fashions that were loose and flowy, as far departed from the formal threads he favored as possible.

"Jon," she said, lighting up when he entered her boutique. "It's lovely to see you after so long."

"Likewise, Vicky," he said, giving her a kiss on the cheek as a greeting. "I try to visit more, but you are not always here when I do."

Victoria glanced behind him at Elenora. "Ellie? You're here too?" The two women, similar in bubbly temperaments, smiled widely and waved at each other. The tailor looked between her two guests. "What can I do to help you today?"

"If you could have Elenora fitted with some standard protective gear, that would be wonderful," Jonathan said.

An inquisitive glint sparkled in Victoria's eyes at his request, but she turned to her assistant, giving them instructions to guide Elenora in finding something suitable. Elenora followed the assistant farther inside where the dressing rooms and closets were located, while the cousins remained in the front reception area.

"Why would Ellie need any armor, Jon? Are the chefs starting to toss knives around in your kitchen?" Victoria asked, an amused smirk plastered across her face. She flicked her wrist as if to throw an invisible knife in his direction.

"Hilarious."

"Much like the review you received from that eccentric food critic."

Jonathan rolled his eyes. "So, even you have seen it."

"I couldn't imagine you being very happy. I felt bad."

"I am going to rectify it by hunting for coveted ingredients and proving Labey a fool. Elenora will be lending me her support."

Victoria narrowed her eyes. "You mean... on the level of Mercenary work? She doesn't need to be put in that kind of position. Why don't you just hire someone from the Union instead?"

Founded by and currently still being run by Victoria's father, the Rose Union was a nationally esteemed adventurer's guild in Silver Valley that specialized in preparing talented prospects to earn Mercenary Licenses and distributing missions to those already in this lucrative profession. The senior Tessier was getting on in years and losing vitality, so he wanted either his daughter or his nephew to take over soon.

"I recently discovered there were thieves on my team. The fewer people involved with this endeavor, the better," Jonathan said.

"Sounds like you've been kept busy. You haven't been involved with the Union much lately. Dad wants to retire, so you should think about succeeding him."

"Should it not be you who succeeds him? You are as skilled, if not more, than I am. My combat prowess is miserable compared to yours."

The woman let out a deep sigh. "You know I don't have an affinity for Avidea like you do," she said. "And that's just as important a part to being a Mercenary. At least run it with me? I don't like the idea of doing it alone."

He felt he had a long way to go before he could harness

enough valor to fully partake in the Mercenary lifestyle. The occupation was a constant barrage of duties and risks, a delicate balance between proving one's worth and facing the perilous unknown.

"Forgive me, Vicky," he said. Though he had been hesitant, he gave her a gentle smile and nodded. "I promise you, after Elenora and I handle all of this, and I've gained more experience and fortitude, I should be much better prepared to help take over the Union. How have you been faring?"

"You know how it is," she said with a sigh. "Always running around the country from one job to the next."

"Has there been more work than usual? Or not enough people to handle it?"

She shook her head. "They mostly just take a lot out of me. And a lot of time."

They briefly discussed Victoria's most persistent case, which involved a bewildering disappearance. She described the missing person as a reputable nutritionist who mysteriously vanished several months ago, but even in these late desperate stages they were working on sparse leads to find him.

Elenora reappeared, having changed into an outfit better suited for the type of excursions Jonathan had in mind: a sturdy tactical jacket that Victoria described as having flexible light-weight metal plates between layers, durable cargo pants with sleek but spacious pockets, and comfortable combat boots.

"How do you feel, Ellie?" Victoria asked. "Are these to your liking?"

"They're great. Everything is so well-made and comfortable,"

Elenora said, diffidently adjusting the collar of her jacket. "I feel that I might be past the age to pull these off, though."

"Nonsense," Jonathan said. He took out his wallet to pay. "You look properly prepared and capable. Age has nothing to do with anything."

"He's right, for once," Victoria agreed, ignoring the glare her cousin shot in her direction. "You give off a very cool vibe. Have some confidence in yourself, girl!"

Jonathan reviewed the bill for Elenora's outfit and paid for it in full. Victoria insisted on giving them a discount, but he would not relent. She made him promise to update her on all the happenings of their upcoming excursion in return.

The two of them made it back to their restaurant by noon. On the ride to the Taverne, Jonathan learned that Elenora's favorite component of the outfit was the number of pockets simply by how much she gushed over them.

From all the items on his list, the plan was to begin with something called the radiant cabbage. These cabbages were said to be located in a small forest outside of the city in the southwestern direction, and though they were challenging to spot among the foliage during the day, their fluorescent leaves would be sure to draw attention after the sun had set. Jonathan's contact had informed him that the patches where they could be found might be guarded by dangerous creatures. His efforts to conduct additional research did not provide much more information on what these creatures might be.

"Wouldn't they just be bears or wolves?" Elenora asked. "I know some wilderness survival tips."

Jonathan shrugged. "These instances of scarce documentation almost always point to things of abnormal origins. Be prepared to encounter something odd tonight."

Though it would be more expensive, they decided to rent a car that Jonathan could drive rather than burden a cab driver to wait for or come retrieve them so far outside the city, especially at the late hour they expected to return. Elenora slept in the passenger seat for most of the ride, which required almost three hours to reach the edge of the forest.

The soothing orange glow of evening sunset shone through the gaps between the outer tree trunks, flickering like dancing blazes in the thicket. In the distant horizon toward the south lay the emergence of a mountain range that continued on for a significant length, joining numerous other summits that weaved through the land until they reached the western Amezan coast.

After finding a safe place to park the car, Jonathan woke Elenora, and they began trudging through the forest that encompassed the base of a few smaller mountains. As the beginnings of darkness cloaked their surroundings, he thought they should try to look for any hidden caves or alcoves that might obscure the glowing plants from view, in case the luminescence did not become blatantly obvious to them.

The farther they traveled, the denser the trees and the shrubbery underfoot became. Elenora tripped over fallen branches and uneven ground with increasing frequency, so Jonathan offered his arm for her to hold on to as they patrolled.

She started grumbling. "Is this even worth the effort? This place is awful! What if we don't even find anything?"

He said nothing for now and let her air out her frustrations. She muttered under her breath for a few moments more.

"Will people even care if we used radiant cabbage instead of some normal cabbage?"

That felt too redundant of a question to ignore. "Did you already forget how the lotus tasted?"

"No," she groaned. "I didn't. . . Did you know that memories associated with the sense of taste are incredibly fleeting?"

"Second only to smell in terms of memory recall, Elenora."

"Well, wouldn't it be easier to just buy these ingredients?" she asked.

"We only have one week. The supply is incredibly lim—"

He was interrupted when, despite his support, Elenora yelped and stumbled over something underneath her feet once more. They both stopped and looked back.

"A grave marker?" Jonathan muttered. It was a rickety one made with two wooden scraps nailed together into the shape of a cross. He did not dare tamper with the man-made heap sitting near it.

Elenora shivered and inched away. Jonathan leaned in to peer more closely at the marker, noting a roughly scrawled message written across the horizontal scrap of wood.

I shouldn't have survived.

A chill ran through his body, and he turned to Elenora, expecting her to express aversion toward this discovery. She instead seemed to be spurred to action, brandishing the butcher knife she brought along and steadying herself.

"Let's get this over with," she said as she walked past him and led on. "Cowering in fear is not going to be useful to us if we want to stay alive."

Despite her complaints, Elenora had always been one to step up to face dire situations. Last night proved that to him more than anything. He laughed quietly to himself and followed her, though reading that ominous message in the middle of a darkening forest had him on edge. It seemed to hint at something harrowingly sinister.

While the sky above them continued to lose light, they came upon a sloped area of the woods where a small clearing opened below them. Near the bottom of the slope sat a sizable mound of rocks, twigs, dead leaves, and moss that had naturally formed over long periods of time. Perhaps the most remarkable part of it was the faint purplish glow that emanated from a cavity on the side of the mound, indicating that a sort of cavern might be concealed within.

Remembering the words of warning his associate gave him, Jonathan stopped Elenora before she headed down the clearing. They stood still and waited with apprehension for any signs of activity.

Without the noise of brush crunching beneath their feet, the sounds of the forest took center stage. Soft breezes rustled the leaves of the trees above them while distant owl hoots and cricket chirps kept the forest from being absolutely dead silent.

Minutes passed as the two of them kept their eyes trained on that mound. Elenora was the first to glance at Jonathan questioningly, clearly a sign that she was wondering when he would be satisfied with their monitoring efforts. Mere curiosity soon transformed into terror. He saw her eyes widen, and the scream she let out resounded in his ear when she shoved him away with impressive force.

He stopped himself from falling over by planting his arm against the ground just before a shadow whizzed past him. There was no time to think about what filth he had just stuck his hand into for balance when the entity stopped abruptly and spun around with rabid swiftness to face him and Elenora.

The creature resembled a wild dog in shape, but its coloration was so incredibly inky that it did not reflect a lumen of light. Even though night had yet to completely engulf them, he was unable to discern if the dog had fur or was merely some kind of phantom with black-hole similitude.

Jonathan rushed to position himself back on his feet when the dog charged at them once more. Its dim gray eyes were its only feature not darker than everything around it. He retrieved his rapier and took a swing at it, attempting to time the strike right as the beast came within range.

The wild dog instead took a sharp turn just beyond the reach of Jonathan's sword. Before he could be disappointed that he missed, it darted in Elenora's direction and she brought down her butcher knife with faultless tenacity at the perfect moment. As she cleanly decapitated the shadowy creature, a fearsome howl rumbled thunderously throughout the forest.

For a number of reasons—the sheer volume of the cry, the beast's spectral appearance, the fact that its head was now disconnected from the rest of its body—Jonathan had trouble mentally registering whether that soul-shattering sound came from the wild dog's mouth or from the depths of an otherworldly dimension.

Afraid that their quick victory was only temporary, Jonathan used his Avidea to transform his rapier into an oversized carving fork that almost doubled his reach. Both he and Elenora stood, stances ready, as they surveyed their surroundings, waiting to witness the consequences of that yowl.

Two eagle-like creatures with the same dark phantasmal effect swooped in on them from overhead, releasing eerie screeches to announce their presence. One eagle targeted Elenora and managed to claw viciously into the side of her neck. She recoiled and grimaced as jagged lines of red formed on the exposed skin above the collar of her jacket. Her reprisal swing using the duller side of the butcher knife knocked the eagle onto the ground but did not provide enough power to finish it off.

The other eagle homed in on Jonathan. A violent swipe of its talons across his arm shredded the fabric of his coat and barely managed to catch flesh, but it was the amount of force in the bird's dive that caused him to stumble backward. Another of those wild dogs suddenly appeared and darted from the clearing below them to join the mayhem, immediately trying to nip at any ankles in sight. Its jaws chomped futilely in the empty air.

There was no elegant way to evade the snarling maw of the feral beast at his feet. Jonathan yanked his legs away from the nightmarish canine, hopped frantically around its hyper movements, trained his eyes up at the eagle that had come after him, and threw his entire body behind the thrust of his weapon. The carving fork pierced right through the flying creature like a spear, hitting what he could only assume was its heart when it then fell limp.

It certainly felt as if he had struck a real, physical body. When he swung his weapon wide to dislodge the corpse off the tines, it traveled the expected trajectory of a carcass until it collided with the ground.

"Look out! Another wolf!" Elenora shouted to him. Her fallen eagle had already taken to the air again, and in its mindless desire for vengeance, would not leave her alone.

A third wild dog bolted toward them, this time from above the clearing. Jonathan ran through the trees to reach the more open space. There were fewer dead branches lying about and the grass was uniformly flat. He would have better footing here if evading them was going to make him dance like a fool anyway. The two nightmare beasts sprinted after him, but their crazed attempts to close their teeth around his legs were all made in vain.

Almost at the same time, Jonathan pierced his carving fork through the skull of one of the wild dogs, while Elenora found her chance to slice the eagle in half. The multiple bloody scratches peeking through both torn sleeves of her jacket indicated that her triumph had not been an easy one.

Still scampering about, Jonathan shook the lifeless form off his weapon. A heavy grunt was wrenched from his throat when he found himself hitting the ground hard.

Instinct guided his hands to hold his weapon out horizontally. The remaining dog had fiercely tackled him in retaliation and kept him pressed down with its phantom claws. He had positioned the extended tang of his carving fork just in time to stop the dog's fangs from sinking into him. The beast tried to close its mouth around the metal rod and gnaw away at it, causing Jonathan's arms to tremble as he desperately maintained the defense.

Out of the corner of his eye, he saw Elenora stumble onto her knees as she tried to reach him. She must have been overwhelmed by adrenaline fatigue again.

After a bout of struggle, Jonathan summoned a burst of strength and shoved the wild dog off him. He hurriedly pushed himself upright and turned his polearm around so when the dog went after him again, the sharp points of the fork impaled its chest from its own momentum.

The dog's body slumped. Before he could shake off its corpse, black wisps began to float up from it and dissipate into nothingness. He met Elenora's eyes, and they both watched with astonishment as the five carcasses evaporated into the night sky, as if they were never there to begin with.

CHAPTER 6

A STILLNESS LINGERED FOR a stretch of time before Jonathan felt assured that nothing else would be coming after them.

He stood up and plodded over to where Elenora was resting, though as he came closer his face involuntarily twisted at the waft of an atrociously sweet scent.

"What's wrong?" Elenora asked.

"Just the blood," he answered. "We should have your wounds covered up." He retrieved a compact first aid kit from an inner coat pocket and knelt down next to her. Though he tried to suppress it, a grimace slipped through onto his face every few seconds.

Her bemused expression put him on alert for a follow-up question regarding his sense of smell.

"What were those things anyway?" she asked instead. She rolled up her sleeves and took the gauze pads and bandages from him to wrap her own arms while he tended to the scratches on her neck.

He took a moment to conjecture a few possibilities. "I suspect they could have been magically created. Or they could have crossed over from a different realm," he said. "From how they looked, a darker realm that may have diverged from this one."

She narrowed her eyes. "What do you know about this realm?"

With a grunt, he stood back up. The offensive scent remained, but it had been adequately stifled. "I know some people who have the abilities to manipulate that realm, but I myself have never tampered with anything like that before. Why do you ask? Have I lost your trust?"

Her expression softened and she laughed. "No," she said as she pushed herself to her feet. "It's all just so fascinating to me. I didn't know there was so much to our world outside my tiny little bubble."

"Technically, we are still within the Silver Valley area," he noted, earning himself an unamused look from her. He hurried to change the subject to avoid laughing. "How are you feeling about all of this, Elenora? Even with a proper jacket, you were hurt, and that worries me."

She shook her head. "I've never felt that kind of thrill in my life. Even when that awful bird nicked me, it just gave me more energy and concentration to fight back."

"I hope not every ingredient will be such an intense experience," he said as they started treading carefully into the clearing together. "Should I take that to mean you want to continue the search with me?"

"Yes," she said. "As far as I'm able to. I can't deny how curious I am. I thought I already knew everything there was to know about being a chef."

When they reached the mound, it took some work to pry the glowing opening wider to where they could both ease inside, but they were soon led down a mossy path toward a small cavern where a patch of the radiant cabbages thrived.

Except for the soft light enveloping each one, and the green leaves mottled with various shades of pink, blue, and purple, these plants were similar in shape and size to normal cabbage plants. Some of the heads grew along the cavern walls, though most emerged from the ground. Not one individual plant was so excessively bright that they could not look at it directly, but conjointly they rendered the inside of the cave as bright as day. Some of them were ready for harvest, and many more had gone to seed from having been untouched for a relatively long time.

They picked out a total of ten heads of cabbage and collected a small bottle of the seeds. Elenora picked at the leaves, displaying an obvious fascination for the colors and luminescence that set these cabbages apart from the kind they were more familiar with. Jonathan made sure they did not harvest so much that the plants' natural growth cycles would be disturbed, but he desperately wanted to know if they could be cultivated outside of caves like this one.

By the time they returned to the car and drove back to Silver Valley, it was past midnight, a mildly unhealthy hour. He dropped Elenora off at her apartment complex and instructed her to rest as much as she could because the search would resume once they were refreshed.

It was late morning when they reconvened at a spice market near the edge of the city, where the streets were vacant enough to block off without inducing heavy traffic. They had their minds set on tracking down a special type of fennel pollen, one that held such likeness to the usual varieties that most vendors and consumers were unaware they possessed any in their own stock. He had yet to sample it himself, but Jonathan was considering featuring the spice in a pasta dish.

"We should have asked Vicky to fix your jacket," Jonathan said to Elenora as they casually glanced around the first few stalls. "It would have taken her no time at all."

She glanced down at her jacket sleeves. In the areas where they had been ripped by the abysmal eagle, she had crudely sewn the holes back together with threads of a mismatched color. Her handiwork served its purpose, but Jonathan knew his cousin would have made the stitching unnoticeable. At least the makeup she applied to conceal the scabs on her neck looked flawless.

"I know it doesn't look great," Elenora agreed with a laugh. "I figured it wasn't worth slowing down our week for it. Oh, look! That's fennel pollen, isn't it?"

He stopped walking and leaned in to see where she was pointing. The stall displayed a wide assortment of small transparent jars filled with different spices all tagged with homemade labels and topped with black plastic lids. Locating the fennel pollen, he picked up one of the bottles and examined it closely, rotating it in every direction and even shaking it.

He proceeded to do the same for nearly every bottle of the spice. While the polite merchant raised her brows toward his painstaking inspection, she did not say anything through her smiles and nevertheless seemed content that someone was taking interest in her wares.

Unfortunately, Jonathan ended his assessment with a shake of his head. "But pick out a few bottles of thyme and paprika," he said to Elenora. "I like those prices."

Moving from one stall to the next of those that offered fennel pollen, they ended up with identical results until they reached a more crowded section of the market. The senseless din of dozens of separate conversations overlapping with each other and having to squeeze past narrower channels of people had Jonathan itching to claw at his own skin. He attempted to glance over the heads of the crowd, desperate to find a section of the market with a lower density of people, or just an escape from the venue altogether. How he would have preferred that their search took them to some sort of secret marketplace instead, the kind with the whimsical allure Elenora would have found delightful. The kind that, while great for the imagination, would be too hidden and too sparse to be sustainable.

He was ready to give up early, but Elenora tugged on his sleeve so that he would squat down to her height. She still had to raise her voice to tell him that she thought she spotted something promising.

He promptly followed her to confirm. Disregarding all other spice varieties, he saw that this merchant had skinnier and taller plastic bottles of fennel pollen stacked in a neat pyramid. A precarious arrangement, but one that allowed full visibility of the available stock. Sure enough, there were a handful of bottles that contained particles of a paler yellow color compared to the rest. A subtle difference, but when he stared at them for longer, the bottles appeared to shift and distort a small perimeter of light around them, warbling the air like a heat mirage.

When the merchant looked away to engage another potential customer, Jonathan discreetly pulled out an ultraviolet flashlight. He kept it mostly concealed in his hands when he pointed the light at the bottles, and upon seeing the specks gleam a faint electric blue, Jonathan nodded to Elenora.

The merchant then turned back to him, and he asked to purchase four of the bottles, trying not to sound incessantly picky as he pointed to the exact containers he wanted. The spice was already quite expensive on its own, but the type he was looking for would explicitly sell for a hundred times more than its ordinary counterpart. Here, he was able to buy all the bottles at the regular price. If the merchant wanted to blame anyone for that, he could direct that attention to his own ignorance.

Either way, the fennel pollen of the "fairy" variety was secured. Likely the easiest of the ingredients to find, checked off Jonathan's list.

Next on the agenda was a lunch appointment, facilitated with Victoria's help. She promised that Bray Akpan, the man they were going to meet and a fellow armor enthusiast, would be useful in finding the two remaining ingredients. Much to Jonathan's dismay, she arranged the rendezvous point to be a rather unremarkable sandwich shop. Upon seeing no one matching Bray's description sitting alone, Jonathan and Elenora picked a secluded table snug in the corner of the small establishment and ordered first.

Elenora delighted in her chicken cheesesteak hoagie, while Jonathan was unimpressed with his roast beef sandwich. Their orders were cheap in price and quality, and rudimentary in culinary preparation. Jonathan poked at the bread with annoyance, thinking that this was the true epitome of being uninspired.

His companion looked up at him between ravenous bites. "Oh, come on, Mr. Tessier," she said. "I can see your thoughts written all over your face! You can't keep being bummed out by that review, even while we're working on getting better ones. And this isn't bad! Just try it."

He only raised a brow and pulled out his phone to message Bray that they were ready to meet him.

Irritatingly enough, more than thirty minutes passed before the man showed up. Elenora had already asked for a box to take Jonathan's sandwich home for herself.

"You the people looking for me?" A youthful man approached their table, light on his feet.

Bray was clad in a mechanic's overalls, the sleeves of which were rolled up high enough to expose his toned biceps. He adjusted his glasses as he sat across from Jonathan, grinning widely.

"Yes, Mr. Akpan? Pleasure to meet you." Jonathan reached out for a handshake, but Bray insisted on turning it into a fist bump. Jonathan awkwardly obliged.

"Same, same!" Bray said, punctuating his words with a carefree laugh. "I was told my skills were needed? What can I do for you, Tessie?"

He could do without the undue familiarity, but Jonathan knew he needed to maintain a focused professionalism.

"You specialize in tools for supernatural phenomena, correct?" he asked. "I happen to need something that can detect invisible arcane fires or burn marks. Do you have anything like that?"

Bray wore an amused smirk as he rested an arm on the small surface of the table, bumping his knuckles softly against Elenora's empty plate. The smile then disappeared, and he lowered his voice.

"What is it exactly that you're looking for?"

"I just told you."

"No," Bray said, shaking his head. "Why are you looking for a gadget that can detect something like that?"

Jonathan hesitated. "I would really prefer for that to remain my own personal business."

"No, no. Secrets so soon? I only work with those I trust, my friend! Spill."

For a brief moment, Jonathan's gaze wandered to Elenora, who was now leaning fully back in her seat with arms crossed over her chest. She was watching him with intense, sparkling eyes. She might have agreed to be his partner in the search, but he was ultimately still the one responsible for all the consequential decisions.

"Fair enough," he said finally. "We want to look for burning truffles near the city's recreational trails. I know they appear indistinguishable from the normal burgundy ones to the naked eye, which is why we need your help. I've also been told that we might find spiral cashew trees nearby, if you have anything to aid us in navigating those trails."

Bray clapped once, much too loud and crisp. The other patrons in the shop spun their heads at the sharp sound, most looking away when Jonathan glared back.

"That's more like it! I heard you were cooks, so I'll bet you're about to whip up something real awesome with that stuff, aren't you?" Bray said. "There's just one little problem. . . I have the right tool for you, but it's out of order. If you two help me repair it, you can borrow it free of charge. I'll even give you discounts to rent my custom-built ATVs. How's that sound?"

Another type of vehicle he had never yet driven. Jonathan was fleetingly reminded of that clunky boat trip two days ago. He glanced at Elenora, and seeing her excitement, he quickly decided.

"That works perfectly for me," he said.

"Great! Just let me order something to go, and then I'll lead the way to my lab."

Bray's lab was just like any other modern artificer's shop Jonathan had ever seen. Anything that could not fit on the cluttered workbench or the shelves lining the walls would be haphazardly strewn across the wooden floors. Metal parts, wires, engineering lab equipment, and mechanical tools filled his vision when he entered.

It looked like a disturbing mess to him, but Elenora seemed fascinated by every strange gadget. She was all questions and awestruck eyes, which Bray welcomed with great warmth.

The tool of the hour was, for all intents and purposes, a flash-light. It was much more cumbersome and complexly built than a typical one, adorned with external gears and thin pipes that left little space to actually hold it correctly. Jonathan did not fully comprehend the intricacies of the repair process, though most of it boiled down to him and Elenora fetching tools and materials for Bray to do most of the work. Bray made it sound as if their assistance would have been integral, as if their absence was the primary reason he had not already repaired the flashlight on his own.

At one point, Jonathan noticed that the mysterious batteries used to power the torch were encased in something other than steel and a plastic label. The surface of the cells had a matte finish of a neutral brown color instead.

"What are these batteries made of?" he asked Bray.

"Clay," the mechanic answered.

Jonathan stared at him incredulously. "What? Is that a joke?"

"No, I'm serious."

"Electricity cannot be generated from clay."

"You're looking for arcane burning fungi," Bray said with a snicker. "I don't think you're in any position to worry about the bizarre ways of my alchemy."

That earned a scoff from Jonathan. "No, I suppose you have a point." He thought he heard Elenora giggle from the other side of the room.

Bray ran a few functional tests on the flashlight by turning it on and off over his hand before he deemed it suitable for use. The beam shone mostly white, though the edges of it were tinted an unusual neon green.

"There you go, Tessie," he said, handing the flashlight to Jonathan. "That should help you distinguish the truffles. Now, let's get you sorted on the ATVs. They're sturdier and faster than the ones you can rent near the trails. I must've put their keys somewhere around here. . ."

Bray held true to his promise to give them a discount, even if Jonathan did not feel their contributions were enough to earn it. Jonathan thanked him for his help and told him they would return the torch and vehicles later that day. Sometime tomorrow at the latest.

"Don't sweat it," Bray said. "It's not like I have much use for that thing if I let it stay broken for so long. Let me know how it all goes down with your hunt. Didn't know cooks were so involved with their food these days. I should come by your restaurant sometime."

"If you do, I would be happy to return the favor. With the discount."

"My man! Then I definitely will, whenever you're open again."

"I look forward to it, Mr. Akpan."

Jonathan and Elenora left the workshop and began driving their vehicles down Silver Valley's paved roads toward the popular recreational trails that lay just outside the city's border, with her speeding ahead and him struggling to keep up. She needed little guidance from him on where they were headed, and he remembered that she enjoyed inviting their coworkers out to hike sometimes.

These trails were sectioned off by accessibility, the easy and intermediate ones being very popular with the city's residents. Not only were those highest in difficulty generally avoided, with their fluctuating altitudes and uneven terrains, the staff in charge required guests to undergo training and initial supervision before they could make the trek on their own.

Unfortunately, Jonathan was just as ungraceful steering the ATV as he had been with the boat, and while Elenora was enthusiastic, her driving was best described as reckless. The poor staff member in charge of being their tour guide showed an incredible amount of patience toward them even as she was wrought with stress in overseeing their progress.

She let them go after about an hour. Whether it was because she no longer had the energy to freak out over them nearly ramming into the next tree, or because she genuinely felt they were ready, Jonathan did not think to ask. He was simply relieved they could finally be left alone to search for those coveted truffles and cashews.

"Hey, boss, how about a race?"

"Absolutely not, Elenora. Please stay focused."

They put on the brakes every few hundred feet to disembark and walk off from the main trail. Each time, Jonathan would crank the flashlight and aim it at the ground between exposed roots of several nearby trees, examining the area for any unnatural flames.

"This is wild. How do these magical truffles even come about?" Elenora wondered to herself, using her foot to push dead leaves out of the way.

Jonathan pondered silently over her question, a negligible part of him also curious about the answer. Then again, where did the truffles they deemed normal come from?

"How does anything in our world come about? I suppose they just exist. They don't care whether we know about them, whether we studied them in school," he said.

"I guess that makes sense. In a way, I could even say those deep-sea creatures we know so little about are also magical. Anything that lives underground might as well be in a fantasy land too... Mr. Tessier?"

"Yes, Elenora?"

"I'm glad to be doing all of this with you now," she said. "If I had known about all these new things years before, or even when I was a kid, I don't think I would've fully appreciated what I'm feeling now."

"And what would that be? We only just started."

"Amazement. Wonderment. The excitement of adventure."

"Did you enjoy poking around in Mr. Akpan's workshop that much?" he asked, chuckling.

"Okay, look, he had so many cool things in there! A robot octopus with extendable arms that can grab anything you need, a box that shrinks and expands no matter what you put inside it, a gun that shoots out little floating clouds that you can step on..."

Elenora continued to gush over the unfinished projects in Bray's lab that had yet to prove they could be successful until Jonathan noticed trace amounts of dark reddish flames under the beam of the flashlight.

They carefully dug around the area with hand trowels and found a few of the precious morsels buried within the dirt. Jonathan knew he should not have been surprised, but what they found truly appeared no different from normal burgundy truffles when not blindingly illuminated by the torch. When they were, the gentle flame fully enveloped each morsel and flowed with a tranquil rhythm, leaving behind phantom burn marks that could not otherwise be perceived.

After trying a few more spots farther down the trail, they obtained a total of twelve ounces of the burning truffles. Jonathan figured it was a satisfying number to stop at, even if he wanted to keep searching for more. There were a few pieces of the non-scorched variety in the mix, which he considered a pleasant bonus for their efforts.

It took them three hours to drive to the deepest part of the trail. There was little indication whether this was the end of the trail, or rather, if there was an end at all. Jonathan doubted any normal person would have ever come this far.

The deciduous trees of the forest gave way to a secluded boscage that logically should not have been able to grow here. Tropical and evergreen, a group of six cashew trees stood isolated and framed by an arena of bright orange.

Getting off the ATVs, they approached slowly in case they might be greeted by a monstrous ambush, but they only encountered the usual docile wildlife of birds and small rodents timidly scampering out of their way.

"Whoa, look!" Elenora had her head tilted back under one of the trees. "The branches are so curly."

Jonathan peered upward as well. The branches twirled neatly into spirals that wound tighter the farther they stretched. Vibrant leaves sprouted along the branches in every direction, and at the lowest point of each loop were fruits at various stages of their flowering cycle.

The spiral cashew fruit was rounder than its more common equivalent, and a gradient of green to blue in its ripest form. But while the fruit itself might be a decent ingredient, the real prize was the cashew nut, which grew into the shape of a small coil rather than a thick, curved bean.

Jonathan and Elenora began examining the branches within their reach. Any of the fruits that passed their inspection with minimal deformities and abrasions were plucked off their delicate stems.

"I used to go apple picking with my family every year when I was young," Elenora said, clearly enjoying herself. "The beautiful sights of the orchard, the fresh air. This reminds me of that."

Jonathan had partaken in nothing of the sort during his own childhood. He knew bringing that up now would drag down the mood, and while he still regarded this as work, he appreciated the chance to unwind just a bit.

"I suppose you could call this relaxing," he agreed. "Careful where you step. The roots are very dense over here."

They found and collected a total of thirty-seven of the fruits and cashew nuts. It was in trying to find a way to store what they had overzealously harvested that they realized Bray's spatially defiant storage boxes would have been tremendously helpful. Instead, they settled for carefully stuffing all the fruits into two of the woven sacks they had brought along.

"That was fun," Elenora said as they began driving back toward the city, the sacks of spiral cashews tied to the cargo carriers behind them. The evening sky had already been losing light while they were hard at work. "Especially compared to yesterday. And the day before."

"A fortunate turn of events."

"And we've already gotten half of the ingredients on your list! We'll be finished with the whole thing in a flash at this rate."

Jonathan chuckled. "While that would be most ideal, these were the easiest of the ingredients to obtain," he said. "Given that we have less than a week, I would be happy if we ended up with a total of five or six out of the eight ingredients."

"Oh, wow," she said, glancing back at him. His stern glare commanded that she keep her eyes on the road, a warning she quickly heeded. "Are the next ones that hard to find?"

"In a manner of speaking. Tomorrow, we head to Lismai," he said. "So pack for an overnight trip, just in case. Yes, your overtime and travel expenses will be covered." He knew he had to dip into his Mercenary savings to cover the restaurant's hiatus, but he found that he did not mind doing so to have her by his side.

"I like the sound of that," she said cheerfully.

"Stay vigilant. We still have much work to do."

CHAPTER 7

RADIANT CABBAGE, FAIRY FENNEL POLLEN, burning truffle, and spiral cashew.

Next on the list was something called ghost bone marrow. The ingredients Jonathan and Elenora had secured up until now could be written off as regular ingredients with whimsical names, but in no universe should someone name anything they wanted to sound appetizing after the spirits of the dead based on whimsy alone.

Jonathan arrived at the Taverne early the next morning to review his research notes while he waited for Elenora. He stood in the dining room, his overnight bag on the table next to him packed with hygiene supplies and two changes of clothes in preparation for the trip to Lismai, a city located to the south quite a distance from Silver Valley. His rapier needed to be concealed in a separate case, but he found a way to tuck his favorite cast-iron pan snugly into his bag.

All of this was purely precautionary. Ideally, there would be no need to get his hands dirty, but he did not want to be caught in a fight without his dependable gear. And if he could help it, he would rather return to the city and sleep in his own bed at the end of the night regardless of the lengthy commute.

A sudden loud knock on the restaurant's locked front door demanded that he look up and away from his notes. Elenora had her own key and would have simply come in.

On the other side of the glass stood an older man, likely in his fifties or sixties in Jonathan's vague estimation. The man, dressed in a full tuxedo, was staring directly at him with that expectant gaze he was much too familiar with, and Jonathan narrowly kept from rolling his eyes when the man rapped his knuckles against the door a few more times.

Jonathan shook his head and mouthed through the window that the restaurant was closed, but that did not stop the man's incessant knocking. When he pointed to the sign indicating that the Taverne was not open for business, the man escalated his absurdity by rattling the door handle instead.

Maybe he could hide in the kitchen until this stranger went away. No, Elenora had yet to arrive, and no doubt this man would end up bothering her too. Jonathan reluctantly went over to the door, unlocked it, and pulled it open by a sliver.

"Hello, sir. We are closed right now. Do you need something?" he asked.

"Finally!" the man exclaimed. "Just let me in, will you? Show some respect, kid. Can't believe you made me wait so long in the cold!"

He brashly attempted to push his way in, but Jonathan's foot blocked the door from opening any wider.

Jonathan's jaw dropped, just slightly, from the audacity. "Um, sir. Please listen to me," he said. "We are not serving any customers at all right now."

"That doesn't matter! Do you know who I am? Let me in!"

Whoever this man was, he unfortunately surpassed Jonathan in physical strength, and with a rough shove against the door, and then Jonathan's shoulder, the man successfully barged his way inside.

"What a dump this is," he grumbled, standing much too self-importantly, with his feet in a wide stance and hands on his hips, as he scanned the dining room. "Well, your food wasn't half bad at the memorial, so. . ."

"What is it that you need?" Jonathan said, rubbing his shoulder. "I will be leaving soon myself, so if you do not make this quick, I have no choice but to call the police."

"Oh, shut it, will you? The name's Hayes Berat."

The name only earned a blank stare from Jonathan.

"Berat! You know! Closest companion of Clifton Askew? And I know you're trying to get in Lucille's good graces so she'll boost your restaurant, so you'd best be accommodating to me in every way if you want that to happen."

Before Jonathan could ask what Hayes's request would be, the man noticed his research notes and snatched them out of his hands.

"Sir, that is—"

Hayes held up a hand to hush him.

"Ghost bone marrow sells for that price? No way. That must be a scam," he said under his breath. "Well, if you're out trying to get a supply of this stuff, you might as well fetch some for me, kid."

"What? Oh, are you looking to purchase some of the bone marrow? If you are willing to pay the price, I could try to secure additional quantities for you."

"Don't be stupid. You will give your supply to me for free. I've got great connections in the culinary industry, so you should be thankful for this opportunity to serve me."

Jonathan, despite his years of experience dealing with the entitlement rampant in the service industry, did not quite know what to say.

"I'll be back here tomorrow around this time, then," Hayes said. "And I expect you to have my supply of that valuable bone marrow ready for me."

After the man left, Jonathan immediately dialed Lucille's phone number, and to his utmost relief, she picked up.

"I apologize for calling without warning and at such an early hour, Lady Askew," he said. "But a man by the name of Hayes Berat came by my restaurant, claiming to be an associate of yours and demanding that I supply an expensive ingredient to him free of charge. Can you verify any of this?"

A drawn-out sigh came through from the other end. "I know him," she said. "I have nothing to do with the demands he's making. But whatever opinions you have of him, I do advise you to be mindful of his status."

"What is his status? He claimed to have connections in my field that he thought I should view with reverence."

"I suppose in a way, that is not untrue."

Jonathan frowned, noticing something odd about her tone of voice. He let a few moments of silence hang between them before he spoke up again. "Hayes said he will be back tomorrow morning. Do you happen to be free during that time, ma'am?"

"Perhaps." He might have been too optimistic, but he thought he heard a smirk in her voice.

"Then I humbly ask that you come by the Taverne as well. I think this might lead to something worth seeing."

She did not answer right away. He thought he might have stepped too far, until—

"I see. Very well. Tentatively," she agreed, and they hung up.

At that moment, Elenora finally helped herself into the restaurant. She had her own duffle bag slung from her shoulder and a bright attitude that was more than ready for the trip.

Maybe they could intentionally spend the night in Lismai to avoid having to deal with Hayes again. But after the call with Lucille, an idea of how to properly handle his outrageous request started brewing in Jonathan's mind, and he did not want that opportunity to slip away.

"We needed to account for staying overnight, but if at all possible, we should try to come back to Silver Valley tonight," he told Elenora as they left the restaurant together.

"I'm fine either way," she said. "But did something happen?"

On their ride to Lismai via intercity cab, Jonathan explained what had occurred during Hayes's unwelcome visit.

"Do we need to rough him up too?" Elenora asked eagerly. "Because you know I'm down to if he gives us trouble."

Jonathan shook his head, and his lips curled into an amused smile. "Last time, it was clear the thieves were in the wrong," he said. "This time, we need to be careful. You should never underestimate the cunning of those with high social standing. We may not have the law on our side if we act rashly."

"But we can't let him walk all over us," she said worriedly, then raised her brow in interest when he gave her a knowing look. "Oh? Do you have a plan?"

"I might," he said. "A battle of wits, you could say. There may be only a slim chance of victory, but it could be entertaining."

Elenora snorted. "When have you ever done anything just because it was 'entertaining'?" She shook her head. "But I guess standing by doing nothing isn't really you either."

"These last few days have been bizarre. I should not be blamed for also being a little bit strange."

It took five hours to reach the city of stone bricks, rugged wood, and traditional architecture, its clearly divided districts evidence of its feudal origins. A higher altitude correlated fittingly with a more upscale neighborhood. Even from the edge of the city, the fancy mansions of the central district could be seen towering over all the lowly abodes of the commoners, exhibiting the aesthetic of castles for residents who no longer possessed any real royal authority.

For the city closest to the modern capital full of tall metal skyscrapers, the stark contrast between Lismai and Silver Valley was mildly disorienting. Ameza was a nation with its most significant and populous municipalities spread far apart, as towns often became absorbed into the city nearest to them before they could properly develop into their own. In between any two names on the map, one could typically find nothing but wilderness and villages too small to be recognized. Traveling from one to another was akin to moving between the counties or states of other nations.

The cyberspace still had worldwide influence, though. When Jonathan and Elenora had been dropped off in one of the middle-class districts and were heading toward a local park, a group of people rudely obstructed their path.

"Oh, aren't you the owner of that restaurant in SV?"

"He is! It was one of the places we ate at when we went there last week."

"Before the bad review."

"Hahaha! We had no idea it was such a pathetic place. You should reimburse us for having eaten there. You overcharged us!"

"Yeah! Pay up, and then close your lame restaurant."

Fools, all of them. They had no complaints during their visit, and yet they thought they were entitled to waste his time rambling utter nonsense. Jonathan could hardly wait for the next victim Labey claimed to take his place in the spotlight.

He suppressed his irritation and stealthily unzipped his overnight bag as they continued hurling their smug insults. Finding the handle of the cast-iron pan, he summoned the scent of durians in a controlled radius that included only him and his mockers.

"Eck! What is that disgusting stench?"

The group backed away from him and glanced around. Seeing that the passersby around them were unaffected and were instead giving them disapproving looks, a damper seemed to have been put on their fun.

"Whatever, let's get out of here!"

Jonathan did not know them, nor did he care to, but he could not help but think that some individuals in this world were simply completely useless.

The supply merchant they met at the local park was not very helpful either. Nicknamed the Squirrel, he would hoard into his possession anything a buyer could want, the absurd prices he placed on them a reflection of his hesitation to let any of it go. The Squirrel had vials of extracted ghost bone marrow among his wares, but he asked for far more than Jonathan was willing to pay.

"Let's pay the lower price for information," Elenora suggested. "And then find it ourselves. I mean, that's our routine by now, isn't it?"

There was a graveyard on the outskirts of Lismai, reserved for those who passed on with no family or friends to arrange their burials. No one had any reason to visit, and the cemetery's location was known only to a handful of city officials. And those nosy enough to poke around.

"Graveyard's quite far from the city. And if you're not looking for it, it seems to disappear in your peripheral vision," the Squirrel had claimed.

It was better kept that way. If a regular Lismaian citizen stumbled across the dome of perpetual night that gloomily shrouded the graveyard, peace in the city would likely be disrupted by panic.

Yet Jonathan was here with Elenora thirty minutes later, having received the information from the Squirrel in exchange for money. He was neither concerned about how the merchant's loose tongue proved to be quite a liability nor keen to sow such chaos himself, but at least the Squirrel was more eager to let go of information than he was of his goods.

Jonathan had been skeptical about it at first. But when he approached the gates surrounding the graveyard, a lantern in one hand and his cast-iron pan in the other, he could see the outline of an enormous creature slumbering in the far back corner.

Elenora followed noiselessly behind him as he carefully opened the front gate and walked in. When they snuck closer, the creature's prominent features became more apparent, confirming it was the double-ribbed chameleon the Squirrel told them they were looking for.

A gentle beast that would not attack unless threatened, the chameleon often roamed this graveyard, presumably to lend companionship to the spirits that dwelled here before they moved on to the afterlife. The Squirrel claimed that the ghosts enjoyed hanging out on its back between the giant bone ribs that curved upward, leaving behind an otherworldly residue on the spikes. These spikes could be harvested for their marrow without hurting the chameleon, and they grew back quickly afterward. The greatest obstacle was in trying to get close without sending the creature into a frenzy.

Out of the blue, a harsh clanging sound broke the silence. Jonathan froze and peered down. He had been careless and walked right into a metal flower vase, knocking it over so it collided with a nearby headstone. Weird. Who could have left it here?

His gaze immediately shifted back to the creature. He watched with awe as it opened its eyes, heaved its bulky gray body to its feet, turned its head in their direction, and gradually vanished.

They knew where the beast had been right before disappearing, but if they acted too slowly, they would lose track of it and miss their chance.

Jonathan gripped the handle of his cast-iron pan, concentrated the stubborn aroma of onions into a ball of aura, and flipped the pan to hurl the shoddily made stink bomb toward the location where they last saw the lizard. His aim was skewed right, but the stench spread over a large area when it exploded in the middle of the air.

He kept still, waiting for any visible indication of where the creature had gone. The graveyard became deadly quiet once more. When the stink cloud faded away, he glanced back at Elenora. She inhaled deeply, and then shook her head. The chameleon had failed to walk through his trap.

"Should we swing wildly to see if we catch it?" she asked, keeping her voice low.

He could not tell if she was joking. "Too dangerous," he whispered back. Though he could transform his rapier to something with incredible range, he would not be prepared for the counterattack. "And the Squirrel told us under no circumstances were we to hurt the creature."

"What should we do, then?"

He beckoned her closer to the gravestone he was standing in front of, staring at it as if he had only intended to pay a visit to his dearly departed the entire time. She stood next to him and did the same.

"A direct approach may not serve us well here," he said. "We will calmly walk out and regroup outside."

They did not stop to begin formulating a new plan until they reached a street brightened by the afternoon sun.

Their goal was not to fight, and the lengthy walk from the front gate to where the chameleon seemed to enjoy sleeping had been a difficult path to navigate in the dark. Elenora thought they should find a way to scout the fence from the outside and look for a place she could climb over. It would be a shorter distance for her to sneak closer to the beast and harvest as many spikes as she could safely get her hands on.

Jonathan had reservations about taking such a risky approach, but he could not come up with any better ideas.

So they took a more roundabout path back to the obscured graveyard, crouching low to the ground to hide themselves within the tall grass that grew outside the fence. He saw no sign of the double-ribbed chameleon, but they were prepared to sit still even if it took hours for the beast to let its guard down and drop its veil of invisibility. Patience would be critical here.

But when surrounded by an eternal nighttime, it was easy to lose track of time. Jonathan began looking for other things to stare at, like the spindly trees, the sparse shrubbery, and the hint of fog in the distance.

Elenora's nudge directed his gaze back to the cemetery. He saw the hazy outline of the giant lizard appear first, and then its full image filled out completely. It lowered its body to relax, but as the minutes passed, its round eyes did not seem ready to sleep again.

It was now visible, though, prompting Jonathan and Elenora to inch closer to the fence. As they stealthily circled its perimeter, they examined the metal pickets and posts until she pointed out a smaller gate near the back of the graveyard. He felt immense relief to have an alternative to her original plan to climb over, which risked making noise or putting her in the way of harm. This gate would help them avoid such outcomes, though they quickly discovered it would be a tight fit even for her. He would have to assist her from the outside.

When they tried to open the gate, they noticed an intricate tangling of thick warped vines binding it tightly closed. Elenora took her butcher knife and attempted to saw through them, but the vines bent and twisted like flexible rubber around her blade, preventing it from slicing through.

"Give it here," Jonathan muttered, and she handed the knife to him. He reshaped it into a serrated knife and gave it back to her for another go.

The vines remained stubborn and unbroken. Elenora sulked for only a second before she looked at him with a peppy expression of enlightenment.

"The thing you did with the cautery, when you stopped yourself from bleeding," she whispered.

He reached forward without much confidence, showing her that he could only burn a narrow line with his fingertips, leaving shallow trails of char along the way. It would take too much time and energy to sear every twist that held this gate shut.

Then he had his own look of realization. He gestured for her to step back, spun his pan, and summoned a banana foster inside it, right at the point the alcohol was ignited. With the flambéed dessert held close to the vines, the flames took hold and began to spread.

Elenora observed this performance with her mouth hanging open, making the tiniest tapping sounds with her hands in a subdued round of applause.

"I will keep an eye on the lizard from the side while you sneak up from behind," he said as they watched the fire slowly eat away at the vines. "I can hopefully warn you if it gets dangerous."

The tightly wound vines burned away and the flames died down. Elenora eased the gate open with care and slipped inside. She shuffled behind the chameleon, and as she studied it, she raised a brow at its impressive tail. It presented itself as the best way to climb onto the creature's back.

"Wait," Jonathan whispered. "Do you like the scents of lavender and rosemary?"

Her immediate reaction was one of confusion, but she paused to think. "I guess so?"

He nodded and assumed his position where his Avidea could still reach her. A part of him felt guilty he was sending his head chef to do the most challenging part of the job, but he was not entirely powerless just because he was outside the fence. If there was any time to maximize their chances for success, it would be now.

The soothing herbal scents drifted over to her, and a moment hung between them where she looked like she was on the verge of laughter before her brow furrowed, her expression focused and determined despite facing a stressful situation.

He watched as Elenora slinked closer to the chameleon. She stopped when the creature stirred, holding her breath until it settled down. When he held out his open palm to indicate it had not noticed her, she scaled the chameleon's tail with delicate steps and skillfully made it to its spiny back within seconds.

She realized most of these ribs towered high over her, so she picked one of the shorter spikes and used her serrated knife to cut near the base. They exchanged looks when she sliced through it with ease, both having expected that it would take her much longer. She tossed the piece over the fence and it landed in the grass a few strides away from him.

The chameleon began shifting around, forcing Elenora to instinctively grab another nearby spike to steady her balance. As far as either of them could tell, the creature was awake and trying to get comfortable, but it did not seem to be aware that she was on its back.

Still, Jonathan did not feel it was safe to continue, so he closed his fist, gesturing for her to hurry up and come back down. She raised her own hand to signal that everything was fine, and she went to cut off another bony spike.

One more rib, and then another, all landing in the same general spot in the grass after she threw them over. He signaled again for her to come down as he went to pick up the three spikes and put them neatly into his bag. This would be plenty to work with. She did very well.

A shriek pulled him out of his gratification, and he spun around to a frightening sight above him. Having finally noticed Elenora on its back, the chameleon had panicked and risen to its full height on its hind legs. Elenora had saved herself from a nasty fall by wrapping her arms around one of the remaining intact spikes and was now dangling from it. If she fell, she would be seriously hurt.

"Elenora! Jump over here!" Jonathan shouted, now that it was no longer imperative for them to keep their voices hushed. He dropped the pan and held his arms out toward her.

She regained footing on the spike below her, and with a yell, she launched herself over the fence toward him. Despite him not having much power to boast about, the need to protect Elenora helped him muster the strength to catch her and cushion her fall.

They stumbled onto the ground, and even in her perilous situation she had the sense to guide their momentum to reduce the impact of their crash. She demonstrated more of a knack for falling than he had for catching. After they rolled across the grass a few times, he hurried to stand and pull her onto her feet. They both took off, barely escaping the reach of a giant tongue that whipped out between the fence pickets to snatch one of them up.

CHAPTER 8

Night transitioned into early evening as they ran toward safety. Their footsteps slowed to a stop when they reached the paved streets of Lismai, with Elenora huffing out a chortle and Jonathan groaning from the temporary pain in his shoulder.

"That was insane," she said in between breaths of laughter.

He smiled back at her, simply grateful that they both came out uninjured. It was not worth it to scold her for staying on the chameleon's back longer than he felt she should have and ignoring his warnings.

When they recovered from the excitement, he arranged for their ride back to Silver Valley, with an estimated time of arrival set at midnight.

"I do feel bad for putting you through all of this, Elenora," Jonathan said as the intercity cab drove through the city limits.

Elenora chuckled. "I love the thrill of it, and with all the danger we're plunging ourselves into, this is about to be the best menu in the whole world!"

"It is still a lot to ask of you," he said. "Asking you to shoulder the responsibilities of a head chef shortly after you started at the Taverne, then asking you to accompany me in this search. I seem to have hired you under a misleading job description."

She waved a hand to dismiss his concern. "If only you saw the place I was working at before I came here," she said and sighed. "You're a fair and reasonable boss, Mr. Tessier, even if you often scare the newbies. That's more than most can ask for in this industry."

He glanced out the car window. In the distance, he could spot the same mountains they saw from their first day on the hunt together.

"If you really feel that bad," Elenora said. "Then maybe you can make it up to me."

"How so?" He turned to glance at her.

"You can tell me more about your magic," she said. "Your abilities certainly aren't close to what I would think of when it comes to supernatural powers."

"You want me to reveal all my secrets, Elenora?" he asked, his tone teasing and his brow quirked.

She grinned. "As much as you're able to tell me."

"The flashy powers and brute strength you might be thinking about do not suit me," he said. "I modeled my abilities after some of the elements of cooking I consider to be the most important: quality utensils, enticing aromas, and the right amount of heat."

He gestured to the silver rapier that he had sheathed at his hip. "I usually use this and temporarily transform it into a much larger version of any kitchen tool I can think of. But I can also use existing utensils, like your butcher knife, for a more permanent effect."

"Oh, yeah," she muttered, glancing at her bag where she had put the knife away. "It's still a serrated knife. Can you change it back?"

"Yes. Do you want me to do it now?"

"Maybe when we get back. I don't think that's a good idea here," she said, jutting her chin toward the driver, who could clearly see them in the rearview mirror. Even while he had a sword on his hip, Jonathan understood she might not want to wave around a knife and scare their chauffeur. He nodded reassuringly.

"But you can tell me how you made it smell so good, or how you did that thing with the fence."

"Hmm. Well, when I conjure recipes in a utensil like the poor pan we left behind, I usually do so to create scents that either distract my enemies or boost my allies," he said. "But I can also summon actual food, and I have the flexibility to utilize it in various ways. Like the flambéed banana foster."

"The food is real?" she repeated. "Then can't you cook dishes up instantly at the restaurant rather than doing it manually?"

He shook his head. "It is incredibly draining and inefficient. I can complete maybe ten recipes before I am completely spent. I would rather conserve my energy, but maybe with further training I might someday be an infinite food machine and solve world hunger," he said jokingly.

"And the heat?"

"My most underdeveloped skill. The smaller the area I focus it in, the higher the temperature. I can warm something up with my palm, or as you already know, cauterize a minor wound with a fingertip. Really, I tend to work better as support."

There were a few minutes of quiet as Elenora mulled over this information. He waited patiently for her subsequent questions.

"What about other people? And the kind of powers popular in TV shows and comic books?" she asked. "Stuff like flight, invisibility, telekinesis."

"Those are terribly broad. Such bland powers are generalized in the media for the sake of appealing to wider audiences. Grants are not like that at all."

"But are these grants responsible for all supernatural abilities?"

"The majority of them," he said. "Usually by Avidea, which is through training, or by Warrants. But Warrants are out of fashion now, because they require a significant personal sacrifice in exchange for immediate power."

"Oh, yuck," she said. "Warrants must be why I thought grants were super dicey. I heard people were losing limbs to become exceptionally strong, which baffled me. But it was all for magic. . ."

"Body parts are a common sacrifice. Or they would swear to follow a strict rule with a severe consequence, such as losing their loved ones."

Elenora wrinkled her nose in disgust.

"If you were bestowed a power by someone else through some sort of deal, or if you were born with special abilities, these would generally not be considered grants," Jonathan continued. "Because it would be near impossible to train that type of magic to be stronger or to gain additional skills in the same way."

"Oh, I see," she said. "Then, since you use Avidea, does that mean there aren't any limits to what you can do, as long as you train at it?"

"Not quite. There is one more thing to consider. When you determine the parameters of your powers to match your own personality or strengths, you also have to keep your grant class in mind."

"What is that?"

"There are five known grant classes," he said. "The Condense class concentrates energy to boost traits like physical strength, speed, or endurance. The Convert class molds aura to mimic other substances. The Construct class creates real, physical entities out of energy. The Control class influences existing objects and sometimes other people. And the Connect class sends power over great distances without losing effectiveness. If you try to wield powers outside of your class, their full potential is heavily reduced."

She ventured a guess. "And you are? Convert or Construct?"

"Construct," he confirmed. "Versatile, advantageous against obstacles with magical resistance, but tangible and perceptible to everyone, even those with no experience in magic. Those who use Convert abilities, or any powers that remain in energy form, can conceal their aura from ordinary people who have yet to learn how to use grants."

"Ah, cool. Would I be able to find out what class I am?"

"If you are prepared to dedicate the next few years of your life to training."

"Oh, no, thank you!" she said through nervous chuckles, shaking her head and recoiling at the thought. "I think I already have enough to worry about as it is."

He laughed along with her, calling the discussion finished at that point. They allowed themselves to relax during the ride, with a few naps and some small talk about their recent hunts to pass the time. When they arrived back at the city, Elenora was dropped off at her home before Jonathan returned to his own to rest for the night.

There were only three ingredients left on his list, and three days before he would have to impress the new critics. More than anything, he wanted Lala Sweet to acknowledge the skills and effort they poured into this operation.

They could stop now and still have something decent to present with five rare ingredients. Six, counting the chomping lotus Jonathan had obtained on his own. Two of the remaining ingredients were said to be found in the same location, though, so he had been hopeful they could squeeze every single item into the schedule and really exceed all expectations.

But today, he needed to worry about Hayes and ensure that the old man did not threaten their progress.

On his way to the restaurant for another early morning, Jonathan ran into Natalie, one of his waiters, in a fashionably casual outfit, strolling along at a relaxed pace.

"Hi, Mr. Tessier," she said as she waved to him.

"Good morning, Natalie. Enjoying your time off?"

"I am, thank you! Are you on your way to the restaurant? How are things going with you and Ms. Kerras?" she asked.

"We are working hard to boost the Taverne's reputation, and we have some critics who have arranged to visit. In three days, I might need support from you and the team."

Natalie smiled warmly. "Yeah, I'd be happy to! We probably shouldn't open the restaurant to other guests yet, if we want to give our undivided attention to these critics. And maybe we can add more decorations. A nice little centerpiece on each of the tables for just one day, perhaps?"

Without the presence of rowdy kids in the dining room, flower vases or candles in the middle of the tables are less of a safety hazard and more an elevation of the ambience in the restaurant.

"I do like both of those ideas," Jonathan said.

"Awesome! You know, some of us might complain a lot, but I appreciate you as a boss. I know you're probably too busy to mingle with us as the staff, but you treat us and the customers very well."

He felt a little guilty considering he was heading to the restaurant with a plot to take Hayes down a few notches, underhanded and disrespectful schemes swimming around in his mind. But then again, Hayes did not intend to pay him, so he could not be called a customer.

"Thank you, Natalie. Your words mean a great deal to me. I will see you soon, then," he said. "I promise you will be able to come back to the restaurant with pride."

"I'm holding you to that, boss! We'll come back so strong that we'll get a 'reservation only' status, or even move to a new, bigger location."

He chuckled when she winked. "I do hope so," he agreed.

Jonathan felt reassured as they parted ways that he had at least one employee other than Elenora who was so optimistic about the restaurant's future. Even if Natalie would never see the full extent of the work poured into it, or if she left the team for the next best opportunity, their short conversation offered comfort to him.

He dropped by his office after he made it to the restaurant. This was where he kept his precious milkweed tea, separate from the other teas stored in the kitchen, to mitigate the risk of them ever getting mixed up. Just for today, he was going to make an exception.

Lucille Askew was the first to arrive after him, and they exchanged knowing glances upon meeting.

"The lotus platters you delivered for the service were phenomenal. I heard you were in the market for other rare foodstuff to revitalize your menu," she said, avoiding any mention as to why they were here this morning. "I hope that is going well."

"I would have liked if Hayes was not here to disrupt our work." He then bit his lower lip, hoping his snark had not come off too strongly.

She seemed entertained and raised a dainty hand to her mouth to cover a laugh. Jonathan was cautiously eased by the thought that she might have sympathized with him.

"I will be present as a neutral party," she told him.

"All the better," he said. "I do prefer for you to not interfere, for your benefit. This is a matter between myself and Mr. Berat, though I am glad to have you here as a witness."

Hayes walked in at this point, his assertive steps jerking to a halt at the sight of his fellow member of the elite.

"L-Lucille!" he stammered. "What are you doing here? You're not poking your nose in my business, are you?"

Expecting this man to have any tact with even his own acquaintances was something Jonathan should have known better to do. He was rendered speechless, but Lucille seemed rather amused by this unruly behavior.

"And you!" Hayes went on, pointing an accusatory finger at Jonathan. "Are you trying to mess with me here? You think you can get away with defying me, huh? Calling someone to try and get out of what you owe me so you can cause trouble for me? You best think twice, then, you commoner kitchen help."

"Mr. Berat," Lucille said. "There is no need for that. I was the one who sought out help from this restaurant for Clifton's memorial. Naturally, it should not be much of a surprise that I have come back for business reasons."

Hayes grumbled under his breath.

"Though it is true," she said. "Mr. Tessier did contact me to verify your identity." She held up a hand to silence any complaints Hayes was about to spew in reaction to this admission. "This was a wise and sensible thing to do, Mr. Berat. Imagine if he believed every person who claimed to know me and foolishly did favors for all of them. That would be a little bit silly, wouldn't it?"

She ambled over to a table near the corner of the dining room, making sure the skirt of her dress did not catch on the legs of the nearby chairs and tables. "I am here at my own discretion, but I do hope you can be mindful of your words and actions," she said as she sat down, giving both the men a pleasant, chilling smile. "Please handle your business first. I can wait for my turn."

The silence was brief. Hayes turned his attention back to Jonathan. "So, hand over the supply you owe me," he demanded, with far less spunk than he had yesterday. "Don't you dare try to charge me again or skimp out on me like a filthy con artist. Well? Get to it!"

"Of course," Jonathan said, bristling at how the man implied he had provided any compensation at all. Exasperating as it was, he pushed to ignore it. "I am waiting for my head chef, though, so that we may prepare something spectacular for you. These ingredients are so special, I want to ensure that you fully understand their exceptional value with a fine breakfast only those of us with a keen and developed palate can enjoy."

Hayes appeared reluctant to take the bait, but he could not outright refuse with the lady watching. "I really would prefer if you would just give me the ingredients and we can finish our deal here."

"Hmm?" Jonathan raised a brow and tilted his head. "Would you not want to verify the quality of the ingredients yourself? You were worried just now that I might find a way to trick you. In a span of mere seconds, do you trust me enough to know I will not hand over cheap imitations of the ingredients you requested?"

"Is that what you're doing?" Hayes snarled. "Why, you—"

Jonathan raised a hand. "I would never do such a thing, but I expected more scrutiny from someone who claimed to be a prestigious figure in the culinary space," he said, shaking his head in a display of disappointment. "In fact, I would only feel comfortable entrusting such precious merchandise to a true expert with a refined taste."

"What about Lucille, then?"

"What about her? Lady Askew is discussing a different deal with me," he said. "And she has always been a generous client, more than willing to pay for what goods are worth. To me, she has already demonstrated that she can recognize the value of these fine ingredients. But your payment. . . has been suspiciously lacking."

"No, it hasn't!" Hayes was quick to protest.

"I would love to impress an esteemed figure like yourself, who is as knowledgeable about gourmet cuisine as you claim, but that is all the more reason I want to be assured I can believe in your expertise."

Elenora entered at this time, mildly taken aback that Lucille was also here, but she wordlessly nodded a greeting to everyone and stood politely off to the side near the host station.

Hoping the pressure he applied was sufficient, Jonathan waited for Hayes's answer. Having another pair of eyes on the old man certainly helped to boost his cause.

"Fine, whatever," Hayes relented. "Just make it quick and don't waste my time!"

Jonathan asked Hayes to stand by while beckoning Elenora to follow him into the kitchen. He leaned back against the door after he closed it and ran his fingers frenetically through his hair.

"Goodness, boss," Elenora said. "I've never seen you like this. Are you okay?"

His hands stopped moving and he dipped his head. "I know I said I wanted to handle this without aggression to avoid legal hassles, but there is still a risk that this could end up worse."

"Maybe. But if you don't deal with him now, he sounds like the type to keep bullying you for freebies until he runs you dry."

He nodded and stepped forward, away from the door. Before he could say anything more, Hayes barged into the kitchen.

"Ah, Mr. Berat," Jonathan said. "I thought I told you to wait out there."

"You'd like that, wouldn't you?" Hayes spat. "So you can get up to your tricks in here while I'm not watching you."

"Considering we hardly had the chance to do anything yet, you waver quite severely on whether you trust us or not."

"I don't care. I'm keeping an eye on you to make sure there's no funny business here."

"If you must," Jonathan said, pointing to a spot near the kitchen door. "Then stand here so as to not contaminate our cooking stations."

The man insisted on being defiant and standing just slightly too close. Jonathan shook his head and moved over to Elenora, instructing her to prepare some of the stir-fried lotus roots the way he showed her while he worked on other items.

He went to fetch a portion of previously prepared chicken soup from the storage room and then heated it in a pot over the stove. His hands shook a little when sprinkling in some of the crushed ghost bone marrow and handling the stirring spoon, but he knew there was nothing he could do in the kitchen that Hayes would catch as abnormal.

Jonathan put a lid over the soup, and while he waited for it to boil, he rinsed and dried out a couple of teacups. He braced himself for prying questions when he poured the dried milkweed particles into the teapot, but Hayes did not seem curious enough about the type of tea he was preparing to ask.

"Elenora is working on a simple but very special lotus root dish," he started to explain. "Even without spices, it is an incredibly savory delicacy." Whether it was a result of guilt or a need to continue selling the illusion of innocence, Jonathan decided to be upfront with the specifics of what they were making. If Hayes did not realize the truth here, that was his own fault for declaring expertise where there was only ignorance.

Hayes merely grunted. It was obvious he did not care for a lecture, but he could not say so or he would undermine his own claims.

"I added some of the bone marrow to the soup, which will enrich its flavors. And this is a nice, sweet tea to round out the meal, made from flowers that are a vibrant red color," he said, glancing up at Hayes. The disinterest he was met with was indisputable. "Some call it the blood flower, which I admit sounds intense, but the flavor is pleasant and something I find I cannot do without."

At this, Elenora turned her head to look at Jonathan, hiding from Hayes an inquisitive expression. Jonathan nodded once. Everything was laid out on the metaphorical table, so Hayes could not contend that they lied to him, either outright or by omission.

When Elenora finished cooking the lotus, Jonathan moved out of the kitchen to sit at one of the dining room tables. Hayes glanced between him and the head chef before joining Jonathan across the table. She followed them and placed the plate of lotus root slices with chopsticks between them.

"The tea and soup will also be ready to serve shortly," Jonathan said to her. "Please bring them out when you can."

Hayes waited for Jonathan to start eating first, which he did. Elenora prepared the dish amazingly well, having only seen him do so once, but he could always count on her reliable skills. Jonathan had to hide his smile when Hayes picked one of the slices farthest from himself, as if he assumed the slices on his own side might have been tampered with.

Regardless, the older man was visibly impressed after tasting the root. "Oh," he muttered. "This is delicious."

Jonathan smiled and nodded. "I am relieved to hear that, Mr. Berat," he said. "Certainly, a response I expected of someone with a sophisticated palate."

The soup was served next, and both men enjoyed its delightfully scrumptious flavors. A hot chicken soup was already inviting on its own, but the addition of the rare mysterious marrow elevated its sublime taste to a new level.

As soon as Elenora set the tea tray down on the table, Hayes picked up his teacup to examine its interior. She furrowed a brow but said nothing.

Jonathan spoke up instead. "Do you really still suspect foul play? This is not the behavior I imagine a guest would show to his host. Good thing this is not a formal event, right?"

Hayes paid no heed to his words and ultimately switched his cup with Jonathan's before insisting on pouring the tea himself.

When he all but snatched the teapot, Elenora lifted her hands and backed away a couple steps.

"Only the best epicures can truly appreciate this tea," Jonathan said. "While most others cannot manage to stomach it due to feeble taste buds." Though he wanted more than anything to admonish Hayes for his conduct, it was very clear that for many reasons, it was too late to try to change his ways.

So, Jonathan made a show of drinking his own tea first, which he allowed Elenora to pour for him. She quickly recovered her composure and stood off to the side, keeping a safe distance from their guest.

Seeing that Jonathan partook in the tea without issue, Hayes picked up his cup and put it to his lips. He took a sip, and his face contorted as he tried to hold it down, but after a series of strong grimaces and nearly gagging, he rushed toward the restroom and slammed the door behind him.

With the faint sounds of retching in the background, Jonathan met Lucille's eyes; her mouth had parted into something halfway between a gape and a smile. None of the three remaining in the dining room said anything.

Hayes reappeared, bow tie loosened and hair disheveled. His visage betrayed signs of rage as he stomped back over to the table. He pointed accusingly at Jonathan, and the speed at which his outstretched arm came flying into his face caused Jonathan to flinch.

"You! You tricked me!" Hayes yelled.

Leaning back so he did not get poked in the face, Jonathan calmly shook his head. "I think you are the one who tricked me. I am disappointed that your sense of culinary excellence was not as outstanding as you had me believe."

Hayes pulled his hand back and clenched it tightly. "Shut up! You did something because you wanted to deceive me and damage my credibility! This is sabotage!"

"It was due to your own lie that I was even willing to hand over such expensive rare goods for no payment at all," Jonathan said. "I think on every front, you are firmly in the wrong."

"No, you definitely messed with my tea," Hayes insisted. "Drink from my cup. Do it now!"

"I can drink from all the cups, and it would not make a difference."

"DO IT! NOW!"

The volume at which Hayes yelled reached an absurd volume, offensively unfair to the ladies in the room, so Jonathan found the untouched side of Hayes's teacup and drank the rest of it. He even took another long sip from his own cup to demonstrate that they had not been switched while Hayes was busy vomiting.

"See?" Jonathan said after putting down the cup. "Nothing strange at all."

"You!" Hayes whipped around to point at Elenora. "You drink the tea."

The head chef raised a hand in refusal. "I don't consider myself to have a refined enough palate for that tea, sorry."

When Hayes turned to face Lucille, she sent him a searing glare. "Leave me out of this and spare yourself the embarrassment, Mr. Berat," she said.

The man looked mortified.

"Knowledge of the blood flower is common among the elite, and even then, very few in our circle should claim to be able to enjoy it," she continued. "If you feel you were conned, this was still a shameful way to behave, and you have only shown your business sense and finesse as a socialite to be humiliatingly untenable."

Hayes sputtered a few incomplete words, but when he realized the futility of any argument he could possibly muster, he turned and marched indignantly out of the restaurant.

CHAPTER 9

THE QUIET PERSISTED AFTER HAYES departed, leaving the three of them to wonder who would break the silence first.

Elenora volunteered for that position when she announced behind a smile that she would clean up, taking all the plates and cups with her into the kitchen. After the head chef disappeared, Lucille's chuckle pulled at Jonathan's guarded attention.

"So, you actually are a Spectral, aren't you?" she asked.

"Ah, you knew all along?"

"I had my suspicions."

"Never liked that name for us. We are not ghosts or undead," he said with mild indignance, and she laughed. The label described a subset of individuals who exhibited characteristics, his own being some of many, with underground origins. Some even called them cursed. He knew how stories and urban folklore perpetuated exaggerations based on the slightest Spectral oddities that diverged from the common eduran race. "How did you realize?"

"That day I came to order catering from you," she said, "I had a few moments to observe you and your staff hard at work, rushing around, sweating, out of breath. But near the end, throughout our conversation, you had not let out so much as a sigh to give away your exhaustion. And today, the otherworldly red color of that tea... I've only seen it once before, but it confirmed you might not be like the rest of us eduro sapiens. I certainly appreciate you using it rather than the real thing."

He chuckled sheepishly. "Thank you for not giving me away to Mr. Berat."

The noblewoman smiled and shrugged. "You did not lie to him, so I felt no obligation to elaborate in your stead," she said. "Perhaps I should be the one thanking you for your cunning. Hayes had always been a thorn in my side, and I doubt my brother ever really considered him a true friend. How could he, when that man only sought to take advantage of our positions for his own personal gain? But I did not want to dishonor Clifton by assuming how he felt about Hayes, and I remained polite up until now."

"So, this was an opportunity for you to cast doubt on his intentions?"

"You could say that. Far be it from me to gossip about him, but if he stops showing his opportunistic face around me and my associates, you will not find me complaining."

"Seems this worked out well for both of us," Jonathan said. He had wondered why she so readily agreed to be present during this matter that seemingly had little to do with her, but it appeared she was in control of the situation the entire time.

"To express my gratitude, I will ensure my recommendation for your Taverne reaches all my friends and colleagues," she said. "I promise you they are nothing like Hayes. All I ask in return is that you continue making excellent food, and try to expand, if that aligns with your aspirations."

"Thank you, Lady Askew," he said, elated by the extent of help she was offering him. She had been vague with her commitment before, but she was starting to be more explicit about it now. "With the new critics coming in a few days as well, I am feeling rather hopeful."

"Oh? Who do you have visiting soon?"

"Um," he stalled. "It was a Mr. Glass and a Mr. Kelly. Have you heard of them? And we might also have the honor of hosting Lala Sweet." Jonathan's tone was one of cautious pride, since he still had trouble believing his good fortune. He could not be sure if the slightest incorrect muscle twitch in this unrelated conversation might cause the arrangement to fall through.

"Glass and Kelly are known for reliable and honest reviews, so that will be a step up from Labey. Though I am extremely impressed," she said. "What kind of connections do you have that Lala Sweet is willing to visit? Are you actually a member of high society in hiding?" She raised a brow, a playful expression of mock suspicion on her face.

He shook his head, hiding his smile. "No, I left that life a long time ago. I only ever wanted to be a normal restaurant owner and make extraordinary food for normal people. Without understanding struggle. . . I do not believe the same appreciation can be taught. So, even if I use connections such as the one you have graciously offered me, I will see to it that the Taverne's success is based on the hard work of me and my team."

"A respectable ambition, and humble beginnings," she said. "I do wish you the best with your new critics. I can see new investments coming your way, and maybe some partnerships that will promote steady growth for you."

"I do have a question, Lady Askew," he said, and she nodded. "While I am incredibly grateful, why do you seem so confident in the Taverne? We have only completed one job for you, yet you have given us an abundance of flattering words."

Lucille pursed her lips, buying herself a hesitant moment to deliberate her answer. She then sighed. "The short of it is, I am a businesswoman," she said. "I have had the privilege of sampling many other great culinarians' dishes, and while you have a ways to go compared to them, you deserve more recognition than you have, and I am snatching up that opportunity to realize your potential while I can. It is a bit selfish, I know."

Jonathan shook his head. "No, that is fair. Everyone is simply looking out for themselves. Nothing wrong with that."

"Not to mention, I can hardly resist a business partner who can manage to be both shrewd and honest," she added with a smile.

Wrapping up the conversation with a few more pleasantries, Lucille then bid him farewell and left the restaurant as well. Jonathan gathered the teapot and any napkins lying around on the table onto the tea tray and brought it into the kitchen to lend his head chef some assistance.

For a few minutes, only the sounds of running water and ceramicware clinking against each other filled the room. Then

Jonathan heard Elenora giggling while she did the dishes, and that giggle turned into full, hearty laughter before she shook her head and sighed.

"What do you have on your mind, Elenora?" he asked. He put the tray away and rinsed out the teapot.

"Everything that just happened. That was a legitimate prank, Mr. Tessier," she said, her voice full of delight. "I never expected you to be such a trickster!"

"Debatable," he said, though he could not help a grin forming on his face. "Were they tricks, or was it his own fault for being so ignorant? Even you knew that tea was not for regular edurans to enjoy."

"I did have my moment of curiosity. I'm just grateful I wasn't humiliated in front of other people when it happened," she said with a snort. "You don't think that old man's going to do something underhanded to ruin our reputation, do you?"

"If I had outright refused to submit to his demands, he might have," Jonathan agreed. "But Lady Askew witnessed everything, so we have some safety in her support."

Elenora smiled as she began drying the plates and cups and handing them to him to store away. "I feel like I've learned so much about you in just these past few days."

"These are special circumstances," he said. "For the most part, I am hoping things will return to normal once we get through this food critic appointment."

"That's a shame. This is shaping up to be the most eventful week in my entire career."

It was midmorning when they finished cleaning up, which

allowed them the rest of the day to resume their search for ingredients. Fortunately, Hayes had not robbed them of too much time. They were out the door within minutes and tucked into another rental car, picking up their usual gear and some hiking supplies along the way before they drove outside of the city once more.

Today's destination beckoned to them from the southeastern direction, where a forest blanketing a swath of canyons was situated equidistant from Silver Valley and Lismai. All things going well, they might conveniently find two of the remaining three sources of exclusive ingredients on the list.

Jonathan filled Elenora in during the long drive. "According to my research, there are no records of what the symbiotic bird looks like or much about its behaviors, but we do know it likes to make its nests in the bottom of shallow ravines."

"Oh, is it a flightless bird?" she asked.

"I would hope so. We have to find a way to sneak close to steal an egg or two, so it certainly would be ideal to not have the bird dive after us."

"I guess we'll form a proper plan when we get there," she said. "And the colossal beef? Will we have to slaughter any poor cattle to get that?"

Jonathan shook his head. "Fortunately not, for this ingredient. The wild colossal cattle beast apparently forms growths over its body that we need to cut off. We just have to do it without getting mauled."

"Like the chameleon."

"Yes. But instead of ribs, we will technically be slicing off its warts."

"Ew! That's disgusting!"

"Indeed," Jonathan agreed with a laugh. "But they happen to be the only part of the cattle beast that is even remotely appetizing. Patrons will enjoy it with ignorant bliss if we simply 'forget' to tell them."

Elenora scoffed and reclined leisurely in her passenger seat. The rest of the three-hour drive was uneventful, outside of the thirty-minute window where Jonathan got lost and Elenora scolded him thoroughly as she worked to recalibrate the navigation on her phone with limited connection.

When they arrived at the edge of the canyon forest, they gathered their hiking supplies and gauged their surroundings. The mountainous terrain varied severely in altitude, with cliffs that reached impossible heights and valleys that dipped dangerously below into denser woodlands.

They maneuvered the lack of defined walking trails by choosing the most-level surfaces to traverse over, and they attentively scanned the nearby areas for either source of the ingredients they sought out.

Jonathan must have dedicated too much of his attention looking for signs of either an unusual bird nest or an oversized bovine, because by the time he realized he was hiking over a particularly rockier area, his weight loosened the stones underneath him and he tumbled with an undignified yell into the clearing below.

The world became a blur to him until he stopped rolling, and he seemed to have avoided any major injuries outside of the few skin abrasions he now had along his hands and face.

"Mr. Tessier!" Elenora shouted from above. "Are you alright?"

He lifted his head to see her crouched down and peering over the edge of the precipice at him.

"Yes, I am fine," he answered back. "Be careful, Elenora!" They were separated for now, and he did not want her to reunite with him using the same method of descent down the rock face.

"I'll try to find a safer way down! Don't move too far, okay?"

He brushed off his clothes and pushed himself off the ground. He looked up and down the clearing, seeing a scattering of trees, broken logs, and shrubs. The glade seemed to stretch on this way for quite a distance, and there were no giant animals or nests to be seen.

It appeared to be taking Elenora more than a few minutes to find a way to climb down, so Jonathan decided to walk in the same direction he saw her heading. His plan had merely been to explore nearby and then return to where he had fallen before he wandered too far, but after walking for a bit, he thought he heard something rustling in front of him.

He stood in place as an individual appeared from within the trees and approached him with much less caution than he used to regard them in return. From what he could tell, it was a younger woman, with androgynous facial features and messy black hair, clad in the tattered clothes of fabric patches and leaves that only a reclusive forest hermit could wear.

She only stopped a few steps in front of him to study his machine-sewn outfit and the weapons he had at his hip. "What's a man like you doing out here?" she asked him, and several exaggerated expressions flitted across her face.

"I just wanted to source some natural ingredients," Jonathan said, hoping a simple answer would suffice.

However, the hermit woman shook her head. "You're here for the twin bird eggs, aren't you?"

Her guess made it pointless to be vague about his intentions. "Yes," he said. "Not that it has been going well, considering I fell down a slope within my first hour of searching."

She giggled shrilly at this, then stared up at him eagerly. "Let me help you, then!"

He frowned, eyeing her with blatant skepticism. They were complete strangers, and even if he paid for her services, she resided all the way out here in the wilderness. Urban currency would be useless to her. "Why would you want to help me?"

"Oh, y'know. Never a bad thing to be kind and all," she said. "What else should I be doing with my time? Always take the chance to spice up a regular ol' day."

It seemed that anything that strayed from her normal routine came across as excitement to her, but the glee in her nebulous response irritated him just a tad.

"I need to catch up with my partner first," he said. The mention of another person did not appear to cause a shift in her joy, so it was unlikely she wanted to take advantage of his solitude. "What is your name, by the way?"

"I don't really have a name, but you can call me Indigo. It's my favorite color!" She waved him over to the cliffside and he followed. "What do I call you?"

"Jonathan," he answered, and watched her walk toward a jagged slant that was not as steep as the other adjacent slopes.

There were several protruding stones that she began to grab and use to pull herself upward.

"Come on, you too!" Indigo prodded, so he lumbered on after her.

They met with Elenora soon after they reached the top, since she had also identified this area as her best chance to descend, though she evidently had some trouble mustering the resolve to do so.

"Oh, thank goodness you're alright," she said, rushing over to wrap her arms around Jonathan. "You had me so worried!"

He chuckled and returned the embrace before she stepped back to study the stranger. "Ah," he said. "This is my partner, Elenora. And this is Indigo. She told me she might be able to help in our search."

"Yup!" Indigo chimed in. "If you'll follow me, I'll take you right to where the twin bird nests."

Jonathan and Elenora followed cautiously, trailing behind at a comfortable distance and peeking ahead to confirm that Indigo was not leading them into some sort of trap. When they came upon a fairly wide glen measuring about twenty to thirty feet deep, they were relieved to find that Indigo had not led them astray.

A nest of large branches and leaves had been constructed directly on the grass and out in the open, five speckled brown-and-white eggs held snugly within. A two-headed bird with a pheasant's appearance and twice as big as an ostrich hopped aimlessly around the nest. For the size of the bird, the eggs appeared quite small, and Jonathan figured he could easily grab a single egg with just one hand.

"If you fall down there, that bird will tear you apart," Indigo told them. "So don't go expecting me to come rescue you."

"How are we supposed to get any of the eggs?" Elenora asked.

Indigo pointed up at some thick vines hanging from some lofty, sturdy trees that stretched over the valley. "You'll need to use those to swing across to the other side of the clearing," she said. "You snatch an egg up when you swing past."

"Have you done this yourself before?" Jonathan asked.

"Yes!" she said, reaching up to grab the end of one of the vines. "Here, let me show you." After pulling the vine down, she grasped tightly onto it with her hands and legs and jumped without reservation toward the other side when the bird's heads were looking away.

She whizzed right over the nest at the lowest point of the swing, and Jonathan could see that if she had extended her hand out at the right moment, she could have grabbed one of the eggs with no issues. Of course, she did not do this, ignoring the nest and pushing herself off the opposite cliffside with her feet. With a flail of her legs, she returned back to their side of the glen, landing with a stumble but otherwise safe and sound.

Elenora let out a groan that expressed her ambivalence, and Jonathan could not help thinking this to be quite an extreme method to secure the eggs. But comparing it to what they had already experienced to obtain these rare ingredients, they slowly agreed to give it a try.

"I will go," Jonathan said, picking out a vine for himself after meticulously testing several of them. He would be willing to try multiple times if it meant Elenora would be spared the trouble. "I think you should only swing in if I find myself in a pinch."

Elenora had one hand on another vine and the other on the handle of her butcher knife. "You got it, boss," she said.

He tied the end of the vine into a perfection loop wide enough to fit his thigh into. Indigo might have had the expertise to swing through the cavern without relying on anything more than the power of her grip, but he was not going to take any chances. Even if his hands slipped, he would not fall straight down into the clutches of the symbiotic bird. It would still be unfortunate for him to lose grip of the vine, but the odds of recovering would be much better for him this way.

Only when Jonathan felt totally secured in the strength of his vine did he hold on firmly and run off the edge of the cliff, timing it when the bird happened to wander off farther from the nest. There was a weightlessness to the drop, until he felt a sharp jerk throughout his whole body at the point the vine was fully extended, and the air grew stronger in his face as he picked up speed.

He trained his eyes on the nest as he flew closer. He had one clean opportunity to do this right. He held out his arm as he cut through the air and managed to scoop one of the eggs right when he swung over the nest, which he quickly slipped into his shoulder bag. He then imitated Indigo in pushing off the other side of the ravine to maintain enough momentum that he could hoist himself up on the way back.

Elenora grabbed his arm to help steady his landing while Indigo giggled and clapped unhelpfully from the side, clearly using their endeavors as her personal entertainment. Jonathan ignored the hermit and muttered his thanks to Elenora.

"That was good," she said. "You did well, boss."

"Here, take this." He pulled the egg out and handed it to her. She had special containers prepared in her bag that would protect the egg's shell from cracking.

"I will go for just one more," he told her. Mostly because he could not stand the racket that woman was making, but he also did not want to push his luck. One wrong move could lead to significantly more problems than this was worth, and two of these eggs seemed plenty enough to work with.

He launched himself down again, successfully swiping another egg without catching the bird's attention. Elenora had to dig her heels deeper into the ground to help him up this time, and he handed this second egg to her with a slight wince of pain.

"You would think a simple swing would not be too much to handle," he said with a groan. "But it really does take a toll on you." The effects of such rapid stamina loss were obvious by the way his muscles trembled, and he knew if he tried to swing down another time, he greatly risked falling into the valley.

Right as Elenora was about to zip her bag closed, Indigo approached them with a smug grin.

"You should give me one of those eggs as payment for helping you," she said to them.

Jonathan looked at her incredulously. "That is a hefty price to pay for only showing us where a nest might be. We hardly walked far to get here."

Indigo shook her head and waggled her gnarled finger. "The two of you could've wandered in the wrong direction for a long time. This forest is huge! Let's face it, you really needed my help. So, I shouldn't even have to ask. You should've just offered to give me an egg in return." She then held her hands out expectantly. "But I'll forgive you."

"Could we simply pay you instead? A fraction of what one of these eggs would cost on the market should be more than fair. I was the one who still had to collect them myself."

"Well, now that you know where the bird nests, you can come back and gather eggs all you like!" Indigo insisted. "And what am I going to do with your money out here? C'mon, it's such a small fee. Don't be so stingy!"

Jonathan clenched his jaw. The thought of giving a whole egg to this hermit pained him, especially when Indigo never warned them that there would be a price for her assistance. And he did not have enough energy to get one more egg just to appease her.

There was a tense, silent standoff that lasted for a while, but then Elenora spoke up.

"No problem. I'll go grab another egg for you, Indigo."

CHAPTER 10

"No, you will not, Elenora," Jonathan objected.

There was no reason for her to unnecessarily put herself in harm's way. They could probably run away from Indigo now and avoid paying her altogether. What was she going to do about it?

"It's okay, boss," Elenora said. "I can do it, I promise. Besides, we've been through worse."

For a grand total of two occasions, but he decided not to say this out loud. During their search for the radiant cabbages, the nightmare creatures they encountered, which he later discovered were called farewell dogs and afterlife eagles from a quick online search, had been a highly unexpected part of the night. As he had suspected, these creatures lingered in an alternate dimension, seldom crossing over to stalk unsuspecting victims in the forest for the chance to send them to their deaths, like bestial versions of a grim reaper.

And they had no other way to slice the chameleon's bony spikes without her climbing onto its back. The tiny cemetery gate made it so Elenora had to be the one to take on that task. Their circumstances gave them very little room to work around the danger.

Besides, those events had already happened. Nothing to do with the present.

"But we already have the eggs we need. And the eggs are heavier than they seem." Having held the eggs in his hand, Jonathan knew that they were slightly larger than those ostriches would lay, and a single unit was more than enough to feed three of even the hungriest of critics.

"Don't worry, this will be a piece of cake," she countered, already preparing the vine for her swing.

Elenora was not always a stubborn woman. No one was ever one thing, all the time. But she was determined, and he could not think of a way to stop her outside of dragging her away from the scene with the crumbs of energy he had left to support him.

Cursing Indigo's quiet enthusiasm as she observed their conversation, Jonathan reluctantly relented, exchanging bags with Elenora before she went for the jump.

The second the soles of Elenora's feet left the edge of the cliff, Indigo started yelling at the top of her lungs, her voice brassy at a piercing volume. Jonathan froze in shock, but Indigo was far from finished. She bent over to pick up some fist-sized stones from the ground and tossed them below at the symbiotic bird.

A few of the flying rocks smacked one of its heads squarely in the face, and the other head instantly straightened its neck out in alarm. Jonathan watched with wide eyes as the bird's unharmed head twisted around to scan its surroundings, and seeing only Elenora in the vicinity after she had just passed by the nest with an egg in her arm, did not care that the culprit was actually the hermit standing on the plateau above.

The bird charged at Elenora, disrupting her trajectory as she swung the rest of the way back. Though its beaks had seemed rather proportionately small, the bird snapped at her with vicious fury, and she screamed out as she flailed her legs. The frantic scuffle consisted of her barely avoiding its bites, kicking at the top of its heads, and dangling in the middle of the canyon as she quickly lost any momentum she had left in her swing. She dropped the egg in the confusion, and it cracked easily upon hitting the ground.

Indigo's grating laughter rang out, and she leaned over to pick up another stone. Jonathan rushed to shove her aside before she could throw it, his jaw tight with restraint. He could not waste time erupting on her. Not concerned with how she fell over, he then grabbed his vine and ran along the bluff. He stopped when he had gone far enough to set himself up for a different angle and turned to aim for a crag on the other side with a lower elevation.

With a running start, he launched himself into the canyon. A surge of pain shot through his arms, but he held on to the vine with desperate resolve.

"Elenora!" he called out to her.

As he flew closer, she rushed to climb a little higher on her vine and then extended her arm outward. At the moment his swing reached her, she grabbed onto his waist and he used one hand to hold tightly on to the back of her jacket. She abandoned her vine and they both lifted their legs to evade the bird jumping up to reach them.

Catching Elenora had slowed down his momentum, but he hoped they had enough to soar above the lower crag at the height of the swing.

"Get ready!" he shouted to her and let go of the vine.

They held on to each other tightly as they flew just short of the crag, tumbling over rocks and dirt down the side of the main cliff. As they slowed down near the bottom of the ravine, Jonathan felt certain they were going to develop a lavish collection of bruises later on, but that seemed an inconsequential thought at this point in time.

Clenching his jaw, he looked up toward the bird, which had spotted them with one of its heads.

"We need to run," he said, urgently pulling Elenora up. She allowed herself to be helped onto her feet, and he gripped her hand tightly as he began to bolt away from the bird.

His partner followed him as best she could, until she let out a pained groan. When he looked back at her, he was surprised that it took as long as it did for her to protest.

"Your leg," he said, stunned.

A red gash glared through a tear in the right leg of her pants. The bird had succeeded in scraping away a significant piece of her skin. The injury was more raw flesh than it was bleeding, but it appeared painful all the same.

He looked behind them to see the bird tottering after them.

It did not seem capable of moving very fast, but it was tall, and its legs long enough to lurch.

"Don't stop running," Indigo called out from above, her cackle making her words taunting rather than warning. "Hasn't had a proper meal in a long time!"

His muscles trembled, but he could not afford to collapse just yet. He quickly stood in front of Elenora and crouched down.

"Get on, now," he instructed, and she complied. He put his hands under her thighs to keep her up on his back as she wrapped her arms around his shoulders. His legs shook as he pushed himself to stand. A few grunts escaped him as he took one step after another, picking up speed into a jog.

The bird had closed the gap, and he glanced behind him in time to see one of the heads lean back, winding up to bash itself into them. He and Elenora both shrieked as he jumped out of the way, and the bird's head crashed into the ground instead.

In a moment of disorientation, the bird tripped over itself, and Jonathan used the opportunity to keep dashing down the ravine. The walls of the cliff felt towering, like they were closing in on either side of them, so when he found an opening on the right side of the ravine where they could hide, he did not hold back his strangled exclamation of relief.

A pile of logs and rocks helped to further obscure the cave, and he gently put Elenora down inside. He slumped over next to her before he crawled to peek in the direction from where they came.

At a distance, the bird stood in place, its two heads rotating independently to scan its surroundings. After a minute or two, it turned away and waddled back to its nest. When he was certain that it would not come dashing after them, Jonathan instructed Elenora to climb onto his back again so they could slink farther down the ravine. He stayed close to the wall, on the same side Indigo would be. He doubted she would come after them with how far he ran, but if she did, he did not want to make it easy.

Around the curve of the cliff, he found a sliver of sloped land leading up to higher ground and away from the canyon.

He helped Elenora to a nearby tree where she could sit and lean against its sturdy trunk while he examined her wound. When he reached for the first aid kit from his coat, he noticed a stain on the front of the bag he was carrying. He opened it, and they both saw that one of the special containers had broken during their fall, and its egg along with it.

She gave him a look, and he frowned, deciding to focus on her wound instead. His first aid kit contained supplies for minor wounds, but this one was proving to be no easy matter to disinfect or bandage up.

"Why did you do that, Elenora?" he said, his lowered voice verging on a hiss. "I told you not to, but you went anyway!"

She did not respond, and whether her brow furrowed with discomfort from her injury or irritation at his scolding was unclear to him.

"I said nothing about you ignoring my warnings in Lismai because no harm came from it, but look at you now. And for what? To heed the nonsensical drivel of that fool?"

"Jonathan," she muttered, and his hands stopped shuffling in search of which ointment or disinfectant would work best to clean up her awful gash.

He looked up at her and squinted his eyes. His name sounded foreign coming from her, but his anger seemed to subside for just a moment when he heard her voice saying it.

"Looks like we could've just given Indigo that egg," she said, "and avoided this altogether."

He made a sound, disgruntled. Elenora had wanted to be kind, but neither of them knew the hermit would crave chaos instead. "No, we should have ignored her, like I wanted to. This was her fault." He bit his lip, stopping himself from continuing. Lowering his gaze, he found an antibacterial ointment and put on a pair of vinyl gloves.

She gave him a weak smile. "I'm sorry this happened, I really am. I never want to cause trouble for you. But I'm my own person. Even if it means disagreeing with you, I'm always going to want a sense of agency. I've gone through life holding on to that, you know?"

As he lifted her leg and checked for any bleeding, the smell of which was almost impossible for him to withstand, he found he could not readily disagree with her outside of his own bullhead-edness. He did ask her to be his partner in this endeavor, which meant they were equals out here. He understood the risks of pulling her into this, and he did it anyway, thinking his bond with her easily trounced any trust he could have had working with some stranger he hired separately for the job.

It did not mean he was any less incensed about how that interaction with Indigo had gone down, and how he thought Elenora should have handled it.

"If you were able to use Avidea, you might be able to accelerate your own healing," he said as he did his best to clean her wound. "I really need you to think twice about these things."

"I know that I'm new to this and that you know much more than I could hope to understand about the crazy work we're doing, the work you've done before we ever even met. No matter what, I have to try to do what I think is best. I have to make my own mistakes. Who am I, if I—"

Elenora winced and gritted her teeth together to endure the pain.

"Listening to that woman was definitely a mistake," he interjected. "We never promised to pay her, and she demonstrated that she could have easily stolen one of those eggs on her own."

"I didn't think it would be a big deal, honestly." Her voice faltered and she panted heavily as Jonathan began wrapping the gash up in bandages. "You were getting tired, so I thought giving it a go just once would be easy if it was to pay Indigo back for her kindness."

"But it was not."

"Who could've expected her to act like that?" A breathy, exhausted laughter heaved from her chest. "I guess there aren't any rules when you live out here in the wilderness."

When he finished dressing her wound, Jonathan stood again, grimacing from a dizziness that lingered. Though the smell of Elenora's blood did not turn his stomach as much as before it was bandaged, he still had to contend with the fatigue creeping up on him.

"Well, I hardly think we can continue today," he said. "It would be best to get you back and admitted into a hospital."

She had her eyes closed as she tried to steady her breathing. "That seems like such a waste, though."

He frowned. "What?"

"We came all the way out here anyway," she said, now looking up at him. "You'll miss the chance to get the colossal beef in time if you don't get it now."

"I hardly think that matters when you are hurt, Elenora," he said.

"And I don't think I can even walk that far right now. If you tried to carry me to the car, you'd collapse for sure. Maybe we'll even fall off a cliff. And die."

He could not believe she was trying, miserably so, to be funny. "What are you getting at?"

"I know you'll say I won't be reliable in helping you when I'm in this state," she said. "But you can at least look around to see if you find something, right?"

"I am not leaving you here on your own."

"I'll be fine!"

"I am not doing it," he said sternly.

She sighed, then held out a hand. "Can you turn your rapier into a crutch? I'll use it to follow behind."

He stared at her curiously. "I can only transform it into a kitchen utensil. But could we not then walk to the car?"

"You don't even want to look around a little bit?" Elenora asked. Her persistent selflessness, or rather foolishness, irritated him, but she clearly understood his own shameful desire to hunt down the elusive ingredient. Perhaps even better than he did. If the circumstances had been different, he would not have hesitated.

"Also, a crutch is just an upside-down potato masher with some adjustments," she added with a cheeky grin. "You can do that, right?"

"An hour, maximum," Jonathan said. Her idea was ridiculous, but he could maybe convince himself that this short amount of time would be no different from getting lost or taking a detour path. "If we do not find anything before then, we are heading back to Silver Valley."

He traded his rapier for her butcher knife, but since he could not transform his silver sword for more than a few minutes at a time, he lent himself as her support for most of their search through the forest. When he did turn it into an improvised crutch so she could walk on her own, he made sure not to wander too far from her.

In any case, they had agreed that she would stay back while he handled any of the challenges expected when encountering a colossal cattle beast, and that neither of them were fit to confront such a beast head-on.

He eased around the other small canyons spread across this forest, peeking over the edges to see if his mark was hiding in their valleys, like the symbiotic bird had been. He also strayed toward any clearings he could find, because he could not imagine a massive cattle beast being very comfortable wedging itself through the dense thickets.

As he checked the ground for droppings or flattened foliage, Jonathan happened upon a series of giant hoofprints. The grass and leaves that bent around the shapes formed clean edges and were as lush as the vegetation around them, so he turned to Elenora and formed his rapier into a crutch for her to hold.

"Follow at a comfortable pace while I go on ahead," he told her. "If anything happens, call out for me."

She nodded. "You do the same, even if it'll take me a while to get to you." She had been allowing her injured leg to touch the ground more often, even if it was only to limp.

He returned the nod and stalked forward, swiftly following where the tracks led while minimizing the noise of his steps. Soon enough, he peered through the trees around him and caught sight of the animal grazing in an open area of overgrown grass and ferns. The creature was colored a striking red, a sharp contrast to the neutrals and greens of its backdrop. With shorter legs and a rounder build than normal cattle, it moved slowly, carrying the bulbous warts he was after all over its body.

With the lush grass around it, the beast already had enough to feed on to sate its appetite, so Jonathan did not feel particularly optimistic when he scanned the nearby surroundings for something that would help him cut pieces off the growths without disturbing the bovine. As he tried to close the distance, he kept his eyes trained on its legs out of fear he would be trampled or kicked. One wrong move, and that would be it.

He remembered reading somewhere that, very similarly to domesticated cows, the colossal cattle beast might be partial to the aromas of alfalfa and clover. If he could summon something that mimicked those fragrances, he could distract the beast long enough to keep it occupied.

That was going to be tough. There were only two ways he could reliably conjure an accurate scent profile: he would have had to practice after someone else confirmed that he did it right, or he would need a comprehensive understanding of its source, the actual dish that went with the smell.

As luck would have it, he had not often cooked with either alfalfa sprouts or clover. As he took hold of the replacement cast-iron pan he brought with him, he tried envisioning the flowering plants using the mere power of his mind, to connect their images to reality, to things that were said to give off similar smells.

The forms of the plants appeared within the pan. Purple flowers for the alfalfa and white ones for clover, though whether they were distinct from other flower varieties of comparable colorations, he did not have the botanical expertise to know for certain. Just like he did not have the olfactory expertise to adjust the scents wafting from the pan.

"Mr. Tessier," Elenora called from behind him. She had slowly caught up to where they could see each other from a distance again, but she spoke with an urgent tone of voice.

He turned to look at her questioningly.

"It's way too strong," she warned, wrinkling her nose. She then lifted the hand not gripping the reverted rapier like a walking stick and pointed toward the bovine.

Jonathan looked back and watched the large creature lift its head from the grass. It started turning toward him, but this simple movement dragged its low body across the ground and created a rumble through this area of the forest.

Trying not to panic prematurely, he tossed the pan into the air. It spun around the axis of its body and flew over the head of the cattle beast, landing in some shrubbery on the opposite side.

He readied himself to dart away if it still wanted to come after him, even if it meant having to carry Elenora with him while he did.

He waited with figuratively bated breath, his shoulders relaxing only when the creature wiggled its snout and turned toward where the pan had landed. Jonathan inched backward until he arrived at where Elenora had taken the liberty to sit under another tree.

"How are you holding up?" he asked her.

"Still hurts, but it's not too bad right now." He thought she might be lying, determined to act as if she had gotten used to the pain.

He picked up the rapier that she had set on the ground while she pulled out her phone. She had no service, but she only wanted to show him the time.

"Looks like our hour is about to run out in just a couple of minutes," she said, a smile pulling at the corner of her mouth. "Aren't you going to jump after that hunk of beef now that its back is turned?"

Jonathan scoffed at her teasing before glancing over at the giant cow. It must have found the pan, as it alternated between aggressively shoving its snout into the overgrowth and digging at the ground with its stubby legs. He had magically embedded the scents into the metal of the pan, so no matter how eagerly the creature plowed into the dirt, it would not find the aromatic forage it yearned for.

"You're going to wait?" Elenora asked. "You're the one who said. . ."

He handed back her butcher knife and sat down next to her. "And you are very well aware that I am not going to simply get up and leave after coming this far, regardless of what I said."

"I knew it," she said, much too smugly.

He shook his head before she could continue. "I can want something while knowing that getting you home was the right thing to do. Now, shush. You were the one who wanted me to do this."

She giggled and accepted his offered shoulder to rest upon, and they both took this time of respite to recover some of their strength.

About ten minutes later, the ground shook again when the colossal cattle beast exhausted itself with its doomed attempts to find its favorite food. It collapsed onto its stomach, resting its head near the pan to enjoy the evasive scents as much as it could.

Leaving Elenora to continue resting by the tree, Jonathan eased over with his rapier, changing its blade into that of a long carving knife. He took careful steps to sneak in closer and then cleanly sliced off one of the animal's rear warts at the base. The mass came off without any difficulty, and he backed up warily, but the cut surface was solid and did not ooze any blood or nasty fluids. The creature gave no sign that it had felt him sever the growth.

He cut another one, and that was about as much as he could carry with ease. His empty bag was still in Elenora's possession, and the bag he had was packed with one whole egg and the remains of another one. After sheathing his sword, he grabbed the two chunks just as the beast stirred. He made sure to stay out of its line of sight as he retreated.

Its attention remained on the pan, another lost cause he could not rescue, but the bovine showed no intention of getting up. He was going through these cast-iron skillets thriftlessly fast, a trend he hoped not to bring with him after the end of the week.

When he reunited with Elenora, she helped him wrap the pieces of beef in butcher paper and pack them up. Jonathan volunteered to carry both of the bags and slowly helped her walk back to the car.

On the drive to the capital, he kept his eyes forward. The sunset guided their way back with spectacular gradients. His facial expression tensed rigidly as he pulled his thoughts together into one conclusion.

"You should stay behind tomorrow," he said. "I will get the last ingredient by myself."

He could feel her stare on him. She held it there for a few seconds, then turned to look out her window for the rest of the ride.

CHAPTER 11

JONATHAN ESCORTED ELENORA BACK to her apartment, telling her to get to the hospital as soon as it would be convenient for her. Ideally, that would be tonight. Right now, really, yet she had protested. He had done his best to dress her wound, but no amount of amateur care would compare to the professional competence of a real doctor.

She had kept her eyes downcast throughout the interaction, only speaking up to wish him good luck for tomorrow.

Disheartened mood aside, this was undeniably the best decision he could have made. He figured that was why she relented to his suggestion despite her clear reluctance. She knew she should use the time to rest, and it would most certainly avoid putting her at risk of sustaining additional injuries. It was for one day only, and then they would resume working together to test recipes and finalize their special menu.

The final ingredient Jonathan included in his list was the

volcanic clam. He wanted seafood, or something that resembled it, as the perfect component to round out his collection of eccentric ingredients. It was honestly such a shame. If it had not been so downright unsustainable to gather these eight ingredients, he might have been content to never change his menu from such a masterpiece ever again. Beyond the critics' visit, he would be lucky if he could regularly feature even just one chef's special of such high caliber at a time.

The trip to the dormant volcanoes between Harbor Town and Sorense, municipalities so far to the east of Silver Valley that only a large bay and the nation's most derelict town separated them from the eastern Amezan border, was easily going to be the longest distance he would have to travel since he had begun this quest.

Having to retire as early as he could last night and get up when the sky was still dark helped him feel additionally justified that he had not subjected Elenora to such a burden. A heavy drowsiness stuck to his body as he trudged to the city's airport, got onto the charter plane he booked, and slept through most of the eight hours the flight required. Given the structure of the country, private jets were one of the most practical ways for people to move between the central capital and destinations near Ameza's borders. Mercenaries could often get incredible discounts as a perk since travel was an integral part of the job, but every part of this quest of his was still racking up a hefty bill for him to pay.

"I'm going to stay here, but come back to the plane when you're ready and we'll lift off again. Our flight isn't cleared for overnight travel, so try to be quick, okay?" the pilot told Jonathan after they landed in a vast open field.

A light drizzle fell over the land and desaturated the late-morning sky. The field surrounded a series of mostly dormant volcanoes spaced far apart, mountainous areas of grayish bronze stretching over expanses of green and yellow. Jonathan had brought along a brimmed hat to ward against the day's sun, but now it mostly served to keep raindrops from getting into his eyes.

He walked toward the nearest volcano and started maneuvering around its craggy base. The uneven terrain proved difficult to navigate, and the rain was beginning to make the dirt slushy and the rocks slippery. He took careful steps because falling over here would be of the utmost inconvenience.

Volcanic clams hid in plain sight, though they often appeared indistinguishable from the abundant volcanic rocks lying around. They would not stand up to inspection, but the odds that someone looking for a rock sample would pick one up inadvertently from millions were exceedingly slim.

So, it was not a surprise to Jonathan that he could not find anything out of the ordinary. Every few dozens of feet, he would bend over and lift a few loose rocks to examine them, only to toss each one behind him when he found nothing remarkable about them. It seemed like a hopeless task every time he gazed back over the space in front of him, endlessly bestrewn with magmatic stones.

When he had circled about halfway around, he noticed a group of older women gathered together, each one of them busy sifting through piles of rocks in and out of several metal buckets.

As he approached, he saw they had a variety of stones and obsidian chunks collected, and a few among them resembled mollusks, with shells of pumice-like texture.

"Hello," Jonathan said to them from a respectful distance. "I was wondering if you knew where to find any volcanic clams." He was almost certain that was what those shells were, but the extra confirmation would hardly hurt.

"Ooh, look at you," one of the women cooed. "What a fancy man who has come to visit us!"

Jonathan watched as a few of them motioned with their hands to mimic his hat, coat, and vest, and chattered among themselves about his outfit. It was then he noticed, belatedly after having been more concerned about their rock harvest, that these women were all some type of Hunter. Their long hair ranged from dirty blond to grayish brown and was embellished with uneven streaks and spots of black, greatly reminiscent of a wild cat's fur.

Hunters were the only variant of edurans that largely maintained homogeneous communities separate from urban societies. The rest of the variants, including Spectrals like himself, had taken to blending in with the people that outnumbered them for centuries, unbeknownst to their ordinary eduran neighbors except for those who might have learned about them through higher education. Other than the few little quirks that he learned to work around, Jonathan had never found himself pondering too much on all their differences.

Now, he was curious if their flowy woven skirts hid any tails. He knew Hunters could take on any number of physical characteristics to mimic a specific animal, or even a mythological creature, on top of traits like heightened senses and agility. Perhaps their tendency to stick together with others of their own kind was what helped to maintain those characteristics over stretches of time, but eduran variants had existed since ancient eras too early to know for certain.

"About the volcanic clams," he tried again.

"Are you going to dig around in your pretty clothes like that?" another woman piped up. "You'll be sure to ruin them."

"It's backbreaking work too, fancy boy!" the first who spoke added. "You're so lean, you couldn't handle it." Sure enough, it did look like any one of them could easily overwhelm him in a one-on-one brawl. If they decided they wanted to have him for dinner, he could only hope they would not match him in Avidea magic.

"I am only looking for a couple of clams," he said pleasantly. For some reason he could not explain, Jonathan did not feel threatened by them. Their teasing only evinced their jovial personalities, and he did not feel the wariness or displeasure he might have if this situation had taken place in the city.

"Well, you're too late anyway with this area," said one Hunter woman in the back, lifting her bucket of rocks in demonstration. A few of the stones toppled onto the ground. "They're so scarce to begin with, and we've just finished doing all our work. Actually, we don't expect to find more than one each a day, if any at all."

That was unfortunate news. Jonathan did not want to spend too much time having to hunt for something so rare it could take him days to find.

"Is there any chance I can buy some off you, then?" he asked, then thought to explain further. They had been so honest with him. "I want to create a new recipe for my restaurant using those clams."

The women all seemed amused by this suggestion.

"Where is your restaurant?"

"In Silver Valley," he answered.

"Oh, that's too far..."

"Yeah... I bet that would be a dream for Drift. Ever since she went across the river to that underground city, she's been so fixated on trying new dishes."

"Can you blame me, Meadow?" the one called Drift said. "Our village is small, and we don't have much experience or the tools to try new cooking methods. We just roast our seafood and eat it plainly."

"You say it like that's a bad thing," another woman spoke up. "Our fish is very delicious that way! And the city people spend so much time preparing food just to eat it in one gulp. What's the point?"

"But don't you ever wonder if we're missing out, Tan?"

Jonathan insisted on introductions before they distracted themselves with a heated conversation. After learning all their names—Drift with her braided hair, Meadow who gestured gracefully with both hands as she talked, Tan with many stunning bracelets on her wrists, Sunny who smiled with her eyes, and Reed with her tall and willowy form—he offered monetary compensation that they could use in Harbor Town, or that underground city, Sorense, for the cooking supplies Drift might want. They refused, momentarily and bitterly reminding him of Indigo, but elaborated that they earned enough money with their obsidian jewelry to meet their basic needs, and any extra currency would be useless within their village.

"Then, how about this?" Jonathan said, pausing to think. "Would I be able to take a look at what you have in your food stores? I can help you create a new recipe or two and see if you all like it."

The women stirred up a commotion, and it fascinated him that his idea was being met with so much more enthusiasm than when he had offered money.

"It'll be like participating in a cooking class with a fine young man," Reed gushed. The others hummed their eager agreement.

So, the women picked up their buckets and led Jonathan to their village, located by a lake northwest from the volcanoes. This body of water was immensely vast, and unlike Purity Lake, it stretched so far he could not see the other side of it. Ripples decorated its surface as raindrops added themselves to its volume. A river extended from the eastern side of the lake and would find its final destination at the bay.

"Does your village have a name?" he asked Meadow, who was the only one who walked at his pace, and not dozens of feet ahead.

"We have one in our dialect, but for everyone else, we can call it the Fishing Village. We'd call that the Fishing Lake too," Meadow said as she pointed toward the shore.

Straightforward, simple names. He nodded respectfully as they guided him through their village. There were people strolling about with carefree strides as they went on with their day. Children played games with each other using simple wooden toys. All of them had similarly patterned hair under their rain hoods, and indeed, no tails could be seen. The women led him to their food storage house and showed him around the many shelves and boxes inside.

Divided into sections of fresh, chilled, smoked, and dried, they kept the meat they extracted from common wild animals. He noted that they were usually from smaller and tamer animals, such as hares, grouse, and deer. The women explained that they usually stayed away from larger beasts in the area that were not safe to hunt, which would have been more alarming to him if he had not been facing colossal creatures all week. He wondered aloud how they dealt with that, but thinking him a sheltered coward, they earnestly assured him that their village was situated far from where any of those beasts wandered.

They also had a small selection of grains, vegetables, and fruits harvested from their farmlands. Another section featured eating utensils made from clay and metal, some that looked handcrafted and others he assumed they had purchased from one of the nearby cities.

Fish and other types of seafood occupied the bulk of the storehouse, naturally. Most of what could be had been smoked and dried, and they used various types of iceboxes to preserve the rest.

"Tell me how you usually prepare food other than your fish," Jonathan asked the group. "Like your potatoes." He noticed that they had a good number of those.

"We cut them up and boil them in a pot," Sunny said. She and Meadow were part of the team of villagers that regularly handled meal preparation, so they stayed behind to chat with him. The others had left to take their pretty stones to their artisan workshop. "We do that for most of our vegetables. It's easy to do over a central fire and feed some to everyone here."

"What about the meat?"

"We grill it over a metal grate, or we roast it over an open fire," she answered.

"What else do you usually prepare for your meals?"

"If there isn't much work for us to do around the village, we might prepare bread with our grains and create spreads from our fruits to put on them," Meadow said. "Otherwise, we have rice or oats as a staple, or we cook everything into a stew."

They seemed to have a good grasp on all the basics, and that seemed enough to satisfy the villagers day after day. There were people in the city who could not even manage this much. When the women showed him their village's central kitchen and left him alone for some time to brainstorm over what he could teach them, Jonathan quietly conceded that there was a sense of madness in caring this deeply about how food was prepared merely to be swiftly consumed.

Even with his level of expertise, perhaps he did not have much he could offer them. The Fishing Village could continue without his contribution and be just as happy as they had always been. They might even come up with new cooking techniques on their own. Drift sounded curious enough to find out how, and with a few more adventures she would bring that knowledge back to everyone else.

Nothing he could show them was a recipe or technique that he invented. The list of ingredients he compiled to create a new menu for the Taverne contained not a single thing he discovered on his own. Something nebulous gnawed at him before he realized that he was already here, he had offered to do this, and he might as well earn those volcanic clams to get that list over with.

Two seemed like a good number, with a third recipe for backup if they despised one of his offerings. Jonathan knew that he did not want to overwhelm the village chefs with something that required too much labor or would be too far of a departure from what the residents already loved to eat. All he was here to do was to inspire some creativity that they could use to keep on experimenting.

The village chefs gathered for his class, all facing him with keen attentiveness from their own stations while he stood at the front. For him, teaching others had only ever consisted of training juniors at old restaurant jobs or working individually with chefs at the Taverne, so having all these anticipatory eyes on him was newly daunting.

"The first recipe I would like to demonstrate to you all uses what you already have to create a filling," he said.

Murmurs filled the room.

"You already mix different ingredients together when you make stews, but you can put a mixture like that inside a type of shell or wrapping for convenient dining. Today, we will be trying a recipe using mashed potatoes."

"That seems like a lot of work if we can just have stew in our bowls and mashed potatoes on the side," Meadow said.

Jonathan smiled and nodded. "Yes, that is true. I am not trying to replace what you already do so much as I am presenting options. You will be using the same ingredients, but you might find that they result in very different experiences."

Tasks were soon divided among the chefs. A couple of them began boiling some potatoes to mash and separating corn kernels from their cobs. One chef started cooking some ground meat while another chopped bell peppers, garlic, onions, and tomatoes into small pieces to mix in. Meadow prepared plenty of egg wash and Sunny tore up old bread into incredibly fine crumbs.

After Jonathan demonstrated the final assembly only once, they divided themselves into two teams of three. One group handled scooping a portion of the mashed potatoes, creating a hollow where they could deposit some of the meaty filling, and wrapping it into a ball to hand over. The other team would then dip the balls into the egg wash and bread crumbs to place onto a metal sheet for Jonathan to arrange and bake until crispy in their ovens.

They learned quickly, and had deft hands. In just over five minutes, they had prepared nearly a hundred stuffed mashed potato dumplings, which he sectioned off into four sheets to bake for around fifteen minutes.

"Very well done, everyone," he said as he helped them set their bowls aside to be cleaned. "While we wait for those to finish, I will show you one more cooking technique."

He had them gather some older pots and utensils, some so worn down they should have been thrown away. The Hunters were intent on watching his every move, so he hid nothing and transformed them into skillets and tongs in front of their eyes.

"Look, he's doing magic!" he heard one of them say. Their voices of amazement began to overlap as they reacted to his ability.

"That's impressive! I've seen tricks like that before, but this is on another level."

"Let's have him change our other tools! To better ones!"

It took almost three full minutes for him to get the commotion to settle down.

Taking a juicy chunk of venison loin, he went through the process of seasoning it, searing each side, adding rosemary and thyme for aromatics, and basting it until it was ready to rest off the fire. There were a few gaps in their supply that he had to substitute with his Avidea, but he figured a few grains of salt, sprigs of herbs, swirls of oil, and dollops of butter would not drain his magical stamina too severely. He instructed them throughout his presentation that this method gave them the freedom to incorporate flavors of all kinds using seasonings and ingredients from the cities that would otherwise have dripped into the fire when they grilled or roasted their steaks.

Every chef was given the opportunity to emulate the technique on their own, and they finished their attempts just in time for the potato balls to be taken out of the ovens.

Drift, Tan, and Reed joined them for the taste testing. Samples of the venison steak were distributed first, and as soon as everyone had a bite to enjoy, the conversations began. Jonathan partook as well, though he kept the opinion regarding the lacking flavor to himself, because the excitement of the village chefs buzzed throughout the kitchen as they discussed shopping lists of other herbs and seasonings they could buy on their next trip to a major city. Some of them speculated on how they could similarly prepare the other types of meat they had in their storage.

Then it was time to sample the baked potato balls. They were passed around so that each taster in attendance could pick one for themselves, and the rest were piled into a wide wooden bowl. Sounds of chewing could be heard, followed by awed remarks about the crispiness and texture as the villagers became baffled at how the soft bread had become a satisfying crunch.

Jonathan thought again that they could have achieved higher quality with better tools and more spices, but their reactions only made him wish he had more time to teach. They had a talented team in charge of their meals, but their small and isolated village had been kept in the dark of the full potential the rest of the world was reaching for in culinary advancements.

The group of women who had brought him to the Fishing Village thanked him and presented him with one volcanic clam from each of them. When Meadow also tried to give him an obsidian pendant suspended on a dyed black string, Jonathan widened his eyes and raised his hand in protest.

"No, I cannot accept something so beautiful for what little I offered you," he said. The natural glass had been expertly chipped away and polished to reveal the elegant form of a wild cat catching a fish, and the elite level of craftsmanship would put urban artisans to shame. If he ever had doubts about how their village sustained themselves primarily on the sales of their stunning jewelry, they were forgotten at the bestowal of this gift.

"Silly man," Meadow said with a grin. "Don't be so rude to refuse us."

"At least allow me to pay you," he said.

"We told you already, we make enough on our own."

"Yes, but the deal had always been for the clams only."

"Your class really impressed us. A bonus gift, as gratitude!"

"I would be remiss if I did not treat you fairly in this transaction."

Meadow groaned. "Ah, you're such a stubborn one, aren't you? Fine, fine, as long as you take it."

Jonathan chuckled and asked how much on average they earned for a masterpiece like this one. Suspecting that she was lying by claiming a lower value, he held out cash totaling twice as much. Another argument ensued, and he won again.

"You're welcome back here anytime," Reed told him when the exchange had finally been made. "In fact, I think we'd like if you visited us regularly."

"If time allows, I will certainly try to come back," Jonathan said.

"Show us a new recipe each time too!" Drift said, the sparkle in her eyes flashing brighter.

The others nodded. "We never knew cooking to be so exciting," Meadow said. "We never really tried. We thought it would be a waste of precious time. Just getting enough food each day and using our crafts to buy what we couldn't grow or gather ourselves was sometimes all we could worry about."

"Now we know there are ways to cook our food without too much extra time or effort," Drift said. She seemed the most pleased, her curious city excursions validated through today's events.

"Hey, why don't you stay for a little longer?" Sunny chimed in. "We can cook up what you taught us for dinner while you're still here, and you can eat with us before you go."

And though he should have politely declined, to not keep his pilot waiting and to return home sooner, Jonathan did not hesitate to agree.

CHAPTER 12

BECAUSE HE WAS THEIR GUEST, the Fishing Village chefs rejected Jonathan's suggestion that he should help with dinner preparations, and they would not allow him to sway them on this point.

So, because the rain had subsided in the late afternoon, he took to wandering the village while he waited.

He noticed now that most of the houses had been built using a combination of carved rocks and clay, with the ones near the lake's shoreline suspended on taller foundations or stilts made of stone.

With their dwellings out in the open, he wondered how the villagers protected themselves from wild animal attacks. The houses were well-constructed and appeared sturdy, but as unfair a comparison as it may be, they had nowhere near the same ability as the metal structures of a metropolis did to withstand attacks of greater ferocity. The women had informed him that they maintained distance from beasts of monstrous sizes, but he could not imagine what would keep those creatures away.

He found none of the urgency he was so accustomed to in his kitchen among any of the people he strolled past as they went about their activities. Those crafting trinkets or weaving reed baskets treated their work as nothing more than a leisurely way to occupy their hands. People often interrupted their placid gaits to converse with each other like they never had destinations to begin with. A few even gladly put their possessions down to fulfill requests from merry groups of children to be goalie for a ball game or to play a villain that they could battle.

This was a community full of people willing to aid each other without the plague of currency. They seemed to want nothing more than to ensure no one among them was ever in need or suffered alone.

He was not entirely unfamiliar with the concept. Books described smaller towns and uncharted societies with words he understood, but immersing himself in an experience of simple living provided him with a different source of fascination. All he had ever known, even with the time he spent as part of a noble family who should have had the privilege of avoiding struggle altogether, was an eternally busy city life, full of intense dreams and individualistic goals that motivated people to hoard money, power, or some other material thing.

Did his own goals make him happy? Ever since he had found himself under the care of an old couple who ran their own small diner, Jonathan had spent his teenage years diligently studying the science of recipes and restaurant operation. He used the culinary skills his adoptive guardians taught him to form soaring ambitions. He wanted to be someone who could claim humble beginnings when he made it as a top chef in Ameza. This week was proof that though he still had a long journey ahead of him, he was making progress with drastic steps. Maybe a passion for food did not need to be loud to be authentic.

There was also the matter of his looming Rose Union obligations. Victoria and her father were his only true remaining connections to the family, and though his promise to her was important to him, he had another reason he would consider fulfilling that responsibility. He had always seen it as another avenue to gain national recognition, a nice little line to add to his Mercenary resume. Though taking on leadership of the Union might put him even more at the mercy of the upper class and bog him down with managing other professional adventurers, he might still have the freedom to align the dangerous work with his desire to earn prestige.

He convinced himself that he did not mind the hustle, but now he was at least a little bit curious if a simple life might be any better for him.

On his way back to the communal kitchen, Jonathan paused to observe a group of teenagers and children who had taken notice of him. They gawked most openly at his hair, which lacked the warm coloration and striking patterning of their own.

He gave them a polite smile when they realized he was aware of their stares, and that seemed to invite them to approach. One of the oldest girls in the group decided to be their spokesperson.

"Mister? What village are you from?" she asked. The younger boys and girls behind her looked at him with interest.

"I am from Silver Valley," he said and was met with not an inkling of recognition.

"Is that far away?"

"Yes, it took me a while to come here."

"Ooh! Really? Is it like Sorense? Do you have your village built deep into the dirt?"

He chuckled. "No, we live in buildings out in the open as you do."

"Does everyone there look like you? Do they all have hair like the sky?"

"A few of us might," he answered. "My family does. People can have almost any color of hair you can imagine. Some even choose to change it."

There were gasps of amazement in the group before the girl continued. "Do you all make jewelry too? In your silver village?"

"I suppose some people do, but nothing quite like what you make," he said. "Do you all know how to make jewelry?"

Everyone nodded in unison. "We all learn stone carving and obsidian shaping first," the girl told him. "Then we learn the skills of a job we want to do to help the village. Things like cooking, sewing, fishing, and farming."

"Well, I guess I am similar to your chefs in that way. I am also part of a team that cooks food to feed a lot of people." The fact that it was for a profitable business and not a cooperative endeavor for the good of the community did not seem an important aspect to bring up.

"But you don't make any crafts at all?"

"I do not."

"Why have you come to visit us if it wasn't to trade for our jewelry?"

"Well," Jonathan said, pausing to consider the reason. "It seems that I came here to trade information instead. Knowledge from my village for access to ingredients from yours."

"What kind of knowledge?"

"About cooking, of course."

"What do you mean by that? Our chefs already know how to cook."

"They certainly do," he agreed. "But every village has their own special recipes, and we can share that knowledge to come up with new flavors and textures."

His explanation did not seem to earn him any less confusion from the youngsters, and he chuckled.

"The chefs are preparing a new kind of dinner today," he told them. "You will get to try it soon and realize what I mean."

One of the chefs soon left the kitchen to put out the call for everyone to receive their meals. Adults and teens were each handed a plate containing a cut of pan-seared venison and five potato bites, while the younger children were given steaks half the size and three dumplings instead. There seemed to be an unspoken rule that servings were to be distributed to everyone in the village first, and then whoever experienced a lasting affliction of hunger could return for a helping of the remaining rations.

From the line that gathered outside, Jonathan estimated that a population of around two to three hundred people called the Fishing Village their home. It was impressive to him that the chefs took recipes they were unfamiliar with and still managed to cook enough to sufficiently feed everyone in the span of just a couple hours.

It seemed they liked to eat in groups of family or friends, once they had retrieved their plates. Drift found him standing aside and came to give him one of the two that she was holding.

"Oh, thank you," he said, taking the food from her. "I was going to wait for the line to thin out."

"Now you don't need to!" She smiled with all the warmth of a loving mother. "Besides, I bet it would've felt awkward to join the line when you feel like a stranger here."

"I assume that was the insight you gained during your travels outside the village?"

She nodded and laughed. "I learned real quick what it was like to feel out of place. Not that it stopped me. The excitement of discovering new environments and cities was much too tempting."

"Have you ever been beyond Harbor Town or Sorense?"

"No," she said. "I couldn't travel that far without neglecting my responsibilities here. As much as it would be my dream to explore the world, I still love my home the most."

"That is very noble of you."

"I do want to visit your Silver Valley someday, though. To see you and your restaurant."

"I hope you do," he said, sincerely meaning it. "You might find it startling, how different it is from your village."

"Then you'll have to be my guide."

"Naturally."

"Of course, I shouldn't ask that of you without offering to do it first," she said. "Come on, let's eat before our food gets cold, and then I'll properly show you around our evening activities before you have to leave."

Jonathan could not refrain from making mental notes on how the food might be improved, but he reminded himself that he should simply enjoy the love and care that the chefs poured into the meal. The villagers nearby exclaimed with delight about the new flavors and textures they were experiencing, with the older villagers favoring the luscious texture of the steak and the youth enraptured by the crispiness of the potato balls. Given that the feedback was predominantly positive, it was an easy matter to call this entire undertaking a resounding success.

Several villagers made rounds to collect empty plates as everyone else began dispersing from the kitchen. Drift led Jonathan to where a group of mostly youngsters and a few adults gathered around a kindled fire pit. At what would be the head of the circle, set apart by sagely appearance alone, sat a man upon a wooden stool. Two tufts on the top of his long-faded hair resembled the ears of a wild cat, and though his grayish whiskers and hunched posture made him seem wizened with age, his face had far less wrinkles than Jonathan would have expected an elderly eduran to have. Most of the others in the circle either stood or sat on the ground, and they seemed to be respectfully waiting on this man to speak.

"What is this?" Jonathan whispered to Drift. They stood on the outside of the crowd so as not to disturb anyone who had come here first.

"Legend is a beloved storyteller," she said. "He's been telling stories, three or four tales every few nights, for decades now. You came here on a good night. I try to catch them when I can, and when I can't, I try to find someone who did, even though I know it won't be as good as when he tells them. But I don't think he's ever had to repeat a story he's already told."

"Incredible that he has not run out in all that time."

"I know. I'm still not sure if he's heard thousands of stories himself and he's just retelling them to us, or if he makes them up in between."

The elderly man glanced up, his eyes sweeping over his audience with an easygoing tempo. He paused for a little longer when he made eye contact with Jonathan, and it seemed a nearly undetectable smile appeared on his face before he looked away and opened his mouth. Any ongoing conversations taking place hushed into an anticipatory silence.

"Tonight," Legend began, his voice gentle and deep, "we will open with a fun, silly fable. How's that sound?" He received a few nods, and the extremely young children who had been indulging in their distractions during the wait calmed down from fidgeting and sat close to their friends.

"This tale is about two fishing cat Hunters who were acquaintances. They had known each other as long as friends did, but they often treated one another like rivals instead. Always competing, always trying to surpass the other.

"One was named Wiles, and the other Wish. They both loved to travel, they loved to attend parties, and most of all, they loved to eat. They especially craved fish, shellfish, and water amphibians. Sometimes when they were served such appetizing meals, they would forget their manners and eat more than their share.

"A friend invited Wiles and Wish to a dinner party where delicious shellfish, both crustaceans and mollusks alike, were the featured items on the menu. More specifically, there was said to be plenty of oysters, both Wiles's and Wish's absolute favorite.

"After they arrived, their friend greeted them and went on to chat with other guests. Wiles and Wish dashed over to the serving table and filled their plates with heaps of oysters. They settled themselves at the dining table and helped themselves right away. One after another, they slurped up the yummy contents and left behind two messy piles of empty shells.

"Seeing their friend approaching the dining table, Wish suddenly felt very embarrassed to have eaten so much when the party was still young. Not wanting to look bad in front of other people, Wish quickly pushed their pile into the one in front of Wiles.

"'Wow, look how gluttonous you are, eating so many oysters,' Wish said, pointing to the pile now doubled in size. 'You should be ashamed of yourself.'

"Wiles stopped eating and looked at Wish.

"'That's nothing compared to you,' Wiles said and then pointed to the residue of juices and sauce and tiny bits of stuffing on the table in front of Wish. 'You were so gluttonous, you've even eaten all the oyster shells.'"

Some of the children burst into fits of laughter, and the adults chuckled at the conclusion of this story. Jonathan smiled, mostly entertained by how Legend had built the tale up to such a simple punchline. He exchanged looks of amusement with Drift, who seemed glad that he did not despise the story.

Legend told three more stories of similar lengths, a couple with moral lessons intertwined within the plots and a charming tale of ancient Hunter heroes. Even though Jonathan felt ignorant of some of the cultural significance behind these stories, Legend certainly knew how to capture attention when he spoke.

While a fraction of the group stayed behind after the storyteller finished his last tale to ask him questions and engage in curious conversation, everyone else scattered to find other activities to occupy their night. Drift pulled Jonathan over to where Tan was teaching some teenagers and children how to shape larger chunks of obsidian.

Tan cheerfully welcomed Jonathan into her class, handing him a rock and an oblong hammer stone. She demonstrated how to position the obsidian in her lap and strike its edge with the stone tool to split the glass and then gestured for him and the other students to try.

He was no stranger to finesse, being a proficient wielder of the rapier, but this skill thoroughly eluded him. Strike after strike, he only chipped away minuscule pieces, excruciating shock traveling down his hand to his poor wrist no matter what angle he tried.

Shaking his sore arm as well as his head, he passed the rock and hammer back to Tan with a sheepish grin. As if he did not already regard their art as outstanding, this was really rubbing it in how masterful the villagers were at their craft.

Instead, he watched Drift handle the tools far better than he could to knap her rock into a piece that mimicked the waning crescent of Eduryae's moon.

She gave her crude design to Tan for smoothing and promptly ushered Jonathan to the final stop of their tour.

Near the lake, where the air blew cooler, an ensemble of three musicians sat together and granted a euphonious ambience to a small crowd of nearby listeners. One instrumentalist held a lyre in their arms, the second struck rhythmically upon a thin drum, and the last blew into a wooden flute to produce bright melodies.

Log benches were spread out in the area, so Drift and Jonathan found one unoccupied where they could sit. She leaned forward, elbows propped on her knees and chin resting in her palms, closing her eyes to enjoy the music. He caught himself smiling before he peered up into the darkening sky, now variegated with grayish clouds reflecting shades of orange against a dull blue backdrop.

He was not, or at least he had not considered himself to be, one to choose these types of activities as a worthwhile use of his spare time. To be fair, it was unclear if he ever really allowed himself spare time at all, or if he did anything for the sake of leisure. The last time he properly absorbed himself into anything he could call a hobby was likely a forgotten memory from more than a decade ago.

Despite it all, today had been incredible. As he sat there appreciating a playlist of local songs, Jonathan felt an unfamiliar sensation comforting him. A feeling of relaxation that he had lost when he became accustomed to living so guardedly. If not within the walls of his restaurant where every business decision could incur lasting consequences, he kept his heart closed off from cultivating deeper friendships outside of his work as well, in case his trust, which was already scarce, would be betrayed.

Participating in a community like this village, even for just one day, felt refreshing. People cared for each other freely and cooperated for the benefit of the whole. Isolated from nasty politics, greed, and modern technology. Jonathan laughed to himself at that last train of thought. Labey's review had been off his mind for more than an entire day, and no one here would have reminded him. Even if they somehow had seen it, he doubted that anyone in this harmonious village would care.

Elenora should have been here.

He had formed this thought a while ago, and it kept coming back no matter how many times he tried to wave it away.

He maintained that it had been a wise decision to have her stay behind, but he regretted the possibility that he might have been much too harsh. Sure, she would have had difficulty navigating the volcanoes and the trek to reach the village, but she would have loved this. She would have been completely in her element making new friends with these villagers, running her own cooking class, relishing in these nuggets of fishing cat Hunter culture.

This cruel mistake was his alone. He might have been the one trained to handle bizarre creatures, treacherous individuals, and rare artifacts, but that did not mean she brought no experience with her at all.

Elenora was the one with the perceptive eyes that saved him from the ambushing farewell dog and found the bottles of fairy fennel pollen. She was the one with the strength and stature to climb onto a giant lizard to take its bony spikes. And she was the one with the vibrant personality full of an inquisitive spirit and hopeful empathy that balanced out their partnership.

But perhaps most importantly, and he very plainly needed to admit it, he missed her. She should have been here.

Jonathan sat for an hour more, then told Drift that he should get going.

"Aww, that's too bad," she said. "I wish you could've stayed longer, but I get it."

"Just like you, I have to tend to my own responsibilities."

"But you really don't want to go, do you?" Her playful sneer made him chuckle.

"Thank you for the clams and for showing me around. Pass my gratitude to the others as well," he said. "I will look forward to the next time we see each other, and I hope to even bring a friend."

Drift's eyes sparkled. "Yes, please! That'll be so much fun. Don't take too long before you visit us again."

He waved to her as he set off, past the stone and clay houses until he was greeted by the open expanse of fields and distant volcanoes again. He hurried to the place where the plane had landed so he would waste no time returning to the city for an important day, and a very important conversation.

CHAPTER 13

"What for?" Elenora had been all smiles and restless excitement when she entered the restaurant in the late morning, but the apology transformed her expression into one of bewilderment.

"For leaving you behind yesterday," Jonathan said.

Her shoulders relaxed. "Oh, Mr. Tessier. Were you worried about that the whole time?"

He kept his eyes down when he nodded.

"Look, you weren't wrong. I got a few pretty strong reactions at the hospital with how bad my injury was."

"How is it now?" He glanced at her leg, but since she always wore long pants, her slight limp when she walked in was the only visible indication that she had been wounded.

"I'll still probably have to take it easy. So really, there's no harm done in me missing out on yesterday. I've pretty much forgotten all about it."

"It was unfair of me to not let you make that decision yourself, after you had confided in me," he said. "About how much that meant to you."

"I mean, I am glad you realize that now," she teased.

"I feel awful for making you upset, Elenora."

"At the time, maybe. But I'm all good now."

"And I was afraid that I might have caused a rift in our friendship."

"You didn't."

"So, I understand if you have reservations about continuing to work with me."

"Goodness!" Elenora exclaimed. "Even when you're apologizing, you're so dramatic, boss." She let out her delightfully hearty laugh and that eased him enough to stop speaking.

He did not think he could be blamed for it, though. It was already an odd event if he found himself willing to admit misconduct, and the stakes for any transgressions he committed against his head chef were that much higher than they would be for almost anyone else.

"Listen," she continued with a soft smile. "I've gotten over it, and I understood where you were coming from. A little dispute is not going to drive a wedge between us after years of trust, okay? I forgive you, and I'm sorry too, for causing you so much worry. But let's move on and get to the exciting stuff already! Where did you put those volcano clams?"

She bounced over to the kitchen so that he would not be able to argue, even though he had not wanted to.

"Wait," he said, following after her. "Before that—"

"I said I'm not going to dwell on it!"

"No," he said, pausing for a quick chuckle. "I mean to bring something else up." When she turned to face him, he pulled out a box from his bag and presented it for her to take.

"What's this?" Her hand hovered over the lid, but her gaze fixed on him for an answer.

"A gift, as thanks for the tremendous help you have given and continue to give me. And because when I received it yesterday from the village I visited, I thought you would probably make better use of it than I would."

Inside was the obsidian pendant he received from the Hunter women, laid out upon a velvety cushion within the container.

Her jaw dropped and eyes widened, and she brought the box closer to her face to study the intricacies of the carving. She ran a fingertip over the flow of the wild cat's movement until she ended up at the fish, then pulled back to grin at Jonathan.

"It's beautiful," she said, closing the box and holding it to her chest. "I'll definitely treasure it. It feels almost too precious to do anything but display it in a glass cabinet, but I'll figure something out."

"I am glad you like it," he said.

"You're the best boss I've ever had."

Jonathan raised his brow. "Do I now need to provide gifts to be considered a good boss?"

"You know I'm just teasing. Your status as a good boss is based on other positive qualities, of course, but this didn't hurt." Elenora waved the box in the air. "Let me go put this safely away, and then you need to tell me all about this village while we get to work."

When she was gone, he spread all of the ingredients they had secured during the past six days over the metal counter: three chomping lotus roots and two of its flowers, ten heads of radiant cabbage, four jars of fairy fennel pollen, twelve ounces of burning burgundy truffles, thirty-seven spiral cashew apples and nuts, three spikes of ghost bone for its marrow, one symbiotic bird egg, two colossal beef chunks, and five volcanic clams.

Elenora joined him again and they began deliberating on possible recipes. They agreed that variety was essential, and that the menu should include at least one soup item, one salad, and one dessert, with the rest designated as appetizers or main entrées. They scribbled notes on scrap pieces of paper at first, but their brainstorming rapidly forced them to turn to the kitchen whiteboard for more space.

Before they contemplated their options, they sampled each of the ingredients to get an understanding of their flavor profiles. Having to resist the temptation of tasting too much, especially when the ingredients offered such tantalizing experiences with minimal preparation, became a challenge for both of them, though they were keenly aware that they needed to reserve their supply for tomorrow.

For a few of their items, they tried cooking them with different methods in minuscule proportions. One of the clams, sectioned into three pieces, endured trials of being seasoned in-shell with cumin and paprika, subsumed into pasta, and boiled into a chowder. They tried the cabbage fried and then tossed in a salad, meticulously noting down their observations. The fennel pollen allowed them the most freedom to sprinkle it over a selection of roasted meats, spaghetti, and homestyle sauces.

Four hours of laborious toil and a mess of sullied utensils and cookware later, they beheld the prize for their efforts: a satisfying finalized menu.

Jonathan and Elenora agreed on the clam chowder as the best use of the mollusk by a large margin, each small spoonful an intensely piquant journey of flavor. The ghost bone marrow, with its sharply savory and richly sweet combination, worked fantastically in a bone broth chili stew.

Diced warts from the colossal cattle beast disguised themselves seamlessly into a spicy beef salad with lettuce and assorted vegetables, providing the kind of powerful heat that avoided lingering out its welcome with a painful burn. Slices of the lotus roots found their way into another reliable salad of their own, and adding some chili peppers and bits of the flower petals for some tangy goodness enhanced the already phenomenal dish.

Their lone appetizer offering utilized the radiant cabbage leaves as wrappings for stuffed rolls, lending the meaty recipe a beautiful appearance and a piercingly fresh bite despite being drowned in sauce. Elenora helped herself to a couple rolls for lunch, since the cabbage heads yielded plenty of leaves to go around.

Jonathan feigned agony when they stirred a portion of the symbiotic bird's egg into fried rice, lamenting the awful memories associated with their acquisition. Elenora only rolled her eyes as she stored the rest of the vibrantly orange mixture in a tight mason jar and put it inside the fridge. The finished dish had a hint of smoky bitterness, startling but unusually enticing. Their other main entrée, garlic noodles with fairy fennel pollen, upgraded a mellow comfort food using a complex and citrusy spice comparable to the most expensive of gourmet relishes.

It would be a crime to forget the desserts. The burning burgundy truffles had flavors reminiscent of cinnamon and a tart version of sweet honey; they performed excellently in a truffle custard. The cashews worked overtime as part of a cheesecake masterpiece, with the mildly sweet fruit blended into the filling and the crushed nuts scattered on top of a chocolate drizzle. A shame they lost their distinctive spiral shape, but each bite of the cake would be a crunchy delight all the same.

With this menu scrawled out on the whiteboard, Jonathan and Elenora together took a step back for a holistic review. He was of the opinion that some of these could be improved further, but she expressed relief that they managed to work within their time constraints and had not used any of their ingredients to a dangerous excess.

"I should look into finding reliable vendors to keep up with this kind of menu on a regular basis," Jonathan remarked.

"Yeah," Elenora agreed with a laugh. "We're really condensing our best offerings in one sitting. If we run out of everything, it's back to a normal menu for our other customers."

"My thoughts exactly. Finding suppliers for everything here would be unreasonably expensive, and out of the question. But we also cannot keep closing the restaurant down just to go hunting again," he said. "I had the idea that we might be able to feature one such item regularly, at an elevated price."

"That's not bad. Probably the best we could manage. We'll just have to make sure to keep our other 'normal' dishes at top quality too, so we don't look like we're compromising."

"One day at a time, I suppose."

"Are you going to call any of our team back for tomorrow?"

"I was keeping my options open. It might be a lot of work for just the two of us to handle, though I am cautious about having anyone else involved. Would it not be better to keep things contained?"

The head chef frowned as she considered this. "Maybe call in just a couple of our chefs then. I think I can keep a close eye on them, and we won't have any slips in quality, or even more surprise thefts."

"Alright," he said, giving her a nod. "Then you are free to go home, Elenora. You worked hard today."

"What about cleaning all of this up?" She gestured quite grandly to the piles of mixing bowls and pots around them.

"I will do it. You get some rest. I planned on staying behind to design and print the menus anyway. Presentation and atmosphere will also be of utmost importance, after all."

Elenora grinned, unabashedly glad to be relieved of the mundane variety of chores. "Awesome! Thanks, boss."

He returned the smile. "As much as I will try to help with the cooking, I will be counting on you to impress with these recipes tomorrow. So rest well and take the time to relax."

"I will. I promise I won't let you down."

Orla and Marshall seized the chance to return to work sooner, and early the next morning, the four of them were already busy preparing for the critics' arrival. Elenora walked the other chefs through the recipes, communicating relevant instructions but not the details on how certain ingredients were obtained or any acknowledgment that they were exceedingly special. Even though it seemed obvious that a few items in their storage room were of a rather peculiar nature, neither chef reacted conspicuously and instead focused on diligently following Elenora's guidance.

Jonathan made his rounds throughout the building ensuring that every surface, and then every hidden corner, looked presentable. He finished his surveillance back in the kitchen, where he clasped his hands together, cracking a few joints as he watched his staff through a scowl.

"Are you nervous?" Elenora asked as she walked by him, carrying a stack of bowls.

"That, and excited as well," he said. "In only an hour, an unbelievably famous gourmet chef is going to be visiting us."

"So you've said, many times."

"Because it is a huge deal. We may be a decent restaurant, but we do not have the renown to warrant this honor," Jonathan said, dragging his fingers through his hair. His motions were not as frantic as they were the day Hayes came by to pester him, but his hands were shaking nonetheless. "And I think, despite having had this on my mind for a whole week, I am reeling now that the moment is here."

Elenora smiled at him sympathetically. "It'll be alright. Just calm down and breathe."

The vacant, unamused expression he gave her as he dropped

his hand to his side caused her to let out a laugh, which she tried to stifle by covering her mouth. The stack of bowls in her arm clattered as she rebalanced them. Orla and Marshall glanced over at them briefly before resuming their work.

Elenora leaned in. "I was wondering, that one power of yours," she whispered. "The one where you summon those magical scents, for better or worse. You can't use that on yourself, can you? To calm yourself down with some nice lavender or something."

Jonathan thought of the times he brought an ingredient to her so she could tell him if it had gone bad. The times he borrowed her nose to make sure the paste he picked up was made from avocado and not horseradish. The times she showed him up by mixing spices on instinct and aroma alone, while he had to follow strict recipes and conduct frequent taste tests.

He also leaned forward, narrowing his eyes in confusion as to why she was bringing this up now. "No, at least. . . I am not too sure that it would work anyway. I always thought of it being like trying to tickle yourself."

"There are other things that work when you try them on yourself. Pinching real hard hurts, giving yourself a pep talk gets your head in the game."

Her musings made him chuckle. "I suppose we will never know."

"But why did you develop your abilities like that anyway? Couldn't you have chosen something that primarily benefits you over others?"

"Well, if you put it that way, it does sound rather foolish," he said. He had not been a particularly selfless person at the time of his training, and he had already lost his respiratory functions by then. "But perhaps it all depends on different situations and working around personal limitations."

She smiled, seeming pleased with herself. "I think I'm curious because I was introduced to your strange set of abilities first. While it was fun to watch you use them, maybe I'd understand more if I learned about other people's abilities too."

The phone at the host station rang, so Jonathan left the kitchen to receive the call. He realized the manager who worked for Lala Sweet was on the other end, pushily informing him that she would be arriving ahead of schedule to receive a tour of the establishment. Hearing this, his hands started trembling again.

Not to say that Elenora's mild attempt at a distraction was futile, but it was quickly forfeited thanks to this new development.

Though he knew it would be pointless to insist, Jonathan tried to affirm the originally agreed time, but the manager was having none of it. Even the tone with which the manager expressed commiseration was uncharitable, and in the next sentence he transparently warned Jonathan that it would be unwise to refuse Lala Sweet's wish to receive a personal tour of the Taverne.

So Jonathan relented, and the manager informed him that they would be arriving in ten to twenty minutes. After hanging up the phone, Jonathan went back to the kitchen to fill his chefs in on the situation and then up to his office with a portable kettle for a serving of his red milkweed tea. He could think of nothing else that could steady his nerves at this stage better than his dependable Spectral craving.

As he sipped the calming brew and reviewed his notes regarding the critics, time charged forward out of his control. It was the fastest ten minutes of his life, and it felt as if he had only just sat down in his chair when he needed to return downstairs to receive his eager guests.

He made it in time to see a sleek black car park along the curb in front of the restaurant. The celebrity gourmet and her manager stepped out of the car, and he watched them from his position at the host station as they glanced around to confirm the correct location.

The manager's appearance proved consistent with how he came across over the phone, his face wearing a visage more stoic than anything Jonathan himself could muster and his suit and tie a very clean black over a simple white dress shirt. An outfit with no outlandish flourishes. Other than being unyieldingly formal, there was nothing that stood out about the man.

Lala Sweet, on the other hand, had an intriguing look about her. If she had not starred in televised baking competitions and aired a few cooking shows of her own to a widespread audience, Jonathan might have been surprised by what he saw in person. With a stage name like what she had and a specialty in scrumptious pastries, as stereotypical as it might have been, she was someone he had expected to appear demure and cutesy prior to the first time he saw her on TV.

She was instead a broad-shouldered woman, standing at a height slightly taller than his own, which was further accented by the high ponytail that gathered her curly reddish-brown hair. She wore a flattering loose black tank top tucked into a long maroon chiffon skirt, and her exposed arms featured impressive muscles that hinted at a remarkable physical strength. Her face was softly feminine, though, all round shapes along her jaws and cheeks that made her invitingly approachable. He knew by way of public knowledge that she was around five or six years older than he was, but her youthful energy could have fooled him into thinking she was no more than thirty.

That cheerful spirit made its announcement as soon as the two walked inside, and the manager beside her seemed to shrink in size as he struggled to keep up with possessing even half as much of a presence as she did.

"Welcome, ma'am," Jonathan said, and she did not let him get much further than that.

"Wow, so this is the Taverne Tessier?" she said, giving the dining room a thorough inspection from ceiling to floor. She turned to him and gave him a confident smile. "And you are the owner, I presume?"

"Yes, ma'am."

She walked over and held out her hand, which he graciously took in his for a firm, nearly crushing, handshake.

"I have to tell you, I am so excited to be here. I can barely get away with my busy agenda, all my research work and then being invited to all the uppity events that just want the status to boast. It is suffocating to be around snobby people who think they know so much about food, or pretend that they do, maybe to impress me or the other top chefs like me. Anyway, that's why I snatched this chance to dine somewhere less flashy, a little more local. And boy, am I glad! This place is cute. So quaint. So cozy."

He could only interject when she paused to take a breath. "Ma'am, I am extremely grateful that you agreed to visit—"

"Call me Larkin. I know you're trying to avoid using my very charming nickname. Or Ms. Swetnam if you're dead set on being so mannerly."

"I wanted to ask, Ms. Swetnam, why here? There are many local restaurants, and honestly, the only thing I believe that stood out about mine are my social connections."

She giggled melodiously. "You're a little starstruck and can't wrap your head around it, is that it? I mean, all it really is. . . I just love when a person is so devoted to their restaurant or their culinary journey that they'll go this far to rectify a bad review. We all started somewhere, and I'll never lose the admiration I have for hardworking people who push through their struggles."

He dipped his head in a respectful bow. "I am honored and humbled to hear that."

"I've been where you were once. So I am more than happy to help someone like you out when I can." She leaned in and cupped her hand around the side of her mouth as if she was imparting a secret. "I also so much more prefer working with culinarians who haven't become arrogant. I have some colleagues at the top with attitudes I can't say I'm very fond of," she said, her voice hushed, and then she pulled away to laugh again.

Her words and demeanor made her seem less intimidating, even if not by much, at least convincing Jonathan that she was here more to have a pleasant time than to bring down harsh judgment upon him and his establishment.

"So, about that tour!" she said. "Please, show me around, if you don't mind."

He obliged immediately, leading her around the dining room and outdoor seating area, where she commented her affection for his choice of color palette and furniture, and then bringing her to the kitchen, where she vocalized heartfelt encouragements to the three busy chefs.

With a bizarre determination to ignore his protestations, Larkin even had him guide her through the break room and his office upstairs, an experience he could not liken to anything other than exposing a vulnerability to a stranger. Fortunately, she only had kind things to say, comparing her endearment for his restaurant's atmosphere to her disdain for the blacks, whites, and browns of interior designs that were preferred by rich clientele.

The one benefit of a small restaurant was a short tour, and before long, they returned to the dining room so Larkin and her manager could settle themselves at one of the tables. She chose one near the front window for the view, and that was how she reported the arrival of the other two critics, only a tad bit earlier than scheduled.

Mr. Austin Glass and Mr. Davin Kelly, both distinguished-looking older gentlemen, chose their own tables before Jonathan handed the menus out to everyone. While they mulled over the selection of dishes, he escaped to the kitchen to recover from how tense his body had been during that entire affair.

Elenora came around to tell him he did well. He appreciated her doing so when he knew she had to be as burdened, if not more so, than he was. She gave him an update that she, Orla, and

Marshall were keeping up on their end, and he knew she was right when she urged him to hone his focus so that they could finish this together without a hitch.

CHAPTER 14

A FEW MINUTES LATER, when he had mostly regained his composure, Jonathan returned to the dining room to take his guests' orders.

He was abruptly interrupted by a commotion occurring right outside the front door, with clamorous noises and an insolent rattling of the door handle. Hoping he had managed to mask his frustrations before any of his guests could see, he excused himself to address the matter.

The source of the disturbance was a rowdy group of individuals ranging from young children to elderly, presumably a family spanning multiple generations. They all talked at him at once, their jumbled voices leading Jonathan to scowl and hold up his hands. It took the group a while to notice his gesture and gradually fall silent.

"What seems to be the problem?" he asked them.

"Why are your doors locked?" demanded a man he assumed to be a father or an uncle.

Jonathan's eyes flashed as he did everything he could not to point at the sign next to the door and ask if any of them could read. People who acted as if they thought businesses were never allowed to be closed might come rarely, but they certainly made themselves memorable every time they emerged from their indecorous bubbles.

"The restaurant is not open at the moment," he said instead.

A woman stepped forward. He guessed that she might be a mother or an aunt in this family.

"We saw other people walk in," she said, a hint of aggression simmering under her tone. She looked toward the window and pointed an accusing finger. "We can see them seated at the tables right there!"

"Yes, they are special guests for a private event," Jonathan said. "I do apologize for the inconvenience, if you were planning to dine here. There are many good restaurants nearby, so I am sure you will find another one worthy of your patronage."

"No, no!" the man cut in. "We should be able to eat here too. You have plenty of room. It shouldn't be a problem."

"Yeah, just consider us special guests too, and welcome us in for our own private event."

As everyone else in the group began to raise their voices with complaints that they had been looking forward to eating at the Taverne today, Jonathan entertained the fleeting and amusing thought on how powerful his extraocular muscles must be that he had not yet rolled his eyes at them.

"How about this?" he started, and they quieted down again. "I will offer your party a twenty percent discount if you come back tomorrow instead, when we reopen."

The most outspoken pair muttered among themselves, something about being inconvenienced, but finally accepted this compromise and herded their group to leave. Jonathan stayed to watch them walk away, briefly wondering if they were a group who wanted to see the Taverne's failings for themselves or just a bunch of entitled patrons, then closed his eyes for several seconds to will away his irritation.

It was not an entirely uncommon interaction to have at his restaurant, and on any other day, it would not have been a bother at all. Today, however, even the slightest upset seemed primed to throw him off-kilter.

He turned and walked back inside, pressing on with a smile as he offered much more sincere apologies to his guests. Since Larkin arrived before the others, albeit quite forcibly, he approached to wait on her first.

"Actually, I was thinking," she said. "You put all this effort into arranging such a deluxe menu for us, why don't we just order one of everything and share with these gentlemen, so nothing gets left out?" She glanced inquisitively over at the other two critics, who both nodded their agreement to this plan.

After acknowledging this order, he went to relay it to the kitchen and contributed where he could with plating and final touches. After the soups had been boiled again and stirred to prevent sediments at the bottom of the pots, one bowl was filled with the bone broth chili and another with the clam chowder.

Jonathan took extra empty bowls and spoons with him when he delivered these to Larkin's table, letting the critics distribute however they saw fit.

When he checked in with them later, the feedback was unanimous. The chili was up to standard and had a riveting combination of flavors, but everyone agreed that the clam chowder was uniquely intense and exceptionally delicious.

The cabbage rolls finished baking, and he prepared to bring them out with the salads. Elenora reminded him to relax, as he was getting into a bad habit of tensing up every time he left the dining room. Along with extra forks and plates, his hands calmed from quivering, he placed the dishes on the three tables.

Mr. Glass and Mr. Kelly were not avid fans of the beef salad, but Larkin appeared to derive great enjoyment from its spicy kick. They all agreed it was a dish for a very particular palate. The hot and sour lotus salad was a major hit, and the cabbage rolls scored somewhere in between.

The egg fried rice, having taken a while to fully prepare, still became a decent winner with all the critics. Mr. Kelly decided to skip out on the garlic noodles due to personal preferences, but Mr. Glass and Larkin appreciated both entrées.

With the finish line in sight, Elenora joined Jonathan in plating and bringing out the desserts. As they placed the truffle custard and cashew cheesecake in front of the guests, he thanked them for their time and for giving his restaurant the privilege of their visit.

"Good job, Orla. Good job, Marshall," he said when he was back in the kitchen, relieved the challenging portion of the day was finally over. "You both did very well, and you are most definitely receiving overtime rates for today. And a hefty bonus for you, Elenora, of course."

Orla grinned at him as they all began cleaning. "I'm just glad things are starting to look up," she said. "I know I was really worried about losing my job here, but maybe I overreacted."

"Not at all," Jonathan said. "That had been our first review from a major critic, and with such extensive influence, even I thought it looked rather bleak. We had people who had previously dined here taunt us when we were in Lismai looking for new ingredients."

Both the other chefs wore expressions of mild surprise.

"Wow, really? I can't believe people would do that," Orla said.

"And you went that far away during the break?" Marshall asked. Jonathan and Elenora nodded in unison, and though neither of them elaborated, Marshall seemed impressed.

"I think there will still be much to contend with moving forward," Jonathan said. "But having some big names endorse the Taverne is much better than nothing."

"Does this mean the restaurant will go back to normal operation soon?" Orla asked.

"Tomorrow. Most of the team will be able to return by then," he said. He put the stack of pots and bowls he collected into the sink and walked toward the kitchen door. "I will leave the rest of this to you three; I want to check on them one last time."

Jonathan stood with his hands clasped in front of himself with the deference of a child receiving a lecture from their parents, though he had no reason to believe this final assessment would be parallel to such a scenario.

Mr. Glass volunteered to be the first to provide his summary of the meal.

"It was not perfect, though these experiences very rarely are," he said. "I will be very clear in my publication that I was invited, and the menu was specially curated for us."

Jonathan expected as much, but he stood rigidly, awaiting further comments.

"Regardless, I understand that any flaws I find are often very much based on individual taste, and I can't expect every dish to be to my liking. I enjoyed the majority of the food and came across some complex and delightful flavors I've never tasted before. You experimented boldly with flavors in classic dishes without being afraid of stepping outside the norm, and I will highlight such positive traits in my review."

"Thank you, sir." Jonathan's stance slackened a bit upon hearing this, a welcome contrast to how Labey described the restaurant.

"I agree." Mr. Kelly spoke up next. "I'm very sorry I wasn't able to partake in every single dish, but I enjoyed your wide variety of flavors and presentations. It's almost guaranteed that people will be able to find at least one thing they like here that they wouldn't be able to find anywhere else. My personal favorite was your lotus salad."

It felt almost bittersweet that Mr. Kelly favored the dish made with the very first ingredient Jonathan obtained this last week, on his own, no less. "I am glad to hear that, sir. If you would like, I can pack some extra for you to go?"

"Oh, certainly! I'd love that. And I hope to come by a couple more times during your regular operation before I finalize my review, to ensure it is honest and thorough."

"Me too," Mr. Glass readily agreed as the two stood up to leave.

Jonathan took care of the take-out lotus salad for Mr. Kelly and the two gentlemen settled their bills. It was only when they both left the restaurant that Larkin finally said anything.

"They'll let anyone be a critic these days, won't they?" she said, laughing softly and shaking her head.

"What do you mean?"

"Apparently, you don't need to know the intricacies of food to be one. You only need to know how to use the right words to make a review sound positive or negative."

"I apologize. I still do not follow."

"The double-ribbed chameleon, hidden volcanic rock clams, the warts of a colossal cattle beast, a chomping lotus's rhizomes and flowers, cabbage patches located near nightmare rifts, the two-headed symbiotic bird, a fairy fennel plant, burning burgundy truffles, and cashews from the spiral tree." As she listed out each entity, she pointed to the corresponding bowl or plate, most of which contained only crumbs or residue left over from the meal. "Did I get them all right?"

Jonathan's eyes widened, but he said nothing. He was impressed by her ability to accurately pinpoint the highlight of each item when he did not disclose this information anywhere on the menu, but maybe he should not have expected any less from a top-tier expert in her field.

"Maybe I'm showing off a little, but you don't reach a position like mine without having the keenest sense of taste."

"I am blown away by your mastery," he said.

"And you used some pretty elusive ingredients in every dish. The fact that you were able to secure a collection of such rare supplies in time for our visit is quite the accomplishment in itself."

"Thank you, Ms. Swetnam."

"Surely you didn't just purchase everything, did you? Even the best chefs of the nation would envy your menu, so I doubt you found all the suppliers you needed to put it together."

He hesitated, debating whether to tell her the truth. He thought it sufficient that she discerned how unique the ingredients were and was impressed by that alone. Maybe the methods he used to obtain them could remain a business secret.

But if there was anyone he should do everything in his power not to disappoint if he wanted to grasp onto that bright future he coveted, it would be Lala Sweet.

"I received information about these ingredients from some contacts of mine," he admitted. "And then I found them myself with the assistance of my head chef."

"You found them yourself?" she repeated. "As in, directly from the source? Even the chameleon? The lotus and the cattle beast? Just the two of you?"

He nodded at each segmented question, and she whistled, the high to low slide that expressed her amazement.

"Are you both Mercenaries?"

"She is not, but I am."

"That explains it," she said. "Good, because so am I. You can't be considered an elite culinarian if you can't go out and discover new ingredients yourself."

"Of course," he agreed, though he had not ventured to do anything like that himself. He still had to rely on existing information.

Larkin's manager leaned in toward her and whispered something in her ear, which made her sigh.

"Looks like I'm nearly out of time," she said.

He tried not to look devastated that this might be the end of their interactions. To receive a review from her was a marvelous opportunity already, and one he should be content with, but there was always the question of whether he could be doing more.

"But actually, this makes me even more glad I came here."

"Why is that?"

"I've been looking for someone capable of helping me in my own everlasting search for ingredients and cooking methods that have yet to be discovered. And I think you're exactly qualified for such a position, if you're interested."

The sudden proposal stunned him for a moment. He could not believe that she was extending an offer of precisely what he desired so soon. This would be a serious step above using intel from other people to find rare ingredients, and he would receive full credit for discovering new ones in an arrangement guaranteed to boost both his Mercenary and culinary careers.

"You don't need to answer right now," she added. "I want you to think about it." She gestured toward her manager, and he swiftly produced a business card that he passed on to Jonathan. "You can contact me later when you feel ready to make the big decision."

"How much later?" he asked.

"Really up to you," she said, standing up with her manager, who stepped forward to take care of the payment. "I don't see myself ending my search for extra assistance anytime soon, even if I manage fine on my own. If you do decide to take me up on my offer, we'll arrange a separate meeting to discuss the finer details."

She approached and reached out her hand for another handshake.

"Understood," Jonathan said, accepting it gladly. "Thank you so much for visiting us."

"No, thank you for the invite, Mr. Tessier. I had a wonderful time, and I hope to hear from you soon."

Once the two were out the door, Jonathan ensured that it was locked. Any excitement that threatened to bubble forth he had to suppress during the process of gathering all the used plates and bowls, washing them clean, and putting everything away.

He waited until Orla and Marshall were also almost ready to leave before he asked Elenora to stay behind and meet him upstairs in his office. While he waited for her, he noticed how much his hands were still trembling, this time from excitement.

"Our chefs have gone home. What happened, boss?" Elenora asked when she entered the small room.

"Things... went better than I could have ever expected," he said. "Everyone gave us positive feedback, and Ms. Swetnam herself wanted to continue working with me."

She gasped. "No way? That's such great news! Congratulations!"

He let her see Lala Sweet's business card, which was printed on a dark purple cardstock with letters and bakery motifs done in gold embossing. She inspected it with awe as she slowly settled down into her favorite chair.

"So, what did she say?" she asked as she handed the card back.

"When she correctly guessed every ingredient we used, I decided to be transparent with her. She was impressed that we had obtained those ingredients ourselves directly from their respective sources."

"Oh, you gave me credit too?"

"Of course I did," he said. "But the opportunity she presented might only be suitable for a Mercenary, those of us who can use grants. Though I could try asking if she has any work for you."

Elenora immediately shook her head. "No, that's alright. I imagine if you say yes, you'll be pretty busy, and I'd rather help hold down the fort here."

"Are you sure?"

"Yeah, I'm very happy just cooking good food for our customers. And I don't think I have nearly enough skills to take on something as grand as working with a celebrity chef."

"I beg to differ. Not only are you a monster with the butcher knife, you were integral in our endeavors over the last week."

She let out a laugh. "And I will cherish those experiences forever. But it's just not something I picture myself wanting to do, you know, all the time," she said. "I might be curious about learning Avidea someday, but I'm already well into my forties."

"I understand your reasoning, but I have heard of people learning at all ages."

"I already have a stable career and enough culinary expertise to not have to worry for the rest of my life. I'm satisfied with that. What kind of work did she say you might do if you accepted?"

"It would involve the discovery of new exotic ingredients and cooking methods, the kind of innovation and work that could gain national, maybe even worldwide, recognition," he said. "Essentially, the same kind of work Ms. Swetnam did to earn her fame."

"That's exactly what you wanted, isn't it?"

"It is."

"And you're still young," she said. "I hardly think you have as many reasons as I do to hesitate."

He pondered this for a few moments. "I do have some doubts," he eventually said.

"Really? Like what?"

"The biggest one is the idea of splitting my devotion between the Taverne and this new opportunity. I do not want to entirely abandon the restaurant, and I question whether I am ready for such a gigantic leap into a new endeavor."

She hummed in thought. "Well, you can always try it out and see if it's a good fit for you. We'll still be here if you decide it isn't and want to return."

"Do you remember how many close calls we had?"

She pressed her lips together into a flat line and did not answer.

"This kind of work could potentially be even more dangerous," he continued. "Even a trial run could end up altering my life forever. I would be stepping into truly unknown territory, compared to what we did, where I had the chance to research beforehand."

A heavy sigh escaped her. "It's not an easy decision," she conceded. "But ultimately, it's up to you to make up your mind or be miserable as you regret missing out."

"How brutal."

"Getting worked up more than necessary won't change this fact." She gave him a sympathetic smile anyway.

He leaned back in his chair. "I will think about it," he said. "For now, it may be best for us to regain some normalcy before I invite even more chaos into this timeline."

"It feels sort of nostalgic to be returning to normal business again," she said. "Almost like I went on another vacation."

"Is that how you would describe what we went through?" he asked, amusement in his voice.

She chuckled and stood up. "I guess I'll see you tomorrow for our first regular shift in an incredibly long time, boss?"

He nodded, lifting his hand to acknowledge her departure. "Yes, have a good rest of your day, Elenora," he said. "See you tomorrow."

CHAPTER 15

BUSINESS DURING THE LUNCH and dinner shifts of the following day began with a lull, before more passersby realized that the Taverne was open again and decided it was worth their time dropping by for their meal. And yet the family that had pestered Jonathan yesterday did not even bother to show up to claim their discount.

Jonathan kept the dish items he served to the critics under their own special section in his newest menu, putting in a special note that these were in limited supply, and highlighted their elevated prices. Where he usually listed the descriptions under each item, he chose alternative names for the rare ingredients he and Elenora secured, hoping that they came across fancy enough to entice willing consumers without giving away too much infor-mation. Vague labels like "exquisite cabbage leaves" and "premium bone marrow."

He had put up listings for chef and waiter positions on multiple popular online job sites that morning. Though his team had shrunk, everyone had returned refreshed with plenty of energy from the break, and did not seem to have any issues handling the flow of customers. Still, if he could fill those vacant positions as soon as possible so his staff would be allowed more flexibility, that would be one less thing he needed to worry about. Over the course of the day, several people requested application forms for the waiter opening, but none yet for the chef.

He quickly set up interviews for the next few days, as soon as the candidates were available, but it was not until his third candidate came in that he saw any promise. When she first sat across the desk from him, she appeared to have trouble letting her eyes rest on one spot. They darted between the wall, the edge of his desk, a vague spot behind him, and his chin.

"Is something the matter?" he asked as he prepared a notepad and pen.

"Oh, no," she said. "Interviews make me quite nervous, and it means a lot for me to get this job."

He offered her a pleasant smile. "I know it might be easy for me to say, but I think you should be able to relax," he said. "Please rest assured that your resume has already impressed me."

"Thank you," she said.

"So, Ms. Phoebe Magoro. You had previously worked at the Eclectic Bistro for over six years, is that correct?" As he scribbled down notes, the establishment's name felt vaguely familiar to him, but only in the negligible way he concluded was due to merely having heard it in passing. She had a number of other restaurants listed from much earlier in her career.

"Yes, sir."

"I was wondering, though, what happened since you left three years ago," he said. "You did not have anything else on your resume beyond that."

"I had some personal matters to tend to in the meantime," she said.

"I see. And though you worked there as a waitress, you stated that you wanted to be a hostess here instead."

"I know your listing asked for waitstaff. I think I should be able to handle that, but I don't mind the lower pay if I could lean more toward being primarily a hostess."

He looked up and raised a brow. "You put down that you are deaf on one side. Is that why?"

She nodded. "I have trouble locating where sounds come from, so it's much easier for me to communicate with customers if I can see them before they talk to me. I saw that your host station is in the perfect position for that," she said. "Of course, when things are busy, I don't mind also helping where I can with waiting on customers."

Tapping the capped end of his pen against his bottom lip, he studied her. She looked to be a woman in her late twenties, which was confirmed by her birth year on the application form. His eyes kept being drawn to her long side braid, which shifted from a dark reddish orange at the top of her head to a bright yellow at the end, a blazingly striking gradient. She had a tendency to turn her exposed ear toward him whenever he spoke.

"But it seems it would be a hassle for you to work at a restaurant when they are so often crowded, does it not?"

Phoebe looked down at her fidgeting hands. "I know, but I don't have many options when all my experience is in food service. It was from an accident only a couple years ago. . ." Her voice trailed off.

"I understand. Let us talk more about that work experience, then."

Despite her skittish temperament, she answered Jonathan's questions with ease and a confidence in her abilities that she did not display with her body. She told him about efficient systems she devised during her time as both a waitress and a hostess to keep her duties organized and had outstanding examples of how she handled customer complaints to avoid trouble for her supervisors without hurting the restaurant's revenue. It pleased him greatly when she admitted she also preferred offering upset patrons future discounts, saying it tested their honesty and mitigated their attempts to get away with a free meal that they had wholly consumed.

"How do you feel about taking on some administrative duties as well?" Jonathan asked. "You would be able to work up here away from the noise, and you would be paid fairly for your time as with the rest of the team."

She appeared intrigued by this suggestion. "Could I really? I didn't know that would be an option."

"I am just thinking of possibilities," he said. "For the shifts where we have enough waiters on the clock to handle the dining room, you would be able to step away. The rest of the time, though, I would need you on the floor."

"I think I would be very happy with that."

"How soon can you start?"

"Whenever possible," she said. "The sooner, the better."

"Glad to hear it," he said. "I do see you being a very good fit for the Taverne, so I believe we could get you onboarded with an official offer and any necessary paperwork within the next couple of days."

"Thank you so much."

Jonathan glanced at the clock. "Actually, since today's lunch shift should be wrapping up now, would you like to take a quick tour?"

She gladly accepted, so he led the way back downstairs to the dining room, left empty with the wait team having finished up and headed home first. He began with the host station.

"We have our phone and POS system here, and employees use this to clock in and out as well. Storage underneath. There is a latch here that unlocks its wheels, so you would be able to adjust its position however you wish."

It seemed a simple thing to be thrilled about, but Phoebe looked on with interest. He then pointed to the group of two tables directly in front of where the station currently stood.

"I would probably have you handle tables like those," he said. "If you do think of other accommodations you might need, I hope you do not hesitate to let me know."

"Of course, thank you."

He briefly took her to the outdoor dining area, stating that the tables there were filled with lower priority or by special request. The next destination was the kitchen, where a few chefs remained in the process of cleaning up.

Elenora looked up when they entered, and her face lit up with recognition.

"Phoebe?"

A similar expression swept across Phoebe's face. The other chefs slowed down in their work to observe her.

"I didn't know you worked here, Ellie," she said. Jonathan noticed that her smile shifted from one of surprised relief to something more conflicted.

"Come, come," Elenora said, wiping her hands and ushering both him and his potential hire back into the dining room to not get in the way of the chefs' work.

Jonathan stood off to the side while the women caught up so that he would not be in the way either.

"It's been so long since I've last seen you, sweetie," Elenora said. "In fact, ever since I left. Have you been at the Eclectic Bistro this whole time?"

So that was why he remembered hearing about the restaurant before.

"Actually, I quit only a couple years after you did."

"Goodness, I'm still shocked you stayed as long as you did at that awful place. You were always a little too loyal, and they didn't treat you what you were worth."

"I know. I finally had enough and wanted a change from big corporate restaurants like that one. But I didn't expect to run into you here. How has it been for you?"

"Oh, it's been amazing. I'm the head chef, for one."

"Ah, congrats!"

"And you applied to work here as. . . ?"

"Technically a waitress, but I'm hoping to handle hosting and admin duties here instead. It'll be easier on me."

"Good, you must be exhausted from working as hard as you did for the Bistro just for the supervisors to completely ignore your dedication."

"You've been here since then, right? I assume that means you like it here a lot better."

"Yes, and I'm sure you will too. I can say with absolute certainty that the owner is someone who has true passion and is nothing like our old bosses." Elenora glanced over at Jonathan and winked.

He pretended to be looking away and not blatantly eavesdropping on their conversation.

"Mr. Tessier," Elenora continued. "I don't know if you have any doubts about hiring Phoebe, but she is amazing. Absolutely trustworthy and dependable. I'm also a bit selfish and would love to work with her again."

"Chances are you will," he said.

With a grin, Elenora turned back to Phoebe. "After I finish up here, why don't we hang out for a bit? I want to know all about what you've been up to these past few years."

"That sounds wonderful."

When they began discussing possible excursion ideas, Jonathan slipped away to head back upstairs, deciding to occupy himself with profit review.

Phoebe was an excellent candidate to handle some of his own tasks for the time he would be away, but more than likely, he would need to keep the waiter posting up to fill the gap Finley left behind. Interest in taking the place that Rhea vacated was low, and still a concern.

Maybe a week ago, or even a few days prior, he might not have been willing to leave even a fraction of his own duties to someone else. Even if he had been left with no choice, he would rather they go to Elenora, or a member of his team who had been around for longer. He would have horrified a past version of himself by hiring someone new for this responsibility, no matter how qualified or dedicated to the restaurant they seemed to be.

There was a popular program in Silver Valley academies that had been around for years, and it rotated between several skilled Mercenaries to serve as teachers. Jonathan had taken part in this program when he first began his Avidea lessons over a decade ago. He had enrolled in classes and training sessions so rigorously tedious that he hardly remembered any of his instructors, only the pain they subjected him to. One had put him through a course that drained his stamina long before he came close to completing it, and no amount of willpower carried him any closer to the finish line.

He had initially run the course too safely, taking every step to avoid danger and conserve his best maneuvers. It took him far too long to realize that until he risked harm to himself and chanced moves that had a possibility to fail, he would never get past the stubborn obstacles of the course, and they would exhaust him into incapacitation.

It was quite an extreme memory to parallel his current situation, but Jonathan remembered that familiar feeling. After years of hard work, he had found security in the Taverne. It was his sanctuary, and he wanted to hold on to it with fierce protectiveness. He wanted to hold on to his ambitions just as tightly, the ones that grew beyond these walls, and he had now been given the opportunity to reach for them. His hands were going to be full.

A knock on his office door interrupted his thoughts, and Phoebe timidly walked inside.

"Really sorry about that interruption," she said. "I hope it wasn't a bad look for me to get caught up with my reunion with Ms. Kerras."

"Not at all," he said. "You could say that I trust Elenora with my life, so the fact that she vouched for you can only mean good things."

"I'm so glad."

"She does not know about your accident, does she?"

"No," she said. "If it's not too much to ask, I'd appreciate if you didn't tell her. I know she'd worry endlessly over it when I'm really doing fine."

"Very well, I will not say a word about it to her. And I look forward to having you on the team," he added. "If you do not have any questions for me, you are free to go. Once the paperwork is processed and all checks have been run, then I will reach out regarding your orientation. You could also reach out to me in the meantime if you need anything." He passed along a business card that had his cell phone number.

"Thank you so much for the interview," she said as she accepted the card. She nodded politely before making her way out.

Minutes later, Elenora waltzed into his office, a wide grin stuck on her face.

"Hey, Mr. Tessier," she said. "Just wanted to drop in to say goodbye before I spend my break hanging out with Phoebe. Boy, am I glad to see her again. I always thought she was the sweetest girl, but she was always working extra hours, so I couldn't get to know her outside of work."

"No wonder she wanted a change of pace."

"She reminds me a little of you. You could stand to take some days off to relax too, you know."

"Maybe. Not anytime soon, though."

"Right. Have you thought about Lala Sweet's offer? It's been a few days, hasn't it?"

"It has, and of course I have."

"And?"

"It is not an easy decision to make, Elenora."

She let out a sigh. "You're overthinking it too much," she said. "Look, with Phoebe joining the team—" She paused and raised a brow. "Because she is joining the team, right?"

"Most likely," Jonathan said with a chuckle.

"With someone as reliable as she is, it just might be a sign that you need to take that offer and rest easy that your restaurant will be in good hands."

"That may be," he said. "You will be the one left in charge, though."

"As long as I can count on her and everyone else to assist me, that's fine."

"And if something were to happen to me, the restaurant should go to you."

Elenora instantly winced. "Huh? What in the world are you

saying?" she said, giving him a look of disgust. "How could you say something like that?"

"Why? I do not imagine Vicky to want the Taverne, and I do not have any other family I am close—"

"Stop! Stop it right now," she insisted, raising both her hands in a defensive position. "I can't listen to this. Don't even speak like that."

"We cannot ignore the possibility, though."

"But there's no need to invite such bad energy either," she said. "Call me superstitious or irrational, but I will not hear it. It won't happen. You will come back safely no matter what."

"I simply do not want to leave you in a situation you were unprepared for."

"I would rather have you back than ownership of the restaurant. Obviously. I don't even know if I like the idea of being an owner. Wouldn't that mean less time for actual cooking? You know, my true passion?"

"No one would deserve to have it after me but you. Not that it would matter to me at that point, but I trust only you to make the best decision for the Taverne, whatever that may be."

"I don't want to think about it right now anyway," she said, scooting her way to the door, a stern finger pointing his way. "I'm going to meet with Phoebe before you continue to bring down my mood." Her voice still had a playful quality about it, but he could tell that there was genuine upset underneath. "You make that decision, don't think so negatively, and do everything in your power to stay alive, okay?"

She disappeared before he could respond. Left in his solitude,

Jonathan let out a laugh at how similarly they went about scolding each other. Admonish and abandon.

He took out Larkin's business card and dialed the number. The ringtones led to voicemail, so he left a message expressing his interest in accepting her offer and that he would like to discuss the details.

Not even ten minutes later, her manager called back to arrange the meeting for tomorrow.

Jonathan treated the meeting as if it would be his own interview, adding a tie and vest to his usual dress shirt and trousers combination, with a reliable coat to ward off the autumn chill. Larkin's manager informed him of the location of one of her own restaurants, one of many that she had not only in the capital but also in every major municipality throughout the nation. Silver Valley was better known as a center of corporate business and academic institutions, though someone like Lala Sweet would have no difficulty ensuring that the city made room for her powerful culinary empire all the same.

He followed the manager's directions and arrived fifteen minutes ahead of schedule at the establishment called the Helix of Zest. Matching the other towering buildings around it, it stretched upward for at least twenty stories. He wondered if every floor was being used for the restaurant, and deeming that notion ridiculous, he reasoned that the upper floors surely must be occupied for other purposes. To emphasize its name, a decorative structure of rose-gold finish began with an arch over the front entrance, twisting up into two intertwining bands along the height of the building until they tapered to a point at the top.

He never had a reason to think a building intimidating when he had lived for years surrounded by this concrete jungle. He had even researched some of the top restaurants in the city using prominent names like Lala Sweet's only to discover far less imposing results, so he was not surprised that something as grand as this restaurant was also being run under her name. But comparing it to what he had to show for his work made it clear how wide the gap between his accomplishments and hers was, one that he could not imagine bridging in just the few years granted by their age difference.

Before Jonathan could muster the courage to walk inside, he stalled by idly checking his phone for the unnecessary confirmation that this was the right place. He noticed that he had received a text message sometime during his ride here from an unknown number.

First appearances deceive many.

What a nonsense message. Jonathan thought it might be from a scammer but waved the notion away when he read the four words again. This would be an awfully strange way to try to trick someone into giving personal information or sending money to an undeserving recipient.

Since he was in no rush to head inside, he decided to respond.

A wrong number, perhaps?

It was the only explanation he could conceive, since something so vague from an unsaved number could not possibly be meant for him.

A minute later, a reply came back.

Just be careful.

Scowling, Jonathan glanced around him. Other people were walking by, not paying him any mind as they went about their days. No one seemed to be looking his way, even as he stood awkwardly out in the open. He lifted his phone back up.

Who is this?

What is the meaning of this?

Hello?

He sent message after message, each a minute apart, hoping to receive some clarification of the cryptic nature of these warnings. He already considered himself a careful person, and there was no way of knowing what first appearance this mysterious sender was referring to.

But as his time ran out before he was due to head inside, a response never came, and he had to put his phone away and walk toward the double doors of the Helix of Zest.

CHAPTER 16

ORNATE. PERHAPS THE ONLY PROPER and expected word to describe the interior of the restaurant. With glass-paneled doors and an excessively spacious lobby, Jonathan felt as if he were ready to check into a resort rather than to ask for a table to dine at. There were even several luxurious couches placed on one half of the room, as if a wait could be possible in a building commodious enough to feed everyone in the city who wanted to eat out.

He approached the host playing receptionist, stating that he was here for a special appointment. The host nodded knowingly and gestured for Jonathan to follow him upstairs. They took one flight of stairs and walked along the wall past a semi-occupied dining room until they reached a line of private rooms, and the host stopped at the first one.

"Please wait inside," the host said. "Would you like anything to drink in the meantime?"

"Whatever hot tea you have available, thank you," Jonathan said.

The room was bright, off-white walls illuminated by a central chandelier and a massive window on one side. The table was much too large for a meeting between two people; it was able to seat at least a party of eight.

He picked a chair to settle into near one of the table's corners. A waiter entered to bring him a teapot containing jasmine tea and a fancy gilded teacup resting on a matching saucer. The waiter worked incredibly fast, leaving Jonathan on his own again within seconds of appearing.

In the silent minutes of sporadic tea sipping that followed, he thought about the text messages from earlier and wondered if they were truly intended for him. His own messages were still the most recent in the conversation thread. Within the last week, he had given away his details to a considerable number of people, on top of everyone who had ever been on his team and a handful of people he had worked with from the Rose Union. There was no telling who each of those individuals could have given his number to either. A situation beyond his control. But being unable to figure out why the sender felt the need to conceal their identity nagged at him the most.

The waiter reappeared with a collection of appetizers ranging from stuffed mushrooms to pickled shrimp, amounting to too much food for him to consume on his own. Before he could begin to express any form of a refusal, the waiter had already gone.

Larkin Swetnam did not seem to be one for early arrivals at appointments of her own request when ten minutes after the designated time, she finally showed up.

"Sorry I'm late!" she said, hoisting a briefcase onto the table. She patted down her blouse and slacks while taking her seat on the other side of the table from Jonathan. "Hello, hello. Thank you for your patience, Mr. Tessier." She shot him a brilliant smile to accompany her happy salutations, then took a stuffed mushroom to treat herself.

"Not at all, Ms. Swetnam," he returned. "It is a privilege to meet with you at all."

"You're too much," she said. "I've actually done a little research on you while waiting for your call." She waggled her eyebrows playfully.

"And what did you find?"

"You're of the family in charge of the Rose Union. No wonder your name sounded familiar to me. I was able to contribute to that guild as a guest Mercenary a couple of times before."

"You say that like it was more an honor for you than it was for the Union to have you."

"Isn't the Union also nationally famous? The Mercenaries on its full-time roster, what are they called again?"

"Couriers."

"Yes. Your couriers are all amazing, and it's not easy being a guest either. That's why I haven't been one as much as I'd like."

"I find that hard to believe."

"Really?" Larkin asked, frowning and tilting her head. "I mean, it's true I might have earned some of the highest credentials in the culinary space, but we're talking about the pinnacle of grants and Avidea. A foodie isn't going to compare to the likes of crime fighters, monster slayers, and treasure hunters."

"But not every talented Mercenary would want to be tied down to a single guild, so those of us who do might actually be quite average in talent," he said. "Did you have a special interest in the Union, Ms. Swetnam?"

She shrugged. "I just found it fascinating that you're a significant part of it."

"I really am not."

"Aren't you a candidate to take over?"

"It is a mere possibility." He had not forgotten his promise to his cousin, but he did not want to elaborate on it to an unrelated third party. "I am only a minor courier of the Union at this time."

"I'm sorry if it's a bit selfish," Larkin said. "I just can't help envisioning how great our partnership would be, if you did. Picture it, setting goals for Union Mercenaries to discover new lands and the ingredients they might contain, sending Merc prospects out to fetch you a consistent supply for experiments. Think of how it'll catapult our dreams into reality."

Jonathan wanted desperately to change the subject or voice his objections against exploiting the Union in this way, but he also loathed the idea of shutting her excitement down.

"I doubt I would be so convincing," he tried instead, "when everyone there has their own aspirations."

"I'll teach you how to handle the business side. After all, I have a lot of experience with connections and how to use them right."

"Maybe this is a conversation better saved for if I do inherit the guild. There are other candidates."

"Alright, alright, that's fair," she said with a cheerful giggle. "I'll be patient. We'll focus on the project that I wanted to propose to you in the meantime."

She reached over to her briefcase and opened it, retrieving a few papers and a tablet from inside. After sorting through her documents, she pulled one out and handed it to Jonathan, an outline with points that Larkin went on to explain verbally.

"Like many other top gourmet Mercenaries, I have a personal laboratory where I deliver the special ingredients that I find. It's where I conduct experiments to observe their flavor profiles and find their optimal methods of preparation."

"Your lab is all the way out in Spectervale?" he asked as he read along.

"Yeah. I know it's a bit far, but its location is amazing," she claimed. "The city is surrounded in every direction by a wilderness full of undiscovered resources, as well as nearby towns and villages with distinctive diets and culinary cultures. Here, the capital is too set in its ways and people are accustomed to 'safe' tastes and textures."

Perplexed, Jonathan gestured toward the ceiling.

"What is the rest of this building used for, then?" he asked.

"Oh." She laughed sheepishly. "Above the restaurant, I have several administrative offices for my businesses, as well as a few studios for my cooking shows. Nothing too interesting."

He should have guessed. One day he might need to think with an entrepreneur's mindset like the one she possessed. If he wanted to carve a way for himself beyond the city, or even within it, cooking talent alone was not going to be enough.

Larkin turned the screen of her tablet to face him, and it displayed an image of her laboratory. The building was only one story high, but it was expansively wide. Like the adjacent structures peeking in along the sides of the picture, its walls were a vivid teal green and its roof a muted purple, with whimsical radius windows and a cozy architectural design. If he had not been informed it housed a food science laboratory, Jonathan would have assumed the building to be an oversized cottage for an eccentric individual.

"I want this to be an open lab kind of situation," she said. "You, and others like you that I hope to bring on board, are free to conduct research on any subject you take interest in. You would then compile and present your findings directly to the Mercenary Triumph Board under your own name. Your discoveries and new recipes will then forever be accredited to you."

"How does that help build a partnership with you?"

"Well, you're using my lab, so I get some credit. But even without that, all I really want is more knowledge circulating the industry. Most Mercenaries dream of making historical or magical discoveries, or just want to get rich. Very few of them see worldwide exploration as an opportunity for culinary expansion."

"But that hardly seems to be personally beneficial to you, for all that you will be investing into it," he said. "Why would I have any reason to not accept something skewed so advantageously toward my own interests?"

"You're very thorough with your thinking, aren't you?" she said, chuckling. "Look, once a Mercenary's work is published, the information is available for anyone to put to good use, and you can bet I'll be doing so as well."

"Still, that is a minor gain compared to what you would be affording to others. Someone could end up gaining overnight fame from your generosity."

"And good for them if they do," she said. She leaned back against her chair and crossed her arms, firm in her eye contact with him. "I told you before, I'm more than willing to help give talented folks like you a boost, because you deserve it. I hope you don't have such a bad impression of me that you think I'm too greedy to be capable of kindness."

"No, it is not that at all," he said, dipping his head. "I do apologize, Ms. Swetnam."

She lifted a hand to wave dismissively.

"It's fine. It's not like I don't understand you," she said. "I'm careful of others' intentions too. Right now, I do have a personal project I would appreciate some help with, but only if you're interested."

"Please tell me more," Jonathan said.

"I have a few supplies I just can't figure out. I catch myself doing the same things over and over," she said. "A symptom of being in this field for much too long. I want fresh minds and ideas to give me a refreshed perspective."

"Have you not reached out to anyone before me regarding this? I would think you would be able to find people willing to work for you quite easily."

"You're the first since I've started looking," she said. "And I'm starting out with pretty high standards for the people I want to collaborate with. You confronted those giant beasts to obtain those ingredients and survived, didn't you?"

"With some help."

"But that makes you more suited to that type of work than most who deal with food, no matter how apt they might be at preparing it. I don't want partners that are restricted to doing research only within the lab."

"I see," he said. "I will admit that I am interested in aiding you before attempting something on my own."

"Love to hear it," Larkin said. "Eventually, I do want to assemble an unstoppable team of people who can attach their names to mine. If this goes well, we'll even be able to set out into unexplored lands together. You'll see, working with me will launch you into opportunities you couldn't even imagine you'd be having in this lifetime."

Waiting for a chance like this to land itself within his reach had always felt like a test of patience, that no matter how hard he worked he could never be sure when the toil would end, when it would become a fruitful effort. Jonathan had envisioned many more years of arduous labor before he would deem himself to have earned the right, so for Larkin to have presented him with something that aligned so perfectly with his goals, it felt simultaneously exciting and gratuitous. Who was he to think that he could become renowned for bringing the most exotic flavors to the people, to be known for cultivating a list of recipes that would be widely regarded as a masterpiece?

"This in itself is an amazing opportunity," he said. "It is precisely the kind of work I have always wanted to do."

"Perfect," she said with a wide grin. "I'm glad I found you when I did. There might be others like you waiting for the right connections and resources to take this step, and I'm going to look for them too."

"I feel incredibly fortunate. I did not think I had the right connections either, before you arranged to visit my restaurant."

"You know, crazy things can happen in our lines of work. Both of them," she said. "Let's plan around whenever you can come to Spectervale, so I can give you a lab tour and show you my ingredients of interest."

"I will only need a couple of days to prepare for the trip."

"That works for me."

"How long should I expect to stay in town?" he asked.

"It's up to you. But we can start with a week to get you acclimated, and then you can come and go however you want afterward."

"Sounds reasonable to me."

"Great," she said, handing him a few more papers for his review. "This should cover all the logistics. You can go over it in your own time, and I'll be eagerly waiting for your arrival."

"Thank you so much, Ms. Swetnam," he said, standing up.

She did the same, so that they could part on a handshake. After she left first, Jonathan sampled each of the appetizers, and then requested for a waiter to pack the rest in boxes that he could take with him and share with his favorite chef.

In between packing for his trip to Spectervale, which in fact did not earn its name for being the origin of Spectrals like himself, he reached out to Phoebe Magoro to complete her paperwork and initiate her orientation. The restaurant continued its regular operation while she became accustomed to her shifts. She adapted extremely well, giving Jonathan the confidence that he could leave the Taverne in the care of his team for at least the week that Larkin had recommended.

As promised, Austin Glass's review became the first to go online and gained a decent reception from his audience. It did not garner nearly the same virality as Trevor Labey's review, but having it no longer be the restaurant's only review from a renowned critic was every bit the solace Jonathan had so painfully sought. It was exactly what he needed before he could step away.

Other than clothes and hygiene products, he made sure to pack his trusty rapier and another cast-iron pan. Within Silver Valley and thanks largely in part to the prominence of the Rose Union, the Mercenary profession was sufficiently commonplace that people could carry sheathed weapons and not earn themselves excessively nasty looks. It was still bad practice to wield them haphazardly, but people generally understood that Mercenaries were legally allowed this privilege for the sake of their work.

Jonathan had always preferred to avoid equipping his weapon within city borders, and not because he was worried there would be severe consequences if he misused his privileges. Since he was not currently responsible for protecting the city from criminals or warding off unwanted creatures from encroaching on residential spaces, the need to gear up had rarely arisen. He had stepped away from Mercenary work for so long anyway, and when he finally decided to do anything remotely close to it again, it was to travel into the wilds and other territories with Elenora.

Lismai and the Fishing Village did not seem to mind, having seen their fair share of tourists who were either Mercenaries or carried weapons for their own protection. Jonathan did not know if Spectervale would be the same, so he found a special case specifically made to conceal his sword. It had been considerably easier to hide his pan inside one of his bags.

On the day he decided to set off, he paid the Taverne one last visit so he could say a proper goodbye to his staff.

Most of his team had never experienced him stepping away for more than a couple of days, and the only other time he had not been actively involved with running the Taverne for so long was when he closed it down. All his brief conversations with the waiters and chefs consisted of intrigued looks when he revealed he would be taking a vacation and a few curious questions regarding his return.

He saved his farewells for Elenora and Phoebe until after the lunch rush was over. He had observed Phoebe throughout the shift, not to scrutinize but because it was such a pleasure to watch her work. In between handling her own assigned patrons, she treated all the guests with gentle kindness, seating them efficiently with an impeccable balance between each waiter so that no one was left idle or overwhelmed. Every time she leaned in to hear better with her good ear, customers seemed to appreciate it as a gesture of courteous attentiveness. They usually left the restaurant appearing quite elated to have received the premium service they felt entitled to.

"Thank you for staying behind," he said to her and Elenora when the three of them were the only ones remaining in the restaurant. "I just wanted to check in with you before I left, since the two of you will be left in charge while I am away."

Phoebe furrowed her brow and glanced uneasily between him and Elenora.

"Me? Are you sure, sir?" she asked. "I am the newest on the team, after all."

"Yes, but I hired you for responsibilities where that is irrelevant," Jonathan said.

"People hire new managers and bosses all the time," Elenora chimed in. "Doesn't always mean that they're great for the job, but you definitely are more than capable."

"And you have no deficiencies in your hosting and waiting skills," he said. "So, you only need to be mindful of the administrative duties I walked you through."

"I can handle the rest of the team and make sure we carry on as usual," Elenora added. "And if you need any help, you have me for support, even if I don't care that much for paperwork."

"Thank you both," Phoebe said. "I'll do my best not to disappoint."

Elenora smiled tenderly at her, then turned her attention toward Jonathan.

"I am going to miss you so much," she said.

"Now you know what it felt like when you were gone," he said. "This is your last chance to change your mind and join me."

The head chef snorted. "Who else will you trust to keep the

Taverne running?" she asked, and he knew she did not expect an answer. "And I still don't want to. Our search for ingredients was thrilling enough. But you be safe, and also, try to enjoy yourself. You've dealt with a lot of stress over these past couple weeks, so try to take it easy."

"I hope you know how grateful I am for everything you have done to allow me to even get this far. I would have loved to take you with me if it meant closing down the restaurant again."

"So extreme," she said, somewhat bashfully. "And so cheesy."

"I just wanted to make sure you knew."

"Okay, get out of here before I start crying and begging you to stay."

By private charter sponsored by Larkin Swetnam, it was a six-hour flight to arrive just outside of Spectervale. A good bit shorter than it took to travel to the volcanoes, but Jonathan could hardly tell during the ride.

Spectervale's borders spread quite broadly, even as one of the smaller cities in the nation. Just as in the picture of the lab that she showed him, many of the buildings featured hues that shunned neutral tones, barraging his eyes with a flurry of colors that would inspire painters or illustrators of children's fairy-tale books. His vision was filled with pink window frames upon yellow-and-orange walls with bright green roofs, and other such flashy color combinations.

He walked upon rainbow cobblestone paths, phone in hand to figure out his way between streets. The color palettes shifted slightly the farther he walked, the buildings beginning to feature some shades of white and black and brown.

The structure he finally stopped in front of was about ten stories tall, and geometric in design. The base consisted of the first two stories, with exterior walls in powder pink on two sides and canary yellow on the others. On the rest of the floors above, its wide windows glowed orange against the early evening sky, and sleek black accents distinguished the different levels, matching with the lower windows and doors.

Larkin's all-inclusive vacation package included a week's stay at the Transcendent Smoothie, which sounded more like a drink shop than a hotel. Perhaps that was why she picked it for him. He checked in and went up to his suite, one that was equipped with a king-sized bed, a desk with commodious working space, a living area with a couch and coffee table, a small kitchen, plenty of storage, and a spacious bathroom. Expenses were a nonissue for someone like Lala Sweet.

Jonathan placed his bags and weapon case into the closet before walking over to the window, not having much energy to unpack just yet. Though the view outside did not lend itself to his personal taste, this hotel was one of the most luxurious places he had ever had the chance to stay as part of any Mercenary-related work. Elenora's words came to mind, that he should use this rare occasion to finally relax.

The short flight and easy search for this resort had allowed him the rest of the evening to explore the city. He tended not to enjoy spending his time so idly, but it was much too early to turn in, and he had nowhere to be before tomorrow. Leaving behind his gear to play the part of an unremarkable tourist, he went back downstairs to take to the polychromatic streets again.

243

CHAPTER 17

THE CITY'S NAMESAKE BECAME AXIOMATIC when Jonathan no longer focused on finding his lodging and had the luxury to spare a glance at every building. One in five storefronts belonged to a charm shop, one in ten was a fortune teller. He traveled several blocks before he found a small business that departed from the mystical nature all the others shared.

Having already been taught about the otherwise inexplicable magic and mythical beasts and such many years ago, he did not believe in anything that could not be elucidated by logic. Grants originated from the vivid energy contained within each eduran being, dormant when born and awakened through methodical means. If someone was able to telepathically manipulate and move objects, they were likely using some sort of Convert or Control ability. If people saw images of a haunted entity or witnessed random items appearing, perhaps someone with Connect or Construct skills was involved. Even powers beyond grant classes, like those that the fortune tellers claimed to have, would need to be powered by that same energy, and did not simply come from nothing.

The residents and tourists of Spectervale centered their culture around all things otherworldly, even though to him, a "mythological" creature drawing breath was equally as reasonable as it was for any common animal. In some ways, perhaps, this city was not too different from Silver Valley, esteemed for its academies in the study of Avidea. The attitude of awe and reverence toward magic was where the cities diverged, where here it was due to willful ignorance and curiosity, and in the capital, it would take its form as the scholarly desire to learn more.

Jonathan, against his better judgment, picked one of the oracle shops and walked inside. He was already betting that the one he selected was among the many that were not legitimate, houses built to prey on the gullible and steal both their hope and money.

The interior was an echo of the exterior, its patches of bright colors placed indiscriminately with no eye for proper design. This, quite unintuitively, made the oracle dressed in a black-and-white suit with a black silk top hat stand out when he walked through a beaded curtain to greet Jonathan. The only splashes of color upon his outfit were the reds of his cravat and top hat ribbon.

"Qiliya An, at your service," the man said, bowing deeply with a hand on his hat to keep it from falling. When Qiliya straightened his posture, he had on the most unnatural smile Jonathan could recall ever seeing, which was not helped much by the tacky makeup drawn over the supposed fortune teller's eyelids.

"What are the services that you provide, exactly?" Jonathan asked. "I apologize, I have never done anything like this before."

"A first-timer! How lovely. I offer general readings for soul searching and future milestones. I can also tailor a session based on advice you might be seeking or any specific questions you have."

"I will try the general reading, then."

"Very well! Right this way, sir, if you don't mind," Qiliya said, parting open the curtain and sweeping his arm in a polite gesture of welcome.

Jonathan walked slowly through the arched doorway into a somewhat darker room with no windows, where in the center he saw the draped table and set of chairs he expected to see from the start. The walls were painted a dark hue he could not readily discern and were minimally decorated, supporting only a couple of small shelves that held various trinkets upon them.

"Sit, sit, please," the oracle said when Jonathan hesitated near one of the chairs.

Upon the surface of the velvety tablecloth sat a collection of small hollow spheres made of thin painted metal bands curved around each other, looking something like round cages or steel tumbleweeds. They came in three sizes of four colors each: black, gold, red, and purple.

They had been scattered all over at first, but as Qiliya walked over to sit at his side of the table, he raised his hand to hover over the spheres, and they rolled around until they aligned themselves into a neat arrangement. Size by row and color by column.

Jonathan fixed his gaze on the oracle, wondering if the man had been born with some power of clairvoyance by magnetism, or if this was nothing more than a Control ability, where Qiliya could move the spheres to his own whim while pretending that the "forces" were speaking to him.

"Comfortable?" the man asked, to which Jonathan simply nodded. "Let's start by establishing a baseline for you, alright? If you could, please extend your dominant hand over the table."

A slight tremor jolted Jonathan's movements before he fully stretched out his right arm, palm facing up. Smiling, Qiliya drew a circle in the air with his finger to indicate that Jonathan should rotate his arm downward, before he slid his own hand underneath. Their palms faced each other, far apart to not touch.

Unable to keep his brow from furrowing and his eyes from looking away every few seconds, Jonathan maintained the awkward positioning for what felt like several minutes. The oracle finally removed his hand, using his other to gesture a polite command to not move, and Jonathan was beginning to feel the fatigue in his shoulder as he complied.

Qiliya closed his eyes as he spoke. "Hmm, I see. Despite people having the impression that you might be an avaricious individual, you actually care much more deeply about people than you let on. Perhaps not unconditionally, but you hold your close ones far above material gains."

An easy thing to say about anyone, even if it was not true.

"Not immediate family, though... maybe an extended or distant family member?"

Jonathan felt his bicep involuntarily twitch at this, but he found that he could not willfully pull his arm back. Something invisible held it in place. He did not know if vocalizing a confirmation was allowed or if it would disturb the oracle's vibe, so he did not risk it.

"And a professional partner, it seems. You're quite profoundly fond of them too."

He waited quietly to see if the man might say anything else.

"But your energy tells me that there's something most pressing on your mind right now. A new project that you hope will go well. Shall we now see what that future holds in store for you?"

"Yes, I would like that," Jonathan said. "Could I put my arm down?"

Qiliya chuckled, raising his palm and nodding. Whatever it was that held Jonathan's arm in place released him, and he rotated the soreness off his shoulder as he retracted his hand from the table.

The oracle then proceeded to pull out a gridded mat to place in the center of the table before gliding his hand over the metal spheres. The tiny metal balls began rolling onto the mat and skittering like little creatures that did not know where to go.

Jonathan regarded this procedure with a skeptical expression but reasoned that anything the fortune teller did was going to feel bizarre and unfamiliar to him. There were people out there who would find this utterly fascinating. Eventually, the spheres slowed in their movements and each rested on a different node of the grid, creating a pattern that Qiliya took some time to interpret.

He began with a few negatives, pointing out the judgmental and stubborn tendencies that Jonathan should be mindful of, and then manually removed the red spheres with his gloved hand. The black spheres corresponded with the apparent hidden desire to redeem a stronger familial bond, which Jonathan doubted he had, and the gold spheres specified a possible shift in his professional journey, which he had already been anticipating.

"You're not really one to trust someone easily," Qiliya said when only the purple spheres were left on the mat. "Despite that, either very recently or very soon, you have or will come to trust a person because you see something good in them, and that will obscure you from their truth."

"With a warning so vague, I might be wary of everyone moving forward anyway."

"Don't worry," Qiliya said. "You'll likely forget I said this all to you. Most people do. In the heat of the moment, you will not be thinking of advice you paid a fortune teller to tell you however long ago."

Jonathan then paid the fee and left, resuming his tour around Spectervale's streets.

He soon reached an area where the occurrence of charm shops increased dramatically. Without having to walk inside any of them, he could see the various trinkets made of metals, wood, crystals, and porcelain through windows or wide-open storefronts. Many of the stores featured no clear signs describing what purpose these charms could possibly serve, being nothing better than jewelry or decorative home goods to a nonbeliever like him.

"Hey, you!" a voice called out to him. "You there, blue-haired boy."

Whirling around to find the source of his heckler, Jonathan was not surprised to see an elderly woman standing outside one of the shops he had just passed, so much older in age that few other than her would regard him as anything but a fully grown man.

Still, his strides came to a halt, and he turned back, dipping his head politely as he approached her. "Yes, can I help you, ma'am?"

"You're one of those Avidea users, aren't you?" He did not enjoy the way she jeered at him, though he could not rightly tell if that was just how her countenance happened to default. "You've got a bit of that energy flowing all around you."

"You can tell?" he asked. She spoke as if she was not a grant user herself, which made her a rare case if she could sense his aura. Idle energy was not easy to perceive, especially if a user was not actively looking for it. Most of the time, he ignored it if it came from someone else.

"Of course I can, I'm no hack," she said indignantly. She began gesturing for him to follow her inside. "Come here, I'm bored, and I want to show you a few things. Don't really care if you don't plan on buying."

She intrigued Jonathan enough for him to walk in after her, where he was received by a scene of dark brown. All the display tables, shelves, walls, floors, ceiling, everything but most of the merchandise was the same shade of coarse wooden material. At least this shopkeeper did not feel the need to oversaturate her décor with colors as a strategy to sell her wares.

Hanging on hooks that protruded from the walls were rows upon rows of beaded necklaces, silver pendants, earrings that looked like they would weigh heavily on the lobes, and chain bracelets that permitted charms to be easily added or removed from them. The display tables and shelves featured larger items, such as sculptures, dolls, bottles, and strange gadgets he could not begin to guess what they would be used for.

The woman waved Jonathan over to her checkout counter and motioned for him to give her his hand. He obeyed, and she placed a beveled wooden cube on his palm. He looked questioningly at her.

"Focus your energy around the cube," she instructed him.

When he did, a smaller identical cube appeared on top.

"You're a Construct," she said cheerily.

"I could have simply told you that."

"And deprive me of the fun in trying this gadget out? I like seeing for myself."

"What happens for the other classes?" he asked.

"Condense would make the cube bigger, Convert would change its color or material, Control would make it float, and Connect would topple it off the palm."

Jonathan hummed in response, not entirely impressed. It was only one of countless methods developed to identify grant classes, most of them using very similar categorization systems. One of his teachers simply had him summon a minuscule ball of fuzz once he learned basic control of his aura.

"I did not think anyone here would have such knowledge about grants and Avidea," he remarked.

"What? Are you an idiot? Did you sleep through all your history lessons when you were in school?"

"What do you mean?"

"My goodness!" she exclaimed rather loudly, causing him to flinch. "Either schools are completely lacking these days, or delinquents like you just don't pay attention anymore. Specter-vale was a front-line city during the Devout Wars. Hundreds of years ago."

The insults seemed uncalled for, but he honestly could not remember anything on the subject. Most of his childhood had been a haze to him anyway, including any education irrelevant to what he used regularly as an adult. His blank expression stirred the old woman to continue.

"You know, the supporters of the Warrant and followers of the emerging Avidea grant went to war against each other, wanting to prove the superiority of their own magic. Devastated the city. Non-magic users lived in terror," she said. "Only those who had not been struck by fear wanted to remain, and everyone else fled. Avidea won the war, but it took decades for my ancestors to rebuild."

That made sense to him. Someone unenlightened might think the Warrant and Avidea grants to be similar, since they both followed grant class rules and could be honed to grow continuously in power. But a Warrant demanded an individual to give of himself for each leap in skill until he could empty himself of no more, while Avidea would teach him to painstakingly train his body as a vessel to contain more and more strength. One method would hit their cap faster than the other.

"I apologize for my ignorance," Jonathan said. "I thought with all this fortune telling and selling of trinkets, it meant less of an interest in grants."

"It is a shame," the woman said. "This all came about for the sake of drawing in tourists and boosting our economy, rather than to preserve our history. But I'm the real deal, okay?" She leaned in over the counter, eyes lighting up. "So, what is it that you're able to create with your Avidea?"

"Basically, I make weapon shells over other objects," he said, simplifying it for a stranger unaware of his profession. "To make them sharper, longer, or better for a certain application in a pinch."

"Not too bad," she said, then squinted her eyes at him. "But can't you make anything without a catalyst?"

"Nothing very concrete," he admitted. "I had always trained with existing tools."

He understood why she twisted up the corner of her mouth. For someone who might have been exposed to superior Avidea wielders, his level of skill was nothing to boast about. It had been enough to earn his License and survive a number of situations that would have been considered dangerous to ordinary people, but since he had not dedicated his entire life to training like many other Mercenaries did, he knew he was at a level that still had plenty of room to improve.

"Wouldn't you like to be able to manifest objects at will? That's the least you should be able to do."

"Are you about to sell me something?"

The woman snickered and walked over to the wall with the hanging bracelets. She picked one comprised of thick metal links and urged him to try it on.

Jonathan felt some of his aura flow around the chain, marginally easing his cynical thoughts that this might be a complete hoax.

"Picture something in your mind and see if you can form it. Make it simple to start," she said.

What came to his mind first was a butter knife. Flat and dull on the blade side, round and thicker on the handle side. Not too strict with either shape in order to be useful.

Particles formed over his palm within the light blue aura, splotching in patches of an image that might resemble the utensil, but it was incomplete no matter how much he tried to picture it.

"Concentrate!" the shopkeeper prompted him.

His forearm muscles strained when he did as she said, and the knife finally took shape, silvery and shiny and recognizable in form.

The old woman applauded, likely thinking this would be enough to sell him on the bracelet. Letting the knife dissipate back into energy, Jonathan wordlessly moved the bracelet from his wrist to his palm, and it took no time at all to become the bigger loop of a pair of kitchen scissors, which put an abrupt stop to her clapping.

"Sorry," he said, turning the shears back into the bracelet and handing it to her. The demonstration only confirmed how much more challenging it was for him to create something out of energy alone, whereas he had already mastered conjuring husks over existing objects. "If it takes me that much effort to do something so simple with an aid, I would have better luck hoping I am not left empty-handed."

She clicked her tongue in disappointment, but took back the bracelet anyway and did not insist. He thanked her for her time before he left her shop.

Feeling the call of his stomach, Jonathan figured he would end his tour by sampling one of the most popular restaurants in Spectervale. The owner had nowhere near the prestige of Lala Sweet, but the man named Antoine Coulis was prominent enough in the industry that Jonathan suspected he might also be some kind of gourmet Mercenary. Though the culinary space had so much competition, he did not follow closely enough to know much more about the man besides his moniker.

As expected of a restaurant in such demand, there was a line of hopeful patrons waiting outside the front door. Staving off his evening hunger to put himself at the end of that line would be an inconvenience, but also a sacrifice he was ready to make if he could witness firsthand what set these culinarians apart. A bit of a learning opportunity he could savor as a side dish to his meal.

The pastel yellow brick building had trims in fuchsia and was two stories high, each level lined with evenly spaced windows that were obscured by navy blinds and draped by matching awnings. Other than its locally appropriate color scheme, nothing about the design of the Dining Portal stood out from other restaurants, so the fuss over this place should reliably be attributed to reputation more than anything else.

A group of people waiting directly ahead of him was having a quite clamorous discussion. If they hoped Jonathan would not eavesdrop, they should have provided him earplugs, free of charge.

"Is this really the place you wanted to eat at?" one person asked.

"Has to be, right? Why else would so many other people be waiting?" said a second.

"But I'm so hungry, I don't know if I can wait," a third grumbled.

"This is probably the shortest this line has ever been, actually. Every time I pass by here during dinner, it's ridiculous. Got me curious, so I looked it up."

"Is it worth the hype?"

"Yeah, we can probably find somewhere else and not have to wait at all."

"It's worth trying, right? It's one of those celebrity-chef restaurants, anyhow."

"I don't really understand how you can be a celebrity chef. It's just food. Who cares?"

"Well, for some people, food is life. But I don't get it either."

"This had better be worth bragging about."

Jonathan tuned out when he could not stand the immature moaning any longer, and his thoughts wandered aimlessly until he was at the front of the line ready to be seated. The host picked a small table for him tucked in a corner and handed him the menu before she left, not sparing him even a dribble of friendly small talk.

He was willing to excuse it with the restaurant being so busy, but having just hired Phoebe as a host for the Taverne, he was proud to have someone like her on his own team. Glancing around, he noted that the spacious dining room was decorated with elaborate chandeliers and embellishments so ornate and tawdry that only a conscious effort could achieve.

When a waiter came to the table with an upturned angle of his nose, Jonathan avoided looking into his nostrils and selected a savory chickpea pancake dish as an appetizer and cedar-plank salmon as his main course. Satisfied that his picks were compelling enough in ingredients and preparation without being too experimental, he hoped to give this establishment a fair chance to impress him.

He did not have to wait long before the waiter brought him his two orders together, placing them both on the table with excessive flourish. But he had not been prepared for what he saw.

The slices of the savory pancake were splayed on something that resembled a wide hair comb, with teeth spread too far apart to be useful or to even hold the slices in place. Some of them were already threatening to droop over in a sad display. There was a presumed dipping sauce drizzled over this exhibit, but none of it came close to touching the food it was supposed to enhance. The thought of having to use the pancakes like a sponge to wipe sauce off the teeth or the board holding this bizarre presentation together repulsed him.

He could not tell if the cedar-plank salmon was any better. The Dining Portal seemed to despise normal plates, because a structure of dowels supposedly meant to resemble a tree was to be his dinnerware instead. The salmon, so generously precut into chunks to save him time, was pierced upon each branching dowel like miserable fruit for harvest.

Clearly, none of this restaurant's food was arranged with any thought to real artistry or inspiration, though it seemed whoever was responsible thought themselves to be a creative genius.

Jonathan sat frozen in disbelief, afraid to accept that someone who had earned a coveted status would present his food in a manner meant solely to be over-the-top and sensational, with more regard for viral pictures than a respect for food.

The waiter who served him, whom he did not realize still remained at his table, suddenly leaned forward to get far too close to him. Jonathan's eyes widened and he recoiled, because he never thought a member of any waitstaff would intentionally invade a patron's personal space.

"What do you think you're doing?" the waiter asked him, rudely and nearly shouting. "How dare you make that face?"

CHAPTER 18

JONATHAN THOUGHT HE HAD sufficiently masked his aversion toward the gaudy tackiness of the Dining Portal's food, but the waiter's resentful confrontation made it clear he was mistaken.

"Excuse me?" he managed to utter. Perhaps there was the slim possibility that he had misheard or misunderstood.

"That wrinkling of your ugly nose and frowning like I served you a pile of garbage! How dare you have that kind of attitude at this fine establishment, that you are privileged to dine at?"

He was going to have to work on discerning who deserved the benefit of his doubt.

Before he could get a word in about this absurd expectation, the waiter appeared fully capable of getting a rise out of himself with no help.

"Huh? Where do you get the nerve to be so disrespectful? You have the undeserved honor to eat a meal inspired by a top chef of the nation, and you make a face? Do you think you're greater than the mind that designed this menu?"

The nearby patrons looked on with furtive wariness as if poorly pretending to not have noticed the commotion, and Jonathan could not tell if it was he or the waiter who appalled them. He, for one, could hardly believe this was actually happening.

"I really do not want any trouble."

"Yeah? Did you not want any trouble when you walked in here like self-important vermin, with your mind set on spitting all over the talent and hard work of everyone who works at this amazing restaurant? You drag your dirty feet in here to desecrate our beautiful establishment, and then you trivialize our esteemed status with your disgusting lack of etiquette."

"How is that fair?" he said when the waiter needed to suck in a huge breath to fuel his long-winded rant. "Is every guest here aware of a rule that they must maintain their composure at all times? How is a restaurant supposed to operate if no one is allowed to have facial expressions without being scolded by the staff?"

"What. . . what did you say? How dare you?"

"I thought someone who worked in the hospitality industry would have a modicum of humility, to at least not yell at a patron."

The waiter's jaw dropped as if he had just been dealt the most wounding insult.

"How dare you?" he shouted, very much an imitation of a parrot. "You'd better apologize, right now!"

"For what?" Jonathan asked. "For a reaction? How do you behave if a guest expresses legitimately negative feedback?"

"You imbecile! The owner himself will come deal with you, and teach that inferior, stupid brain of yours how to properly show respect."

Speechless as the waiter walked off, Jonathan was too stunned to do anything but sit there and glance around at the curious eyes fixed on him. How did this escalate so out of control? Surely it was not the standard practice of these celebrity-chef restaurants to berate a customer before they even had the chance to partake in the dishes they ordered.

Indeed, Antoine himself stormed out of the kitchen and marched between tables of now intently observant patrons to approach Jonathan. It was a clumsy task, given the man boasted a bulkier, muscular build. He had a beard, mustache, and an abundant head of hair, all in a striking jet-black. He was likely in his fifties, his face full of fine lines and proudly aged scars, and as he nearly flew over to Jonathan, his nostrils flared with evident fury.

"Are you the rude jerk who had the audacity to look down on my craft?" Antoine bellowed.

"I was not looking dow—"

"Do you think you're all that to be judging my work? Huh? A nobody like you?"

"Look, I was only surp—"

"You're nothing compared to an accomplished chef like me."

"If I could get a word in, I would expla—"

"An annoying little gnat is what you are," Antoine continued to interject.

Jonathan honestly did not think his reaction had been so extreme to justify the treatment he was receiving. Only when the owner began huffing out angry breaths did he find the opportunity to provide his explanation.

"I was only surprised at such extravagant presentations of the food," he said, with a gesture to the neglected pancake and salmon. "Regardless, this is no way to treat a patron. Everyone should be entitled to their opinions, be they positive or negative."

"No patron of mine is ever going to disrespect me," Antoine announced, looking pointedly around the dining room before glaring at Jonathan again. "All of you should revere my talent and consider yourselves lucky to be able to eat at my restaurant."

"I am sure some people do, but that should never be a requirement."

"Shut up! We're settling this outside, now! See if you can talk back once I'm through with you."

"You must be joking," Jonathan said incredulously. "I only came here to try out your restaurant, not to look for a fight."

One moment, he was defiantly remaining seated, and in the next, his body felt heavy. Everything in his vision shifted downward. Spots of dull pain bloomed over his arms and thighs as they knocked clumsily against the hard edge of the table, and in his hazy confusion, he realized that Antoine had violently yanked him from his chair by his shirt and was dragging him away.

His hands shot up to grab at Antoine's sturdy arm, clawing at it in a struggle to free himself, but it was no use. Only in his desperation to reclaim his dignity and his footing on firm ground could he ignore the fact that this man was many times physically stronger than him. The rest of the restaurant disappeared and became irrelevant as his focus homed in on resisting this humiliation, to not be treated like common riffraff that had caused enough trouble that he needed to be thrown out.

Antoine walked with what Jonathan could only describe as a misplaced and seething determination toward a side door near where the dining room joined with the kitchen. Using his unoccupied hand, Antoine forcefully shoved the door open, taking an unwilling Jonathan with him outside. Once the door swung back closed, leaving the two of them alone in the area behind the restaurant reserved for dumpsters, he aggressively threw Jonathan against the wall with a loud grunt.

A stinging ache spiked over Jonathan's left shoulder that caused him to let out a yell and collapse onto the ground. As he propped himself up against asphalt, he could not tell if anything was broken or if he was simply in excruciating pain.

"You wanna say what you said back there again to my face? You get one chance to apologize."

Jonathan wondered if the man had ever humiliated another patron like this before, and if so, surely they would have wasted no time to grovel. Surely this was merely an intimidation tactic based on nothing more than useless pride.

As soon as he tried to get up, a fist came flying at him from what he was certain was the direction of the brick wall he had just crashed into and hit him in the face so hard it multiplied his disorientation a few times over. Enough for the fight to be decided.

Jonathan had thought this many times before. The eduran body, on its own, was not very suited for physical battle. Once the upper hand was lost, disadvantages piled on top of each other to slide any hope of victory further out of reach. Even the brawniest, well-built fighter would find themselves in a bind if attacked endlessly with no reprieve, no opportunity to recover. Would it not have been ideal for an individual struck senseless to unleash strength instead, so that they had a reasonable chance to fight back?

Counting how many times he was being pummeled became an impossible task, and he only knew there was going to be swelling and most definitely bleeding. If he had been angry before, it was nothing compared to what he was brewing now as he held on to his consciousness. As far as anyone was concerned, he was a defenseless patron, victimized by an asinine response to mere facial expressions. It could have happened to anyone who was eating inside that restaurant, and most of those patrons would have actually been incapable of standing up to this non-sensical treatment.

It was unfair. It was cruel. He despised this with his entire being.

He began to feel a frustrated burning, not from the blows he had been dealt, but from deep within. It grew hotter and hotter, a searing sensation that somehow did not hurt no matter how sharply it scorched. Rather, it was looking for a way out, an over-whelming agitation that was growing too fast, needing an escape from the confines of his physical form.

Something burst, and then everything became calm. Calmer, at least. After a few seconds, the boiling subsided, and it finally registered with Jonathan that he was no longer being punched. In the place of thwacking, ringing, and dizziness, a distant sound of retching and choking replaced the clamor that had plagued him when he had nothing to protect himself but the basic aura he had instinctively pulled around himself.

Not that it did much. Users of the Condense class were significantly better at bolstering their defenses using their energy than he would ever be. Jonathan lifted a hand to gingerly press against his tender skin, on all the spots over his face, neck, and arms that stung with each touch. His fingers found a few patches of fresh blood, especially around his nose. He imagined that he looked a mess.

The gagging noises felt closer, now that Jonathan was able to sort out which direction was which. Antoine was doubled over several yards from him, heaving uncontrollably.

Strange, for two reasons. One, unless Antoine had backed away a considerable distance, he had been too far to throw any useful punches. And two, usually, whenever Jonathan witnessed this type of affliction from others around him, there should have been a cast-iron pan in his hand. He stared blankly as he stumbled to his feet, relying heavily on the wall to steady himself. His attempts to straighten his clothes did very little to reduce their dishevelment.

"What happened?" he asked, his voice hoarse. "Is there still a stench?"

Antoine only coughed harshly, which was much more of a response than Jonathan was expecting.

He kept leaning against the wall as he turned to fully face Antoine. His brow furrowed into a scowl as he simultaneously hoped the lightheadedness would fade and harbored that simmering rage, though it did not feel half as intense as before. He briefly wondered if he could do that again, intentionally.

"You. . . you have the gall to drag someone out in full visibility of all your other patrons," he said, his voice low and angry. "And you apparently have no problems treating them like this."

Whatever scent his desperate instincts had picked to disperse in that moment of outrage seemed to have a lasting effect.

"What if your victim was not a grant user?" he asked. "Have you done this before? What if they had been a normal citizen, just wanting to spend their money for a lovely meal? You would have knocked them senseless too? You would have killed them. And for what? For a muscle twitch? You would throw away your career for that?"

Antoine's retching dwindled into wheezy gasps, but it gave Jonathan plenty of time to continue. He did not care if he was being listened to or not.

"All because I did not give you absolute adoration. This is a disgusting way to resolve a situation," he said. "You are not entitled to have your work liked by everyone. You should have merely let it go. Ignore the people who do not judge you favorably, not assault them."

Jonathan paused to grunt. He was riling himself up, though unlike that waiter, he had justifiable cause. It still hurt to move too abruptly.

He studied the man while he was still bent over. This certainly was not how Jonathan imagined an accomplished chef with a mildly familiar name in the industry to be. That alone could have been worth something, but who knew that the reputation this man truly deserved was one of shame and belligerence? Only a failure would act like this, and Jonathan concluded that to be the truth, unconcerned whether or not it was an assessment too unfair.

"I did not even need a reservation to dine at your embarrassment of a restaurant," he added. "Your own actions are what will drive people away soon enough. You are an idiot for wasting your energy harassing your customers rather than finding a way to improve. I might not be influential enough to convince the public that Antoine Coulis is a pathetic individual and a terrible representation of what an excellent culinarian should be, but you do not need my help to destroy your career. I would bet anything it is already dying. Why else would you have been here, arms deep at one of your restaurants, rather than ruling an empire from afar?"

He thought of the prestige Lala Sweet had achieved, and others like her at the top. They had enough power and wealth to entrust the operation of every restaurant they built to the teams they hired, and so they were able to dedicate all their energy to research efforts and the creation of revolutionary new recipes that would stun the world. They did not need to slave away in one of their own kitchens, hoping to earn the approval of their customers, or to demand it, in this case.

When Antoine managed to croak something unintelligible, Jonathan finally figured out that the debilitating odor was still present, and that he could control it easily. Wielding it felt very familiar to those times he would construct the scent of the durian fruit, only this time it had been devastatingly amplified. The novelty of this power existed in the fact that he was unarmed and using no aid, which alarmed him since he had declined to buy that bracelet from the charm shop.

Despite his excitement at this new development, he eased the scent back down, allowing Antoine a chance to catch his breath.

"You had better use your words," Jonathan warned, "or I will layer that stench until you suffocate. Everyone saw you drag me out here, so this is considered self-defense against misuse of power from a fellow grant user, even if it is to the death. Whatever awful portal nonsense you were using counts. Along with your dying career, do you also want to fall in shameful defeat?"

"Shut up," Antoine hissed. "If you don't know what you're talking about, then shut your stupid mouth."

Jonathan relented completely with the unpleasant aroma and waited. Though they were disagreeable, Antoine was in fact using his words.

He also began hacking to suck in breaths of air, still wearing severe resentment on his face as he did. Jonathan regarded him cautiously, though the man hardly looked ready to lunge at him. When Antoine glanced up to meet his eyes, Jonathan was surprised to see his expression soften, though he did not trust it for a second.

"It's been so difficult," Antoine said coarsely as he assisted himself into a sitting position. He talked slowly and quietly, as if mumbling the rant he had been holding back for far too long. "I've been in this business since I was a teen. Do you even know how long that is? Probably longer than you've been alive. I devoted countless hours to perfecting my cooking. I've fought every beast, crawled through every cave, and explored every spot on the planet to find new ingredients."

Jonathan held himself back from interrupting.

"I've tried every existing cooking technique and even invented new ones for every ingredient I've been credited to have obtained. I thought that would put me in contention to be an esteemed figure in the industry. I even learned how to use Avidea to become a Mercenary, even though I hated it. I hated the training, and I hated my limitations. I don't want to be flinging projectiles like a monkey throwing around its defecation. I only wanted to cook. I wanted to be the best at it. But no matter what I tried, I still couldn't pass the likes of those irritating top gourmet Mercenaries. Especially that Lala Sweet. What in the world could you be doing with pastries to make you that popular?"

The vitriol with which the man spit out those last few sentences caused Jonathan to flinch. "Do you not look upon people like that as inspiration?" he asked. "To spur you to try harder? I am a restaurant owner too, and I enjoyed my time looking for unusual ingredients."

Antoine shook his head vehemently. "No, you can't know what it's like," he objected gruffly. "You've probably just started, haven't you? Naïve idiot. You can't know how frustrating it is, to still not know how the top chefs can concoct such amazing dishes that they consistently create a national stir. How customers keep comparing and judging my work to be subpar since they've tried the dishes that others have made."

What seemed like irrational, brash behavior was starting to make some sense, if Jonathan was willing to allow Antoine the courtesy of believing him. All the negative feedback must have hurt his pride until he could not tolerate it anymore. Could not stand people like Jonathan who had the insensitivity to make faces at his dishes.

"I only made one face, hardly," he countered. "And I was not even permitted to try the food first." Mentioning it reminded him of his hunger that was yet to be sated. "I was only taken aback by what I considered to be excessive presentation, like the chef was trying too hard on appearance over the quality of the dish."

Antoine glared at him but said nothing.

"Even so, how do you expect this type of conduct to solve any of your problems?"

The man snarled before answering. "I don't know," he said. "I'm just done feeling hopeless and wanted to take back some control."

"I think this will only send you down a worse path," Jonathan said.

"I don't care what you think."

"Where you will wake up to find you have nothing left," he continued, unperturbed. "Not even your most loyal customers will be there for you anymore."

"Shut up," Antoine said, but soon quieted down for a moment. He let out a burdened sigh. "I hate what I'm hearing, but I know you're right."

"Just something to think about."

"Don't get comfortable telling me how to feel," he said, refusing to look Jonathan in the eyes. "Get yourself to a hospital, a premium treatment under my account so that you'll be fixed up overnight. And then never show your ugly face in front of me again."

After pushing himself off the ground, Antoine reached into his pocket to retrieve a business card, shoved it at Jonathan, and then marched petulantly back inside the building.

Health care, for the most part, was covered by lavish government programs, at least within the most developed cities of the nation. A minor checkup or treatment was never going to run up a bill on a poor patient already suffering from an ailment, and surgeries or medication that would be costly for a hospital to provide were subsidized by systems that would not pile that detrimental financial debt on the individual whose life needed to be saved.

The majority of facilities had their own teams of talented staff, but even above them, there were those who used grants or powers they were born with to heal at an enhanced level. Expedited healing even for the most severe wounds, reversing injuries and preventing scarring in a way that would baffle most of the general population. So, their talents were usually offered only to Mercenaries, who already understood the healers' abilities and would be the most likely to find themselves in situations to require this premium medical service.

But those healers were paid extremely well, and that had to come out of somebody's paycheck. Jonathan had always been told to think of it as motivation to never get himself injured to this extent, which had never been easy in a job that was meant to put one's life at risk.

He handed Antoine's card to the receptionist of one such clinic in Spectervale, who regarded him with a compassion he wished to ignore. She handed the card back to him after giving Antoine a call and led Jonathan to a treatment room where he would be seen by one of these distinguished healers.

With his face sculpted back to its original form and mostly removed of bruises, and a subpar fast-food meal in his stomach, he returned to the lobby of his hotel, ready to call it a night.

"Are you okay?" a stranger asked, approaching him unprompted. She appeared to have separated herself from her family to talk to him.

Jonathan frowned. "Who are you?" he asked in return.

"Oh, we were at the Dining Portal too, and saw what went down with the owner," she said. "But it looks like you were able to talk things out. And what a coincidence, we're staying here as well."

"Ah. Thank you for your concern, ma'am. Yes, everything turned out fine," he said, which in its twisted, convoluted way, was not a total lie. He suspected that Antoine usually succeeded in scaring his naysayers into place, and Jonathan had been an outlier. It was best to spare her the details of the confrontation.

"Good," she said, sighing. "It's never a fun time when fights break out when you're just trying to eat."

"Unfortunately, I was unaware that the owner took things so seriously," he said. "It could not have been a good look for everyone else at the restaurant."

The woman nodded. "It's pretty ridiculous, especially to any average resident or tourist." She lowered her voice. "But it's actually not uncommon."

"What do you mean?"

"That these B- or C-tier celebrity chefs hold a grudge since they can't break through to an A-tier status."

"So, they lash out against patrons?" he asked. "Surely that is not sustainable."

"I know, it doesn't make much sense. But they squeeze by on the wallets of patrons who want something really good but can't quite afford a meal at a top chef's restaurant. So, it's become this weird culture where customers are willing to behave a certain way and ignore transgressions and lower-tier gourmets try to figure out how far they're able to push the limits. I'm sorry you had to learn the hard way."

He could not envision it. However, he had no proof to deny it. He still had not had a meal at a restaurant that qualified for this description, never mind the years of not eating out anywhere but at his own restaurant. Still, he imagined an incident where an owner lost his temper had to be an isolated one. The notion that it could be happening anywhere else was ludicrous.

"Well, thank you for checking in on me, and for this conversation," he said to her. "This is incredibly enlightening."

She giggled. "No problem, it's just such a relief that you're unharmed. You never know what could be going on these days. Have a good night!"

"You too, ma'am."

She waved an enthusiastic farewell, returning to her family as he called an elevator to take him up to his suite.

CHAPTER 19

ONLY AFTER HE REACHED his room did Jonathan study the card Antoine had given him. It listed a personal cell number and some Mercenary information, including what allowed the receptionist to bill his premium medical account.

Jonathan had once given out his own cards very similar to this one, though he had since left them all behind at the Union. He tossed Antoine's card into one of his bags and went to throw himself sideways onto the bed. He lay there, accepting whatever rag doll configuration his limbs flopped into, and let his mind wander.

There had been a particular thrill in discovering that he was able to conjure one of his abilities without channeling it through an instrument that he did not get to relish in until now. He was still buzzing from that excitement, even if it had been for an already familiar aroma he often employed whenever he wanted to drive some nuisance away.

But many other questions began to linger in his mind. Why had it been so much harder during his training to do the same? Would it always require him to lose his temper? He loathed to think of it as only a desperate last resort rather than a practical and reliable application of his Avidea. Even more so to accept that he was unskilled. Back during his lessons, other Construct users easily created replicas of objects through touch, formed gauntlets over their hands, summoned temporary shields to block flying weapons. He only stood a chance when his teachers allowed him to hold a wooden training sword, so he knew he should not expect to be able to make a weapon from nothing but aura without the help of his rapier anytime soon.

Still, he was itching to try it again, to feed that burning power from within until it burst outward, granting him a wide radius in which he was able to bring his foes to their knees. He would need to find a willing participant back home to test this out and confirm he was forming the aromas correctly, and maybe choose something less nauseating to start.

Rolling onto his back to stare up at the ceiling, Jonathan recalled the other events of that scuffle. It could not really have been called a fight. Despite getting out of it fine, he was not the victor. How embarrassing it was that he had spent most of the confrontation cowering and feebly protecting his head from blows with flimsy arms not made for the job. Not that he would make it a priority, but running some practice drills at one of Silver Valley's training centers to prevent this sort of situation in the future did not seem so bad an idea.

It was the conversation after everything, though, that stuck most with Jonathan. In his anger, he had spewed every grievance and criticism he could think of in relation to Antoine's behavior, dealing verbal blows for every physical one he received. He considered himself lucky that anything he said had registered with the man at all. He could have just as easily lashed out once Jonathan let down his guard. Instead, he agreed to have a conversation. Antoine's furious words, though they did not excuse his actions, gave Jonathan clarity from a perspective he never thought to consider before. And yet, concomitantly, he learned that he wanted the very same things Antoine had once wanted as well.

Jonathan had his doubts now, after hearing from that woman in the lobby. The possibility that the industry could be so tense, maybe even toxic, was not enough to dishearten him, until perhaps when he would see the truth for himself. But it was enough to have him ponder the things he truly wanted. If he could maintain his devotion to a field of work riddled with such complications. He had no problems dealing with rude customers, the betrayals of his subordinates, the entitled socialites that hoped to bleed him dry. For those who shared his passion for cooking, however, they held adequate power to wear down his resolve.

With this opportunity given to him directly from Lala Sweet, Jonathan wondered if he could skip the troubles of being a B- or C-tier culinarian. It seemed rather delusional to think that this alone would shoot him straight to the top. Maybe he would instead end up being resentful, like Antoine, if things did not go his way. If he lost sight of his ambitions and let them become overtaken by jealousy and frustration.

He did not sleep well that night, a fact even the luxurious mattress could not remedy. Coupled with the mediocre complimentary breakfast the following morning, he showed up at Larkin's lab clearly lacking energy.

"You doing okay?" she asked when she met him in the laboratory reception area. "Didn't sleep well? I can arrange for a move if the suite I booked isn't to your liking."

"No need." Jonathan yawned. "I just had a lot on my mind."

Larkin nodded. "Being far from home, about to start an exciting new project. I guess that takes some getting used to. I hope you sleep better tonight." She handed him a plastic card with his name printed on it. "This will be your limited access key, so you can come in whenever you're able to work."

"Thank you, Ms. Swetnam," he said, accepting the card and squinting at it. His name, an identification number, and a few small symbols were printed on one side.

She grinned widely. "Now, let's start the tour," she said.

He followed her dutifully as she guided him through the storage area with pantries and huge refrigerators, test lab rooms, test kitchens, classrooms, conference rooms, a couple of libraries, and an extensive tech room. The exterior of the lab might have been colorfully designed to match its local surroundings, but inside, every surface was clean white, silver, or a light wood stain.

Having expected to only see maybe the first three types of rooms and nothing beyond that, he was impressed by the scope of this facility. This is what it meant to be a genuine food scientist. A gourmet Mercenary. He obviously did not have access to Larkin's main office and a few other private offices, but even then, he could not imagine needing to use every function of the lab that was available to him.

"Ah, here," Larkin said, gesturing for him to get a closer look at a few boxes that had been set aside in one of the storage fridges. "These are the special ingredients I mentioned the other day. Isle sturgeon roe and the bird's nest from the fire swiftlet."

"What have you done with these so far?" Jonathan asked, reaching to pull out a jar of the fish eggs for closer examination. Each egg had a greenish tint when held to the light and was bigger than roe should be for a sturgeon, more than a centimeter in diameter. He assumed they had already been cleaned.

"Well, since I thought these were just very rare versions of ingredients we already have circulating the culinary space, I tried preparing them the same way," she said. "The roe with a bit of salt, the bird's nest boiled into a drink or soup. I ran these recipes through a committee for feedback, but none of us think they're inspiring enough to make any impact on existing recipes."

"Have you tried anything else?" he asked. The bird's nests were stored in plastic bags, and though each piece was similarly sized to their more commonplace version, the stringy substance was tinged an orangish-red.

She shook her head. "Not yet. I imagine something crazy has to be done to make them worth paying extra for. Good thing we have plenty to experiment with. There's more in the other fridges."

The tour rounded off with her showing him a small office he could use if he needed a place to store documents or work in peace. Though there were only a few assistants walking around today, there were days Larkin used the lab to meet with her own clients or invited professors and other Mercenaries to teach students, and she assured him it would get plenty hectic during those times.

"Well, that's pretty much it," she said when they ended up back at the lobby. "For the rest of the day, I suggest you just get comfortable with the lab and where everything is. If you can't stay more than a week in Spectervale this time, then you can get started with some research tomorrow."

"Yeah, I probably will head home soon. Better that I come more refreshed to take on such exhilarating work. Thank you for the tour."

She chuckled and gently patted his shoulder. "Thank you for agreeing to help me. This is going to be a great partnership. And if you ever have any questions, make sure you call me, okay?"

After she left, Jonathan spent some time getting familiar with the array of lab tools and kitchen supplies that she had stocked, finding nearly everything he could think of and some other items that surprised him. Silicone egg-yolk separators, circular rolling knives, a baking pan made specifically for the bumpy shape of corncobs. The kind of gadgets made for very narrow applications that he would expect to find in only the most gimmicky of kitchens, solving problems of fickle ease with modern, innovative solutions.

He pulled out his phone to do some research. It was no secret to the general public that this facility was attributed to Lala Sweet, so he looked into similar information on Antoine. A few recipes he was given credit for developing, an article here and there telling stories of his old exploits, but no laboratories or research centers associated with his name. Not even failed research operations. Jonathan had hoped to find something, a clue, that helped him understand what set Lala Sweet apart from Chef Coulis, but he should have known a simple online search was not going to hand him a straight answer.

Soon after, he called it a day. Back at the Transcendent Smoothie, he decided to request room service for his meals instead of eating out. Some light reading and a lengthy phone call with Elenora during her break hours to catch each other up put him in a better state to sleep well that night.

Jonathan's experiments the next day began with raw taste tests. Or at least that was what he intended. He had to soften the bird's nest in hot water for a more palatable texture and find a way to consume the roe without risking an assault on his taste buds from popping far too much of that briny flavor at once. Plain toasted bread was barely enough to even out the potency of just two to three of those emerald eggs.

Larkin had left some notes behind for him, describing exactly how she executed her recipes, which he reviewed so as not to duplicate her work. He went on to assay the ingredients through boiling, seasoning, stir-frying, baking, and even smoking.

The area just outside the lab room became distractingly raucous sometime in the middle of his work, when he had lost track of the hours. People were filing into the building, and oblivious to Jonathan's preference to work in quiet, were talking among themselves with no discretion for their volume.

Figuring he needed to take a break anyway, Jonathan

gathered his items and shed his lab coat to investigate what was going on.

"Hello," he greeted a young man standing on his own off to the side. "Excuse me for bothering you, I happen to be a new researcher here. Could I ask what is happening right now?"

"Oh," the young man said, looking up from his notebook. "We're here for one of Professor Uden's lectures."

"What about?"

"He's been doing a short course on. . . well, courses. The components of a meal and the order they come in. Today is lecture three out of five."

"Interesting. Is this Professor Uden here right now? What does he look like?"

"I don't know if he's here yet. But he's kind of short, with buzzed teal hair. Has glasses and likes his earrings."

"Thank you," Jonathan said and went to look for the professor.

Once he found him on the way to one of the classrooms, Jonathan requested permission to sit in on the lecture, and Professor Uden very kindly granted his request. Jonathan sat in the back of the classroom, enjoying the air-conditioning in contrast to standing in front of burning stoves and ovens for most of the day, and scribbled down whatever stood out to him as the professor spoke. He took notes on fermentation and glucose levels and metabolism, things that merely fascinated him now, but could prove useful for when he might care about designing full-course meals.

The next day of research passed very similarly, and without disruptions. Jonathan began ranking the different experimental cooking methods in his notes. After he left the lab, he felt brave enough to have a meal at a local, much smaller restaurant.

When he arrived back at his hotel room, he found that he had received a pair of messages from the same mysterious number that had contacted him the day he went to meet Larkin at her restaurant.

Everyone has secrets to hide.

Should you seek them out?

He typed a response back right away, asking again who this sender was and why they were sending messages of this nature. He did not get an answer.

It became a disturbance to his focus while he tried to work the following day, one that wandered into his thoughts every now and then for him to have to push away. Fortunately, most of his experiments were wrapping up anyway.

From his three days of effort, he found that frying the roe turned the substance inside into something with the consistency of a delectable, juicy meat that featured very intensely delicious flavors. While he could not be sure this was going to be the optimal preparation method for the ingredient, it certainly was unexpected that frying something usually made into caviar would turn up a positive result.

Broiling the bird's nests over steaks or filets had been his technique of choice when he discovered it enhanced the flavor and texture of the meat. Considering the ingredient was almost tasteless in wetter food preparations, he considered this an impressive upgrade.

Jonathan wondered if grilling would improve the result even more, especially if done over coal. But there was no suitable grill in the kitchen he had been working in, so he decided to check the other kitchens and test labs.

He rummaged through cabinets and only found quantities of equipment he already had access to. So, he moved on to look around the storage area, which held mostly ingredients. There were a few devices designed to peel fruits or vegetables in a flash, but no grill. He then tried the small courtyard outside near the back of the campus, and it had been his best bet to find a grill, but his search ended fruitlessly.

He tried texting Larkin first, since it seemed less disruptive than outright calling her. But even after he finished taking his lunch, she must not have had the time to look at her phone. He had anticipated working more closely with her over these past few days rather than being left on his own. Not that he was complaining, as the work was engaging. This type of Mercenary assignment emulated his path moving forward, if he were to continue it. It would be one taken primarily in solitude.

Despite the lecture that took place during his first full day here, he quickly learned that the lab was more often empty than it was occupied. He might have missed seeing whether Larkin had come in today for her own projects, but if he could not find her in her office to ask if she had a grill available, he was resigned to call it a day and talk to her later.

It took traversing a few winding hallways to reach her office from the lab rooms. Though he would be slow to admit it, Jonathan had avoided the embarrassment of becoming lost on his first day by not moving around the building too much outside of the lecture. The second day, he gave himself another tour to memorize the rooms, and this search for the elusive grill on the third day gave him a great refresher.

When he reached her door, he lifted his hand to knock. The impact caused the door to crack open, and it very slowly slid to a stop after producing a small gap. Still wearing his nitrile lab gloves, he gripped the doorknob, realizing that the door, while locked, had not been properly closed all the way.

Jonathan had no thoughts of entering without permission when he peeked inside, expecting to see a busy Larkin within. He would apologize for barging in on her and leave right after asking his question.

But the office was empty. Of any person, at least. Jonathan gazed with confusion at the inside, failing to immediately recognize what he was seeing.

The room was dark, but he could discern the faint outline of a desk thanks to the dim light sources behind it, light sources unlike anything he had ever seen. Two giant cylindrical containers, transparent and glowing in soft white, sat near the back of the office. They both appeared empty, aside from their luminescence, like a pair of oversized light bulbs on the verge of dying out. It was difficult for him to make out what the bases of these containers were made of, his best guess being that they were some type of dark metal or dense plastic.

His attention shifted to the side when he noticed something else. Next to these illuminating bulbs was another large gadget, tall enough to almost touch the ceiling. He squinted to find its shape. A wide metal box for the base, with some sort of panel he figured was used for manual controls. A monitor off to the side.

An extension that reached up and forward, into a clawlike protrusion with long spikes surrounding a central nozzle. He could not think to describe it as anything other than some type of extractor.

Despite his better judgment, Jonathan opened the door wider and walked inside to get a closer look. These gadgets seemed excessive for a food research lab, and imagining why Larkin had them in her office only led to more disconcerting questions. But they were questions that begged answers. Demanded them. He hated that he was doing this. She had been so generous with her offer to boost his career, and here he was, violating her unsparing trust. How could what he was doing be considered much different to what those thieves he hired did to him?

He silently vowed to be quick, just a swift glance to satisfy his curiosity. When he neared the glowing containers, an unpleasant sensation crept invasively under his skin, causing him to wince. It was a dirty feeling, something inexplicably disturbing. He attempted to peer inside at what the containers might hold near the bottom, but he could not see anything out of place. He stared for a moment, or maybe more, at the light. It grew brighter and brighter. No, that was only his eyes getting used to the luster. It was a strange dichotomy, the itch that made his skin prickle accompanied by this hypnotizing light. He needed to stop staring at it if he wanted to be brief with his trespassing.

The extractor was immaculate, though he doubted she never used it, for whatever purpose it was intended to be used. Unless it was meant to merely be decoration, Jonathan assumed it had been cleaned rather thoroughly. Walking close to it made him grit his teeth, though, its appearance alone unsettling enough, so he hastily turned to glance at her desk instead.

He noted that it was incredibly organized, mostly empty other than a pen holder and a closed laptop. The drawers were locked, and there was only one folder not stored away, placed neatly off to the side.

The temptation to investigate the folder was too strong to fight off. Jonathan picked it up and skimmed through the papers inside. Page after page, he found profiles of various individuals, outlining information including names, ages and birthdays, occupations, proficiency with Avidea, relation to the culinary field, and notes on other special characteristics.

It did not take long for him to stumble across his own profile. The birthday field was left blank, and his age was listed incorrectly by a year. Other than that, much of the information was impressively accurate. This must be a collection of the people Larkin had a particular interest in bringing onboard for her ambitious endeavors. She did her research well.

He was about to put the folder down and prepare to leave, feeling extremely apologetic that he had infringed on her privacy. The gadgets behind the desk must be for one of her top secret projects that he had no business prying into. He needed to work hard to earn that honor, if she would ever consider him worthy of participating.

Then a name caught his eye. It was a mundane name. Very ordinary. Would not have stood out to him if but for one factor.

It was the name of the reputable nutritionist Victoria said the Rose Union had been looking for, for several months.

At the bottom of his profile, a note was written in red ink, while the rest of the information had been written in black or blue.

FAILED AND DISPOSED OF.

CHAPTER 20

Jonathan did not know how long he had stood there, frozen, staring at this ominous red remark. It was an undeniable fact that the nutritionist had been declared missing for a while. Was *he* disposed of? Or merely something belonging to him? What did Larkin have to do with this?

He flipped through the next couple of profiles, finding that they also had the same comment written in bleak capital letters.

Failure should not mean that someone needed to be eliminated. Was there a possibility he could end up failing too? What would happen to him if he did? He dropped the folder back onto the desk where he found it and glanced around the office, not sure if he could believe that anything insidious was happening here.

One more look. He promised himself to take no more than that. Maybe he was misunderstanding something, drawing a flimsy conclusion based only on a handwritten phrase. There were a few short bookshelves toward one side of the room, and the wall behind them was designed with rows of decorative panels. He sifted through a few books, then ran his gloved palm along the wall.

As the heel of his hand glided across the bottom corner of one of the panels, it pushed inward. He narrowed his eyes and pushed it farther with his finger, until it rotated and retracted inside to reveal a small nook. In the center of the back wall was a combination keypad.

Jonathan hesitated for a moment before pulling the panel back and making sure there were no obvious signs he had been there. He stepped outside of the office and pulled the door closed, but only right up to before the latch bolt clicked into place. Just because he was not a gambling man, that did not mean he should not do everything he could to keep his options open.

She might return to the lab tomorrow, and this might go nowhere at all. Maybe he should rethink his nosiness and get in contact with the Union team responsible for the case in the first place. This was not something he should be doing on his own.

After he finished his work and hurriedly returned to his hotel suite, he mulled over what he saw in that office. The moment he informed Victoria about this lead, she would send a whole team of Mercenaries to raid the lab. But what if Larkin was innocent and he ended up blowing things out of proportion? The investigation would be such a hassle for her, a smear on her reputation, and she might think him the ingrate he made himself to be.

But if she was hiding something sinister, Jonathan could not in good conscience stand by and do nothing. No matter what specialization a Mercenary decided to pursue, a License bound them to an obligation to fight crime. Beyond standard law enforcement, this powerful profession had always been one meant for the duty of maintaining justice and keeping the peace.

That did not make it easy to know when to act. If this took him down a foolish path, he needed something more concrete before he decided what to do.

As he ran himself through this deliberation several times over, he searched online, asking a series of questions about Lala Sweet that might divulge her relationships to other professionals in the field. He skimmed through articles, clicked on corresponding links, spaced out as nothing interesting stood out. Any of her scandals that he stumbled across were incredibly trite and inconsequential. Minor disagreements or deals that fell through with other generic names, events that had mishaps where the fault was placed on someone else, though he found nothing that specifically mentioned the missing nutritionist.

With a frustrated groan, he took out his phone and found his text thread with the mystery number.

Apologies, but do you happen to be talking about Lala Sweet?

He would take this chance over calling Victoria, who would demand more information this instant and assemble a team of Mercenaries to fly straight to Spectervale in the middle of the night. Over speaking with Elenora, who would worry endlessly about how he was doing, and then call Vicky for him, despite any protestations. Over contacting any of his other associates, who might either view him unfavorably as a gossip or overreact to rumors about a famous celebrity. Not expecting a quick response, if any at all, he put his phone down and stepped away to take a shower.

When he came out of the bathroom, with a towel around his waist and another to dry his hair, he reached over to press a button on his phone with little anticipation. The phone lit up, presenting a text notification in the middle of the screen.

Jonathan threw his hair towel off to the side and grasped the device in both his hands as he hurried to unlock it. There were extremely few people whose conversations would stir him to such excitement, and yet here he was, so giddy about the reply from a complete stranger.

This is a very specific question. Do you suspect something?

He bit his lip and frowned. The unknown contact did not rescind their warnings or apologize for the inconvenience of being a wrong number. There was a part of him that had hoped they would.

Maybe. I accessed her office and saw some weird things. Not sure what they mean.

A few minutes later.

Do you want to know more?

Did they even need to ask? He typed quickly, rewording a couple of times to avoid sounding too eager. *If it is worth knowing, yes. I think I might need a code to unlock something. I did not waste time trying to guess.*

The response was not immediate, and Jonathan grew fidgety. He glanced at the time at the top of the screen. Almost midnight. There were so many questions he wanted to ask them, mostly regarding what they knew about Larkin and how they came to know, though they did not seem the type to want to tell him anything so specific. Maybe he should look away, preoccupy his mind with anything else. But it was enough to resist the urge to text them again, never mind taking his eyes off his phone.

Look for Lala Sweet's first big success.

He stared at this message for a few seconds. A clue that was only marginally less cryptic than anything else this person had sent him. He typed his response, still wanting confirmation that this would lead him on a productive search.

Is this a hint for the code?

The next text came in impossibly fast. *ERROR: This number is no longer in service.*

With dark circles under his eyes, Jonathan began the next day hoping he appeared immersed in his research to any onlookers, but periodically, he would walk around the lab for no other purpose than to gauge his company. His quest would quickly be abandoned if he caught sight of too many other people here with him.

He could not help feeling a little disappointed that the lab was mostly empty today. The few other researchers or assistants that showed up did not stay for very long. He had no excuse to delay.

As he stood in front of Larkin's office door, his hand instinctively settled on his hip. He hoped the rapier, whose handle he felt underneath the fabric of his lab coat, would not be necessary, but he was comforted by the fact that he had brought it along. Before he reached out, he gave the adjacent hallways one last scan. Only when he was assured that no one was watching him did he tentatively push the doorknob, finding that it seemed to have been untouched since yesterday.

After he entered the room with dithering steps, he quickly glanced over toward the desk and those odd gadgets. Nothing appeared different about them. The floor creaked almost unnoticeably beneath his feet, and he halted, turning to look behind him. Pressing his lips together, he slowly closed the door and stood still for a few moments to calm down. He then moved with a little more urgency over to the wall near the bookshelves, each sound he made like a spasm to his skittish heart, and pried the panel open, exposing the keypad once more.

Over a decade ago, Larkin Swetnam became a national sensation almost overnight, when she entered a festival baking competition and wowed the judges with her first major recipe: astral chocolate cake. Otherworldly, the judges said. Devilishly delicious, she claimed. It was then that she took on her memorable stage name, showcased her lovable persona, and rapidly propelled herself to high acclaim with each new dessert or concoction that she presented to the Mercenary Triumph Board. She had no time to slow down. She steadily climbed the ranks within just a few years until she reached the top of culinary stardom, becoming one of the first gourmet Mercenaries to earn Emblems for major achievements, one after another.

Her influence began to open up the industry to many more questions about food and discovery. They might have been asked before, but now they were given serious consideration. After all, who could remember the first people to craft the recipes that were now so widespread and taken for granted in the modern day? Who could be credited for turning vegetables into chips, fruits into candy, nuts into butter? Lala Sweet revived a precedent in this generation, for fame and prestige to be awarded to Mercenaries who bravely hunted for bizarre ingredients beyond known animals and plants. After that day, she and others like her became an inspiration to all those who wanted to make a worldwide impact on how people consumed their food.

Jonathan entered the date of the festival into the keypad, and it beeped pleasantly. The tiny door that the keypad was affixed to swung open, and he found a switchboard behind it.

Most of the writing on the labels had faded, but one had been replaced and refreshed with new marker ink. "Lab 2," it read. It was the only one that had its switch shifted to the opposite side.

He knew he had already stepped far past the line being here at all. Maybe he had time to walk back over. Maybe this switch was designated only for an unused test lab, like the ones he had already been using. Maybe this futile curiosity would lead him to something hardly worth throwing his career and future opportunities away for.

There was a loud click as he pressed the switch. Remaining ignorant might doom him to sharing the same trajectory of hopelessness that Antoine had fallen down, and the possibility of that was not something Jonathan was prepared to endure.

The shelves next to him shifted as a section of the wall behind them creaked inward, a secret door. He peeked inside, seeing steps leading downward into absolute darkness. The banality of it did not fit everything else he knew of Lala Sweet, but he remembered the building was only one story tall, so if the keypad did not open to a safe like he initially had presumed, she had nowhere to build additional lab space but down.

Jonathan pushed the shelf aside enough for him to slip inside. On the other side of the door, there was a doorknob, and not far from the entryway, a light switch. A line of small light bulbs illuminated the stairs from overhead. He pulled the shelf as close to its original position as he could from the inside and shut the door behind him.

He slowly descended, nervously wondering what he would find down here. Lab 2 might be nothing more than a hub where she kept her ongoing developments before she went public with them, and the thought came packaged with a healthy dose of guilt. But he waved that notion aside. The missing nutritionist's profile and the messages from the now deactivated number both made it exceedingly difficult to believe.

Stopping right before he needed to turn the corner, he waited and listened. The likelihood that Larkin could also be here was slim, but there would be no talking his way out of this situation if she was. He had done his best to track who had come in and out today and saw no one heading toward her office, though he had yet to write off the possibility she might be the type to spend her entire nights in this basement.

The minutes passed quietly, and Jonathan dared to sneak a look. A short hallway led to double doors with small rectangular windows. He crouched down and scooted closer, pulling out his phone to use its camera. Holding it just past the bottom edge of one of the windows, he pointed the lens into the room and watched the screen. The angle was far from optimal, and he could not work around several blind spots no matter how he pointed his phone.

Seeing nothing immediately suspicious, he stood and pulled open one of the doors. The lights had been dimmed, so he narrowed his eyes to study the scene. He noticed first that it was bitingly chilly, as if he had walked into a massive refrigerator. Near the doors, he fumbled for another light switch, this time sliding it to turn up the brightness. Pallet racks neatly lined one side of the room, and a few workbenches and tables were scattered across the other half, with stacks of boxes covering nearly every surface. Next to another closed door near the back, he saw more transparent light containers and extractors, even bigger than those in her office. Compared to these devices, he would not have even taken notice of the mundanely standard lab instruments dispersed throughout the room if he had not made a point to sweep his gaze over every inch of it.

Satisfied that he was the only living being present, he put away his phone and walked farther into the lab. He began with the half of the room with the workbenches, nudging some of the boxes open to peer into their contents. Personal protective equipment wrapped in plastic bags, laboratory consumables, bottles of chemicals. Between two tables was a smaller desk, upon which was a worn notebook, many of its pages protruding from its bindings from passionate study.

Jonathan picked it up and riffled through the pages. A faint smile tugged at his lips from the aesthetically perfect handwriting. The first section was full of drawings and equations that made little sense to him, but he soon caught a glimpse of an intriguing phrase written near the top of one of the sheets of paper.

Avidea as an ingredient.

He stopped flipping and carefully read through the rest of the page, finding notes on how each grant class corresponded to their own flavors. Aura from the Condense class was described as spellbindingly sweet. Convert sat pleasantly somewhere between sour and bitter, Construct was exquisitely salty, Connect was savory with a kick, and Control was bland on its own until made to enhance the foods it was mixed into. All classes were noted to be delicious beyond any other ingredient found on planet Eduryae.

Fascinating. Jonathan had never thought to use Avidea as a component in his cooking. He had created food from his aura before, converting energy to molecules, but never kept the Avidea as pure concentrated energy to use as an ingredient. If it was as simple as injecting it into a mixture or a broth, he felt a little foolish that it had never crossed his mind. The beginnings of regret over not uncovering this sooner began to creep in. Larkin must have been using her own aura or enlisting the help of other grant users to lend her some of their energy. He continued to read.

Small amounts of Avidea evaporate quickly when separated from the body. Not easy to extract, unstable on its own.

The notes went on to explain how to identify the areas of the body that fueled an individual's Avidea, a method likely to work differently from the much rarer Warrant. That even though this precious life energy could be held in certain body parts like the hands and feet, it was in the vital organs that people usually contained the bulk of their aura. The diagrams drawn in the notebook transitioned from complex scientific schematics to illustrations of hearts, livers, and brains, complete with notes on where to make incisions for tidy removal.

His eyes widened. There was no way Larkin kept moving forward with her research after this. Surely she would have seen this as a dead end to her experiments.

With an expensive procedure and moderate likelihood of failure, body parts can actually be extracted and processed into substances without losing their Avidea.

His jaw dropped. His fingers hovered shakily over the corner of the page, terrified to see what more she had written.

Hypothesis: strong Avidea users who can provide large amounts of aura and recover it quickly can keep up with commercial demand without sacrificing available resources.

He closed the notebook and put it back down on the desk, hands still trembling. As his gaze panned up, he regarded those containers with new recognition. The soft glow, the unsettling feeling when he neared them. They were the remnants of debauched eduran energy.

Did he even want to look at the other side of the room? His expression contorted into a grimace as he walked closer to the racks.

A vague syrupy aroma began to fill his nostrils. He lifted his nose to get a better whiff. It was such an unnatural feeling, sniffing the air like this. His airways felt stuffy from lack of use, but a strong inhale rewarded him with a scent so sickening, a hand clasped over his mouth could not muffle his violent coughing. The fragrance was reminiscent of, yet also nothing at all like, the pleasant smell of his favorite milkweed tea.

No. It could not be possible. Though his eyes began to water, he rushed over to the racks, pushing aside boxes to find the source of the awful stench. He knew exactly what it came from, but still recoiled when he found it.

Jars, tall and wide, lined up one after another along a middle shelf on the rack. Labels with unrecognizable strings of letters written on them, until he came across the last name of the nutritionist. The labels were small and insignificant, unable to hide what the jars held within.

Congealed masses of blood. Flesh submerged in fluids. Organs.

He instinctively glanced down, having hoped to look away and steady himself, but the boxes in the bottom rack appeared suspicious too. His jaw was clenched as he pried one of them open, and inside was a freeze-dried, severed arm ready to greet him.

It was all he could do not to throw up right then and there.

Was this what it meant to be disposed of? Their body parts were still here, not completely destroyed, and yet there was no saving them. He wondered if search parties had been sent out for these people under different guilds or authorities, or if the public had already presumed them dead.

It could have been him. He could have been one of them. They had been lured in by their dreams, by their desires, by their devotion to their work. It was too late for all these names.

A new, ghastly thought formed itself in his mind. Larkin must have been feeding her tainted food, her latest creations, to others. Had she fed any to the people who ate at her restaurants? Maybe even at the Helix of Zest? He noticed nothing strange about those appetizers. Surely she could not have been as bold as to risk doing something so diabolical.

But she must have started feeding her transcended recipes to officials on the Triumph Board, for them to recognize her innovations and award her a total of three Emblems, the highest amount a Mercenary could earn. To earn her such prestige that very few chefs could compete. If experts had not detected the use of detached Avidea in her meals, who could?

At the same time, her notes hinted that the procedure to extract Avidea was not worth the cost for large-scale distribution. It was reasonable to conclude that at worst, she only used this forbidden ingredient for the most important of clients.

But that meeting was meant to impress him, maybe even to lure him in like the rest of them. Did she plan for his name to be the next on the missing persons' list? On a label on one of those jars?

Not knowing whether he had consumed someone else's illicitly harvested aura, contained in a morsel of eduran flesh, was a miserable conundrum. He gave the rest to Elenora. The dread gnawed viciously at him.

Pictures. What was he thinking? There was no time for panicking and acting squeamish when his objective to obtain concrete proof was now dire. Jonathan dropped his phone twice onto the tiled flooring before he opened the camera application and snapped some photos.

He retraced his steps to take a few pictures of the notebook too. He knew he flipped through pages, though with his frantic movements, he could not be sure if he skipped any of the most important ones, or if some of his images came out blurry.

Only one would be enough. One good picture. He could text it to Victoria as evidence for her to initiate a thorough investigation, maybe even escalate this to the Triumph Board. No signal down here. He needed to get back upstairs.

He slid his phone back into his pocket and arranged the notebook to how he recalled finding it. He had kept on gloves throughout his infiltration, so he did not need to worry that he left fingerprints. As he hurried back to the double doors, he saw a figure there waiting for him.

He stopped short, biting down the beginning of a surprised yelp.

Larkin.

She furrowed her brow as she stared at him, lips parted. Her irises darted around the underground lab before settling once again on him.

The corners of her mouth twisted up into a sneer, and the vacant look in her eyes did not match her smile.

"Say, I don't remember ever giving you a tour of this room."

CHAPTER 21

A HEAVY SILENCE LINGERED between them for many long seconds. Her cheerful disposition had been replaced by something forbidding and intimidating as she refused to take her eyes off him. He froze in place, as if her gaze had the power to hold him there.

"Well?" Larkin spoke first, her voice menacingly low. "What do you think you're doing here?"

"I... um." Jonathan did not know if there was anything that needed to be said. "I guess I accidentally stumbled across this room," he said pathetically, even while he barely managed to keep his voice from trembling.

"You're not a very good liar. Are you some kind of spy sent by one of my rivals?" she asked. "Tell me, who is it?"

"No one," he said, frowning. "You were the one who invited me to come here."

She only hummed in response, looking around the underground

lab with a displeased expression on her face. He flinched when she took a step closer to him.

"Either way, you didn't find this place by accident." Her glare petrified him. "I know my door's lock has been having some issues, but that's where the 'accidental stumbling' should've ended. Why did you go out of your way to do this?"

"The containers. . . the extractor," he said. "I did not mean to see them, but I was curious why you had those in your office."

"Ah, yes. Naturally, that means you must also look for a hidden entrance and trespass on someone's private business." She jerked her chin toward the back of the room. "What did you find that you weren't supposed to see?"

He could not steady his voice this time, stuttering over his answer and ultimately forming no real words.

"I really don't know why I even asked," she said, shaking her head and laughing to herself. "That's really unfortunate for you."

Jonathan hesitated, very slowly backing away from her. "Perhaps you will never forgive me, but I do sincerely apologize. I know my actions mean the end of our partnership, and I regret them."

Her cackle was harsh and grating. "Oh, you think we'll just part ways and that's it? No, I'm not letting you get past me. You saw everything, didn't you? You're planning to expose me to your Union."

"Please, Ms. Swetnam. We do not have to do this."

She cracked her knuckles and smirked. "Yeah, and what are you going to offer me to spare you? You'll lose nothing if you don't report me, but I'll lose everything if you do. Not really balanced stakes here, if you ask me."

His hand went to his hip, and he took longer strides to create distance, wary of what she might do. He would not stand a chance against a seasoned combatant like her while he had been years out of practice. Escape was his only priority.

"Why do you look so scared?" Larkin asked him, giving him a grin he knew was insincere. "I would've thought you'd be angry. How dare I act like you've slighted me when it looks like I'm the one who has committed the gravest sin? Isn't that right?" She leisurely walked toward him, holding out her hands. They began to glow a fiery orange from her aura. "I imagined being caught so many times, and I always thought I'd be met with at least a little bit of righteous fury."

Jonathan said nothing and stopped when he backed into one of the lab tables. He pulled out his rapier from under his lab coat, pointing it toward her.

"Hmm?" She let out another laugh. "And what are you going to do with that frail barbecue skewer?"

He responded by forming a giant serrated knife over his weapon. She only smirked.

"Please," he said again. "Maybe a part of you is remorseful if you think about being caught so often."

"You're not very good at reading people either. I think about it often because I'd love the chance to show that I can't be stopped. To snuff out the light of heroic eyes as they realize they can't take me down."

Those words gave him chills. "Are you going to continue this way for the rest of your life? If you. . ." He trailed off. If she succeeded in getting away with this, he did not want to think about what that meant for him.

"Why shouldn't I? What, do you think I'll just abandon my passion and turn myself in? That's as wishful as you can get," she said, scoffing. "I might have Ameza under my thumb now, but the rest of the world is still waiting for a taste of my culinary masterpieces."

He could not respond to that. As he stood there in his defensive stance, the crushing weight of realizing a role model he had adored for so long had corrupted herself beyond redemption was far too numbing.

"What's wrong? You still think you can stall this out through conversation?" she asked. "We both know this isn't a mere difference in understanding. We're not going to resolve this by talking. That's why nothing you saw will ever leave this lab."

As her palms joined together, the aura emanating from them stretched and expanded into the shape of a rolling pin. Tendrils from the handles kept her energy connected to her hands. One moment, the rolling pin grew to half the width of the lab, and in the next, she sent the form spinning down the room at him at incredible speed.

Harsh sounds of collision filled the room as the energy, dense with power, knocked tables and boxes out of the way. Smaller gadgets and bottles smashed onto the floor and shattered. The smell of the room grew more nauseating as the jars fell and broke. With little space to dodge, Jonathan lifted his blade to shield himself from the impact, but it quickly overwhelmed him and shoved him off his feet. A hoarse groan was wrenched from his throat when his back slammed forcefully into the rear wall.

Larkin dissipated the form as soon as it hit him, orange wisps fluttering up into nothingness. Having barely remained on his feet, he ignored the pain and dashed toward her, now that she had paved a clear path for him. She gasped and widened her eyes when he swung his oversized knife, leaning away to avoid it. Her visage seemed to reveal relief that she had dodged his attack, until he elongated the blade just enough to slice deeply into the arm she raised to protect herself.

Her sharp yell of pain was charged with vexation, even as the colorless version of her Avidea already began manifesting to heal her wound. She lifted her other hand, and the orange haze around it arranged itself into the mold of a multi-bladed dough blender.

"Glad to see you fighting back," Larkin snarled, swinging the blades down at him. "You won't be for long."

Jonathan blocked her first attack and ducked out of the path of the second. She was relentless, and on her third swing, the pastry cutter aura found purchase, gashing five parallel cuts down his shoulder and upper arm. He winced, trying to disregard the pain as he parried her subsequent attacks, all aggressive and devastating, most of them driving him to find new footing and pivot around her skilled maneuvers. The surroundings, even the pungent aromas, became a blur to him, instinct alone weaving him out of the way of tables, boxes, racks, and debris.

Physical metal clashed with tinted Avidea over and over, desperation on both sides compelling their strikes to grow in viciousness. He succeeded in leaving her with a few nicks, but the cuts she gave him in return were deeper and more expertly landed. If an average person had been a spectator to this fight, they would think he was losing to nothing at all, despite him being the one brandishing the titanic weapon. He closed the smaller wounds as soon as he could, and expended energy to prevent the others from bleeding too much.

He attempted to move himself out of her reach multiple times, to reset, because whenever they exchanged a series of blows, she reminded him how much more fearfully strong she was than he. It hurt his arms to strike back, and his parries became sloppier the longer he tried to delay his complete defeat.

But she would not allow him to recover. If he stepped out of range of her pastry cutter blades, she would mold her energy into huge balloon whisks from both her hands. They would stretch and lurch after him, like the heads of predators hungry for their prey. Once she willed them to spin, they did so turbulently, energy battering into equipment without care and making it nearly impossible for him to block. If he found a way to sneak closer and swing his sword at her, the whisks disappeared and she countered with her pastry cutter in a flash. He had thought the underground lab to be massive, but there was no room to run from her weapons. She could devour him from every corner, even while her aura needed to remain attached to her body.

When he found an opening to glance around, he realized that their melee, or rather the one-sided barrage of her attacks, had led them to circle each other. He was now closer to the double doors that led upstairs than she was.

If he tried to run, she would catch up in no time. Turning his back on her was guaranteed to doom him.

Jonathan reached to grab the post of the rack closest to the doors and yanked hard. The fatigued muscles in his arm screamed in pain as he exerted more strength than his body could handle, but enduring it was trivial in his urgency to create an obstacle to hinder her. The rack and its contents came crashing down between them. He ran toward the doors.

"Oh, so you think this is your chance to escape?" Larkin called after him from the other side, a taunt more than a question.

He looked back to see her jump onto the overturned rack, an impressive athletic feat if it had not been so alarming. She raised her arm, her Avidea now mimicking a large rubber spatula. He did not have the chance to push open the door when his vision blurred, and he flew to slam into the side wall instead.

Having narrowly braced himself against the impact, he struggled to his feet and turned to find her. Her other hand was now surrounded with yellow aura, and it formed into an enormous ball. He frowned, and in that moment of hesitation, her spatula propelled the ball straight at him, leaving him nowhere to go.

Avidea energy in its rawest, most untinted form flowed like air, but as this yellow mass closed around him, its consistency reminded him of dough. Larkin commanded her spatula to fold it once, twice, wrapping him snugly in it so he could not move.

The sword in his hand turned into the simple metal shape of a dough scraper, its size to match the amount of dough that encased him. He pushed upward, meeting formidable resistance, but he cut through a slit of an opening. He shoved one side of the dough wider, until it was enough for him to pull himself free.

No wonder she had been able to abduct subjects for her experiments. How frightening it was to have one of the strongest people in the nation stray from using their abilities for society's advancement and fall down the wrong path instead.

A wretched yell that did not sound like his own rang in his ears, but all he could perceive in front of him was hopelessness. Why was it so easy for her to take lives, to take his life, and so agonizing for him to fight for it? When she moved to block the doors, he lunged at her, and for once, she did not react in time to keep him from thrusting his scraper right down her torso. A critical wound.

She was still standing, though. There was no laughing off the durability of a top-tier Mercenary. He scrambled to evade the dough she sent after him again. With her focus now entirely on immobilizing him, he was able to leave her with a couple more serious lacerations down her face and arm. He needed her to yield her control of his only escape route, even if he had to climb over her collapsed body to get to it, but her determination to ensnare him was unwavering.

The time limit on his ability approached fast. When Jonathan backed up to refresh his Avidea around the rapier for another attempt to bring her down, the shell around the blade shattered into pieces. He tried to conjure some type of blade, anything, to give his weapon a proper edge to ward off her attacks, but the metal only lasted one second before flaking off into nothingness.

He looked up, eyes wide, and for a fleeting moment, Larkin wore a smirk.

"You've been a nuisance long enough," she muttered. She seemed to be reinvigorated despite her significant injuries.

He strained to fend off the ensnaring ball of dough with the thinner blade, but without a wide cutting edge, his efforts were futile. He could cut himself out maybe one or two more times, but in this fight, he was the one exhaustion crept up on first.

His eyelids were heavy as the aura circled him, and for all his panic, the pliant substance it imitated felt tender and soft, as if inviting him to finally rest his aching muscles. The struggle to escape hardly seemed worth it anymore, and his movements slowed entirely as he watched Larkin approach. The annoyed expression on her face morphed into one of gratification. He could not muster the strength to plead with her or glare in defiance as she lifted her hand, no aura around it, and everything faded into black.

Jonathan had gone on vacation with his parents once, and then never again. He had been in his early teens at the time, and though his folks had claimed they were finally stepping away from their elite duties for a break, it had ended up a business trip anyway.

It was a vacation, an ill-advised sort, to Sorense. The under-ground city. The origin and favored residence of those with grim characteristics.

He could not remember if he had been bored the entire trip, or if there had been activities and sights to entertain him. He could not remember if the time spent with his parents had been meaningful or only for appearances. He could only see one scene from that trip right now. Was this a memory? Was it a fabrication of his mind, in its state of distress?

A group of Spectrals had surrounded him, baring their teeth and grinning deviously. Even when he knew he stood no chance, he had tried to resist. He had tried to fight. They had restrained him with ease. When he had seen the ravenous look in their eyes as they peered down at him, all he could do was silently beg for a chance to escape. Before they hurt him. Before they killed him.

Were they the type of Spectrals who could summon fire and burn him alive? Or would they torture him with debilitating sickness or crushing emotions of misery until he became a hollow husk of himself, to throw away once they had their fun? Or maybe they would simply trap him in the nightmare realm, where his mind would be made to suffer eternally, ignorant of what they did to his lifeless physical body.

"We're not killers," one of them had said. "We just like a little mischief, don't you?"

"Yeah, you'll be alright, kid," another had chimed in. If they had wanted to sound reassuring, they did not succeed. He now remembered their words like a threat. "You'll just have to learn how to live differently from now on."

And so, he had been turned by the kind of Spectrals with the ability to do so, the stone-lunged and bloodthirsty variety.

The scene around him began to flicker, changing too rapidly for the visuals to sink in. The imagery of his parents turning their backs on him. The dark loneliness. The confusion and helplessness. The feeling of powerlessness that had been new to him, yet now seemed so familiar.

Day and night had cycled by as he stumbled through the wilderness, and no matter how long he had walked through endless arrays of towering trees, he never felt the sensations of hunger and thirst. He had only walked and walked, not needing to stop to eat or drink. He had lost his appetite, anyway, when he awoke on some days to find that he had plunged his face into the broken carcass of some wild animal. At the time, he did not understand how he managed to catch any of those unfortunate creatures, having been a spoiled brat raised in wealth and luxury, but he learned. He had no choice.

Eventually, the city had become visible in the distance. With the yearning to return home, he had kept mindlessly walking toward it. As soon as the dirt path had given way to paved streets, he collapsed and fainted.

When he came to, he had been taken into the care of an older couple. For several days, he could not answer their questions; everything before he lost consciousness had become a distant haze. He had spent those days piecing together incomplete memories and finding a conclusion to land on.

He had told them that he had been kicked out of his home and convinced himself that was the truth.

"Do you know if my parents were Spectrals?" he had asked Victoria many years later.

She had looked at him strangely, because the question had come out of nowhere. They were only relaxing together at a local park and enjoying the fresh air.

"You know what? I'm not sure. I just know my side of the family sure isn't," she had said with a laugh.

That had been his sole curiosity at the time, so he had thought to leave the conversation there.

She had not. "We were so young then, so I don't really remember what happened to you when you no longer attended our family events."

"They had disowned me, so I went my own way," he had told her, and sincerely believed it.

She had given him an expression like she doubted him, like she had been told something else, but it disappeared when she shrugged. "Well, Uncle became very sick and passed away. Auntie followed him soon after. Imagine my surprise when I found you were alive and doing alright. What a tragedy, that they weren't able to see you again."

He had not understood why she said that. His parents had turned their backs on him and continued to enjoy their high-class lifestyle without their son, and if they had talked about him at all, it was surely to speak poorly of him. So, he had never wanted to know about them and was curious about nothing except why he was the only Spectral in the remaining Tessier family.

They must have worried themselves to illness over his disappearance. Why did he think that they had abandoned him? The scenes that played before him, how much of them could he rely on to be true?

And why was he remembering it all now? No, he knew why. He had always hated the feeling of being vulnerable, of losing control, having thought it was merely a facet of his natural personality. When the gang of Spectrals had cruelly altered his physiology against his will and forced a younger version of himself to deal with unsettling hungers, there was nothing he could do.

When Larkin fought to keep him from leaving her underground lab after he found evidence of her atrocious crimes, the inability to even defend himself became a mirror that reflected those lost memories.

Those Spectrals and others like them must have carried on with their devilry long after they let him go, with no one to catch and stop them.

She must have induced that very same hopeless fear in all her other victims before robbing them of their dignity and their lives.

Her actions were unforgivable, but what was he going to do about it?

CHAPTER 22

MEMORIES THAT WERE ONCE HAZY and jumbled together began arranging themselves back into their proper places.

The first to regain clarity was the moment Jonathan opened that notebook. Fragments of notes and the vague shapes of corresponding diagrams flashed through his mind in turn.

Maybe he had taken what he read out of context, depriving himself of the chance to see another explanation for the contents of Larkin's secret lab. Users of Avidea agreeing to donate their bodies to her research should the worst happen to them made the situation more agreeable. An honorable contribution after death. She would be using their generosity to pioneer scientific discoveries that benefited everyone.

The labels on the jars and their contents resurfaced to join this train of thought. Then it was the missing nutritionist's profile. Months of work on this case with very little progress culminating in Victoria's sighs of frustration. If the news had reported the man as having passed away from natural causes, she might have been spared a few sleepless nights. Though she had not given up, he was sure she had felt the sting of failure looming overhead.

Larkin's reaction emerged from the fog. The way her eyes flared when she saw him there, her body tensed and closed off as he tried to talk things through, her undying determination to corner him. They both knew there was no angle that she could spin everything in that room to make it right, even if she had used willing participants, to incorporate their donations into experiments conducted in a lab centered around food and creating new recipes. The public would panic. She would better mitigate risk ensuring he never left to tell anyone at all.

As the pieces realigned themselves back into a coherent picture, he remembered one final thought right before she had knocked him out. That he never expected to open his eyes again, and being able to recall that notion would have been hilarious if not for what it implied.

Gritting his teeth through the dull pain that greeted his body as soon as he opened his eyes, he quietly gave his vision a few seconds to adjust. The room he saw before him was significantly smaller than the underground lab, and dimmer too. The walls lacked windows and proper paint, and only one side of the room featured a single plain door.

She had her back turned to him and seemed to be preoccupied with something at one of the workbenches, a version of those he saw in the lab scaled down to fit in this room. An occasional metallic clink broke up the silence between them as she worked. In one of the corners behind him, his sword, wallet, and phone had been tossed into a pile. When he squinted, he could see that a hole had been pierced clean through the device.

The only other thing in this barren room was the chair he was sitting in, to which she had tied his hands behind his back with a coarse rope. His ankles were similarly secured to the legs of the chair, as if she could not be careful enough.

His tattered lab coat had been removed, leaving behind a matching pattern of rips in the dress shirt he had worn under-neath. The fabric draped wide in several spots where she had cut deep, exposing the evidence of his injuries. He imagined he looked awful with all the wounds he had sustained from the neck up.

Jonathan glanced back over at her, noticing that the air in the short distance between them appeared murky, contaminated with particles that seemed to dance in the air with more purpose than regular dust. It was then that he noticed the thin tendril of her faint orange aura stretching upward from her body.

Above his head floated the large shape of a flour sifter, its hand press moving rhythmically to fill the room with its contents. It seemed she modeled her Convert class aura to mimic a medley of baking mixing methods, but he could not figure out what this one was supposed to do.

He debated whether he should call her attention to the fact that he was conscious. Maybe she expected him to remain subdued for as long as this ability was active, and giving away how he bypassed it was another advantage he did not want her to take from him.

Before he could decide, Larkin turned to glance at him first. His heart raced when they made eye contact, but her brow only lifted in gratified surprise and a smile formed on her lips.

"Ah, you're finally awake?" she asked, answering his unspoken question. Her tone of voice rang pleasantly, as if she was only encountering an old friend and asking how he was doing.

He kept his eyes lidded, just in case.

"I thought I went overboard and accidentally killed you," she continued. "You weren't breathing when I checked. But then you started murmuring in your sleep, so that was a relief." She let out a giggle like she found the situation endearing.

"Are... are you going to kill me now?" he asked, his voice barely a whisper.

She chortled. "What a waste that would be. No, I'm not squandering away your potential before I've run a full scheme of experiments on you."

He frowned, but he made sure to avoid sharp movements. "Why are you doing this?"

"You sure put up a good fight. I'm going to have to see a healer for these scratches you left me," she said. "But you should've known you couldn't beat me, and you can forget about escaping altogether." She pointed up at the sifter before turning back to her tinkering. "That dampens the Avidea abilities of everyone who inhales the particles. Except for me, of course."

Jonathan said nothing in response, because she did not answer him.

"Oh, and let's talk about the state of my lab," she said, shaking her head and exhaling a breathy laugh. "You were my most expensive catch, so you best bet I'm going to make this investment count."

"Why are you doing this?" he repeated.

She had the nerve to look at him with feigned innocence. "What do you mean?"

When she turned, he saw that the small device in her hand held a suspicious resemblance to the menacing head of the extractor he found in her office. He winced and let out a groan. "No amount of fame or wealth could possibly be worth knowing how many lives you destroyed."

"You sure had plenty of time to snoop around. If only you hadn't poked your nose in my business, I would've played the part of your role model a little longer," she said. "I made the right choice destroying that phone of yours."

"Yet you want to spare a witness. What if I find a way to leak what I saw?"

Larkin scoffed. "As in, to the Union? And what are they going to do without solid evidence? Trespass? No Mercenary is powerful enough to be above the law, and most certainly not your mediocre colleagues."

"What if they look for me? Some people know I came to work for you."

"So?" she asked. "How hard could it be to claim you died in action while we were out hunting some dangerous beast? It happens to people in our line of work all the time. Give it a few years, and they'll forget you existed."

He did not know how much longer he could stand to listen to her.

"And let them come if they want to. I'll definitely remember you as my favorite if you can lure more test subjects into my grasp."

At this point, he should cease all efforts to find any dots to connect. He simply wore a scowl as she emptied her hands and turned to face him. They maintained eye contact as she crossed her arms and leaned back against the workbench.

"If you're so curious, I'll tell you," she said. "After all, it's no fun having to keep a secret for so long and not being able to tell it to anyone even once."

He looked away. Why did he care when she was planning to ruin his life?

His reaction seemed to make her more eager to tell him.

"No, listen. I did great work for the culinary industry for years, finding the rarest and most delicious ingredients in the world," she began. "When that knowledge spreads, other chefs catch up to you fast. I mean, that's how I survived too, on the shoulders of those who came before me. But once you've reached that limit as a top gourmet, you end up getting stuck in this tedious copycat game."

The familiar beginning of her story caught his attention, but he kept his eyes averted.

"I always felt that wasn't enough. That there had to be a way to transcend the status of top chef to ultimate greatness. And I wasn't alone," she said. "I discovered that my competitors were starting to inject concentrated Avidea into some ingredients. The science behind it was still too rudimentary to be lucrative, but the flavors were rumored to be legendary."

He peeked to catch her looking up at the ceiling, as if ready to reminisce about nothing more than a fond memory.

"I first tried with my own. You know, the Convert class was supposed to work well for this. We're typically able to keep our aura in its purest energy form the longest. But even for me, it was draining. I'd lose days of valuable research time recovering and fall behind in the race.

"So, I began researching how to extract energy from ordinary people with the basic aptitude for using Avidea. I didn't harm them, but I guess that doesn't matter now. Not after I realized I needed more powerful users to make real progress. Unfortunately, I still couldn't take the energy integrated with their bodies without taking their lives as well."

She paused and looked at him. Surely that was not the conclusion of the story. He scowled, waiting for her to continue.

Another laugh escaped her. "I hope you're not too mad at me. After all, I'm not the first or the only one to do this."

"How long have I been one of your targets?" He recalled his own profile in her folder.

"Ah, right." He envied how delighted she seemed to be with her lighthearted tone of voice and frequent bouts of laughter. "I might have lied to you a little. I researched your involvement with the Union before ever coming to your restaurant. Think about it. What's a better sustainable source of Avidea than a Mercenary?"

Being forced to entertain such a distorted perspective caused a shudder to run through him.

"And you were the perfect candidate. Relatively new in the culinary space, eager for opportunities, and skilled with Avidea.

Not to mention that our partnership could've given me more influence over the Union, which means more access to other Mercenaries and flexibility in my plans. All I had to do was lure you with this offer and put you in a position to supply me with your Avidea for as long as I needed. Until I figured out how to keep it from evaporating away from the body."

She leaned forward, and though she was nowhere close to touching him, he recoiled back as far as he could in the chair.

"Wouldn't that have been what you wanted?" she asked. "You could've been the hero to help stop the massacre of innocent lives. You could've been the reason we reached the pinnacle of flavors, Mr. Tessier."

His name sounded revolting on her tongue, and he refused to dignify her absurd question with a response.

"Your nosiness skipped us a few steps in my charade, so here we are. I couldn't afford to let you slip away, so you'll just have to do what I want now." She picked up the portable extractor device and grinned at him. "Even with your power dampened, you can release the raw form of your energy for me to harvest, can't you? Why don't we give it a trial run?"

"Why would I ever do that for you?" His words came out like a snarl, which earned yet another chuckle from her.

"You'll want to do this willingly," she told him. "Rather than force me to use methods that leave you no choice but to obey me."

He only stared at her defiantly, counting in his head.

More than five minutes had passed since she noticed he had woken up. Jonathan watched as Larkin's eyes began to droop.

She did not seem to realize her eyelids were becoming heavier until she stumbled in trying to approach him.

Her gasp was sharp. "What did you. . . do?" she drawled, with all the intent to glare at him, before her legs wobbled and gave out, and she collapsed onto the floor.

A wave of fatigue washed over Jonathan, and he wanted nothing more than to close his eyes and rest. But he had no time to spare before Larkin would regain consciousness. If he was lucky, he had maybe a couple of minutes to act.

A naïve, younger Jonathan had only ever wanted to create scents like lavender and jasmine to soothe, the smells of home-cooked meals to inspire, and the aromatics of garlic and herbs to entice.

Instructors kept telling him that he could not just produce smells with his Avidea and expect them to be useful in battle. They questioned the validity of manifesting aromas and argued that nebulous scents were not a physical object to be worth mis-spending his energy.

He had been a stubborn youth, even in his early twenties. He claimed with great confidence that his ability to create molecules powerful enough to influence the people around him without their knowledge was the right choice. So, they convinced him to practice conjuring the scents of stomach-churning delicacies to stun his opponents and hazardous gases to harm his enemies. Complying with his instructors' suggestions gave him more options with the ability and put an end to his naysayers.

And though he practiced filling a room with the gas that evaporated from chloroform countless times, it was an entirely different matter doing so without an implement to aid him. Beads of sweat rolled down his forehead from the effort he exerted to put Larkin out of commission for a sliver of a chance to escape.

His sore muscles felt as if they were going to burst as they tensed up again, this time with the image of that charm shop in his mind. The shopkeeper laughing at his incompetence, regarding him as if he was a silly amateur for needing her bracelet to form a simple knife. A fire seemed to sear through his veins.

And then it was there, in his palm. A measly thing, hardly even a fruit knife, but a blade nonetheless. He ignored the protests of his body as he folded his wrist around and worked to slide the blade back and forth against the ropes that bound his hands together. In his frantic urgency to free himself, he nicked his own skin a few times, but he barely noticed the pain.

Strand by strand, the rope frayed apart, and he groaned as his arms were released from their unnatural position. He grunted as he flopped forward, using the knife to saw through the ropes around his ankles as well. The utensil disintegrated into expended energy as soon as the blade broke through the last strand of the final rope.

When he tried to stand, his legs quivered underneath him, and a wave of panicked fear washed over him. He could not spare any time hobbling like a newborn deer if he regarded his life as worth preserving. If Larkin caught him again, even if she somehow let another oversight slip past her, he would faint from energy depletion first.

He stumbled over to the corner of the room to pick up his wallet, rapier, and broken phone. His hands confused themselves between scrambling to put the smaller articles away in his pockets and opening the door, which fortunately had not been locked.

Unfortunately, he did not find himself back in the massive and frigid underground lab. A hallway greeted him instead, and he threw away time running down a few of the branching corridors that led to nowhere. She was going to wake up any moment now, and she was going to find a confused little rat scurrying about for her to stomp out for good.

Crates blocked his way as he hurried down a new hallway. Really, it was his sloppy running that had him tripping over them when they were too small to obstruct most of the corridor. He gritted his teeth as the loud rattling filled his ears and he stood, pushing forward without looking behind him.

Finally, one of the doors he shoved open with increasingly unhinged agitation reunited him with the secret lab. All he had to do was go through those double doors, up the stairs, through the secret entrance back into her office, and out of the lab to reach safety.

A clattering sounded from the hallway he had just left, with the fury of Larkin's voice following soon after. She still might be disoriented from the effects of his ability, but she was awake. If he tried to leave now, he would never make it in time.

Jonathan dove under some of the workbenches, upon which boxes and debris from their fight had been piled to form a canopy that hid him from view. He pushed into the tunnel of debris as far as he could go and curled himself into a ball. Had he any breath to hold, he would be willing to nearly asphyxiate himself to ensure she did not catch him.

Thudding footsteps indicated her arrival, if her vexed mutterings were not enough of an announcement. He grimaced as the collisions of racks and broken equipment ground against his eardrums, and he could picture her madly yanking objects out of her way.

She let out a piercing growl of obvious exasperation. "Did you actually escape?" she called out angrily. He stayed absolutely still, hoping she continued to remain ignorant that he could hear her.

"I can't believe. . ." Her voice trailed off as she seemed to walk away from where he was hiding, toward the double doors that led back to the ground floor.

Minutes ticked by in silence before he crawled back out. His extremities tingled either with numbness or extreme trepidation, he could not really tell. He knew his hope of evading her only stayed afloat because she had no idea how much time had passed since she collapsed, and her aggravation drove her to rush upstairs instead of thinking he would still be here. The main lab aboveground was a much bigger space. As long as he could make it out of her office without her retracing her steps, he would have a better chance of sneaking outside.

He stepped quietly through the secret lab until he reached the double doors, stopping to listen for any abnormal noises. When he heard nothing, he walked through, his heartbeat ringing in his ears and distorting his ability to gauge his surroundings. Realizing this made him more anxious about every sound—his own footsteps and rustling clothing included—which in turn did little to help him pull himself together.

The door at the top of the stairs had been left open, the bookshelf that had once blocked the way now thrust aside. He hurried out of her office after scouting it a cautious number of times.

Relief teetered like a flickering flame when he saw that the hallways outside her office were empty. She could be searching any of the rooms in this lab, suppressing her apparent anger around any potential occupants and maybe even the urge to break more expensive equipment. The surface portion of the lab would always be meant for appearances, the kind that lured in fools like him.

Every corner, every new corridor, every door he had to walk past, Jonathan looked every which way to map out his next best course of action. Several times, he was convinced he would turn around to see her there, locking eyes on him and preparing to drag him back down into that dingy room.

But he somehow made it outside. The path he took to reach the front lobby and its automatic doors was nothing more than a blur to him as the colors of the city greeted him once more. He cared very little for the spectrum of Spectervale as he dashed down the street, disregarding the stares he earned from passersby.

A shopping center came into view, and he barged inside, darting directly toward the nearest public restroom. He did not attempt to plead with his speeding heart to calm down until he shut and latched the stall door, the cramped, filthy space an unlikely comfort for his frazzled nerves.

He could hear people coming in and out of the restroom, the sounds as they did their business and washed their hands a cycle of normalcy he leaned on to sort his thoughts. Should he gaze upon his situation from the outside, he would have laughed at his pathetic state. But more importantly than that, there was no way she could find him in here, right?

He lost count of how many people had come in and left before his heart steadied enough, before his legs could carry his body upright again. His hands shook as he unlatched the stall door and feebly requested the first visitor of the restroom willing to take pity on him to let him borrow their phone. His eyes avoided the giant mirror that would confirm his appearance and remind him of the fate he had narrowly dodged.

The dread was so painfully familiar, now that he remembered everything. Perhaps having already gone through something like this was how he remained sane enough to have formed a plan in an otherwise hopeless situation. But having the reality of it catch up to him here, his body sought refuge back in the same stall as he waited. Waited until he was certain he had waited long enough.

A cab greeted him right outside the shopping center. He hated to think what it would do to him if it had not been parked there, if it had driven off without him, even though he had requested the driver to stand by until he was able to board.

The driver said nothing when Jonathan slipped into the vehicle, not even to comment on his tattered outfit. Mercenaries used these services all the time, and it would not be strange to see one of them looking worse for wear after one of their excursions. He did not doubt that was what the driver assumed had happened to him, as he silently sat in the passenger seat. After being taken to the airport to catch a private charter back home, it took hours for him to get comfortable on the plane. He sat tensely, his mind plagued with the replaying of events from inside Larkin's lab until he could no longer ward off his exhaustion.

CHAPTER 23

Going to the Taverne, where he would be reminded of the day he met Larkin, was out of the question. When he arrived back in Silver Valley late in the day, Jonathan called another cab to take him straight to his apartment building instead.

At some point, he must have showered and cleaned his wounds, because he only remembered finding himself staring up at the ceiling while lying on his bed in a shirt and pajama pants.

Late the next morning, he woke up in a cold sweat, his mind convinced that she was here and about to break down his apartment door. He stayed inside and wasted the day away in idle apprehension.

On the day that followed, the day he was originally scheduled to check out of the hotel in Spectervale, he still could not leave his apartment. Anything he had lost by not going back to that room was beyond his concern, and easy to replace.

He found sufficient courage to step near his unit's windows on the day after that. As he looked vacantly over the city and its gray geometric buildings, he knew Elenora was waiting for him to return to the restaurant. She might have already tried to message and call him. He could not bring himself to face her yet.

An anger began to burn inside him when he got out of bed the following morning. Where it had once been directed at Larkin for her unforgivable crimes, he now aimed it at himself. In a moment of weakness, he yelled out deep from his throat, balled up his fist, and slammed it against the wall dividing his bedroom from the rest of the unit. As the flesh under his pinky finger stung, he stewed in the self-loathing that he had not been strong enough. That he had fallen for her tricks. That he had revered so highly a horrible representation of culinary eminence.

Eventually, he willed himself to get dressed in at least a hoodie and sweatpants to leave his apartment, anxiety and disappointment clashing inside his stomach in a nauseating mixture.

He knew he could not wallow in self-pity forever, holed up in his home like a rat that barely escaped death. The chances of Larkin coming to the capital to find him were slim. She would better spend that time seeking out her next unsuspecting victim.

Instead of heading to the Taverne, though, he took a cab to the Rose Union. He wanted to let off some steam, so he needed to fetch something from his underutilized office at the guild. The building itself was a block of white concrete, black accents, and red window frames, only three stories tall but sufficiently wide and long enough to house all of its functions. Its most defining feature, a humongous white sculpture of a rose, sat on top of the building's flat roof and broadcasted the guild's name to all who could behold it.

Jonathan walked inside to the lobby, where there were kiosks to submit requests for Mercenaries and prospective adventurers to fulfill, and cozy waiting areas. To his right were the restrooms and a few meeting rooms for clients to meet with their representatives, and directly in front of him was the receptionist desk that usually went unattended.

A restricted entrance permitting only registered Union members to pass led to a computer room, a library, a common room, a mini kitchen, and three smaller conference rooms. He walked down the hallway to the stairs that ascended to the second floor, where permanent Mercenaries of the guild had individual offices and guest Mercenaries could use the desks available in an open central area past the staff restrooms.

He unlocked the door to his office and walked inside. The building was well-ventilated for the benefit of everyone else, so he figured it was his imagination that made him think the room felt stale from neglect. He approached his desk and opened a few drawers, trying to remember where he stored all that he used to access his perks as a Union courier.

Silver Valley was particularly known for its academies on Avidea and a special stadium where grant users could participate in combat matches for an enthusiastic audience or sweat it out in state-of-the-art training rooms. Jonathan wanted to use one of the latter to vent his frustrations, and he knew he kept the card that granted him discounts to rent a room somewhere inside his desk.

A gruff voice interrupted his search. "What a surprise to see you here." Jonathan looked up to see his uncle standing at the door.

He never really saw the man named Zachary Tessier as his family. Victoria's father usually worked on the top floor with his direct reports, and it was his office that Jonathan was meant to inherit once he retired. The man had always been more of a distant boss to him, maybe a mentor at most. Back when he worked more diligently at the Union, Jonathan was left to handle his own, unbothered. Even years away from the guild had not been enough to invite his uncle to get on his case for any disciplinary action.

"Hello, Uncle Zachary," Jonathan said, nodding, eager to go back to searching for his stadium discount card.

"Have you looked at yourself in the mirror lately?" Zachary asked. If he had not meant for the question to be condescending, him looking more dapper and fresh in his late fifties than Jonathan did almost three decades younger did not help.

"Yes, I sure have."

"That restaurant gig you decided to distract yourself with is wearing you down. Are you sure this is what you wanted?"

What Jonathan wanted was to argue. About how there was nothing wrong with being passionate and dedicated to his restaurant. How his sunken cheeks and dark eyes were not the result of working hard for the sake of the Taverne. How he would like his uncle to quit implying that he should instead devote his life entirely to Mercenary work.

Though what would be the point? Was there anything left at

the Taverne that he still wanted? He had always yearned for recognition, for his talent now and for pioneering major culinary discoveries later. He would not be satisfied with the same things Elenora wanted. But now he saw that recognition faded over time, faster than he knew. He could give everything to keep up with the grueling pace of the industry, just to find himself at the crossroads of that fateful decision. One that Larkin made and was bent on never regretting, one that Antoine had yet to fall to merely due to his ignorance.

"You say that like being a Mercenary is any easier," Jonathan said, frowning. "Did you not also chase an ambition in your youth that ate away at your health and sanity? Just to be a glorified errand boy?"

The corner of Zachary's mouth twitched. "Is that how you truly feel about being a Mercenary? Jonathan, my boy. If you cannot see how grand it is to be a powerful warrior, an expert of magic and conquest, I pity you."

"No one here is an expert at anything. Not when there is always someone out there better than you. Stronger than you. Have you never faced crushing defeats before? Times when you felt like the despairing eyes of death were staring at you in the face? Or maybe even when death felt like a better option than surviving in disgrace?"

He knew he was being dramatic again. How he wished he could tell his uncle what was going on. One defeat so insurmountable that his dreams no longer had a vibrant flame igniting them, and he became so hopelessly disillusioned with them.

But he could hear Zachary telling him that this was a serious accusation against a fellow Mercenary. Advising him to get solid evidence before they could spur others in the Union to act.

Still, the older man appeared to soften his demeanor, the crease in his eyebrows loosening. "There must be something that is plaguing you," he said. "I know we may not be close, but talk to me, boy."

Jonathan scolded himself for getting carried away with his ranting and hesitated. "It is not anything worth getting upset over," he lied, an act he did so rarely. "I apologize. There are times I feel inadequate and helpless, that is all." A truth to balance the fib.

"What do you mean?" Zachary did not let him off easy.

"My Avidea. My skills as a Mercenary," Jonathan confessed. "I went down the path of hunting for rare ingredients in dangerous places, and that led me somewhere I was not equipped to handle."

The head of the Union let out a breathy laugh. "You are a talented grant user, Jonathan, even better than my own daughter. But I always thought you devoted too little time to growing your talent. You never stuck to training long enough to reach your potential."

"Well, that is why I came here. I am going to rent a room at the Ascension Stadium to work on my Avidea."

Zachary grinned widely. "I am glad to see you taking this seriously. The sooner you are ready to take over, the sooner I can start all the vacations I have planned."

Jonathan looked down at the next drawer in hopes that the card would be inside.

"Just a reminder for you," his uncle said, causing Jonathan to lift his chin again. "Whether it was a strong beast or a powerful opponent that you lost to and began feeling this way, I care not. But I want you to remember that your strength as a Construct is not in your suitability for combat. There are very few objects you can create with your energy that are better weapons than wielding that energy as the other classes do."

"I know that."

The man continued on without pause. "No doubt there are Constructs out there able to manifest weapons so powerful they would make me sound like a fool right now, but the strength of your class generally lies in its versatility. The greatest heists of all time, the greatest schemes hatched by masterminds, were all made possible because of Construct mastery."

"Thrilled to know I am destined to be a schemer," Jonathan said dryly, even though he knew what Zachary meant. Conjuring physical objects like fake copies and counterfeit credentials to trick people would only be possible with his grant class. The advice would be significantly more appreciated if his enemy was not also a grant user who would know what he was planning.

His uncle chuckled. "You may not think to use your skills for deceit, but consider how you might avoid head-on confrontation, or how you might maneuver your weaknesses by remembering that the objects you create are independent of you, and they no longer exist as mere energy."

Jonathan thought back, reluctantly so, to when Larkin shaped her energy into a sifter near the top of that tiny room. The special effect of her ability could only hamper his Avidea, energy against energy, if he had breathed it in. But what he had created did more than that. He had assembled a dangerous chemical at the molecular level that manipulated the state of her body and caused her to faint.

Could she have achieved a similar outcome with her Convert aura had she been even more powerful? Possibly. If there had been anything he learned during his Avidea lessons, it was that limits were a funny thing when it came to an individual's unique magic. Some people chose abilities with numerous intentional restrictions to drive up their potency, while others seemed to steadily grow their magic without end.

He finally found the card and held it up. "Thanks for the advice," he said to his uncle. "I will keep it in mind."

Zachary gave him an encouraging pat on his back as he made to leave his office. "Do not feel bad about not being the strongest. That does not detract from what you do have. You have the brains to run this establishment, and as long as you strive toward your own potential, I am not worried about you," he said. "And I will still be around to guide you for many years to come."

Jonathan was glad for a fleeting moment that Victoria had agreed to help him run this place.

Once his uncle let him leave, he took another cab to the stadium and rented out one of its training rooms. Each of these facilities was provisioned with mats and padded walls, punching bags, reinforced dummies designed for use with grant powers, standard workout equipment, and a small indoor obstacle course. Without the perks program, having to book a room like this for even a few hours would financially set him back at least a couple of weeks.

He began with some stretches in the middle of the matted area, warming up his body so his muscles would scream less as he accustomed himself to moving around again. Keeping fit enough to wait tables and handle a meal rush was one thing, dodging for his life and matching the pace of a seasoned combatant was another.

The sweat was already flowing abundantly as he switched to focusing his aura, raw and colorless, to surround his body like a shroud. The more he concentrated, the more energy he was able to summon. If only he could have maintained this flow of Avidea during his fight with Larkin, he would have healed his wounds better, he would have struck harder, he might have escaped. Then again, this elementary application of magic came naturally only for the Condense class, and he could have just as easily overexerted himself even faster. For now, he thought only to build up his stamina, whether or not he should ever come to face her again.

With the aura enveloping his arms and legs to aid his lacking physical brawn, he drilled through some kicks and punches against one of the training dummies. Kick after kick, punch after punch, he ignored the pain building up in his body until he could no longer, drenched in sweat and doubling over, vision blurry.

When he managed to recover, with no help from his vestigial lungs, Jonathan sat on the mat and crossed his legs. He rested his hand on top of his thigh and opened it with the palm facing up. For a full minute, he only stared at it.

A fruit knife. How pathetic. And yet it had been crucial to why he was here now, and not still trapped in that basement as her drooling test subject.

He furrowed his brow and envisioned the utensil in his hand again. Fragments began to form in his palm amid pale blue energy, the familiar feeling of tension tightening the muscles in his arm as he imagined the shape, tracing it with his gaze.

And then it was there, a solid object. A rudimentary handle with an inelegant blade. He closed his fingers around the handle and reeled back his arm, aiming to throw it at the nearest padded wall.

It flew, rotating around its center of gravity. And then it crumbled in the air before it could make contact with the upholstery.

Jonathan groaned and leaned his head back, bracing his arms behind him. He knew this was not going to be something he could do overnight, and it was too late to regret not training this from the start, when he thought relying on an implement could propel him to greater feats faster. He might not need to regularly rent out a room at this stadium or even at smaller training facilities, but practicing at every possible moment suddenly felt urgent to him.

The next morning, he dressed to head to the restaurant, despite wanting to delay his return even longer. If he indulged his desire to continue being a homebody, he might end up putting this off forever.

His eyes still sat on top of deeply set bags, and he had clearly lost weight. The temptation to drop by the store and pick up some makeup to conceal his signs of exhaustion brewed vigorously inside him, but the deed would be rendered pointless if he intended to tell Elenora the truth.

He stopped to pick up a new phone first, and after restoring his contacts, he sent a message of apology to Elenora with a promise to be there at the Taverne. He did not need to announce his arrival hours before it happened, but while he was in the right state of mind, he wanted to give himself no room to waver on his responsibilities.

The time he spent stalling and wandering aimlessly around the city had gone too soon.

Phoebe greeted him with warmth, stark and stunning from his lack of it the last few days, when he stepped inside the restaurant just before the dinner shift. But she took one look at him and her expression changed to one of concern.

"Mr. Tessier?" she said. "Are you alright?"

He nodded. "Yes, thank you for asking. The trip away worked me harder than I expected it to. I will recover, though."

She frowned, appearing unconvinced, but she did not press further.

"Has Elenora come back from her break yet?" he asked.

"Yes, she's in the kitchen preparing right now."

"Thank you, Phoebe," he said and headed toward the kitchen.

The moment she saw him walk in, Elenora cried out with joy and rushed over to embrace him. She seemed far less observant of his appearance than Phoebe when she expressed nothing but happiness about his return.

"How was your opportunity with Lala Sweet?" she asked optimistically, causing him to flinch.

"We need to talk," he said solemnly.

The smile fell from her face. She bit her lip and nodded her understanding, telling the other chefs to take charge of preparations before she accompanied him to his office.

With each of them in their respective chairs, the pair sat in silence while she waited for him to say something, to overcome the hurdle of finding the right way to start this conversation.

"Do you need me to help you brew some tea?" she asked.

He shook his head, and the quiet fell over them again. His gaze was fixed on his desk, but he could guess that she noticed his desaturated complexion by now, his dark circles, and was deciding not to say anything about them until he did.

"Was it not all that you dreamed it would be?" she prompted again. Her delicate tone of voice indicated she wanted to be tactful with her question, careful not to make him feel rushed.

"The opportunity, it was a dud," he finally said. "She tricked me. . ."

Elenora stared at him, perhaps hoping that he would elaborate. When he did not, a deep furrow formed in her brow.

"What do you mean? Did she not really have a project for you? No, that can't be it. You were gone for a whole week."

He could see the confusion in her eyes when he decided to meet her gaze. "Things were much worse than we could have imagined. I really did have to fight for my life after all." He let out a humorless laugh.

"On a hunt for a rare ingredient? Was it that much more dangerous than what we did? Don't tell me she thought you were unworthy to continue working for her."

"No, that was not it." With each new speculation Elenora made, he felt more that he should stop dancing around the issue. "How can I say this? Everything was fine at the start. She had me work on some research at her lab. I was enjoying the work and looking forward to when we might go on an excursion together."

Elenora leaned forward but did not interrupt him.

"She had some ingredients she wanted me to work into new recipes that she hoped would be groundbreaking. But when I was trying out different cooking methods, I stumbled across something. I found. . ." His throat closed up, and he propped his elbow on his desk, covering his face with his hand as he coughed.

"Take your time, Mr. Tessier," Elenora said gently.

The memories brought back phantom traces of that horrifying stench, eliciting a reaction from him identical to the one he had then. His chest hurt from his body doing things that it had not done for a decade and a half, experiencing the setbacks of having airways without needing to use them, so much that his vocal cords could barely move any air around to form words.

He managed to recover quickly, though his voice remained only a few notches above a whisper. "It was awful, Elenora. She had been abducting people, and using their Avidea. . . and their bodies. . ."

For several long seconds, she wore a look of confusion, before she gasped, her eyebrows raising and her eyes widening in realization. "No, that can't be true," she said, almost shouting. She pushed her chair back as she abruptly stood up. "You're not saying that she—"

A knock interrupted her, and they both looked toward his

office door to see Phoebe standing on the other side of the glass. Elenora glanced at Jonathan for a brief moment, and when he did not display any signs of objection, she beckoned the hostess to come inside.

"I'm so sorry for interrupting," Phoebe said as she timidly stepped inside the room. "But I think there's something that I really need to tell you."

At this point, it hardly mattered to him. Putting his conversation with Elenora about the horrendous misdeeds of a celebrity chef on hold to address some urgent restaurant issue was almost more of a reprieve than it was a nuisance.

"Go ahead, Phoebe," he said, not bothering to hide his tired tone of voice.

"So, I know you took a leave from the restaurant to work for Lala Sweet, Mr. Tessier," she said.

Jonathan narrowed his eyes. He could not remember if he had ever told her exactly why he left the restaurant in their care for the last week, but maybe he had mentioned it in passing.

"And," she continued, "I'm the one who sent you those text messages urging you to look for her secret."

Something inside him snapped. He had received the first of her messages just the day after interviewing her, the day after he gave her his phone number. He remembered now, without a doubt. He had never spoken of Lala Sweet in front of her before that point. The critics' visit had also been done in private, outside of normal restaurant operation.

He stood up, causing his own chair to shoot backward into the filing cabinets behind him.

"You," he snarled. "How did you know I was offered a job opportunity with her, then? Were you working together with that woman? To lure me into her trap?"

That must have been it. Why else would she have tried to encourage him to look for Larkin's hidden lab? Gave him hints to the code that unlocked the keypad door? Larkin might have wanted him to find something suspicious about her, so she could use it as an excuse to make him one of her victims ahead of schedule.

If Phoebe had left him alone, he could have played his part at the lab with ignorant bliss. He would have behaved, presenting his research to Larkin and perhaps walking down a different path, one where she saw value in him as a legitimate partner and not as a potential experiment.

Phoebe dared to stare at him with surprise and terror in her eyes, as if she had not been the reason his curiosity had become insatiable.

"Well?" he shouted, slamming his hand against the desk. "Answer me!"

"Jonathan!" Elenora exclaimed, stepping between them as if she felt the need to block his voice from reaching Phoebe with her own body. Her height could not obstruct his intense gaze from fixing onto the younger woman. "Please, Mr. Tessier, let's take it easy," she insisted desperately. "I'm sure she had a good reason!"

Was he going to hurt Phoebe? Unlikely, but he could feel the searing anger of betrayal, despite her being someone he only recently hired. Maybe he was the one completely at fault for trusting her.

"Why should I listen to what she says, Elenora? You could never understand what horrors I experienced because of her. For all we know, she not only came here to trick us but she also might have had a hand in that woman's wrongdoings."

"Get a hold of yourself, boss," Elenora said, frowning as she went around the desk and pulled on his arm. "Sit your dramatic rear end down and at least listen to her tell her story. We'll decide what happens afterward. I won't let her harm you. I won't let either of you hurt each other."

He resisted at first, but her pull was strong, and so he complied, retrieving his chair and sitting back down in it. He glared at Phoebe and watched her fidget with her hands as he waited impatiently for her to speak.

CHAPTER 24

WITH TWO PAIRS OF INTENSE eyes on her, Phoebe took a deep breath before beginning her explanation.

"First, I want to say that I really am sorry. It seems my actions led to something terrible happening to you," she said. Her brow was knitted with remorse, which Jonathan did not know if he could believe. "That was not my intention at all."

He opened his mouth to retort, but Elenora lightly slapped his arm and shot him a fiery look. He pressed his lips into a tight line.

"If it helps, since I was hired after you had already received the offer from Lala Sweet, it would have been a big gamble for me to apply for a job and hope that I was given access to your phone number. In fact, if I was working directly with her, she could have given it to me herself, and I never would have had to meet you. I mean, you would have taken her offer whether I interviewed to work here or not, right?"

He attributed his inability to find a flaw in her reasoning to the subpar condition of his mental state.

"So, if those messages were not intended to lure me into digging deeper, what were they for?" he asked.

"They were genuinely meant to warn you," she said. "I'm really sorry I had to be so cryptic. I did it because I didn't think you'd believe me if I told you in person."

He raised a brow. "So, though you were not working with her, you knew what that woman was up to?"

"I had a suspicion. I've been keeping tabs on her activities, which led me here. I decided to apply to find out her involvement with your restaurant, and maybe prevent her from doing any harm to you, even though I knew I didn't really have much power to do anything."

"What made you suspicious of her?" he asked.

"During that three-year gap in my resume, I had actually worked at one of her restaurants. The big, tall one in this city."

"Helix of Zest?"

She nodded. "While I worked there as a waitress, I began noticing something odd about the dishes we served to her most important guests. I. . . um. I was able to detect a strange temperature difference from when we served those same dishes to regular guests."

"A temperature difference?"

"Yes," she said. "I'm able to gauge the temperature of something as if it was another sense, like smell. Or hearing," she said with a wry smile.

"Is that your Avidea? Or a kind of grant?" Elenora chimed in.

"No, but I'm surprised you know about that, Ellie. It's just an ability I was born with," Phoebe said.

"What made you think something was wrong?" Jonathan prompted, wanting to get back on topic.

Phoebe hesitated, looking grim. "The cooling rate of certain ingredients in those dishes... they were identical to when a corpse loses its heat after death."

The office became quiet. Jonathan did not want to get into the science of how that would be possible, whether cooking a body at high temperatures made a difference to its cooling rate, or whether Phoebe's ability detected the presence of Avidea in both living bodies and in Larkin's dishes to be the same. Even if the method she used to draw her conclusions turned out to be wrong, he knew she arrived at the correct answer nonetheless.

"I know it's hard to believe," she said. "But I've been aware of temperatures all my life, even those of people and objects in buildings I can't see through, so naturally I've come across people who had recently passed on before. It was too familiar of a feeling to ignore."

"What did you do when you realized?" he asked.

"I tried to investigate further. I asked the chefs if they knew where the ingredients for those important guests were sourced, and I researched the distributors they named for me. I couldn't find anything reliable," she said, her voice hushed for the latter part of the sentence. "But I still wanted to give her the benefit of the doubt. Maybe she bought from local suppliers, and it wasn't that she was trying to hide her use of illegal or unethical ingredients."

Phoebe glanced at her hands. Elenora quietly invited her to sit but she shook her head.

"I thought to myself, if I could just get a small sample of the raw ingredient, maybe I could examine it, or send it to a lab. I really wanted to clear my doubt, or I'd feel bad working there. So, on the morning of a big event, I arrived at the restaurant early and tried to intercept a shipment. That's when it happened."

Jonathan nodded, remembering. "The accident," he said while Elenora glanced questioningly between them. "Without going into too much detail, can you tell us more about it?"

"Lala Sweet knew someone was snooping around, so she sent her goons to eliminate the spy. I was able to get away, but not without severe consequences."

Now it was his turn to stop Elenora before she could utter her question, with a whispered promise to explain later.

"This was why you omitted her restaurant from your resume?"

"Yes, I left it off entirely, to prevent you from ever mentioning me to her. In case she remembered my name."

"And what have you been doing since then?"

"Of course I had to quit, but the fact that people were sent after me proved that something was wrong. In the two years that followed, I tried to gather more evidence and clues, though it hasn't been easy."

"I assume you lack sufficient evidence to report to the authorities."

She sighed and nodded. "I was laughed out of the police station when I tried it once before."

"Did you come here and encourage me to investigate her hidden lab in the hopes I would find more evidence for you?"

Her eyes widened as she shook her head. "I wasn't trying to use you," Phoebe said with apparent sincerity. "It's just that. . . she's so well-loved, no one would think badly of her. So, when I heard from Elenora about your offer the day of my interview, I wanted to warn at least one other person that there might be more to Lala Sweet than what we all admired."

Now that he had calmed down, it made sense that Phoebe heard about his connection to Larkin through Elenora. There was nothing suspicious about that. "Well, you certainly succeeded in that regard."

"I still want to stop her. In the best-case scenario, I wanted us to join our testimonies against her. I know I can't do this alone, and I'm sure you felt the same way, Mr. Tessier."

"She needs to be stopped," Elenora agreed, then glanced at Jonathan. "Were you able to slip any evidence out from what you found?"

He leaned back in his chair, resigned to his unlucky fate. "She destroyed my phone before I could escape," he told her, recalling the now defunct piece of electronic junk he was forced to throw away. "I had pictures on there."

"Then we need to find a way to get something else," Elenora said, earning herself a terrified expression from him.

"No," Phoebe said. "I think if Mr. Tessier and I go together to report this, our testimonies might be enough. The evidence I have can't really stand on its own, but maybe since you saw something inside her secret lab, it might prompt them to investigate."

"But if you go to the authorities claiming a celebrity is cooking up edurans in her basement without any proof, they're going to think you're crazy," Elenora argued, then stared at him like he was the one who had countered her. "Aren't you the type to want to have concrete evidence, boss?"

When he did not say anything to contribute to their discussion, Elenora alluded back to the repercussions of Phoebe's accident. Phoebe eventually filled Elenora in on how the accident imparted her with a head injury that led to her single-sided deafness, and as predicted, Elenora expressed great concern that Phoebe tried her best to soothe.

Phoebe offered to show them pictures of the damage she had sustained from the incident, to which both Elenora and Jonathan refused. She believed Phoebe wholeheartedly, and he did not think it was fair to require that confirmation. In her eagerness, which he guessed had been to earn their trust, Phoebe displayed a hint of disappointment at their strong denial.

"How about I let you two go back to work, and I will think about what we can do?" he suggested. "I need time to recover and think through our options anyway."

Phoebe was first to be ready to exit the office. "I know you might not trust me completely, and I don't blame you, but I do genuinely want to work with you to stop her. Please let me know what I can do."

Elenora nodded and walked over to follow her out. "Remember, boss. You're not alone. We may not be powerful Mercenaries like you, but you have our support, and we'll do whatever we can, even if you choose not to pursue her."

He gave them both a weak smile as they left and closed the door behind them. After a series of minutes in soundless solitude, he straightened his posture and fetched a notepad to write in.

The notes began as chaotic scribbles, the accurate representation of his muddled thoughts before they slowly morphed into coherent considerations.

What if he did nothing? Phoebe might carry on with the investigation on her own, putting herself in dangerous situations she had yet to understand. She had already figured out clues to the secret code, and he helped her confirm them. Of course she would want to target that hidden lab. Elenora might feel troubled knowing there was nothing she could do about such a disturbing situation. Antoine and chefs like him would forever wonder why they could not break through to a higher status. And Jonathan himself would be burdened by guilt for the rest of his life. How could he deem himself worthy to take over the Union if he allowed a dastardly criminal like Larkin Swetnam to go entirely unpunished?

Could Phoebe still have been putting on an act, even now? As Larkin's last attempt to ensnare him, a puppet to make him believe he might be capable of stopping her if only he had the support of his allies?

But Phoebe was the one who insisted on relying on the authorities, while Elenora expressed an eagerness to seek more evidence. Phoebe seemed sincere about wanting to show proof of her accident when he had not asked. Should he be so unfair to doubt her this much, and imply that she was faking or lying about her disability when he saw for himself how much it had affected her work?

He had made a mistake trusting Lala Sweet. The damage that incident did to further inhibit his ability to trust would never be forgotten. He did not want to let her continue to win over him, though, even with such small victories. She would be elated to have him wallow in his helplessness or isolate himself from any chance to defy her. It seemed his only choice was to trust again. If he willingly walked back into her lair on his own, he would only see a wretched replay of what happened before.

There would be nothing for him if he let his fears and dread paralyze him completely. Elenora might understand if he wanted to take the time to heal from everything he had been through. He would not, if he was in her place. He could not sit by comfortably, allowing Larkin more time to continue what she was doing. He needed to figure out a firm course of action.

Ferocious brainstorming consumed the rest of his day, forcing him to neglect his administrative duties and leave the ladies in charge for a bit longer. Back at home, in between cooking himself dinner and winding down for the night, whenever his hands were free, he practiced conjuring fruit knives again and again. Each time, the process became quicker, the utensil more refined in shape, until his body became too sore to manifest any more new physical particles.

He took the next day off and began his training again. While he watched the mundane news on television, read a book, distracted his mind with any entertainment he could bear, his hand would summon and dismiss cutlery with increasing speed. Occasionally, the ability backfired from overuse, and the feedback stung like electricity through his body. But he pushed on. He wanted the ability to feel effortless, occur instantaneously, and exist independently from his concentration.

As for his plan, every angle he deliberated seemed to revolve around a missing piece. Elenora's strength existed in her ability to physically fend for herself as long as she had her hands on a good weapon, and Phoebe's ability made her a perfect scout. But then what? Even if he teamed up with Elenora to face Larkin, their combined prowess would hardly be enough to bridge the gap. He could improve his own stamina and wield his abilities differently, but nothing within his capabilities would secure him a decisive victory.

The only option he could come up with was highly unlikely to cooperate with him, but not impossible. He needed to make the call.

"Hello?" Jonathan said after the line connected. "This is Jonathan Tessier, from over a week ago. The one you pummeled for not liking your cuisine presentation."

"Why are you calling?" Antoine spat, his vitriol transmitting vividly over the phone. "Leave me alone and don't bother me!"

The line cut before Jonathan could get a word in. He calmly pressed redial.

"What do you want?" Antoine demanded angrily when he picked up again.

"Do you remember telling me that you wanted to know how Lala Sweet and other top culinary Mercenaries were able to exceed the limits of rare ingredients that even expert chefs like yourself could not?"

"Oh, and I suppose you're going to tell me you suddenly have the answer? Like I'll just believe you. I spent my entire life trying to find out, there's no way that you know."

"No, I happened to stumble upon the truth, through no merit of my own."

A pause persisted tensely between them.

"Is this some kind of trick you're playing on me? So soon after we met? Seems a bit too convenient and easy to me."

"I admit I have no physical proof to give you," Jonathan said. "But I was only ever in Spectervale because Lala Sweet had given me an offer to work at her lab there. I can prove that much, if you need me to show you the documentation I have from the arrangement."

"I do know she has a food lab here. I guess I'll text you my email and you can send the proof to me after this," Antoine said. "But why did you decide to call me about it?"

"Because even though we might not get along, you might care. Things at her lab seemed normal at first, but something corrupt is going on underneath it all. I also suspect she is not the only one involved. She mentioned that other top chefs were doing something similar."

"Go on."

"I found her underground lab, where she stored severed body parts in jars and had notes on using Avidea in recipes, often killing her test subjects to do so and incorporating their bodies in her cooking to achieve otherworldly flavors. One of her victims was a missing persons case the Union has been investigating for months."

Antoine did not answer right away, and Jonathan assumed he was letting this all sink in.

"Tch," Antoine finally hissed. "That's outrageous. I don't believe you."

"I think you actually do," Jonathan said. "After all, you told me yourself that you explored every other possibility."

Yet another stretch of silence fell over them, broken only when Antoine grunted in frustration.

"And what do you want me to do with this information?" he asked. "You don't expect me to just partner up with you like we're the best of friends so that we can take her down, do you?"

"Putting it mildly, yes, I do," Jonathan said. "She caught me looking around, and I almost ended up being her next catch."

"Well, you are a weakling, so that's no surprise."

"If you must take every chance to insult me even now, remember that I bested you at least once."

"Shut up."

"But I understand that feeling of hopelessness now, that defeat," Jonathan continued, unfazed. "I felt there was no way to bring her down, and I would just have to watch people like her continue corrupting the culinary space. My own dreams would crumble into nothing, since I will never take part. And I realized that those thoughts started to sound familiar."

"How do you know I won't use what you told me to turn around and do the same thing?"

"Call it a hunch, from how passionately you assaulted me based on a perceived insult of your craft. Maybe you might have followed the trend if you knew about it years ago, but you would not stand for it now."

Antoine scoffed but did not disagree.

"Do you know of any way you can help?" Jonathan boldly pressed on. "I am sure you would love to see Lala Sweet's downfall. Even if you do not have the noblest of motivations, anything you can do would be appreciated. You must have some skills at combat, or maybe a way to expose her?"

"Well, as you know, I can't really fight with anything other than my fists. My Avidea can assist with that, but I didn't develop it with combat in mind."

"Can you tell me more?"

"Promise not to laugh or judge me."

"I promise."

Antoine sighed. "I'm a Connect class. What I do is form portals with my energy that essentially swap two similarly sized things over very long distances."

Jonathan frowned. "I do not see why you thought I would find that funny. That is not a bad ability. How did you use it when we met?"

"I kept my distance, swapped a patch of your face with an area on the asphalt near me of the same size. And punched you from afar."

"What?" Jonathan reeled from this revelation. "You can swap other people's body parts like that?"

"Don't get it twisted. I'd have to be a lot more powerful to say, swap your head with something like a hollow melon, and then also be able to close the portal around your neck to behead you. I don't even know if that's a possibility to begin with."

"Ah. So, while you can temporarily swap a body part with something else, you cannot alter its actual location in reality?"

"Yeah, something like that. I can do it for living and nonliving things in their entirety though, as long as they aren't too big. I used this ability to obtain ingredients that were hard to reach, or to really excel at moving utensils and plates around." Antoine sighed again. "Maybe I should've just stuck to being a waiter. I was an excellent one."

"But you also succeeded as a Mercenary with such an ability."

"The master who taught me was even better. He was able to swap two whole objects of vastly different sizes. I can't do anything like that."

"Yet," Jonathan remarked, thinking of his own training. "No one said you had to stop here."

"I'm much too old for that. But anyway, what is your ability? Is it just to be an annoying little skunk?"

Jonathan decided to ignore the quip, and explained the details of his own abilities, as it was fair to do. He made sure to briefly mention how he escaped from Larkin, the time he spent with Elenora hunting for ingredients, and the fact he had another person working at his restaurant who had independently looked into Lala Sweet's illicit activity. Though he noted that he had yet to fully trust Phoebe, the four of them would make a better team than even just the two of them as Mercenaries.

"So, you have a plan?" Antoine asked.

"Not yet. I have a vague framework of one, but I am starting to put the pieces together. You might be the finishing touch, Mr. Coulis, if you find yourself willing to participate."

Antoine laughed dryly. "Tell me what it is, and I'll think about it."

CHAPTER 25

"DOESN'T SHE LOOK ADORABLE with black hair?" Elenora gushed, after she and Phoebe had finished getting ready in their hotel room and joined Jonathan in his.

"It's just a cheap wig," Phoebe said, blushing as she straightened the hood of her jacket that helped hold it all in place.

Jonathan chuckled to himself as the women examined each other's makeup. They had chosen to experiment with what they usually wore—Phoebe gave herself a smoky-eye look, while Elenora transitioned from her soft everyday neutrals to bold splashes of color.

"What a shame we have to hide your vibrant hair," he remarked, and Phoebe shrugged, smiling. She would have fit in so perfectly with the scenery otherwise. Larkin might have never seen Phoebe in person, but that unfortunate encounter two years ago had left too many witnesses behind. They all understood they needed to play it safe.

Standing together, the two of them looked to be an unlikely pair. Elenora matched seamlessly with the aesthetic of the city, with her outfit and makeup of pastel blues, purples, and yellows. She could pass as one of the more eccentric residents of Spectervale, and Phoebe as the friend devoid of color that she was showing around. They might earn themselves a few strange looks, but they were hoping to turn certain heads less than they would without their disguises.

As he sat in the armchair near the window and gazed out into the colorful streets, Jonathan knew the plan he managed to put together was one that defied his better judgment. When he had worked more regularly at the Union, he always preferred to complete missions on his own. Even when he took bright-eyed prospective adventurers under his wing, he endured through it out of the obligations dictated to him by the design of the Union's training programs. Something about giving practical experience to those who wanted to earn their Licenses, but he had always seen those glorified interns as liabilities rather than true team members.

And here he was, up on an early morning waiting on the call of a despondent Mercenary who was on the last legs of his career, so he could join him with two employees in tow, neither of them with Licenses nor even a modicum of Avidea expertise. Because Jonathan needed all three of them.

When he stopped to carefully contemplate his plan and the structure of his team, with members whose hands would hold the fate of his life, it had struck him as laughably concerning. He trusted Elenora like nothing else, perhaps even more than he felt he could rely on Victoria, his own family. But she would have the smallest role to play today. A part of him wanted to keep her safe, if something terrible happened to him. Most of it was derived from practical reasoning. Her skills, though impressive, were limited in versatility. Antoine, on the other hand, was given the biggest role. Jonathan trusted that man nearly not at all, but he could not deny the value of his Avidea. Phoebe stood somewhere in between, in both trustworthiness and ability.

Despite the nature of this plan, he felt a strange calm resting on his shoulders while they waited. Instead of the debilitating dread and anxiety he had expected to suffer as the time drew near, a tolerable nervousness mingled with the tranquility of fully accepting his own decision to move forward, that he would be happy with whatever outcome he managed to secure. He would have to be.

Ten minutes later, Antoine finally called him and told him he was ready to go.

Jonathan, Elenora, and Phoebe left the hotel, one closer to Larkin's lab and certainly not the Transcendent Smoothie. He would have had to lose his mind to book at that place. Then again, intentionally going back to her lab was not something a sane person should be doing either.

He parted ways with the ladies and checked his phone as he made his way to meet with Antoine a few streets down from the lab.

"You don't look much better than the last time I saw you," Antoine said gruffly.

What a greeting. "Thanks for letting me know," Jonathan said, and they walked together in silent frigidity to find a shop that they could pretend to browse.

Phoebe and Elenora were leading the first part of the plan, as the two people on the team who had the fewest interactions with Larkin. They would stroll up and down the street closer to the lab, posing as a pair of good friends enjoying a lovely day out. After a few minutes, Elenora reported that they were in position.

The earpieces each of them wore fit into walkie-talkies that had been priced within a modest budget, which sacrificed the quality of the audio but were sufficient for handling the purpose of their humble operation.

"I can tell that there's no one inside the lab yet," Phoebe informed them, her voice hushed.

Good. They did not have to wonder if Larkin had already checked into the building or if any other living individuals Phoebe detected inside might merely be other researchers. Elenora and Phoebe would only have to keep their eyes fixed on the front entrance.

Idleness occupied their next few hours, and he exchanged very few words with Antoine as they moved from shop to shop. Elenora had taken to communicating her mundane observations to pass the time.

"Someone with the widest dress I've ever seen just passed by us," she said. "I almost tripped on their skirt. I can't believe they allow tutu assault out here."

Antoine looked at Jonathan from a few aisles down inside their first store, raising a brow and clearly judging him for the staff he hired.

Several minutes later, when the men had moved on to the next shop, her voice came through again. "Phoebe and I bought some pastries from a food truck nearby. They're filled with the smoothest ice cream I've ever had. So delicious."

Phoebe pressed the button only to laugh sheepishly into the microphone.

"We're going to take turns heading to the restroom," Elenora reported next, after half an hour had passed.

"Is she going to keep doing this?" Antoine asked.

"I see no harm in it," Jonathan responded, and so they enjoyed a few more minutes of peaceful stillness.

Until they left another store together and Antoine spoke up.

"I can't believe you dragged me out to waste time like this," he said, though for once, his tone was lilted with lighthearted amusement.

"I told you to arrange for a few days off."

"At this rate, I could've just done my own thing until you called me."

"And waste time waiting for you? How sensible."

Another hour passed and they found themselves in a bigger shopping center with a food court, and so they decided to order something to eat.

"Are you actually nervous?" Antoine asked, while they were standing in line. "I hope you aren't thinking of backing out after putting me through all of this."

Jonathan realized he had been anxiously fidgeting with his hands as they waited for their turn to order. He commanded his fingers to stop moving. "Well, that certainly seems presumptuous," he said. "I know we might not be able to do anything today if she does not show up, but I am itching to get this over with. I will not bow out of my own plan."

"You'd better not, you coward. It sucks to be out here the whole day with you, but if it means finally confronting that witch and bringing down others like her, I'm not going to let you do anything but walk in there and catch her red-handed."

"You made yourself very clear," Jonathan said, rolling his eyes as they reached the front of the line and gave their orders to the cashier. "Hearing you say the plan out loud, it sounds absolutely ridiculous." Someone who had been abducted by a monster like Lala Sweet should not go waltzing back into her clutches.

"You were the one to say it out loud first."

"I like to think it did not sound as absurd coming from me."

They were in the middle of enjoying their food when Phoebe connected the line, her voice barely a whisper.

"Target just arrived and went inside the lab," she told them.

"Now's your chance to shine, big guy," Antoine remarked.

"Should we not finish our lunch first?"

"Don't you dare make excuses now." Antoine stood up and made to drag Jonathan out by the arm. Jonathan quickly slipped out of his chair and walked with determination toward the exit of the shopping center, not letting his nuisance of a partner lay hands on him, even if the man was right. There would be no room in his racing mind to think about wasting all that food.

With Antoine lagging behind, Jonathan passed by the women as they sat together on a bench, casually chatting while holding a line of sight with the front of the lab. He gave them only a brisk nod to relay his thanks for their hard work before he headed straight toward the entrance.

The day before, Jonathan waited until late at night to try the access key still in his possession, and the fact that the doors unlocked both thrilled and shocked him. His plan had revolved around being able to enter the lab after Larkin had done so herself, and he would have had to shift gears if she had already taken his access away. He remained surprised that she had not. It had been over a couple of weeks since his escape. He wondered if she had been hoping, for whatever asinine reason, that he would come back.

Which he did. It mattered not if his attempt to enter last night had been recorded for her to see. Hiding it had not been crucial to his plan, and a part of him wanted her to know. Wanted her to realize not only was he back in town, but that he might be so illogical as to sneak into the lab for another try at securing evidence.

Jonathan put his key near the reader and the lock clicked in response. He pulled the door open and held it there for a while, glanced down at the card, then stepped inside, letting the door close behind him.

All he had to do was wander until he found her, and so he walked, resting his hand on the walls every few steps. Since he did not immediately run into her, he headed toward her office and tried the door. No luck there. He felt relieved that his plan did not depend on entering that forbidden space ever again.

He paced himself through the familiar hallways, making sure he never walked too quickly. He was beginning to suspect she might have positioned herself deep inside one of the bigger rooms of the facility when orange flashed before his eyes.

Instinct moved his body out of the way in the nick of time, and he turned to look at her. Her gaping mouth, which his hunch told him was of feigned bewilderment, transformed into a smile of sinister glee.

"Interesting," Larkin remarked. "You really came back?"

"I cannot let you get away with hurting innocent people and using them for your depraved recipes," Jonathan said. "You must have expected me to return."

She cackled. "You're right," she admitted, pulling out a respirator from behind her. "You're not going to get me with your stupid tricks again. And you won't be getting a shred of evidence from me."

A smirk tugged at the corner of his mouth. "I hope you do not consider yourself to be the only one who made preparations. I will not let this be a repeat of last time either."

"I don't care if you're recording our conversation," she said, and her accurate guess impressed him. She secured the gas mask over her face and readied her stance. "It doesn't matter, if it can't leave this building."

Jonathan braced himself, knowing that though he had significantly improved over the past two weeks, he still had far to go to reach her caliber. The likelihood that he would lose hovered as high as it had in the underground lab. But he would fight, and he would persist.

She made the first move, lurching at him. Her aura mimicked the familiar shape of a large multibladed pastry blender in front of her body. Before she could bulldoze him down, a dozen chef's knives shot out from his palm at breakneck speed, lodging themselves in a trail up the wall. He pulled himself up with urgency, gripping each knife's handle to the top and squeezing his body into a corner where her weapon could not reach him just as she whizzed past.

Still hanging on to the wall, he turned toward her and threw three more knives after her in rapid succession. As they flew in her direction, they began spinning on their own. She reacted flawlessly, swinging her energy to knock them away, but his blades would not simply fall. Exhibiting minds of their own, they slowed the trajectory of their rebound, and homed back in on her, slicing through the air like spinning drones for a couple more rounds of clashing before they finally fell and disappeared.

When he landed back on his feet and met her eyes, she glared at him. He could almost imagine her lips twitching with anger. "So, you want to poke holes in my beautiful lab before you die?" she spat, the venom of it muffled by the mask. "I see you're no longer relying on that skewer as a crutch."

"I was always praised as a fast learner," he said, allowing himself this moment of smugness.

She scoffed. "Don't start thinking that's going to change your odds of victory, amateur," she said. Her aura wisped into those erratic balloon whisks again, slightly smaller than last time but much longer and better suited for whirling down the corridor like missiles.

In response, he created large cleavers with wide blades in his hands to block her attacks, the kind of weapons that used to only be possible with the help of his rapier, but now could last several seconds on their own before he needed to manifest another. His stamina held strong as he parried and dodged, slowly moving closer to her as she tried to keep her distance.

His body felt light, able to move more nimbly than before as he remembered what it was like to be in his better physical form. Even within the compressed space of the hallway, he still managed to evade a good percentage of her barbaric attacks in a battlefield that prevented her from using that rolling pin ability if she did not want to pull the structure of the building down with him.

Whenever she relented to center herself, he conjured an oversized serrated knife, focusing his energy to extend the blade as long as it needed to be to slice through her skin. Though he endured a few hits himself before he could land even one on her, he did not display the same fear he had harbored during their first fight.

"You sure seem confident," she remarked, nearly snarling through her respirator.

"I must have gone through something like this before," he returned, and they resumed their collision of powerful abilities.

Though his endurance had greatly improved, he once again hit his limit first. Sweat dripped down his temples from the exertion as his back collided with a damaged wall, her orange aura digging into the flesh of his arms and legs to pin him there.

Her shoulders heaved with apparent fatigue as she approached him, her presence as daunting as ever. He could tell that even though he would never be a match for her, he fared better this time. More of his attacks landed, and they cut deeper. Though he had been painfully immobilized and once again teetered near defeat, he could not help feeling anything but pleased.

"Congratulations on actually putting up a fight this time," she said, the spite evident in her stifled voice. "But it's over, for good. I'll ensure that you stay a compliant subject for me to use as I wish."

As he stared her down, he kept the vigor alight in his eyes, as if to flaunt a defiant determination to continue fighting, to provoke her with a challenge.

His expression faltered when Larkin pulled out a syringe, filled with what he assumed to be a sedative tranquilizer, and removed its cap. He had expected her to do what she did last time—strike a nerve with her expert hand to render him unconscious. This would be far more dangerous and required more precision to counter. His jaw clenched tightly.

"Any last words before you become a shell of yourself?" she asked darkly, raising the syringe up near his neck. "Before providing me with a steady supply of your precious Avidea becomes your only purpose?"

Jonathan scoffed. "There is no stopping you with mere words. Do what you will."

"If only you had come to this conclusion earlier, you would've saved me a whole lot of trouble."

She brought her hand down, finding a suitable spot of skin and stabbing it with practiced care, as if she had done this a million times before. He did not feel the sting of the needle.

And neither did she.

As they both waited for the drug to take effect, her grip around the syringe loosened and it fell from her hand, plastic clicking on the tiled floor. Her eyes widened as she stumbled over her feet.

"What? How are you doing this again? I have the mask—" She cut herself off when he smiled tiredly.

She placed a hand to her own neck, feeling around with her fingertips until it looked like she found the minuscule bump from the prick of a needle.

"You—" Her eyelids began to droop. She swayed and could not form another word from her lips.

"I do apologize," he whispered, not sure if she could hear him. He was busy fighting his own exhaustion just to stay awake. "That I was the target who fought back. That I will be your last. The one you would come to regret."

He did not see the moment she collapsed, and the next thing he knew, Elenora's voice called out to him through a haze of fatigue and excruciating pain.

"Jonathan! Stay with me!" she called, forcing him back awake. "Tell me where the energy is pinning you down already, before you bleed out!"

Through strained communication, Jonathan guided Elenora's blade, and she swung with trepidation in close proximity to his body. Larkin's Avidea energy was powerful, remaining present even in her unconsciousness, but Elenora eventually pried away and shattered every persisting piece of the aura without being able to see any of it.

He crumpled into a pile on the ground as soon as he was freed, and she went immediately to work tending to his wounds. He made no effort to move, his role finished.

The next couple minutes passed by in a blur. Phoebe and Antoine came running in to restrain Larkin, and then a team of Mercenaries began storming the lab. At one point, Victoria came to pester him about the wounds he sustained, something about unnecessary risks and how it broke her heart to see him like this. Her scolding felt like a dream.

When he could manage enough strength to sit up, he could not do it without groaning and wincing. It had been years since he had sustained such severe injuries. What was left of his sleeves and pants had been pushed up to expose bandages around his arms and legs, and he examined how neatly they were done.

Elenora came around the hallway and ran toward him, engulfing him in an agonizing hug, but he did not complain. When she pulled away, she had tears welling up in her eyes, and he was fairly certain he did too.

"That was unbearable to watch." She sniffled. "But you did so well. I'm proud of you."

"What is happening right now?" he asked, unwilling to verbally express his relief. Elenora, Phoebe, and especially Antoine had all played their parts perfectly. They had granted him time to weep later, as breaking down now might not be so good for his injuries.

"She's been arrested. They're currently investigating the underground lab. They'll find even more evidence there to make a case against her."

He nodded and closed his eyes, letting his body rest.

"Don't. Open your eyes," she requested. "It's really hard to tell if you're alive."

He obliged, chuckling as he did and grimacing immediately after. Her eyebrows knitted with concern.

"We'll get you to a hospital soon, okay?" she said. "The Union and the other Mercenaries in charge will take care of everything."

"Thank you, Elenora," he said. "Especially for keeping an eye on Antoine and Phoebe."

"They were amazing too. And I wouldn't have let them be anything less while you were giving it your all out there."

"Thank you for coming with us and supporting me. You never could have anticipated this kind of work environment when I hired you."

"I'm not here as your head chef, silly," she said. "I'm here as your friend, and your partner in crime. But not that kind of crime." She pulled a face.

"As head chef, as my friend, and as my trusted partner," he agreed. "I am eternally grateful to have you in my life in all those ways."

She tenderly held his hand until paramedics rushed down the hallway with a stretcher and prepared to carry him away, and he finally let himself succumb to sleep.

CHAPTER 26

"She thought you walked in there alone, didn't she?" Victoria asked. He had no time to do anything more than sit up in his bed before she started grilling him with questions.

Jonathan had been discharged from the hospital a few days after being admitted, after that fateful day, and given instructions to rest at home. Victoria came by his apartment to check in on him, though she seemed more curious about how he had pulled off his scheme than about his health.

"I wanted it to appear that way, especially if she had been watching me through the security cameras. Seeing me on my own, I doubt she would have stayed long to observe the cameras over coming after me."

"So, you had your little entourage enter later?"

He nodded. "After I opened the front door and before I stepped inside, Antoine swapped my access key with a blank card, since I would not be needing it anymore."

She smirked. "And then they waited for the right time to join you in the lab. How did they know where you would be? That building was huge."

"Phoebe knew where Larkin and I were at all times, based on our body heat," he explained. "But they would have had little time to refer to a map to get to us through that maze of hallways. So, I heated up my palm and left imprints along the walls that she could follow."

"Can't believe you even thought about that."

"They told me later they had a couple of close calls, where she almost spotted them," he said with a laugh.

Victoria raised a brow. "You're not the type to laugh about things being left to chance like that. You always want everything perfectly planned out."

He shrugged. "There was no perfect plan to catch her, at least not one I could think of."

"Your goal was just to get a recording of her admitting to her crimes."

"I knew if I could get that into your hands, you and the team you had on standby would finally have a reason to act."

"I see," she said, a small smile forming. "I didn't think you had it in you to be so sneaky."

In preparation for a portal swap, Jonathan and Antoine had traded phones before they entered Larkin's lab. Antoine did not want his phone in Jonathan's possession during combat, in case Larkin had her mind set on destroying it again, and Jonathan did not mind risking his new one. Once Antoine's phone had recorded their conversation, the switch took place. Since Phoebe had completed her job leading the others close enough, she had then taken the phone outside the lab and straight to where Victoria had been waiting.

Jonathan would be the first to admit the many risks of his plan, beyond trusting his own allies to not sabotage him. If the others had been caught when they were sneaking through the hallways, he would have been left stranded. If Larkin had been prepared with backup, they could have been outnumbered. He had put his hopes on the likelihood that she preferred working alone. Top chefs who would agree with using similar methods in their cooking were no better than competition to her.

During the scuffle, Antoine had remained hidden in the hallways, keeping vigilant watch for any opportunity to support Jonathan from afar. Jonathan fought with that in mind, making sure Larkin never looked down the wrong hallway to notice Elenora or Antoine. The plan had never been to allow Jonathan unfair advantages throughout the fight, but to wait for the one moment she put him in serious danger. Whether she had planned on neck chopping a nerve or slicing her Avidea blades deep into a vital organ, Antoine would open portals to switch a part of Jonathan's body with the corresponding one of hers. Though Antoine would not have been able to permanently swap sections of their bodies, he could swindle her into dealing the damage to herself instead.

Jonathan had figured he was doomed when she pulled out that syringe. If she had managed to remain standing, any number of awful outcomes could have come about. She would have time to destroy evidence if she knew Mercenaries wanted to search her lab. She could have convinced them that everything was all a misunderstanding or tried to delay their investigation. He had thought it impossible that Antoine could be so precise and quick to save him. But then he saw it. A tiny portal had appeared on her neck, and within it, he knew what he was looking at was the part of his own neck that she had been aiming for.

And so, she had stabbed the needle into her own body. He wondered what would make her angrier as she sat in her cell, awaiting her trial—staying ignorant about the situation, or realizing exactly how she had been outwitted.

The authorities had found everything. The notebook on Avidea experimentation, the glowing tubes of residual aura, the broken jars, and the severed parts that she had tried to stash away. She had been promptly arrested and injected with a temporary Avidea dampener to reduce her chances of escape. A permanent version might be waiting for her, if the verdict decided it to be her fate.

"You said you'd consider helping me take over the Union after you were done with your hunt for ingredients," Victoria said. "With all of this, I think you're more prepared for the job than ever before."

He leaned his head back and stared at the ceiling of his bedroom.

"You think there are others like her out there, don't you? Don't you want to take them down too?"

"I do," he said slowly. "Before I can fulfill my own dreams of creating culinary masterpieces, I have to rid the industry of such corrupt minds, and restore it to a state of legitimacy, of genuine attempts to discover and improve flavors."

His cousin chuckled. "How corny," she said, getting up to leave. "But I don't disagree. I know what decision you'll make, but keep thinking about it while you recover. Come see me and Dad at the Union when you're ready."

The day he deemed himself fit to step outside his apartment, his first destination was the restaurant instead.

His arms and legs were still kept wrapped in bandages to hide under his clothes, as his wounds extended deeper than a healer could fully reverse with just one session, but a few days of rest allowed his limbs to move without debilitating pain. Not many would know about the battle scars he kept concealed under his late-autumn outfit.

Once inside his office, he summoned Elenora and Phoebe to meet with him. Before he could inform them why, his phone rang, the name above the number belonging to an official from the Mercenary Triumph Board.

"Sorry," Jonathan said, standing up to leave the office. "Let me take this first."

Only the most esteemed Mercenaries in the nation could secure positions on the Board, and he felt certain this caller had been one of the Mercenaries who accompanied the Union team deployed to Spectervale.

"Hello?" he greeted. "Jonathan Tessier speaking."

"Yes, thank you for receiving my call, Mr. Tessier." The voice that responded sounded like one of resplendence, but he could have been imagining it.

"Is everything alright?" he asked. "With the case?"

"Oh, yes, of course," the official said. "I hope my calling didn't cause you worry. The case is progressing without issues, though it's created quite a stir within the Board and the Mercenary community. Everyone's talking about it. But I actually called to discuss something else. About your Mercenary status."

"Ah, go on." He knew his voice wavered over these three small syllables despite his efforts to keep it stable.

"It's good news only," the caller reassured him. "You earned your License a number of years ago, and we know you haven't been particularly active in the profession. But since you played a significant role in this investigation and helped us take down a major criminal, we'd like to offer you an Emblem in recognition of your contributions in law enforcement."

His eyes widened, and he could hardly form the words to respond right away. Mercenaries had to achieve amazing milestones to add even one Emblem to their rank, and they were badges to be regarded with the utmost respect. Only the greatest explorers, detectives, and warriors earned the maximum of three Emblems in their lifetimes. Larkin had herself as many before her License was revoked, and Jonathan had resigned himself to the fate that he would never deserve even a single one.

Still, receiving an offer of an Emblem in the field of criminal investigation, rather than for the reason he became a Mercenary in the first place, gave him pause.

"I truly am grateful to be considered for such a promotion," he told the official. "And I hope to not sound rude or unappreciative. But a Mercenary's first Emblem is crucial, and I fear this may take me down a path I hold no interest in pursuing. I do not think I can take this offer."

The official sighed. "I understand. You are a chef, after all. You intended to take a similar path to Ms. Swetnam's."

"Did you reach out to Mr. Coulis?" he asked. "He deserves the promotion maybe even more than I do."

"We did. He already has one Emblem to his name as a gourmet, but when we asked if he wanted to be recommended for another, how should I put this?" The official chuckled. "He essentially said it was far too late for him to care."

Jonathan did not find this surprising. "How about Phoebe Magoro? She may not be a Mercenary, but can the Board do anything to reward her for her involvement?"

"I'll look into it," the official promised. "You can let her know that if she decides to apply for a License and passes the evaluation, her career as a Mercenary would already be boosted from day one. But I'll see what can be done for her in the meantime, or if she never decides to take that path."

"Thank you so much."

"Not a problem, Mr. Tessier. Though it does seem I wasn't able to accomplish my original goal for this call."

"I do apologize for my refusal and any inconvenience it caused. It is regrettable that I cannot accept."

They both stayed on the line for a bit longer, neither of them initiating the routine to end the call. Several quiet seconds passed.

"Wait, I think I can—"

"Well, if there is nothing else—"

"Oh, sorry."

"No, no," Jonathan said. "Please, go ahead."

"I remembered hearing that you came to work for Lala Sweet because you had been doing some exploration yourself and enhanced your restaurant's cuisine as a result of it. Why don't you put together a report of your exploits and the recipes you created, and I can put in a good word for you to get the Emblem you want?" the official suggested.

"Even if they were not original discoveries?" He tried not to sound overly enthusiastic.

"Together with your work on this case, I reckon you still have a decent chance. Weeding out bad actors and reducing unethical behaviors in the culinary industry can be considered a very important contribution to the field, don't you think?"

"Words cannot express how grateful I am for such an opportunity," Jonathan said. "I will work on that report as soon as I can. Thank you."

"A Mercenary being able to achieve a new Emblem is always a momentous occasion for the Board," the official said. "It was great talking to you, and I wish you the best."

"It was a pleasure. . . And thank you, again."

Jonathan stared at his phone after the call ended. He never thought his heart would race this hard to finally receive the recognition he craved, but perhaps he now realized how little he deserved it. The last month had opened his eyes to how much grit, talent, and sacrifice was required to make a meaningful difference where it mattered. Chasing after lofty dreams with tears and perspiration would never be enough. Unchecked ambitions could unravel victories as easily as it granted them.

Realizing such things should have multiplied his unwillingness to travel further down that path. He should want to contain himself in a world he could fully control: the four walls of his small Taverne. But he knew now what he truly wanted, and what he needed to do to make it all happen.

"Phoebe," he said as he reentered the office, and both she and Elenora turned to look at him from where they were sitting near each other. "Do you have any plans on becoming a Mercenary?"

She laughed lightly. "I've been considering it. But I'm not much of a fighter."

"Neither am I. But I think you still have amazing potential."

"Then I'd have to start taking Avidea training seriously, maybe expand my powers with a grant that works in conjunction with my birth abilities."

"Did you already have something in mind?"

"Well, if I was a Control class, I could manipulate the temperature of the objects I touch. Or if I was a Construct like you, I'd want to make something a little quirky. Maybe a system of thermostats that mold an environment exactly how I want it. I'd have to figure out all the rules, but I always loved complex and creative abilities along those lines."

Jonathan noticed Elenora looking on with great fascination. Even if she would never be interested in learning how to use a grant, he could tell she found it entertaining to learn about everything Avidea could do.

"If you need mentors or trainers, I can provide a few recommendations," he offered to Phoebe. "The Board already has a positive record for you, so you will have a favorable resume built up as soon as you earn your License."

"Oh, that's really nice," she said, appearing impressed. "I'll think about it some more. I do want to, since I seem to have taken a liking to challenging investigations. But I also want to keep helping out here, at least for a while."

"It's gotten crazy busy since we've come back," Elenora commented. "You missed out on it while you were recovering."

"Yeah, with the news buzzing about what we did, we've gotten to the point we have long lines stretching down the street every shift," Phoebe said. "People queue up even if they know they might not get in before we close."

"Are we going to expand? We might need to move, and hire a bigger team, if this hype doesn't die down soon," Elenora added. "We need you to make the call, Jonathan, and soon."

"Actually," he said. "I had been thinking of passing ownership of the Taverne fully over to you, Elenora."

Phoebe widened her eyes with astonishment at this announcement, and Elenora looked ready to panic.

"What?" she exclaimed. "No, no, no. I told you I didn't want to be an owner, and you're still here to help run things. I can't do this on my own."

"You will not be on your own. You have Phoebe here to support you with administrative duties, we finalized the paperwork for investments from Lady Askew and some of her associates, and I trust you to make the best decisions for the restaurant."

She frowned. "I really don't know about this."

"And you handled things fine the multiple times I stepped away. I want you to have complete freedom to fulfill your own dreams, the way you helped me fulfill mine," he said. "You create the menus you want, design your dream interiors, move and expand when you deem fit, and hire anyone you need so that you can keep doing what you love."

"I still don't like the idea of me just taking over. Especially when this was your restaurant to begin with."

"I know. It was not an easy decision for me to make. But I will not be able to do much here if I return to the Union."

"Can't we at least be co-owners? I'd be down for that," she said, her eyes pleading.

He could not remain stoic with her looking at him with such a beseeching expression. "Fine," he said with a laugh. "Co-owners."

She smiled widely at him. "Yay, thank you! I know it'll mostly be me running the show, and there's no other restaurant I'd be more honored to be doing that for, but it's reassuring to know you still have your rightful connection to what you've built."

"I suppose you have a point. I do not have to give it all up. The name will have to change, though," he said. "To reflect our shared ownership."

"Ah, right." She tapped her finger to her chin, glancing over at Phoebe, who only shrugged. "Oh! How about something with 'Radiant' in the name? A testimony to the first excursion we went on together that started this all?"

"Not bad," he agreed.

"The Radiant Taverne," she tried out the name. "Actually, this might be fun. If we expand, each new restaurant could follow the same naming scheme. The Radiant Grill, the Radiant Bistro, the Radiant Diner. Maybe even a restaurant that specializes in salads so we can call it the Radiant Cabbage," she said with a hearty chuckle.

He fondly relished in her delight as she turned to solicit approval and suggestions from Phoebe, who added very little to the conversation other than an eagerness to listen.

"Are you really sure about this? You don't want to stay with us and see your business grow?" Elenora asked him after a while. "Are you in that much of a rush to go back to the Union?"

"I think I left Vicky in suspense about taking over the Union long enough. I want to spend some time thinking this through, what I truly want to do, and if I get pulled back into the daily routine of operating the restaurant, I may never figure it out," he said. "There is also much training I need to be doing, if I plan on deserving my title as a Mercenary."

"There are plenty of people who work pretty normal jobs and also happen to have a License," Phoebe remarked. "And there's nothing wrong with that."

"I know," he said. "I was fine being that person for a while. But I would not feel right continuing as a mere restaurant owner knowing there are more corrupt chefs out there taking advantage of people's ignorance."

Elenora hummed, and Phoebe nodded solemnly.

"I do appreciate everything you both have done to support me, and I will now be entrusting everything to you." He then let out a chuckle. "Phoebe, I will admit that I imagined you betraying me multiple times. Ratting out my plans to her, taking the phone and destroying the evidence instead of giving it to Vicky, all paranoia built up from everything that happened. But

I am glad I relied on you, and even more grateful you want to stay on board with us."

Phoebe raised her brows upon hearing this, but her features softened, and she smiled warmly at him. "I'm happy you didn't blindly give me your trust, and that I was able to earn it. If you continue on the path of investigating more scoundrels in gourmet cuisine, you can count on me to support you."

"Same goes for me," Elenora said. She took a deep, shaky breath, as if she was ready to start tearing up.

"I suppose I should be leaving now," he said. "So I can get all the paperwork and everything else in order."

Elenora and Phoebe stood.

"It's goodbye for now," Elenora said, approaching him with her arms spread wide.

He leaned over to accept the embrace. "Thank you, Elenora, for everything. You will be a most excellent owner, just as you were an excellent partner."

"You'd better come visit us whenever you get the chance, alright?" Elenora said, hugging him tight. "Or I'll be very angry with you, co-owner."

"I promise I will, whenever I can."

She sniffled as she pulled away, hiding her face and fetching a tissue from his desk. The desk that would soon be hers.

Phoebe stepped forward to offer her hand, and he took it in a firm handshake.

"We'll be cheering you on in your work," she said. "And don't worry, Mr. Tessier. I'll take good care of her, and make sure she's always happy."

"Thank you, Phoebe."

He stopped by the kitchen and the dining room to tell the rest of the team that he would be less frequently involved in the restaurant, and that Elenora would be left in charge moving forward. He was met with varied reactions, ranging from indifference to surprise, and he kept the interactions brief before he exited the building.

Across the street, he turned to look back on the Taverne's royal-blue-and-beige exterior, thinking of all the years he spent inside of it. Of the dedication he painstakingly poured into its success, only for it to become a small chapter in his journey.

In his bittersweet farewell, Jonathan Tessier reveled in the excitement of pursuing his ambitions, even as they began taking on very new and unfamiliar flavors.

Acknowledgments

I want to express my gratitude to everyone who has supported my journey in cooking up this novel.

First, I want to thank Shepengul for designing the map and bringing the world of this book (and soon series) to life. You were one of the first professionals I reached out to for this project, and your creative and meticulous work was a surreal delight. Seeing the nation I had envisioned come to life through your artistry was truly an extraordinary experience.

A special thanks to Stanislav from Getfast for elevating the cover design of *Ambition to Savor,* and to Paige and Bojan for cover feedback and guidance. You've all allowed me to have an artistic visual representation of my book that I'm incredibly pleased with.

To Sasha Bent and Shawna Hampton, talented editors who refined my manuscript and whipped it into shape, I'm so grateful for your contributions to my novel. Your expertise and thoughtful critiques are the recipe for why I can feel confident presenting my work to the world.

Thank you, Leah Parkhurst and Jackie Lee Morrison, for being my beta readers. Your honest feedback and insights truly helped to fine-tune this story.

My gratitude extends to JD Caron, Liz Poder, and their team, who armed me with invaluable marketing knowledge. I would've felt quite lost in the self-publishing sphere without your guidance.

And to friends and family who supported me in ways big and small, letting me pick their brains for random questions and feedback. Your encouragement and contributions are deeply appreciated. This book wouldn't have been possible without you.

Enjoyed *Ambition to Savor?*

Continue the adventure by joining my email list! You'll receive updates on new releases and all the exclusive content you'll need for a deeper dive into the Lone Thorn series.

Join the party at bbegwyn.com.

Leaving a review on the retailer's site or Goodreads will help me more than you know! Please consider letting other readers know your honest thoughts so more people can discover this story.

Thank you for your support!